MURDERLAND

MURDERLAND

Thomas B. Cavanagh

OPEN ROAD

INTEGRATED MEDIA
NEW YORK

ISBN: 978-1-5040-9462-7

This edition published in 2024 by Open Road Integrated Media, Inc.
180 Maiden Lane
New York, NY 10038
www.openroadmedia.com

For Pam

Empire Realm Map by Thomas Cavanagh, Sr.

MURDERLAND

CHAPTER 1

He was doing the math in his head. $52.95 for each adult to get in. That included Joey. Since when was a twelve year old an adult? That was almost $160. Add in the twins at thirty bucks each, the usual and customary tourist taxes, and Jim was already out a cool $240. And that was just to walk in the gate.

Per day.

Of course once you're in, you have to *do* things. There are the rides, sure. If you can endure the hour-plus wait for each one. But there are a million other little things that get hawked everywhere you turn. Countless street vendors and plastic-smiling guest service representatives, all with their hands out. And you can't turn them down, not with the kids begging, pleading. *Please, Daddy? Pleeeeease?* After all, you're *on vacation.* So you purchase the bonus backstage tours that don't really show you anything and family photos to commemorate the day and ridiculous hats you will never wear in public again and incredibly cheap souvenirs that get lost or broken before you even get on the plane to go home. And don't forget the milkshakes, sodas, hamburgers, cotton candy, and WilberBars. Plus the hotel and the airfare and the rental car. And the night-time movies and the restaurant dinners. And the tolls. Jesus, you can't cross the street in Orlando without handing some joker a quarter.

Jim figured that a week spent in the happiest place on earth was costing him upwards of ten grand. He was utterly miserable.

"Daddy. Daddy, I'm hungry."

Jim looked down at his daughter Stefanie. Or was it Gwen? Damn, why did Claire insist on dressing them exactly the same? It wasn't cute anymore. It was just confusing. "Hungry? You just ate."

"But I want a WilberBar."

"But you *just ate*."

Claire shot him a reproachful look. "Jim," she said.

"Jesus, Claire. She just ate like . . ." Jim looked at his watch, ". . . like *fifteen* minutes ago. I spent seven bucks on her hamburger, which, may I remind you, she did not finish because she was full."

"Don't be such a tightwad," said Claire.

"She was full!"

"Daddy. Daddy, I want a WilberBar, too." This time it was Gwen.

"Me too," said Joey.

Jim closed his eyes.

"Y'know, I could go for something sweet myself," said Claire.

Shoulders slumped, Jim walked over towards the ice cream stand where some guy dressed like a cowboy was selling WilberBars. As Jim walked, he tried to calculate how much time in minutes he would have to spend at work to pay for these ice creams. He ordered four WilberBars and a cup of water for himself. He paid for them with a VISA card. As he signed his name he winced. The thought of needing a credit card to buy four ice creams was almost too much. It worked out to just over thirty-two minutes of work time.

He sat on a bench sipping his water while his kids climbed

on the lifesize Corral Pal figures at the edge of Prairie Park. Twenty-one hours until he was on a plane back to Illinois. Claire sat next to him, surveying the park map.

"We haven't been on Prospector Mountain yet," she said. "And, according to Frommer's, the early afternoon is the best time to avoid lines. The big Roundup Rodeo is in ten minutes and almost two thousand people fit in that stadium. That means fewer people in lines. Since we saw the Rodeo on Tuesday, I think we should cut through Lonesome Pass here—"

Claire stopped suddenly when she heard Stefanie scream. Jim got up and hurried over to where Stefanie stood next to a life-sized statue of Wilberforce the Wilberhorse. An audio recording was broadcasting in a continuous loop from a speaker in the statue's mouth. Wilberforce's familiar baritone sounded incessantly: "Huh-Howdy, Pardners! Are yuh itchin' fer some fun?"

"What's wrong, Stef?" asked Jim. "What happened? Is Joey picking on you again?"

Stefanie, now crying, pointed at the sugary sand at her feet. Jim looked down and saw the remains of a half-eaten WilberBar lying on the ground. He quickly calculated the cost of the wasted ice cream. Then he added in the inevitable replacement.

He reached down and grabbed the ice cream stick so he could toss it in a nearby trashcan. But when his hand touched the sand, he felt something odd. It was soft and rubbery. He moved the ice cream bar aside and recoiled, actually stumbling over onto his backside. He saw why Stefanie had screamed.

"Kids—go sit with your mother. Now!" he barked.

Claire looked over. "Jim, what is it?"

"Claire, call park security. And the cops."

"What is it?" Claire said, the concern in her voice growing.

"Oh, man . . ." said Jim. There, buried in the playground sand of Orlando's third-largest theme park, was the face of a human corpse.

* * *

The neon sign read "All Nude Girls!! Nude!! Nude!!" Very subtle, thought Kevin as he pulled into the parking lot. He watched the Dude walk in the front door with his buddies.

The Dude. That's what Kevin had nicknamed him. His real name was Hank Gordy. According to Kevin's file, Hank Gordy was thirty-eight, divorced, had two kids, and was a contract roofer in Central Florida's exploding construction trade. Hank Gordy was also currently on medical leave because of a work-related injury.

Although Kevin hated these workman's comp cases, they definitely beat the adulterous divorces. Most importantly, they paid the mortgage—always a priority.

Kevin grabbed a small, digital camcorder and shoved it into his coat pocket. It was a hot June afternoon and he would rather not be wearing the sport jacket. Plus, by the looks of the club, he would probably be the only patron in a coat. But he needed somewhere to stash the camera.

The Flamingo Room was located in the heart of Orlando's infamous Orange Blossom Trail. On one side was a pawnshop with wrought-iron bars on the windows. On the other side was a fourteen room motel boasting hourly rates. Orange Blossom Trail. It was a lovely name for a decidedly unpleasant neighborhood. This was a part of town that the tourist campaigns conveniently omitted, presumably because their target consumers were people other than crackheads, hookers, and transvestites. Orange Blossom Trail, or OBT, as the locals called it, was the home of all three. Sometimes all three in the same person.

Kevin followed the Dude and his construction buddies into the lowroofed, block building. A bouncer with a shaved head and arms the size of New Jersey nodded at Kevin as he walked in. Kevin paid the five-dollar cover and passed through a wrinkled velvet curtain.

The room was dark. Loud dance music played from speakers mounted in the corners. A bar curved along one wall. At the far end of the room was a stage illuminated by flashing colored lights. Two girls danced distractedly on the stage for the subdued crowd, twirling around greasy poles. The girls' eyes were blank. Lifeless. This was not one of the classier strip joints on OBT, and that was saying something.

There is a certain clientele that can be found in a seedy strip club bar at four o'clock on a Tuesday afternoon. A half-dozen unshaven men sat alone at tables or at the bar. They drank quietly, staring at the girls with sullen eyes.

Kevin slid into a booth with a view of the Dude and his boys. Kevin thought Gordy looked like a guy hanging desperately onto his youth. Long hair, goatee. Obviously worked out, but was showing the signs of a few too many beers. Probably used the word "dude" a lot on the job site. Currently, the Dude was wearing a neck brace and limping along with a cane.

He had fallen from a roof two weeks ago and hadn't been back since. The construction company's insurance carrier had asked Kevin to do a follow up to see if he was really hurt. Kevin did a good job for the insurance guys, very thorough, got evidence, kept detailed records. They threw Kevin a lot of work. It was grunt stuff but Kevin was a professional and took his assignments seriously.

Five times out of ten the workers' comp cases were frauds. And every time Kevin nailed a cheater he was disappointed. Every time.

The waitress approached. A brunette, she was young, pretty, and wore pink lingerie. Kevin ordered a club soda and shifted in the booth to get a better view of his subject. The Dude was already drinking and waving dollar bills.

Kevin nursed his club sodas and politely declined two lap dances during the next hour. By that time, the Dude and his friends were roaring drunk. Kevin reached into his pocket and pulled out the palmcorder. The digital technology was quite effective in low light. Kevin zoomed in on the Dude. Via the small, external view screen, Kevin saw that Gordy had a crowd of girls around him and they were dancing for him and his friends. The dollar bills were flying and, like moths to a lamp, they had attracted every g-string mercenary in the club.

Apparently, the Dude had had a few too many beers because the spirit overcame him and he stood up. With the music pounding, he danced enthusiastically with two girls at once. His cane was on the floor. He banged his head and shook his long mane, laughing and singing as he danced. Kevin let the palmcorder run.

His waitress passed by and Kevin detected a furtive glance as she went. She might have spotted the camcorder. Kevin stopped recording and quickly ejected the tape. He had what he needed. He slipped the tape into his sock, threw twenty bucks on the table, and slid out of the booth. The bouncer was waiting for him.

"Where you goin'?" said the bouncer.

"Home," Kevin said.

"Uh-huh. Where's the camera?"

The waitress was standing behind the bouncer, watching over his mountainous shoulder. "Look in his pocket," she said.

The bouncer reached into Kevin's jacket and yanked out the camcorder.

"Okay," said Kevin. "Take it easy." The bouncer was a good foot taller and probably had sixty pounds on him. But Kevin had handled guys bigger than him when he was on the job and could probably take him now, if he had to. He decided that he didn't.

"Fuckin' pervert," said the bouncer. He lifted the camcorder up and then smashed it down on the tabletop. There was an unmistakable crunch of highly expensive electronic components being pulverized.

He pushed the camcorder back to Kevin and grabbed his arm roughly. Then he dragged Kevin to the front door and threw him out into the parking lot. The last thing Kevin saw before he was shoved through the velvet curtain was the Dude and his friends laughing at him for getting bounced.

Kevin brushed himself off in the parking lot and thought, *get in all your laughing now, Dude. There won't be many chuckles in your new cell.*

The camcorder jangled in his hand. Damn. That camera was $3,500. He needed it for surveillance. Where was he going to get the money to replace it?

Then, as if on cue, his cell phone rang.

"I understand, Mr. Harrison. Of course, this must have been a very distressing incident." Jerry Engle was doing his best to remain calm. *Keep it together,* he kept telling himself. But his mind was racing. He needed another Xanax, but he dared not take anymore.

"Distressing?" said Mr. Harrison, who sat on a cheap couch in Jerry's office. "Well, yeah. I mean, one minute, my daughter is playing in the sand and then the next thing you know she steps on some dead guy's face. What kind of place are you running here, anyway?"

Jerry tugged at his eyebrow. "This has been very traumatic for all of us. Certainly not part of the Empire Realm Experience."

"I should say not." Harrison looked at him for a long moment. Jerry had no idea what to say. What can you say to a guy whose daughter just stepped on a dead man's face? There's no Hallmark card for it. Jerry tugged again at his eyebrows. At this rate his face would be as bald as the top of his head before the end of the day. Finally, Harrison broke his silence. "So? What do you intend to do about it?"

"Do?"

"Right. Like compensation. As you said, it was a traumatic experience."

"Oh. Yes. Well, I suppose that I could comp your family's tickets for the day. To make up for the trouble."

Harrison's expression was blank. "The day? Forgive me, but this is a pretty bad situation. Did I mention that my seven-year-old daughter stepped on a dead guy's face? She's scarred for life."

"Right," said Jerry. "How many days have you been at the park?"

"The whole family has a four-day Empire Pass. Plus we're staying at the Realm Villas."

"Well, I'm just not sure that we can . . ."

"You know," said Harrison. "This whole event has really tarnished my opinion of both Empire Studios and Empire Realm. I mean, things are gonna happen, right? Nobody's perfect. Although, a dead body in the middle of the park—that's gotta be off the map. Still, you judge people by how they *react* to a situation. Do they do the right thing? Do they make up for their mistakes? I'm sure the newspapers would be interested in how Empire has reacted to this . . ."

Jerry sighed. "Tell you what, Mr. Harrison. Why don't we comp your family's whole visit? We'll pick up the tab for the Empire Passes and we'll also cover your hotel stay. Would that alter your opinion of Empire Studios?"

Harrison smiled. Jerry wanted to choke him. Opportunistic bastard. He was using a man's death and any legitimate trauma his own daughter may have suffered to get a free vacation. Jerry made the arrangements with him and couldn't usher him out of his office fast enough.

When he was alone, Jerry closed his eyes and rested his head on his desk. Lips tight, nostrils flared. Steady even breaths, like the doctor told him. Visualize the palm tree on the island. The warm breeze. The gentle waves lapping at the beach.

All he could visualize was a tsunami crashing over him.

He had been Director of Security for Empire Realm for almost three years. In all that time, nothing like this had ever happened. Actually, that wasn't true. Something just like this had happened only three weeks ago, but he didn't know it until yesterday.

A dead man—also a tourist, like today's discovery—had been found behind a topiary cow. The preliminary cause of death was natural: likely a heart attack, given the victim's age and weight. But according to standard county procedure, an autopsy was done anyway just to confirm it. Jerry finally got the results from the Sheriffs department yesterday.

No toxins in the blood. Nothing unusual in his stomach. No drugs, save for trace elements of psuedoephedrine, a common, over-the-counter decongestant. No broken bones. No lacerations. No trauma at all, except for some bruising and abrasions around the neck. The sclera of the left eye exhibited some redness from a burst capillary, a result of a sudden increase in blood pressure in his head. The medical examiner's conclusion: Strangulation.

Murder.

And now, just a day after that shocking autopsy report, a dead man was discovered buried in the sand of the Corral Pal Playground. This was clearly murder. You don't usually die of natural causes and then accidentally bury yourself.

Oh, this was exceptionally bad.

The cops had cordoned off a huge section of the park as a homicide crime scene. Jerry knew the drill. Fourteen years with the Orange County Sheriffs office, the last five as a detective, gave him an appreciation for what needed to be done. And this clearly wasn't some Parramore Street crackhead knifing some other crackhead for his shoes. This was a homicide in the center of a major Central Florida theme park. Depending upon how it played out, this could be a once in a lifetime case. A cop's career could be made on a case like this. This was a potential book deal. A trip to New York to chat with Maury. Maybe even a TV movie of the week. This was the proverbial big fat one.

And the primary detective on the case was just the kind of guy to take full advantage of the opportunity. Jerry knew Louis Pendergrast well. They had served in the department together, Jerry graduating from the academy a couple of years before Pendergrast. They had worked the streets together, arrested punks together, solved murders together. And they hated each other's guts passionately.

Jerry couldn't stand Pendergrast's overt ambition. He took credit for other people's work. He blamed mistakes on others. Although he had no proof, Jerry also suspected Pendergrast of planting evidence in order to make an especially juicy collar. A certain kilo of cocaine found on a prominent Senator's son came to mind . . .

But Pendergrast was a serious cop. He cleared murders. Jerry knew that Pendergrast would play the Empire Realm murder for all it was worth. His wide, round face would be on the news every night. Newspaper interviews, anonymous leaks to the Internet, CNN reports—Louis Pendergrast would use this case to launch himself into the national spotlight, of that Jerry was sure.

This was exceptionally bad. Jerry tried to swallow but his

mouth was dry. He rubbed his hands over his face in a vain attempt to get a grip on his racing thoughts.

Jerry was an ex-cop and his mind still worked like a detective's. With the recent autopsy results added to today's body discovery, he was looking at two murders within three weeks of each other—both within the confines of the park. It seemed awfully unlikely that the two deaths weren't related.

But how? Did they somehow know each other? There had to be a connection. Drugs maybe. Money. Romance gone bad. Something. But the victims lived in two different states and had visited the park three weeks apart. Jerry just didn't know enough yet. His bowels made a loud gurgling noise as stress-induced stomach juices started flowing.

As his mind churned and he involuntarily tugged at his eyebrow, his gaze drifted down to a desktop picture of his family. He, Janie, and the girls were standing in front of the Empire Palace, its purple spire extending above the border of the photo. The family was smiling. If you leaned far enough to the left you could almost see the spot where the latest body was discovered.

He thought about his $286,000 mortgage for the house on Lake Conway. He had a nice life. Worked an easy schedule—nabbed shoplifters, busted teenagers for hopping the park walls, talked to the kids in local schools. He rarely worked past six, unless there was a TV special being shot or a concert at the Empire Pavilion. He pulled in $85K a year for basically being a theme park Andy Taylor. He had a staff of Barney Fifes and the work was predictable, sometimes even enjoyable, like when he helped a lost kid find his parents.

All of that was suddenly very much in jeopardy.

His job was to ensure that the park was a safe place for folks from all over the world to bring their families. He was responsible for their well being. You don't exactly get a warm, fuzzy, safe feeling when your seven-year-old kid steps on a dead man's face. Oh, Pendergrast would eat him alive.

What the hell, one more Xanax wouldn't kill him.

He shakily opened the pill bottle and popped another 0.5 milligrams into his mouth. He swallowed it down with the last gulp of his now ice-cold coffee.

He had already gotten four calls from various bosses at the studio in Los Angeles. He'd met with the PR lady three times so far. His voice mail was full of unreturned calls from the media. And Bill Oglethorpe had been by to see him twice today. He usually didn't see Oglethorpe more than twice in a month. Oglethorpe was the park president and was clearly under monstrous pressure from the suits in Hollywood. Jerry could imagine the conversation: *Fix it Oglethorpe. Fix it or we'll send in somebody who will.* Oglethorpe had made it very clear that Jerry's ass was on the line.

And there was Pendergrast roaming the sidewalks and boardwalks of the park, flashing his badge and scaring the crap out of the tourists. Jerry couldn't rely on the official cops (and especially Pendergrast) to return the Empire Realm patina of safety. He needed to take matters into his own hands.

But how? Jerry's job was a civilian, corporate role. The cops weren't going to tell him anything, even though he used to be one of them. Jerry was sure that Pendergrast would give instructions to his team to specifically exclude him. So far, Jerry had only had one brief conversation with Pendergrast to coordinate police access to the park. Pendergrast had been positively giddy at the prospect of sticking it to his old comrade.

Jerry needed to be in front of any new developments. He needed to see around corners if he had any hope of preserving his job. He needed to conduct his own investigation. But he couldn't do it himself. Pendergrast would ensure that he was frozen out.

Jerry needed someone on the inside. Under the radar of the cops, the press, even the Empire brass. Someone who knew what to look for. He couldn't trust anyone in his corps of Barney Fifes. They were mostly pimply kids right out of high school or retirees looking to combat the boredom of their last remaining days on earth. Jerry had nobody.

He tugged again on his eyebrow, pulling out a clump of short salt and pepper hairs. Jerry then flipped through his Rolodex and stopped on "L." He found the cell phone number for Kevin Lonnegan. An old cliche came to Jerry's mind. *Desperate times called for desperate measures.* Jerry felt like the freaking poster-boy for "Desperate." He picked up the phone, took a deep breath through flared nostrils, and prayed he was doing the right thing.

CHAPTER 2

As instructed, Kevin turned his Blazer left at the T-Shirt & Souvenir Boutique and headed down the two-lane blacktop road. It was a poorly maintained road, more of a country lane with cracked asphalt. An unkempt pasture containing two sad cows was overgrown on the right. On the left was a scrub pine hammock. The landscape seemed oddly out of place, as if hidden behind a curtain of blinking neon and rental cars. That it seemed out of place was pretty ironic. Only thirty years ago, after all, before Disney and Universal and Empire and Anheuser Busch built their tourist Meccas, this whole area was orange groves and palmetto scrub. Cattle once grazed where Bermuda short-clad tourists now lined up to have their pictures taken with part-time employees dressed like cartoon animals. This particular road was like an echo of those former times, hidden in the shadows of the parasite-like T-shirt shops and Denny's restaurants and discount ticket booths that populated the hinterlands of the theme park kingdoms.

A few miles down the road, Kevin saw a plain white sign with block letters that read "Empire Realm Security Gate 4B." He pulled his Blazer off the road, hitting a pothole. The busted shocks of his '86 Chevy made a telltale clicking sound. Kevin was pushing almost two hundred thousand miles on the old girl. He could probably afford a new truck. He knew he should get some new wheels.

But Kevin couldn't bring himself to sell it. It was the car he bought with Maria so long ago on a blindingly bright April day in Key West. Maria had liked the interior color. Charcoal. She said it looked smoky.

Kevin had bought it on the spot, pulling all his cash in the world out of the pocket of his Navy whites. He handed the man the money and climbed behind the wheel. He had no money, no job, no place to live, and no idea that his world would be turned completely upside down in a few short years. What he did have was a full tank of gas and a long-legged beauty in a blue bikini top in the seat next to him. He found a Bob Seger tune on the radio, cranked up the volume, pulled out onto US 1, and just headed North.

Smoky . . .

The memory was brushed aside as Kevin pulled up to a small booth where a guard wore a uniform the color of a putting green. The guard ignored him and Kevin waited patiently for almost a full minute. Finally, Kevin honked his horn.

"Excuse me," Kevin said.

Without looking up, the guard said, "The main entrance is three miles down the road. Go back to the highway. Go west and follow the signs for Empire Realm Main Gate."

"I know where the main entrance is," said Kevin. "I'm supposed to be here. Gate 4B."

The guard looked up from the science fiction novel he was reading. "Can I help you?" he said. He was maybe twenty-two years old. Maybe. His name badge said Billy.

"Yeah. I have an appointment in Building Three and I'm running late."

"Uh-huh. Name?"

"Kevin Lonnegan."

"Who?"

Kevin repeated his name. Billy punched a few keys on his computer. He waited for the results to post. And waited. Billy hit another key. Then waited again.

"Is there a problem?" asked Kevin.

"You're not cleared."

"Excuse me?"

"I can't let you in. You're not cleared."

Kevin sighed. "I think there's been a mistake. Check again."

"Let me see some ID," said Billy.

Kevin pursed his lips. He was late for his meeting and didn't have time for this nonsense. He reached his driver's license through the booth. Billy examined the picture like he was looking for an al-Qaeda loyalist. He checked the vital stats—eyes: blue; hair: red; height: 6' 2"; weight: 190. Billy's head bobbed up and down confirming each piece of information on the card with the person in the Blazer.

"It's me all right," said Kevin. "Like I said, I'm running late."

"Nope. Still not there." Billy handed the license back. "Sorry, pal."

"Sorry? What do you mean, sorry?"

"Sorry, like turn around and go home. I told you, you're not cleared."

Kevin felt a rush of anger behind his eyeballs. It was a familiar feeling, one that he still struggled to control even after all these years.

"Look, *Billy*, I don't care what your computer says. I was told to drive through Gate 4B and that I would have a clearance and that there would be no problem."

"I think you got a problem," said Billy, chuckling.

Kevin took a deep breath, attempting to lower his rising blood pressure. He gritted his teeth. "I suggest you call Jerry Engle. He's my appointment."

"Who?"

"Jerry Engle. Director of Park Security. Your *boss*"

"Oh. Right." Billy picked up a phone. "You got his number?"

Unbelievable. Kevin gave the kid the phone number. After a few minutes of discussion with an administrative assistant, Billy punched in a code and hung up.

"Got ya. Had your name spelled different." A small piece of paper stuttered up from a computer printer inside the booth. Billy placed it on Kevin's dash.

It read *Kevin Lung Again.*

The gate arm lifted and, with no apology or even another word, Billy pointed Kevin to a parking garage around a corner. The only empty space had a sign prohibiting anyone from parking there except for the Cast Member of the Month. Kevin turned the wheel sharply and parked in the space.

Kevin found Jerry's office upstairs, above the Lone Star Cantina. The distinct aroma of deep fat fryers filled the hallway outside the elevator. It was a smell that could border on delicious when you were starving but was downright nauseating at all other times. Kevin was currently leaning towards nauseating.

Jerry came out from around his desk, arm outstretched. "Kevin." Jerry looked basically the same. Thirty pounds overweight. A horseshoe of graying hair running along the back of his head from ear to ear. Pink, fleshy cheeks. Animated, intelligent eyes. Strikingly straight, white teeth. He looked agitated and very tired.

"Hey, Jer," Kevin said, shaking Jerry's hand warmly. They both remained standing.

"So, how are you, Kevin?" Jerry said it earnestly. It was more than just casual small talk.

Here we go. Kevin knew that this would come up—it always did—he just didn't expect it to be the first thing out of Jerry's mouth.

"I'm good, Jer. Real good." Kevin paused. He knew what Jerry was waiting for. So he gave it to him. "Clean and sober. Going on three years."

Jerry's tensed features softened a little. He seemed physically relieved to hear about Kevin's sobriety. "That's great, Kevin. Really, I mean it. Just great." Jerry clapped a hand on Kevin's shoulder. "You hungry? Let me buy you a Bronco Burger."

Empire Realm is eighteen square miles, not including parking and resorts, making it third only to Disney and Universal in total area. The park averages about 25,000 visitors per day, spiking to its 50,000 capacity during a few days each peak season around Christmas and Memorial Day. With almost $600 million total annual revenue, including restaurant and retail receipts, it accounts for almost 23% of Empire Studios' total profits and has a direct impact on earnings per share.

The park's theme is loosely hung on the "Four Corners" of the globe—the Realm. In the Southeastern corner is the European Alpine Village, which features the Breakaway Toboggan simulator ride, the Ice Haus (an indoor pavilion that boasts both an ice skating rink and an actual mini ski slope—with real snow), and the *Oom Pahs,* a band of roving street musicians in lederhosen. A series of shops offers genuine imported merchandise from Europe and hungry guests can choose between everything from a quick bite of bratwurst and slaw to thirty-dollar-an-entree fare at Les Chalet.

The northeastern section of the park is devoted to the tropical clime of South America. Lush vegetation crowds winding paths that lead to the Uncharted Amazon River Expedition, the Anaconda roller coaster, the one-third scale Aztec Pyramids, and the Machu Pichu Theater (where trained macaws and cockatoos perform three times daily for crowds in excess of five hundred). Shops here offer wide-brimmed straw hats, shirts bearing bold, tropical prints, and precious gemstone jewelry. Dining options include such choices as fried plantains, jerk chicken, and soft tacos.

The northwestern portion of the park is the home of the Asian Experience. Here visitors can get their pictures taken on a full-scale replica of a portion of the Great Wall, wander quietly through the Japanese Serenity Garden, ride a fiberglass Junk boat through the history of China (compressed neatly through the magic of animatronics into just six minutes), and watch dragons dance in the street every night to celebrate the Chinese New Year. As might be expected, the shops in the Asian Experience offer the finest in Far East imports. A woman with a disposable $465 can get a very nice silk kimono to wear back home. For the hungry visitor, dining choices range from pork lo mein to shrimp with lobster sauce to the sashimi platter for $28.99.

By far the largest section of the park is reserved for the United States. The centerpiece of Downtown USA is Lonesome Gulch, an authentic reproduction of an old west mining town. Guests can feel the thrill of being trapped in a runaway mine car at Prospector Mountain or witness the action of *Rootin' Tootin' Ropin' and Ridin'* at the big Roundup Rodeo. Four times a day, the kids can watch a live theater presentation of *Wilberforce the Wilberhorse at the Okey Dokey Corral* where full size cartoon animals (aspiring actors in latex and felt costumes) cavort on a raised stage to the delight of the squealing kids in the audience. All of the Corral Pals are featured, of course. A row of wood-floored shops hawk genuine Native American wares alongside Empire T-shirts and $300 crocodile-skin cowboy boots. The food is equally eclectic from the fast food of the swinging door Lone Star Cantina (above which Jerry Engle's office was situated) to the five-course gourmet feast offered at the Dixie Emporium.

Every theme park worth its salt has a signature landmark. The Magic Kingdom has Cinderella's Castle. Epcot has the giant spherical Spaceship Earth. Animal Kingdom features the Tree of Life. At the very center of Empire Realm is Empire Palace. The Palace is a massive, colorful structure, reminiscent of something that might be found in Red Square. Huge turrets reach into the blue Florida sky, topped with mosque-like rounded minarets. Inside the Palace is a five-star restaurant and the equivalent of a small, galleria-style mall. It sparkles in purple and green and shines magnificently when the nightly fireworks reflect off of it.

Looking at the global theme of Empire Realm, the major continent of Africa is conspicuously absent. One might think that this underrepresentation is yet another example of corporate America's neglect for the Third World. One would be wrong. Empire Studios had seriously considered including Africa in some of the original theme park concepts. But the idea was nixed fairly early in the planning process.

The entire Empire Realm operation began as one big marketing expense. Its sole purpose was to promote Empire Studios' movies. Even the Palace itself was lifted from the classic Empire film *Siberian Summer.* The fact that it now more than paid for itself (quite profitably, in fact) didn't change that single basic purpose. And Africa is a very small portion of Empire's global ticket revenues. Very small. As a result, Africa was excluded from the Empire Realm experience. Never mind that more than 680 million people live in Africa. The cost-benefit analysis clearly stated that the expenditure in promoting Africa within Empire Realm was not worth the return. It wasn't neglect that excluded Africa. It was business.

The park debuted in 1981, ten years after Disney opened the gates of the Magic Kingdom. Sea World was already operational but Universal's Orlando theme parks were still in the planning stages. The resort villas came in 1992, along with a state-of-the-art convention center and a Nicklaus-designed golf course. An animal park concept was currently under development. Empire Realm was a bona fide vacation destination. It was one of the major players in the Central Florida tourist trade.

On the film front, Empire Studios was just coming through a disappointing year. None of their films in the last twelve months had been a box office hit and one particularly high-profile action flick starring Sylvester Stallone whacked the balance sheet pretty hard. Stallone's picture, *Colder Steel,* cost $94 million (not including marketing) and brought in about $35 million (domestic). Even after the global markets finished their runs, it probably wouldn't break even. Empire's stock (NYSE: EMPR) had taken a particularly brutal beating as a result. The only high point that Empire's CEO Henry Jantsen could point to was the performance of the theme park operation. And this year was projected to be a banner year. That projection was pretty much the only thing keeping the stock afloat.

Empire Realm's 20th anniversary celebration was coming up this summer. A giant, month-long jamboree was planned, complete with a special parade (featuring Empire's newest star, Bruce Willis, as Master of Ceremonies) and a two-hour television special on CBS. Attendance was projected to spike more than 20% over last summer's receipts. In addition to the admission sales, revenues were projected to jump correspondingly in the ancillary restaurant and retail merchandise arenas.

The very last thing that Empire Realm needed, especially this summer, was an anonymous killer running loose in the park.

"You want fries or onion rings?"

Honestly, Kevin wanted neither. "Can I get a side salad?"

"How about cole slaw?"

"Fine." Kevin followed Jerry through a nondescript door. It was like some magical portal. One moment Kevin was walking down an industrial cinder-block hallway. In the next moment he was transported to the wild west of the nineteenth century. In theme park vernacular, Kevin had just stepped "on stage." The Lone Star Cantina looked like an old saloon right of a classic John Wayne movie. A mustachioed piano player in a striped shirt and arm garters plucked out a jaunty tune on an antique upright piano. A blonde woman in a royal blue costume hoop dress walked amongst the tables, twirling a parasol and acting the consummate hostess.

The main difference between the Lone Star Cantina and an actual old west saloon was a pretty big one: the clientele. Absent were the grizzled cowpokes sidled up to a whiskey-stained bar, the Derringer-hiding card players, the scarlet women with painted faces. In the Lone Star were close to seventy-five sunburned tourists lined up in neat rows to order fast food and seated at tables munching on burgers, fries, and chicken fingers.

"Why howdy, Sheriff Jerry," said the blonde woman when she spotted them come through the side door. She eyed Kevin flirtatiously. "Who's your friend?"

"Hi, Mavis," said Jerry. "This is Kevin. He's an old buddy from my law enforcement days."

"Doesn't seem too old to me," said Mavis. "Seems just about right to me." She was pretty but up close she looked older than

Kevin originally thought. Kevin guessed her to be in her mid-forties. It was hard to tell under the thick pancake makeup.

"Nice to meet you," said Kevin. Then he added, with a wink, "Ma'am."

She gave Kevin a Mae West smile. "Oh, you're trouble. I can tell already." She turned back into the restaurant. Over her shoulder she said, "Of course, I'm always lookin' for trouble." And then she was gone, back into the crowd of tourists, spinning her parasol and making small talk.

"That's Mavis DuBois," said Jerry. "She's the proprietor of the Lone Star Cantina."

Kevin watched her saunter from table to table. "She really seems to enjoy her work," he said.

Jerry smirked. "You have no idea. Her real name is Doris Anderson. A couple years ago she went through a really nasty divorce. Husband got the kids. She decided to start her life over in sunny Florida and moved down here from Cincinnati or Cleveland or somewhere. She wanted to be an actress and auditioned for a couple different performance roles. When she got the job playing Mavis, she took method acting to a whole new level. Even legally changed her name to Mavis DuBois. Comes in and works on her days off. And she bitterly hates any other actress who's assigned to play Mavis when she's not around. She calls them 'damned imposters.'"

Kevin had no idea how to respond to this information. "You've come a long way from that squad car, Jerry."

"Tell me about it."

Kevin found an empty booth while Jerry retrieved a tray of burgers and sides. In spite of himself, Kevin couldn't help but smile. He was sitting in the middle of a giant game of "pretend." Sitting here, listening to the piano music, winking at Mavis, it sure beat getting tossed out of seedy strip clubs.

Jerry sat down with their food. "I got you a Dr. Pepper."

"Thanks." Dr. Pepper was Kevin's preferred soft drink while he was a cop. Whenever he stopped at a 7-Eleven, something that cops did frequently, he'd grab a Big Gulp Dr. Pepper. Kevin was actually touched that Jerry remembered. "So what's up?" said Kevin between bites of burger.

"What do you know about the guy who died here yesterday?"

"Not much. Just what I read in the *Sentinel*. Some tourist from Detroit died in the park. Didn't say how. An investigation is ongoing."

"Well, there's more to it than that."

"I figured."

"The guy was strangled. Coroner says sometime between nine and midnight the night before. Whoever did it was careful. Buried him in the sand of a playground just around the corner from here. Some little girl found the body yesterday afternoon by stepping on his face."

"Jesus."

"It gets worse. Three weeks ago, same thing. A tourist. Also strangled. Except that one was stuffed in a topiary cow by the front entrance." Jerry put down his burger. "You see where I'm going here."

"Who's the primary?"

Jerry looked downright sick. "Pendergrast," he said.

"You poor bastard." Jeez, ol' Jerry couldn't have gotten a tougher break. Pendergrast. Kevin knew him well. "At least it hasn't leaked to the news yet."

"Not yet," said Jerry. "The department still has a soft spot for the theme parks. You know the drill."

"Right," said Kevin. No unnecessary publicity that might affect tourism. Tourists were the lifeblood of the Central Florida economy and strong tourism meant reelection for Sheriff Tim Gardner. That message was reinforced to the members of the Orange County Sheriff's Office almost daily. "But, Pendergrast, you know how he is."

"Yeah," said Jerry. He pushed his food away, his appetite gone. He pulled nervously at his left eyebrow.

"So, you think these two deaths are related?" asked Kevin.

"I'm afraid so."

Kevin sipped his Dr. Pepper. "I take it there's a reason you're telling me all this."

"You always were a good detective, Kevin."

They finished their lunch and took a walk. Jerry led Kevin down the main street of Lonesome Gulch. As they strolled along, Kevin tried to imagine the alley deserted, no tourists in sight, his spurs jingling as he prepared to draw on an outlaw. Jerry's proposition amused him and put him in an imaginative frame of mind.

"I can pay you a grand a week," said Jerry. "Plus you'll get your regular salary for the hours you're on the clock. Six-fifty an hour."

Kevin smiled. "Don't oversell it, Jer. What's the cover?"

"I figured I'd start you as a loader at Prospector Mountain. I'd prefer to place you into a job that's a little more mobile. Like custodial. But this is all that's available without attracting a lot of attention. The good news, if you can call it that, is that both murders were in this general section of the park, so at least you'd be in the vicinity."

"A loader?"

"Yeah—one of those guys who helps people get in and out of the mine cars."

"I see. Well, I do have some experience getting loaded. Maybe that qualifies me."

Jerry let out an awkward chuckle. He stopped walking and faced Kevin. "Look, I know this is a pretty weird gig. I've just got nowhere else to turn. Sure, this place is kinda ridiculous and basically a big sham. But, the truth is, I really like working here. I like my job. I like paying my mortgage. Once word gets out to the media that there have been *two* murders inside the park—*tourists*—in less than a month, I'm history." Jerry ran his hand over his balding head. He wasn't sure how to say what he wanted to say next. "We go back a ways, Kevin. I know what you've been through. You tell me you're clean, that's good enough for me. I need help. I need someone who can get out in front of this for me and give me some shot at saving my job."

Six-fifty an hour. Plus a grand a week. Actually, that wasn't so bad.

Kevin didn't have another assignment lined up yet, so, technically, he was available. Although something always turned up. He didn't need the gig. He didn't need to be standing out in the hot summer sun all day helping whiny kids in and out of a mechanized ride. But faced with the alternative of another seedy workers' comp case, or a messy divorce, or tracking down some strung out junkie for a law firm, a couple of weeks spent at Empire Realm didn't seem so bad. The place was scrupulously clean. Everyone was here to have fun. It was like make-believe. He could almost hear those spurs jingling.

And here was old Jerry Engle, hat in hand, asking for help. Jerry had been very good to him during his drinking days. Covered for him a few times. Drove him home when he wanted to drive himself. Gave him the number for the department counselor and told him that there was no shame in making the call. They were small gestures, but they said a lot about the man. And Kevin never forgot them.

Kevin knew he owed Jerry, even if Jerry didn't know it. He'd take the gig out of loyalty alone.

Plus, there was this small matter of a killer potentially loose in the park. The thought of it sent a shiver down Kevin's spine. He'd never been a big fan of the tourist trade—to him it was just part of living in Orlando. Like tollbooths on the highway or mosquitoes. He really couldn't care less about how the murders would affect Empire's bottom line. But the idea of some sick bastard strangling someone when they were on vacation, under the noses of their families, that was just awful. Kevin imagined what the plane ride home must have been like for the families of the victims. An empty seat where Daddy should have been.

Kevin could spend a few weeks here poking around. If everyone was lucky, he wouldn't find anything and the killer would turn up with a signed confession at a police station back home in Omaha or Philly or Seattle. If that happened, this would just be like a paid vacation for Kevin. Somehow Kevin had the feeling that he was in for something other than a vacation.

Jerry was waiting for an answer.

"Do we have any leads?" Kevin asked.

Jerry sighed in relief. "Not really. Pendergrast is keeping a lid on everything." They started walking again. Ahead of them was Prospector Mountain. Even from this distance, they could hear the excited screams of the riders as their mine cart swerved around a corner.

"What's your gut say, Jerry? Is this some killer on vacation? Needed a break from the daily grind of homicides back home?"

"I think it's a cast member," said Jerry.

Cast members. Theme park vernacular translation into English: employees.

"Maybe," said Kevin. "Could also be a transient. A new resident who doesn't have a job to go to yet. Both murders were

weekdays, right? Of course that doesn't really mean anything . . ."
Kevin's mind was starting to crank up. He could feel a little of
the old juice coming back. He hadn't worked a homicide in
almost four years. The possibilities started flying at him. "What
about two killers with the same M.O.? What if it's just a freaky
coincidence? What about two killers working together? Still . . .
it seems like an employee—"

"Cast member—"

"—cast member is the most probable. Just in case, did you
pull the ticket receipts for the two days?"

Jerry nodded. "But we've gotta do it by hand. We're not the
FBI. I've got my assistant entering all the names for both days
into a database so we can flag any matches."

"But that's just credit card receipts, right?"

"Right."

Kevin shook his head. "You think our boy would be dim
enough to show up twice in three weeks and pay with a credit
card? That's a dead end. What about cash? Do you have any
record of cash customers?"

"They're not customers. They're guests."

"Christ, Jerry. Whatever."

"These things are important, Kevin. If you're gonna blend in,
you have to start using the right terms."

"Okay. Do you have any record of *cash guests?*"

"Unfortunately, no," said Jerry. "Cash guests just get their
tickets and are shown through the gates. They don't have to
sign anything."

"Any connection between the vics?"

"Nothing yet. Of course, I can't interview the families like the
cops can. I'll see what I can find out."

Kevin nodded, more to himself than to Jerry. "There has to
be some connection. We just don't see it yet. Two victims. Same

M.O. Separated by three weeks. That sounds kind of calculated. More like a plan than a crime of passion."

"That's what I'm afraid of." Jerry's fingers were back at his eyebrow, tugging away.

Kevin wiped the sweat from his forehead with the back of his hand. The afternoon sun was relentless.

"Even so . . ." Kevin said. "Anything going on here we should know about? Harassment claims? Financial troubles? Cast members with drug problems? Extramarital affairs?"

"Nothing that I know of. I hear things now and then, but nothing that would be a motive for murder, let alone a double murder. And certainly nothing that would tie one of our cast members to the victims."

Kevin stopped walking. There was another set of happy screams from Prospector Mountain. He thought for a moment and his eyes wandered up to the plank porch roof outside Lonesome Gulch's Apothecary Shop. Handpainted signs advertised the latest remedies in snake oils and tinctures. The park designers had done a good job. The place looked like it belonged in an old west mining town, even down to the fake bullet holes in the roof overhang. The only part that wasn't authentic was the tinted domed cover of a surveillance camera.

"What about the surveillance tapes?" Kevin asked, eyeing the dome.

"We didn't see anything. The areas where the bodies were found were just outside of any camera's range. Anyway, Pendergrast confiscated the tapes."

"What about the camera at the front entrance? Did Pendergrast take those tapes, too?"

A smile crept across Jerry's face. "No, as a matter of fact, he didn't. I don't think he thought of it."

"Get me those tapes, Jerry."

"Done."

Kevin sat down on the edge of a horse's water trough. There were several coins resting at the bottom. Why the hell did tourists feel compelled to throw change into any body of standing water?

"So when do I start?" Kevin said.

"I think you already have," Jerry said, still smiling.

More screams from Prospector Mountain. Kevin squinted up at the sun.

"Jeez," he said. "I sure could go for one of those ice-cream horses."

CHAPTER 3

Damn, eight-thirty in the morning and it was already ninety-two degrees. If he was lucky he'd hook up with some job in the shade. If he was unlucky, he wouldn't get no job at all. If he was *really* unlucky, he'd spend another day out in the sun hauling chunks of concrete back and forth. His back still hurt.

Lucius Monroe stood in the parking lot of the Church's Chicken restaurant on north OBT along with about a dozen other black men. They ranged in age from eighteen to forty. At thirty-two, Lucius was starting to creep up into the upper half of the parking lot demographic.

Some of the usual crowd was there. Johnny T. And Willie. Arthur was sitting against the wall of the restaurant, looking pretty shaky. He probably had a long night with a bottle.

Lucius was feeling pretty good, all things considered. Every day got a little better. It was still tough. That pipe kept calling.

He had an apartment now. Yeah, it was a shithole, but it was his own crib. He'd been paying the rent for three months. But the money didn't come from nowhere. He'd gotten a couple of odd jobs through the Reverend. And he'd been lucky here at Church's, picking up day labor jobs when he needed them. He was often picked early. Since he'd been off the rock, he put a few pounds back on. He looked stronger than most of the other guys.

He kept telling himself: *one day at a time.* But sometimes it was tough to walk past the crews out on the sidewalk, waving those bags of rock. Coming home from a day's job, the cash felt heavy in his pocket. It would be so easy to buy a bag or two. Or three. Take a hit. Feel all the pain disappear. Feel like nothin' mattered. He had the money.

How many times had he done that? Probably a million. Every time he quit, said he was gonna straighten out, he'd stay clean for a while. But one day, and it always came, that pipe would start calling. He'd fight it for a while. But she's a bitch, man. At first she just whispers your name. *Lucius . . .* A voice dripping with promises. She lures you in. Talks sweet to you. Tells you how good she'll make you feel. And, damn, if she ain't right. She makes you feel *good.*

But if you resist . . . tell her *no, bitch . . .* she gets pissed.

Then she stops calling your name all sweet. And she starts screaming. Screaming in your head. Screaming all day and all night so you can't eat or sleep or do nothin' until you buy a bag, light her up, and take a hit. And if you don't have the money, you'll do anything to get it. Anything. You'd steal your momma's wedding ring. You'd grab a lady's purse. You'd knife some dude in the kidney. You'd do anything to stop the bitch from screaming. Because when she's screaming you can't hear nothin' else. Can't do nothin' else except whatever it takes to make her stop. And when you finally put your trembling lips on the pipe and take that hit—a long, sweet, burning drag—everything gets quiet, like church on a weekday. And the pain goes away. And you're hers forever. Hers until she uses you up and leaves you dead on the ground in some alley behind a dumpster, laying in the broken glass and the piss and the coffee grounds.

Lucius had been four months clean so far. He had never been four months clean before. He felt that he was straight for good now. It wasn't easy, would never be easy. God knew that the first couple weeks were a nightmare. The screaming was loud. Lucius didn't think he could stand it. But Kevin and the Reverend were there. They helped him through it. And eventually the screaming got quieter. It wasn't gone completely and there were some days when the bitch would come back, as loud as ever. But Lucius knew now he could handle it. He had taken the worst she could give.

A green Ford F-150 pulled into the parking lot. The crowd, Lucius included, pushed its way over to it. Two white guys got out and said they needed four men to lay sod in a new home development in West Orlando. Lucius had laid sod before. It was hot, dirty work. But he knew how to do it and it paid forty bucks for the day including lunch. He tried to get the men's attention, but he was near the back of the pack. They couldn't see him. They couldn't see that he was stronger than the rest of these guys. Most of them were either strung out or hung over.

The two white guys picked four men from the front of the crowd. The men jumped in the bed of the truck and were gone. The crowd shuffled back to wait for the next opportunity. That's the way it was. Folks came by, took who they needed, and left. By ten o'clock, if you hadn't been chosen, you weren't gonna be chosen. The homeless guys drifted off to the shelter on Parramore or made the rounds to the soup kitchens. The guys like Lucius looked for work elsewhere. If things didn't work out today, maybe the Reverend could hook him up with a painting job or some lawn work. He liked the lawn work, the way everything looked all neat and trim when he was done.

And some of the guys wandered off, looking for anything that would stop the screaming.

Lucius needed the money. Hell, they all needed the money. But Lucius really needed it. He had a home now, his own place. He was paying for it himself. But the shithole wasn't the dream. The dream was a house. With his own lawn to take care of. A respectable job. Lucius was saving for college. He was one of the few guys out here with a high school diploma. He knew that he couldn't get the dream without college. And college cost money, even with loans and grants. He wanted to learn about computers. Everyone knew that computers were the future.

Lucius recognized the next truck that pulled in. What the hell was he doing here? The pack swarmed on the white Blazer and Lucius had to push his way through. The window rolled down and Kevin leaned his red head out.

"How many you need?" said a short guy towards the front of the crowd.

"Just one," said Kevin. "Hey," he said to Lucius. "You busy?"

"Lookin' for work," said Lucius.

"Good. I need some work done."

Lucius smiled. Kevin always had the best jobs. One time he had Lucius sit outside a restaurant all day and count how many people went in. Lucius climbed into the Blazer.

As they pulled out onto OBT, Lucius asked, "So, Red, what is it this time?"

"You're going to love this one. I need you to watch some TV."

Lucius looked back at the Church's parking lot and the crowd of men waiting for the next truck. Damn, watching TV beat laying sod any day.

She was as beautiful as ever, standing over a dead body, eating a sandwich.

"Kevin Lonnegan!" she said with a big smile, chicken salad filling her cheeks.

"Hey Violet," Kevin said. "I'll never know how you can do this and eat at the same time." The smell of antiseptic was overpowering.

She shrugged. "Lots of people eat at their desks."

Violet Wilkins, M.D., was the Orange County Medical Examiner. She'd been in the job for six years and she and Kevin had always gotten along quite well. Kevin respected what she did and the professionalism with which she did it. She thought he was cute and a damn good cop. When he was a cop.

Establishing herself had been hard enough as woman in a male-dominated field. But as an African-American woman, she had felt extra pressure from both the people she worked with and herself. Kevin had accepted her right away.

Kevin walked over to her and they hugged like family. She put her hand on his cheek.

"It's been too long you know," she said.

"I know."

"You doing okay?"

Kevin gave her a reassuring smile. "Actually, I'm good. Really."

She patted his face in a maternal way. She was only forty-three, old enough to be Kevin's big sister, and that's exactly how she treated him.

"Who's the patient?" Kevin said, nodding at the body on the table. He was a middle-aged Hispanic man, naked except for a thin drape over his midsection. His face was horribly swollen and bruised. Deep lacerations crisscrossed his neck and chest.

"Carlos Petron. Cause of death—not having exact change." When Kevin gave her a confused look, she continued, "He smashed his car into a toll booth at seventy miles an hour."

Kevin had heard this. It was on the local news the night before. "He was in the coin lane and then changed his mind at the last minute," he said. "Smashed right into a booth on the Greeneway."

Violet shook her head. "It's a miracle he didn't hurt anyone else. He went towards the E-Pass lane instead of the change lane. If he had veered right instead of left, I'd have a toll collector lying on the table next to him. And here's the most amazing thing, he wasn't drunk or on drugs or anything. The toxicology was clear. He was just stupid." She threw her sandwich wrapper in a nearby wastebasket and drained a can of Diet Pepsi.

"So," she said. "How did I get so lucky to get a visit by the prodigal Kevin Lonnegan?"

"I'm a private investigator now."

"I heard. A waste of a good detective."

"Violet," Kevin said in a tone of brotherly warning. "I told you, I'm good. I'm happy, all things considered."

Violet leaned back against the examination table and smiled sadly. "All things considered . . ." She paused, lost momentarily in thought. "Funny coincidence that you came to see me today. I was looking for a pen in my desk last week and found this under a bunch of junk." She turned and plucked a photograph from a wall-mounted bulletin board. "The time we all went canoeing at Wekiva."

"I remember."

"I was still pregnant with Tommy and Bill had to keep pulling our canoe over so I could pee. Maria thought that was about the funniest thing she had ever seen. We were all laughing so hard I almost fell out of the boat."

"And then it started raining."

"That's right . . ." Violet trailed off, looking at the photo, lost in the memory. "She had a great laugh. I can still almost hear it."

"Me too."

"I'm sorry, Kevin," said Violet. There was a long pause. "I should have been there for you."

"Violet, please. I wasn't exactly the easiest guy to be there for." It wasn't Violet's fault they hadn't kept in touch. As fond as Kevin was of her, he purposely kept her and Bill at a distance. Although it was good to see Violet again now, it was still hard. Seeing her brought back too many memories. And if Violet wanted to talk about old times, there was really only so much Kevin could talk about before he would have to leave. Even after all this time.

He needed to change the subject. "I came to ask a favor," he said.

She seemed relieved to move onto another topic. She put down the photograph. "Shoot."

Kevin told her that he was working on a case having to do with the two recent deaths at Empire Realm. He couldn't go into too many details but he would like to know what the autopsy results were.

Violet crossed her arms. "You know I'm not supposed to give that information to anyone outside the department."

"I know. Perhaps if you could unofficially give me a few clues, I can figure the rest out myself."

"I assume you know Pendergrast is the primary on those."

"Yeah," said Kevin.

"I assume you also know I can't stand that little pecker."

"Yeah," said Kevin.

"Let me get you the files."

When Violet handed them over, she made it clear that neither was complete. She was still evaluating some findings. Kevin flipped through the reports, starting with the first victim. He read quickly, asking few questions. His old habits kicked back in, skimming through the dense medical jargon on his way to the conclusions tucked in the back. He scanned the first few pages, taking in the description of the autopsy procedures, the weight of the organs. If the guy had a pancreas that was abnor-mally large, or a small liver, or mushy brain tissue, or whatever, Violet would catch it. If it was significant, it would show up in her conclusions. From what Kevin could tell, there was nothing unusual with either victim's primary physiology that would be a cause of death.

Kevin learned that Victim #1—the guy found in the topiary cow—had last eaten a hamburger and fries and had a beer at dinner. His bladder was empty before he died. There was no evidence that he had involuntarily voided his bladder upon death, which would be normal. He had taken psuedoephedrine within two hours of death, which was consistent with some minor sinus congestion. No other drugs were found in his system. He was thirty-five pounds overweight, had high cholesterol, and was on the road to a heart attack, had he lived another ten years.

Three significant items leapt out at Kevin: (1) there was a burst capillary in the sclera of the left eye; (2) the hyoid cartilage in the neck was damaged; and (3), when the body was discov-ered, it had a slight erection.

His name was Kyle Hanratty. He was forty-seven, lived in Kansas City, and, according to Violet, he was on his honeymoon with his second wife. Kevin pulled a manila envelope from the file folder. Kevin knew that Violet liked to take a full comple-ment of autopsy photos. Sheriff Gardner especially insisted on thoroughness when a tourist was involved. He didn't want anything that could be potentially high profile coming back at him at election time. Kevin also knew that Violet liked to include crime scene pictures in with the autopsy pics.

Kevin slid the photos from their envelope. In the first shot, the man looked peaceful, almost like he was sleeping. A cliche, Kevin knew, but it really was what he looked like. Eyes closed, lips slightly parted, like he might start snoring—although the tip of his tongue protruded from his lips. He was Caucasian, with a brown beard turning grey at the corners of his mouth. His hair was thinning. The photos provided close-up shots of various body parts and points of forensic interest. The neck had the most coverage, displaying purple bruises and a raw, pink abrasion in a roughly horizontal line. The hands were photographed and Kevin noticed that they looked clean. The nails were neatly trimmed. There were no defensive wounds evidenced. On the outside of his left shin was a blistered, oval discoloration approximately two inches long and an inch wide. It was subtle, but it was there.

Victim #2—the one found in the sandbox—had last eaten a salad, some chicken and rice, and a cola. He had no drugs in his system except for a little caffeine from the cola. Also Caucasian, he was in much better physical condition. Apparently, he had run a marathon just over a month ago. His name was Frank Wilson. He was forty-one, lived in a Detroit suburb, and was on vacation with his wife and son. His physiology was also normal, with the same type of exceptions as Hanratty. There was no burst capillary in the eye, but the hyoid cartilage was also damaged and, when found, the victim had a slight erection.

Kevin pulled Wilson's photos from the envelope and was suddenly startled at the gruesome first image. It wasn't gory like so many violent crime scenes Kevin had been exposed to in his career. No blood was visible. But the picture was perhaps even more disturbing. The man was buried in the sand, with just his face and half his head exposed. His mouth was open with the tongue protruding unnaturally like a thick, purple sausage. His eyes were wide, bulging in a vacant death stare that looked life-less, yet penetrating. Grains of sand were dotted liberally over his tongue and eyeballs. That was the face that greeted the little girl who found him.

Kevin shook off the image, chastising himself for being startled. He had been away from homicide for too long. His skin had thinned. He wasn't the same person anymore.

These photos were very much like the first victim's. No defensive wounds. Same bruises and marks on the neck. Same blistered skin discoloration, except not on the left leg. There was a smaller round mark on his head behind his ear and another on the outside of his left wrist.

Kevin turned to the last page of each report. Violet's preliminary conclusions were that both cases were homicides and that both were victims of ligature strangulation. The burst capillary, the damaged hyoid, the slight erection, the bulging eyes and tongue—all were classic signs of strangulation.

Violet's assessment of the murder weapon was that it was a fabric or soft cord of some type. It wasn't a wire or hard-edged plastic or leather strap. Or even a rope. The neck abrasion was too diffuse. Violet was unable to offer any conclusive hypothesis on what the precise murder weapon was. All she was willing to say was that the weapon was probably a woven material of some sort because of the inherent flexibility of such a material and the horizontal trauma to the dermis. Some examples she provided were a stretched sock, a nylon strap, and a fabric belt. She was able to rule out a human hand as the primary murder weapon. There were no indications of finger bruises or prints on either body.

The pressure on the trachea had been strong, although probably not aided by any tensioning tool, such as that provided by the fabric being knotted around a stick and the stick turned repeatedly. There wasn't enough trauma to the skin. Plus, the hyoids, although damaged, had not been crushed. She couldn't justify anything but a manual strangulation with a woven ligature. But whoever did it was strong.

She postulated that the killer was tall, at least six-foot three, and powerful enough to quickly gain control of his fully grown, male victims. She believed that the killer approached the victims from behind, caught them by surprise, and overpowered them. They were dead within a few minutes. Skillfully executed, it was an efficient and quiet way to do the job.

Based upon the medical evidence and the nearly identical disposition of the bodies, Violet's conclusion included the statement that the killer of both victims was, in all likelihood, the same person. Of course, it was up to the detectives, and Pendergrast specifically, to confirm that through the course of their investigation. She couldn't testify to it in court except as an opinion. But her gut said it was the same killer and Kevin couldn't remember a time where she had ever gone out on a limb like that and been wrong.

Kevin looked up from the files. "Did you find any connection between the two guys? Something that ties them together?"

"Well, besides the obvious—of how they died, no. I don't have access to Pendergrast's interviews with the families. All I would come up with are physical connections like the marks on the neck. Maybe if they both had hangnails or the same tattoo or something, it could be a start. But there's nothing. As far as I can tell, these are two completely separate guys who were killed by the same person."

"What about these spots?" Kevin said, holding up the image of the blistered oval discoloration on the first victim's leg. "You didn't say anything about them in your reports."

"I told you that the reports were preliminary. Those are what's keeping me from offering final conclusions."

"What do you think they are? Preliminarily."

She made a face. She hated offering half-baked guesses, preferring to present reasoned theories backed up by medical evidence. But she considered a moment and said, "Burns. They look like burns."

"Sunburns?"

"No. Something else. I've got some tissue samples out at a specialty lab for further testing. I'll let you know when I get the results."

Kevin nodded. He trusted Violet's hunches. Something was telling her that these burns were important. It certainly strained credulity to think it was a coincidence that both victims happened to have small, localized burns on their bodies.

Violet informed him that she was told that a personal item was missing from each victim. Theft clearly wasn't the motivation for their murders—both still had their wallets and jewelry. The first victim's sunglasses were missing. The second victim was found without his rental car key.

"There is one more thing," Violet said. She produced a small plastic evidence bag. Inside was a single brown hair found on the first body. It was about five inches long.

"A hair," said Kevin. "You going to run a DNA test?"

"I would, but it's not a hair. It's a synthetic fiber."

Kevin examined it more closely. It looked like a hair to him. "Made of what?"

"Nylon."

"Nylon . . . Part of the murder weapon? The woven fabric?"

"Maybe. I don't know. Honestly, I've never seen one like this. Sure, we get fibers on bodies all the time. But this one is different. It doesn't look like any fiber I've seen come through here before. It's a little thicker than a real hair, no fraying or kinking, like it was pulled by force from a fabric. And it's relatively stiff. It wouldn't make a very good strand for a weave. But, having said that, we can't specifically rule out that it came from the murder weapon."

Kevin held it up to the light. This was a critical piece of evidence. It could represent a mistake by the killer. Plenty of murderers have been brought down by a single fiber. "Is Pendergrast running this down?"

"Of course. Word is that he's checked everywhere. Wig shops, clothing stores. He's spoken to a dozen textile companies and clothing manufacturers. The actual nylon it's made from is quite common. But the fiber itself is a mystery. Its size. Its purpose. Nobody's been able to ID the source yet."

Kevin gave her back the evidence bag. He read through the files again, took some notes, and photocopied a couple of pages and photos. When he was done, he gave Violet a sincere hug and thanked her for her help. She promised to keep him in the loop on any new information.

"Where are you off to in such a hurry?" she asked.

"I'm late for my new job orientation."

It was called Empire University, although the only thing it had in common with an actual university was the average age of the students. Essentially, it was a corporate classroom with movie posters from Empire Studios pictures on the walls. Kevin sat in a chair on the left side of the room, Jodie Foster brooding on the wall over his shoulder.

About a dozen other students were there, mostly kids from the University of Central Florida looking to pick up some part-time beer money. Their instructor was a thin, blonde man of maybe thirty named Kippy Whittaker.

Kippy.

Kippy was dressed in an Empire Realm polo shirt, neatly pressed khaki pants, and had the regulation short haircut (above the ears). Also per regulations, Kippy did not sport any facial hair and had his nametag displayed prominently on his shirt. He began the session by learning everyone's names and asking why they wanted to work for Empire Realm.

Most of the answers were in the neighborhood of "I need to make some cash to buy beer," although there was one Disney hater who went on a long diatribe about the Mouse slashing previously paid benefits and forcing her to quit her job in Disney Guest Services. When Kippy got to Kevin, Kevin thought about answering truthfully: *Well, Kippy, I decided to come work for Empire Realm so I could try to find the killer who's murdering your nice guests before that prick Detective Pendergrast does.*

Instead he said: "I lost my job and I need the money."

Kippy went through the usual routine of explaining the company benefits (which, Kevin thought, were pretty good). 401(k). Medical. Dental. Tuition reimbursement. Same sex partner coverage. Paid vacation (full-time cast members only). Free admission to the park. Discounted merchandise. Discounted tickets to Empire Studios movies. The list went on.

There were a few questions. Kevin only asked one, and it was sincere: "Why is it called Empire Realm? Isn't that redundant?" He genuinely wanted to know. Kippy just blinked silently at him. He had no response. Instead, he moved on to the code of conduct.

There was a long list of rules for conduct. Basically, they all boiled down to one thing: Be insanely nice.

Always smile. When approached by a guest, always ask, "How may I help you today?" Always end a guest interaction with "Have a wonderful day/evening!" Always display your nametag. Whenever you need to point to offer directions, do so with two fingers, never one (which is rude). Maintain the grooming standards. Men: short hair, no beard or mustache, no earrings, no other piercings, no visible tattoos. Women: hair not longer than the shoulder blades, only one earring in each ear, no more than one ring on each hand, minimal make-up, short fingernails, no bracelets, and, like the men, no other piercings or visible tattoos. Clothing was not an issue for either men or women because everyone was assigned a job-specific costume from the wardrobe department.

Although there was a staff of full-time character performers, every Empire Realm cast member was required to don a character costume one day a year. That was because Empire Realm felt that, since the park relied upon the popularity of the Empire Studios stable of cartoon characters, every cast member should be a part of bringing them to life for the guests.

There was a lot to cover and Kippy was a professional. Kevin respected that. Kippy was excessively enthusiastic about Empire Realm and he tried to inspire that enthusiasm in his audience. But it was a tough room.

"You mean to tell me," said one student in a Sigma Chi fraternity shirt, "that I gotta put on some heavy fur chipmunk suit in the middle of August? Screw that." There was muttering of concurrence from his colleagues.

"Actually," said Kippy. "Given your size, I doubt you'd be selected to portray Spunky. You'll probably be Wilberforce the Wilberhorse, which is quite an honor. He's the symbol of Empire Realm, after all." Kippy smiled sincerely. "I was asked to be Wilber once. It was one of the highlights of my career."

"I bet you were the back end," said Sigma Chi.

Kippy's smiled never even twitched. Kevin was impressed. "Let me assure you," Kippy said, "that all of our character costumes are climate controlled. Plus, character performers are not allowed to be on stage for more than twenty minutes at a time. So you have nothing to worry about."

The next section of the curriculum focused on handling difficult guests. Kippy set the stage. "For the most part, people come to Empire Realm to have fun, enjoy themselves, and go home happy. But every once in a while, despite our best efforts, a guest will be dissatisfied. This is an important opportunity to turn a frown upside down."

Kippy explained that no matter how upset or angry a guest became, you never raised your voice or responded in any way but politely and happily. Kippy ran through some role-plays with the students where everyone took a turn being an upset guest. Kippy then modeled the behavior for dealing with that guest. Then everyone got an opportunity to be the cast member in the role-plays.

Kevin got paired with Mr. Sigma Chi, who really enjoyed his role as Angry Guest. He used this opportunity to throw in every profane word he had heard since third grade, all aimed directly at Kevin. Then he got personal and made fun of Kevin's red hair, losing his job, and his breath. Kevin maintained his composure and his smile, calmly asking Angry Guest, "What can I do to make you happy?"

"Go fuck yourself, carrot top." Sigma Chi cackled with laughter.

"I'll see what I can do," said Kevin. "Perhaps you would care to speak with my coach?" Supervisors at Empire Realm were called coaches.

Kippy actually stood up an applauded. "That was *excellent,* Kevin. Really. You maintained your smile. You never got upset. You were accountable and tried to handle the situation personally, but when that didn't work, you offered to get your supervisor. Very well done. Remember, everyone here is a *guest,* and even if they're rude, we still treat them as a guest."

The training session concluded with Kippy printing nametags. Empire Realm preferred the cast members to have informal, friendly, accessible nicknames. A classmate named

John was given a nametag reading "Johnny." Susan was "Suzie." When Kevin approached the table, Kippy seemed stumped.

"Kevin . . ." he said, thinking. "How about Kevvy?"

"You can't be serious."

"Sure! Why not? Kevvy. That sounds great."

"Look, Kippy, no offense, but there's no way I'm wearing a nametag that says Kevvy. That just isn't gonna happen."

Kippy pursed his lips and considered. "Okay. Kevin it is. Just make sure you're extra smiley."

Kevin offered a toothy grin, which pleased Kippy.

As he made his way out of the room, Kevin accidentally brushed against Sigma Chi in the doorway.

"Watch it, limpdick," said Sigma Chi.

Before the kid knew what happened, Kevin grabbed his wrist and twisted it behind his back, pushing him into the hallway.

"Ow—Shit—Let go!" shrieked Sigma Chi.

Kevin pushed Sigma Chi's face into the wall, pulling his arm up firmly behind his back. His wrist was twisted at an unnatural angle and Kevin felt the kid's tendons trembling under the strain. Kevin leaned in close, talked softly into Sigma Chi's ear. "You're a very good actor. I almost believed that you were really insulting me. But I know you were just playing the part, right?"

Kevin gave the wrist a sharp twist. "Ungh—" said Sigma Chi.

"But I know you were just playing the part, right?" Kevin repeated.

"Right—" said Sigma Chi, his face a deep red, his eyes watering with pain.

"Because if I thought that you were actually insulting me, well, I might have to do something about that. I have a pretty nasty temper."

"I—" grunted Sigma Chi. "Just acting."

"That's what I thought. Like I said, you were very good. You should think about being a drama major."

With that Kevin released him. Sigma Chi turned around, rubbing his now-sprained wrist. Kevin could see the anger in the kid's eyes. But even more he could see the fear. Kevin had dealt with hundreds of punks like him when he was a cop. He knew that Sigma Chi wasn't going to do anything. He almost hoped he would. Without a word, the kid turned and left.

Before Kevin left the Empire University corridor, he caught a glimpse of Kippy peeking at the encounter from the doorway. As per regulation, Kippy was smiling broadly.

CHAPTER 4

Louis Pendergrast had a hemorrhoid the size of a golf ball.

At least that's what it felt like. He literally couldn't sit down. When he did, his ass hurt so much that his face involuntarily tightened, like he just licked a lemon.

Despite the pain, he had avoided the doctor for weeks. He just couldn't picture himself bent over an examination table, spreading his cheeks while some doctor shoved his face in there. The image disturbed him.

He had applied every ointment and cream he could buy at the drugstore on the affected area. It would help a little, for a while. But, damn, this was one stubborn pile.

Eventually, the pain became worse than the image of the examination room and he went to see his general practitioner. Thankfully, the doc had been professional and not burst into laughter, as Pendergrast expected. Although, when Pendergrast finally bent over the examination table and the doc shoved his face in there, the doc did whistle and declare, "Boy, that's a beaut, that is."

The doc told him about rubber band ligation, where he would strangle the hemorrhoid with a rubber band and wait for it to die and fall off. Yeah, that sounded pleasant. But the doc actually recommended surgery. Out of the question. *Ass surgery?* He was kidding, right? There was no way in hell Pendergrast was going to have ass surgery. He could just picture what the guys in the department would do with that. As it was, he kept telling everyone that he had pulled a hamstring and that's why he was walking funny and preferred standing up.

He was standing in the break room, pretending to sip coffee (any excuse to get up and stand for a while) when the call came in. Another body in the Empire Realm park. He was in the process of investigating what had surprisingly turned into a murder at the park three weeks ago. An autopsy report had come in two weeks ago informing him that the stiff in the big shrub shaped like a cow had been strangled. He had had the pleasure just the day before of telling that old has-been Jerry Engle all about it. And now there was a new body. This was really getting interesting.

Before he went out to the park, Sheriff Gardner had given him "the speech." He had heard it a million times in various forms. Do your job but don't attract attention to anything that might result in negative publicity for the parks. The same held true for the Convention Center, International Drive, and the downtown Church Street area. This town lives and dies on tourist dollars and our job is to keep the veneer of safety on the whole place. As far as the department was officially concerned, we were just doing a routine investigation of some poor yokel who had the bad luck to croak while on vacation. Blah blah blah.

But Pendergrast could smell the red ball. Most cops hated the red ball—the public scandal. But Pendergrast got off on it. Where better to show what you're capable of than under a white-hot spotlight? Where others ran for darkness, Pendergrast stood up to the pressure and stared it down.

Who would play him in the movie, he wondered? Maybe Harrison Ford.

No matter that Pendergrast was about four inches shorter and had less hair than Mr. Ford. Not to mention more waist.

Finally a case that Pendergrast could sink his teeth into. Actually, as it turned out, *two* cases. Two murders at Empire Realm in three weeks. And these weren't ordinary, garden-variety murders. Like some minimum wage popcorn vendor offing his wife's boyfriend in the employee parking lot. These were tourists. That made them instantly different. Plus . . .

. . . and this was the really interesting part . . .

. . . it looked like Pendergrast was facing two murders by the same killer. Pendergrast didn't have a motive yet, but he'd ferret it out. The case was sure to become a publicity magnet. It could become national news. The thought of what this could mean to Pendergrast's future had rendered him unable to sleep ever since he found out. He immediately began keeping copious investigation notes. He also started locking his files in his desk drawer and password-protecting his computer. As of the moment he got the call about the second body, he officially couldn't trust anyone. Not that he trusted anyone anyway. There was no way he was going to share any of the glory when he eventually tracked down the killer and brought him to justice under the glare of CNN's cameras.

The ride from the Orange County Sheriffs office out to Empire Realm had seemed even longer than usual. The damned hemorrhoid made it impossible for Pendergrast to get comfortable in any seated position.

His latest partner was driving. Pendergrast had a way of running through partners. He knew he could be tough on them, but this was police work. It was no place for pussies, which seemed to be all the academy was providing these days. Either you had what it took or you didn't. Precious few did and Pendergrast had no patience for the wannabes.

The partner's name was Walter Mickelson, just a kid, really. He had recently made detective and Sheriff Gardner thought it would be good to pair him with a veteran like Pendergrast. Great, thought Pendergrast, now I'm a goddamn babysitter. He shifted uncomfortably in the passenger seat.

"Uh, you okay?" Mickelson asked him.

"Yeah, I'm goddamn peachy."

Pendergrast tried clenching, but that just made the pain worse. He stretched out his legs and braced his feet on the floorboard, attempting to surreptitiously raise his butt from the seat.

"Are you sure?" Mickelson asked. "You're making a funny face, and . . ." he trailed off, obviously not sure how to describe his partner's unusual movements.

"I told you, I'm fine," snapped Pendergrast. "I pulled my goddamn hamstring. I was playing pick-up basketball and some asswipe fouled me."

Mickelson looked unconvinced. He glanced back at Pendergrast's butt. "Your hamstring, huh?"

"Will you just watch the goddamn road?"

When they arrived at the crime scene the uniforms had already cordoned it off and were chatting pleasantly with the assembled crowd of gawkers. Pendergrast found one of the patrolmen licking an ice cream bar and gave him a good ass chewing. Instead of gathering evidence or interviewing the crowd, he was eating a goddamn ice cream. What the hell?!

The body was in the sand of a playground at the feet of one of the park's ridiculous character statues. The statue kept repeating the same inane phrase over and over. "Huh-Howdy, Pardners! Are yuh itchin' fer some fun?" Pendergrast had only been there ten minutes and it was already driving him nuts. Maybe the guy in the sand killed himself rather than listen to that one more time.

"Will somebody shut that goddamn thing up?" he said loudly to no one in particular. "I can't even hear myself think."

An Empire Realm rent-a-cop ran off to flip whatever goddamn switch shut it up.

A police photographer snapped the last of a series of shots and the Medical Examiner, who had just arrived, bagged the hands and gave the authorization to dig the body out. Pendergrast's first impulse was to seal the park exits and run everyone through a checkpoint before they could get out. Search shopping bags, purses, pockets, even look under the WilberHats. If someone had a fabric belt or a nylon strap or whatever was used to garrote the dead guy, he would find it. Plus, who knew what else he would find? He bet this place was filthy with drugs.

However, the M.E. declared the body cold. The victim was killed sometime the night before, more than twelve hours ago. Meaning the killer was probably long gone and Pendergrast wouldn't be able to justify sealing the exits.

Oh well. That would have been truly a rush. Single-handedly, Pendergrast would have brought one of the world's largest theme parks to its knees. Nobody would've been able to leave without his permission. Sheriff Gardner would have had a stroke, but so what? If sealing the gates would have found the killer, the end would have justified the means.

Jerry Engle did manage to come by, pulling on his eyebrows and looking like he was hauling a load in his pants. Which he probably was. This couldn't be good for the big Director of Security.

"Hey, Jerry," Pendergrast said. "How you doin'? Boy, this is a pisser, wouldn't you say?"

"Lou," Jerry said. "Do we really need the police tape and the big scene here?"

"Jer, this is a crime scene. A homicide."

"I understand. But we're in the middle of a theme park. Let my crew put out some cones and parade barricades."

Pendergrast laughed. Parade barricades? Was he kidding? "Sorry, Jer. I gotta do my job. You understand." Jerry looked positively sick. Pendergrast thought about how the universe worked. If you just waited long enough, justice would prevail. Jerry Engle had been a royal prick to him when he was still on the job. Well, he was paying for it now. The universe had deposited a dead body in the middle of his pristine, make-believe world.

They could build their fantasy worlds, populate them with costumed animals and happy music, but they couldn't keep the filth out. They pretended they were immune from the realities of the outside world. But they were as vulnerable as anyone. The filth had blown in through a crack in the freshly painted park wall and the result was murder in the middle of happy land.

Jerry couldn't do a goddamn thing about it. Hell, everyone knew that Jerry couldn't handle real police work anymore and had thrown in the towel, talking his way into a soft job at a ridiculous salary to wipe runny noses and direct traffic in the parking lot. But when the filth blew in and real police work needed to be done, they called Lou Pendergrast.

He'd find the killer. He'd clean the filth so the tourists would keep spending their money. But he'd make damn sure Jerry squirmed while he was at it.

They arranged unlimited park access for the police investigation team and Jerry's pager went off. Jerry looked at the number, muttered "Not again," and scurried off. Pendergrast just laughed.

"So, Boss, what do you think?"

Pendergrast turned from watching Jerry hustle back to his corporate master to see Mickelson standing at his side like some goddamn puppy.

"I think this may just be the best day of my entire life."

Kevin opened the door, carrying a pizza box. Lucius was sitting on the couch, a pad on the coffee table in front of him filled with scribbled notes.

"How's it going?" Kevin asked.

"I'm goin' blind, Red," said Lucius. "Seriously."

"Take a break. I brought your favorite."

Lucius shut the television off and stood up, stretching his arms towards the ceiling and then holding his lower back. Kevin noticed that Lucius looked a lot better than he had ever seen him before. Lucius claimed he hadn't hit the pipe in four months. Kevin wanted to believe him, desperately hoped it was true. But crack was an awful drug and once it had its hooks in you it was very hard to escape.

"Not pepperoni again," said Lucius, lifting the pizza box lid.

"What? You love pepperoni."

"I told you, it gives me heartburn."

"When?"

"Last time you got pepperoni. Man, now I gotta get more Turns."

Kevin pulled out a couple of Styrofoam plates. "I could cook you something. You want an omelet?"

"I'll take my chances with the pepperoni." Lucius grabbed a slice and walked out to the small deck off the back patio. Kevin grabbed a couple of Dr. Peppers and followed him.

The sun was just starting to drop in the west and the reflection off the water of Lake Jessup was breathtaking. The rippled water looked painted in bright orange and red. On the horizon the remnants of the daily afternoon thunderstorm lingered. Dark purple clouds flashed periodically with silent lightning. The light show was too distant to offer any audio. It was a typically brilliant Florida sunset.

Kevin and Lucius, neither being overly sentimental, sat silently and just watched the natural show, eating their pizza and drinking their soda. Although neither of them expressed it, they were both mesmerized by the natural beauty around them. A great blue heron drifted across their view, searching for its own dinner glinting under the surface of the water.

Kevin had owned the house since he left the force. It was really just an old cracker shack, all wood—a termite's heaven—but it was in an excellent location. Nestled on the shores of Lake Jessup, the property was worth much more than the structure. Under normal circumstances, Kevin could never have afforded a home on that property, even one as humble as this. But life was funny and cruel. He had come into quite a bit of money from Maria's insurance policy.

Two bedrooms, one bath, it was barely big enough for Kevin to live in and run a small private investigator's office. His office was in the spare bedroom and consisted of a couple of second-hand file cabinets, a fax machine, and a computer.

The place was devoid of photos. There was just one picture on the mantle of the unused fireplace. The picture was of Kevin and his brothers as kids, arms around each other's shoulders, grinning on a beach outing somewhere on the Jersey Shore, a long, long time ago.

He and Lucius finished the last slices of pizza and retreated back into the house as the sun set and the mosquitoes bore down on them.

"So, how's it going so far?" Kevin asked him.

"Damn," said Lucius, shaking his head, smiling. "When you

said you wanted to pay me to watch TV, I thought it was gonna be a piece of cake. But, damn."

"It ain't exactly prime time."

"Damn."

Lucius had spent the day watching a security camera tape from the front gate of Empire Realm. The camera didn't move. Ever. No tilts, pans, zooms, or cuts. Just a locked-off, static angle looking slightly down on the arriving park guests. And there was no sound. It was deadly boring.

"I been through about eight hours so far," said Lucius. "You hear what I said? *Eight hours?* You're gonna kill me watchin' this shit."

"Find anything interesting?"

"Interesting? I think *you* must be the one on crack." Lucius let out a loud belly laugh. It was infectious. Kevin laughed along with him. God, it was good to see Lucius laughing. It had been a long time. Maybe he really was clean this time. Kevin let a little hope seep into his heart.

God knew, Kevin understood addiction. Maybe not crack, but Kevin had his own demons, just as dark and just as powerful. For him it had been alcohol. What had the psychiatrist called it? An event-triggered addiction. Whatever. The booze took away some of the pain. It clouded his mind and helped him forget. Which was exactly what he wanted.

But he had grown dependent on it. He drank at night to fall asleep. He drank in the morning to face the day. He drank during the day just to cope. Then he drank at night to fall asleep again. Because when he stopped drinking, his mind cleared and his thoughts drifted back to happier times. And the idea of getting up and facing a world where all his happiness had been taken from him was too much to bear. When he wasn't drunk, he was sitting in a dark room, unable to move. So the booze was his rehabilitation.

Of course that was a lie. The booze just masked his pain, it didn't take it away.

He understood Lucius' demons only too well.

They had met a few years ago and their friendship began with a most unlikely introduction: Kevin had beaten Lucius to within an inch of death.

It was during the height of Kevin's drinking period. He was coming off duty and was drunk, as usual. As he was driving his unmarked car, he actually witnessed Lucius stepping out through the broken glass of a Radio Shack storefront, his arms holding a brand new Compaq Presario computer. Lucius was much thinner then, strung-out bad. He had a long rap sheet of breaking and entering and fencing the goods for crack money.

When Kevin saw him coming out with the stolen computer, he quickly parked the car and leapt out. Even in his drunken state, he was able to run Lucius down and tackle him from behind. When Lucius resisted and tried to escape, something inside Kevin's inebriated brain snapped. He didn't just restrain Lucius, he started beating him. Severely.

He rained down blow after blow until Lucius quit trying to escape and just begged him to stop. But Kevin couldn't stop. He was out of his mind by then, taking out all of the anger and frustration and pain he felt in his life at that moment on this poor petty thief and drug addict, who happened to be in the wrong place at the wrong time. Kevin let fly punch after punch, transferring all of his rage onto Lucius.

It took three other cops to pull Kevin off of him—one of them was Jerry Engle. Panting and sweating, being held by his colleagues, Kevin finally let the anger drain from him. He looked down and suddenly felt the pain of broken bones in his hands. His knuckles were raw and covered in Lucius' blood.

Lucius lay semiconscious on the sidewalk, the smashed

computer on the concrete beside him. He was making a low, moaning noise and the whole lower half of his face was crimson with blood from his smashed nose. Kevin would later find out that he had broken several bones in Lucius' face and ribcage, as well as caused dangerous internal bleeding.

"Oh, Christ," said Jerry. "Somebody call an ambulance."

Finally coming out of his dazed fury, Kevin realized what he had just done. His knees buckled and he collapsed on the sidewalk, convulsing in sobs. His anger had been replaced by overwhelming sense of remorse. He regretted what he had just done, almost killing a man who in no way deserved it. But on top of that were the events of the previous months. They suddenly pressed on him like a giant boulder and he lost all emotional control.

His colleagues backed away, not wanting to be associated with what he had just done. But they also had no idea what they could do for him, sitting awkwardly on the sidewalk, sobbing his eyes out.

Lucius survived. Just barely. Fortunately for Kevin, the event was handled so quickly by the other cops on the scene, no media were involved. The county picked up the tab for Lucius' hospital expenses and after two months he was well enough to be tried and sentenced for the burglary of the Radio Shack. The official report read that he had "resisted arrest," which was true, but not to the extent that he deserved the beating he received.

Lucius never pressed charges or talked to a reporter, although a story like this would have made him into a Rodney King—like martyr against police brutality. When you lived your life on the streets, smoking crack and scraping every day to survive, violence was just a part of your existence. You accepted it along with everything else. You didn't look for trouble, although, when that was your life, trouble was bound to find you. Complaining about getting beaten up would have been like complaining about getting rained on. It wouldn't do any good and when you were done complaining, you were still all wet. He was a lowlife crackhead, and he knew it. What was his word against a cop's?

Kevin, who had been warned previously about his drinking, was suspended pending a thorough investigation. He never returned to the force. One week into his suspension he turned in his badge. He drove straight from the Sheriffs office to an Alcoholics Anonymous meeting.

He surrendered himself to the proverbial higher power and eventually accepted that he would never have another drink again for the rest of his life. Not a sip, not a drop. There was no middle ground. He was an alcoholic and he would be until his dying day. For something that had become such a part of his daily existence, it was hard to let it go. A fellow AA attendee described it like this: your right hand is a part of you and has been your whole life. You need it. You depend on it to do what you have to do and get through the day. You can't tie your shoes or brush your teeth without it. It's essential. But if that hand gets infected and turns gangrenous, it needs to go. No matter how important it is or how much you think you need it, you better chop it off before the rest of your body gets infected and you die. It's you or your hand. You or your bottle of bourbon.

Kevin had wanted to visit Lucius in the hospital to apologize for what he had done. But the Fraternal Order of Police lawyer that had been assigned to him had forbidden him from setting foot inside the hospital. It would be perceived as an admission of guilt, he told Kevin. He needed to stick to the report of record: "The arrestee was under the influence of controlled substances. When he resisted arrest necessary force was required to subdue him." Kevin knew it was bullshit and the thought of standing by that story sickened him.

As part of the AA twelve-step program, Kevin had to personally apologize to all the people in his life whom he had hurt because of his drinking. He went to see Lucius in prison.

The meeting was short. Lucius recognized him instantly and regarded him coldly. But he sat down and listened to what he had to say. Kevin told him why he was there. He offered a sincere apology, which Lucius neither accepted nor rejected. Before he left, Kevin gave Lucius two things. The first was his home telephone number. He told Lucius that if he ever needed anything, day or night, inside prison or out, to call him. He owed Lucius and if he could do anything to make it up to him, he would. That was a promise. The second thing he gave Lucius was the number for Reverend Jacob Thomas.

Reverend Thomas was the pastor for the Second AME Church of Orlando. A towering black man in his late fifties, the Reverend had a voice so gentle, so understanding, that it reached right into your soul. Reverend Thomas' special ministry was dedicated to working with the homeless and drug-addicted. Kevin encouraged Lucius to talk to him. He could help. Kevin asked Lucius to call the Reverend before he got out of prison, before he went back out onto the streets, before it was too late.

Kevin told Lucius that he knew the Reverend from working with him on several homicide investigations and said that he was truly a man of God. Kevin also told him that he personally understood what it felt like to be addicted and he knew from his own experience that it wasn't something Lucius was going to beat on his own.

Lucius didn't say much in response. But he took both numbers.

Eventually, Lucius called. It was months later at two o'clock in the morning. Lucius had been out of jail for a week. He wanted to know if Kevin really meant what he said. If Lucius needed anything, Kevin would help him out. Kevin told him that he meant it. Lucius said he needed a hundred bucks.

Kevin said he'd be right there.

Kevin picked him up on a street corner in a notorious drug neighborhood. Lucius was jumpy and fidgeting. He clearly needed a fix. He demanded his money.

Kevin asked when he had eaten last. Lucius couldn't remember. So Kevin took him to a 24-hour Taco Bell and bought him three burritos. He ate all three. His mouth full of the last huge bite, Lucius again asked Kevin about his money.

Kevin pulled out a roll of cash and held it up for him. He told Lucius that he would give him the money, but not all at once. They drove out to Reverend Thomas' church and knocked on the door of the residence. Dawn hadn't yet broken in the east and the Reverend came to the door sleepyeyed, adjusting his robe. But when he saw Kevin and Lucius standing on his doorstep, his eyes took in the whole story. Without a word, he offered a gentle smile and stepped aside, allowing them into his home.

Kevin handed the roll of cash to the Reverend and told him that it was Lucius' money. He was to give Lucius five dollars a day, provided he came to the church to collect it. Lucius protested, but Kevin told him that was deal, take it or leave it. Lucius had no choice but to take it.

So Lucius showed up at the church every couple of days, asking for his five dollars. At first the Reverend had given it to him without any comment. But eventually he drew Lucius in and what he said began to stick. Lucius expressed a genuine desire to get off drugs and the Reverend vowed to help him.

The Reverend enlisted Kevin's help and Kevin was glad to lend it. In Kevin's new AA vernacular, he became Lucius' sponsor. Over time, he and Lucius gradually became friends.

They went fishing together. Kevin threw odd jobs at him to assist his investigations. He had Lucius help him with his yard work. Lucius really seemed to love mowing the yard. And Kevin talked to him for hours about college and computers and gave him hope that there was more to be found in his life than the end of a crack pipe.

Lucius tried several times to break the drug's vise grip. And each time he failed. But maybe this time it was different. He had never lasted four months before. That was a long time. A lifetime for some of Lucius' old cronies on the street.

As Kevin sat with his friend in his living room, he couldn't help but smile at his prospects. Lucius was an extremely bright man, a high school graduate, with a wicked sense of humor. He had just made one terrible mistake in taking that first curious hit from the pipe. But now his future seemed full of promise and Kevin was truly happy for him.

"What have you found, so far?" Kevin asked him.

"I'll tell you what I found," said Lucius. "I found out that I wish I took that job laying sod instead of your bullshit TV job."

Kevin smiled and nodded at the pad of scribbled notes on the coffee table. "Tell me what's in your notes."

"Well, you told me to make notes on any single man I saw coming in the park and mark down the tape time code. That's tough, because so many people are comin' through in crowds that it's hard to tell who's alone and who's not. So I started writing down descriptions of everyone that didn't look like some kinda family man." Lucius didn't ask why he was doing this. He had long ago learned that Kevin couldn't give him the details of his investigations.

Kevin reviewed the notes. *Tall white dude in blue shirt, brown hair. Ugly dude with round glasses. Some dude who looks like my 3rd grade teacher. Blonde dude with buckteeth.* Kevin smiled. It was a dude parade. Kevin had asked Lucius to focus on single men just because he wasn't sure where else to start. Given Violet's conclusions, he believed that the killer was a man, probably acting alone for some, as yet undefined, motive. Tall men would gel special attention. Plus, Kevin had an alternate theory scratching at the back of his head, one for which he had no evidence and which he wouldn't yet share with anyone. He felt that the tapes might be the key to that theory and he needed Lucius to help him determine if it had any merit.

Of course, Kevin couldn't know anything for sure. The killer could have been father of the year or a very strong woman, but this was where he felt they should start.

"So let me get this straight," Lucius continued. "I'm supposed to watch everybody who went in on this day . . ." He held up one videocassette. ". . . and then see if I can spot anyone who also went in on *this* day?" He held up another videocassette.

"You got it."

"That's crazy, Red. A needle in a haystack."

"Yeah, I know. Even if someone did go into the park on both days, it's one in a million that we'd be able to find, see, and recognize him on both tapes."

"Try one in a billion."

"So, you don't think you can do it."

"Did I say that? Damn." Lucius gestured with the tapes. "If he's in here, I'll find the motherfucker."

Kevin just grinned. He didn't doubt Lucius for a second.

CHAPTER 5

Kevin parked in a lot that seemed to be at least thirty miles from the theme park. He stood with several other cast members and waited in the 93-degree sun for the bus to shuttle them to a backstage entrance. Once at the park, he found his way to the men's locker room, checked out his costume and changed clothes. A few other guys were in there, putting on big floppy shoes or animal heads. Two of the guys were arguing over the performance of the Orlando Magic in last month's playoff loss to Atlanta.

A certain amount of innocence is forever lost after witnessing a giant chipmunk give a guy the finger and call him a "fuckhead."

Kevin adjusted his costume and looked in the mirror before venturing onstage. He was dressed like a coal miner and felt utterly ridiculous. He wore old, heavy work boots, gray denim overalls, a flannel shirt (in the middle of summer!), and a hard hat with a light over the stubby brim. The hat was extra large and heavier than normal so it could house the battery pack that powered the light. The whole ensemble was covered in faux coal dust stains. Kevin completed the outfit by accessorizing with his official nametag.

Prospector Mountain was located on the perimeter of Lonesome Gulch. As an actual mountain it was pretty small.

As a theme park ride it was enormous. Its peak soared above all other structures in Empire Realm except the Palace, and it was one of the signature rides. The twisting tracks and mine carts were often featured in print and TV ads.

Kevin found his way up a set of concrete steps to the cast member entrance. He could hear the folksy Appalachian music piped into the twisting tunnels that snaked up to the ride loading area. Except for a few off weeks each year, those tunnels were always filled with tourists lined up to get on the ride. At times, the wait could be an hour and a half. For a four-minute ride. (Four minutes was actually excessively long for a roller coaster, but Prospector Mountain had leisurely, themed interludes in between stomach-lurching drops and turns. Besides, the focus groups had determined that three minutes was too short to be considered a "good ride value" and five minutes was too long to keep the line moving efficiently.)

Kevin stepped out into the ride loading area. Four other miners were busily loading passengers into the six-person mine carts. The queue split right before the eager riders stepped onto the platform so that half the line was loaded into carts on one track and half into carts on the other track. There were two different tracks that twisted throughout the artificial mountain, but they both offered the same ride experience.

Kevin spotted a nearby miner and approached her. She was in her mid-thirties, with dark eyes and a tapered, attractive face. Her chestnut hair was tucked up under her hard hat. She was efficiently loading a family of German tourists who clearly didn't understand English.

"Okay," she said. "Step in please. Steppen zee inn. There ya go. All the way. Danka shen. Auf veederzen. Geshundheit." The Germans departed down the track in eager anticipation. As she turned back to load the next group, Kevin approached.

"Excuse me," said Kevin. "I'm looking for—Ahh!"

Kevin felt his legs go out from under him and he fell hard on his butt. He had stepped unaware onto a moving sidewalk and lost his balance.

The woman helped him to his feet. She offered a mechanical smile and said in a rote manner, "Please watch your step at all times as you enter the vehicle. The platform is moving at the same speed as the mine cart."

"Yeah, thanks for that. I'm—"

"Kevin."

"That's right," said Kevin, surprised.

"You're the new guy. Excuse me a sec." She turned to the next group and quickly loaded them into an empty mine cart. "You're looking for Chuckie."

"And you can find him for me?"

She pointed to a ride control podium a few feet away. A thin miner of about twenty-five with neatly trimmed hair stood listening to a walkie-talkie. "Chuckie."

"Thanks." Kevin started over towards the podium, but stopped. "And who are you?"

"Sheila."

"Thanks for your help, Sheila."

Kevin stepped back onto the moving sidewalk and let it carry him over towards the podium.

"Hey, Kevin," Sheila called after him. "Watch out for the Code V."

"Code V? What's that?"

Sheila smiled mysteriously. "You'll find out."

Kevin's coach, Chuckie, walked him through the job responsibilities. They were incredibly simple to grasp but deceptively difficult to execute. Basically, his job was to keep the line moving by ushering guests into the mechanized mine cars. He had to make sure that the safety lap belt was engaged because Prospector Mountain was essentially a roller coaster and Chuckie made it very clear that they couldn't have guests flying out of the car and over the edge of Fool's Gold Tum.

Chuckie was in his mid-twenties, with short, light-brown hair. His coif sported strategically placed blonde highlights. He was slight of frame, thin, and maintained excellent posture at all times, perhaps in an attempt to mitigate his five foot, five-inch height. Chuckie could give Kippy a run for his money in an ultimate Empire Realm cast member showdown.

The reason that the job was so difficult to execute was because, when things got busy, there were just too many people trying to get on the ride. If you weren't efficient in getting groups out of the queue and into the moving cars, you could have a car head off into the ride at less than full capacity. That was forbidden. There is nothing more infuriating to a crowd of people who have been waiting in line for an hour and half in Florida's summer heat than to see ride cars heading out half-full. It was a good way to incite a riot.

In addition to the sheer volume of people, and the speed at which the cars constantly moved, was the human factor. Groups invariably wanted to ride together, even if the car didn't have enough remaining seats to accommodate them. "Oh, we'll take the next car," they would say. That would then force the enterprising miner to locate suitable replacement riders in the line and then get them properly secured into the moving cars before they headed off down the mineshaft. There was an unexpectedly high level of negotiation skills required to fill those seats. It wasn't brain surgery, as Chuckie said several times, but it was a lot harder than it looked.

Chuckie had walked him through the two main priorities of

his job: (1) fill cars to keep the line moving and (2) never break character. He was "Kevin, the Old West miner." If someone asked him a question, he was to answer it in character. For example, if a kid asked him how long the Prospector Mountain ride had been around, his answer was to be something along the lines of "Why, Prospector Mountain has been around as long as the hills. But the old Willoughby Gold Mine has been in operation since Aught Four." The restrooms were "latrines." Chuckie handed Kevin a photocopied page of bullet points outlining the history and heritage of Prospector Mountain. He was to take it home and memorize it. *Yeah, that'll happen,* thought Kevin.

After completing the verbal instructions, Chuckie placed Kevin in the loading area. His first major challenge was a Brazilian tour group of sixty-five kids and chaperones. None of them spoke English and Kevin certainly didn't speak any Portuguese. They didn't understand a word of Kevin's instructions and mostly just stood there confused. The first car went down the shaft only half-full and the rest of the crowd started to grumble. Fortunately for Kevin, he was paired with Sheila, who was clearly an experienced pro. She stepped in and used a series of hand gestures to get the Brazilians loaded and on their way.

"You gotta take control, Miner Kevin," said Sheila. "Otherwise, they'll eat you for lunch."

"Thanks, Miner Sheila."

Kevin worked a five-hour shift and probably never felt so tired in his life. The park was preparing to close and the crowds dwindled. The remaining guests gathered around Empire Palace for the nightly fireworks display. For the first time, Kevin had an opportunity to chat with his partner.

"So how long have you worked here?" he asked.

"One year. My whole life."

"Pardon?"

Sheila took off her helmet and shook out her shoulder-length hair. She was even prettier with her hair down. Kevin noticed that the miner's costume actually looked good on her, the baggy overalls coming off as cute and almost trendy, as opposed the ridiculous nature of Kevin's appearance. As she answered, she readjusted her hair back up under the miner's helmet. "I started working here part-time when I was eighteen. I worked for a couple years before I quit when I was twenty-two." She flipped her helmet light back on. "And I've been back for a year now."

"Why the big gap between then and now?"

She cocked her head at him. "It's not *that* big a gap, pal."

Kevin quickly realized his faux pas. "Sorry—I didn't mean—"

"Have you ever been on this ride?"

Kevin considered for a moment. "You know, I never have."

A mischievous smile crept across Sheila's lips. "Come on." Kevin followed her into an empty mine car as it passed by. "You have to sit in the front for the real effect."

The lap bar came down across their thighs and Sheila looked over at him. She smirked and bounced her eyebrows up and down. And the next thing Kevin knew they were plummeting down an almost vertical mineshaft.

The premise was that they were in an out of control mine car and that's exactly what it felt like. The darkness of the tunnel was used to maximum effect. It made the turns harder to see and more jarring. The railroad-like tracks clicked rapidly as they twisted and turned. Left and right; up and down.

Occasionally the ride would slow down and the car would pass a bit of set dressing that enhanced the old mine theme: a bucket full of simulated gold ore, some old pick-axes, a grizzled old animatronic prospector forever chiseling at a huge chunk of gold lodged in a tunnel wall, repeatedly muttering "It's the mother lode, by cracky!"

A hand-painted sign read "Go Back! Mine Closed! Cave-in Danger!" and the car appeared to plow down a wooden barricade. The wooden beams that supposedly held the tunnels in place rocked and rumbled as the errant mine car passed. Above them a huge pile of fiberglass rocks and boulders started to tumble down towards them and they zipped underneath just in time to avoid getting crushed.

The roller coaster mode picked up again and sent them on a few more twists and turns before ending in a wild corkscrew descent that sent Kevin's stomach lurching. As the car coasted into the exit area, Sheila let out a loud, "Wooooo!" and turned to her companion. "You know, it doesn't matter how many times I go on this ride, I still love it. What did you think?"

"I think I might puke."

"Ah," said Sheila knowingly. "Interesting."

They got out of the car just as the fireworks were starting. Kevin and Sheila walked to the edge of the platform and leaned on a couple of fiberglass boulders. From this vantage point, high above the rest of the park, they had the best view possible for the fireworks show. They stood silently and watched the pyrotechnics. Huge red and purple clusters exploded in every direction with dramatic booms. Bright golden streamers whistled up into the night sky. An impressive finale seemed to thunder on forever and when it was finally over, Kevin's ears were ringing. Neither one of them spoke right away. Finally, Sheila broke the silence.

"I've said it before. The pay sucks, but this is still a great place to work."

Kevin smiled at her and nodded his head.

Kevin was on Interstate 4, just passing the brightly illuminated Suntrust skyscraper downtown, when his cell phone rang. It was Violet.

"Hey, Kev. I hope I'm not calling too late."

"Nah, I'm in the car on my way home. What's up?"

Violet explained that she couldn't call during office hours for fear of being overheard. She had some additional information regarding the Empire Realm murders.

"Remember those burn marks on the skin?" she said.

"Of course. On the left leg of the first guy and on the wrist and behind the ear of the second guy."

"You're going to love this."

"A calling card from the killer?"

"Nothing like that. At least, I don't think so. The patterns seem incidental."

"Can you confirm that they're from the same source?"

"Within a reasonable amount of certainty. We've been able to establish that the burns on both victims occurred right around the time of death. Or even shortly post-mortem."

Kevin looked over his shoulder and checked the traffic. He changed lanes to pass a slower car. "Okay, Vi. The suspense is killing me. How were they burned?"

"Actually, *burned* isn't even the proper medical term for it."

"You're playing games with me, Vi. Do I have to guess? I feel like I'm back on the force."

"It's like old times, isn't it?"

Kevin smiled. Violet was an excellent M.E., but she had a sadistic side when it came to providing information to detectives. She never withheld information, but she forced the detectives to think harder, to ask more questions, to be better investigators. Kevin always felt that she helped him to be a smarter detective, to think about a murder from multiple angles.

"Don't get me wrong," he said. "I really appreciate what you're doing. But you're driving me nuts here. If they weren't burned, what were they?"

"Frozen."

Kevin wasn't sure he had heard her right. "Say again? Frozen?"

"The effect on the skin is very similar. Extremely cold temperatures can damage the skin as badly as extremely hot temperatures. When your skin is burned, the cell membranes are actually being melted, breaking the cells open. When your skin is frozen, the water in the cells freezes, forming crystals that can tear through the cell membranes. We were able to determine that our two victims were both exposed to extremely cold temperatures."

"But only on small, localized areas of their bodies."

"That's right."

"So what do you think the cause is?"

"Could be a lot of things. But I've done a little research and I'm almost positive we're looking at damage caused by frozen CO_2."

"Frozen CO_2? Carbon dioxide? I don't get it."

"That, my friend, is what's commonly called dry ice."

"So. How was your first day?" Jerry Engle was looking eagerly at Kevin from across his desk.

"Exhausting," said Kevin.

"The job's a lot harder than it looks, isn't it?"

Kevin's shift started in an hour. He had come in early so he could brief Jerry on the status of his investigation and make a request. But first, he had a question.

"Have you been able to get any information regarding the police interviews with the victims' families?"

Jerry nodded. "Believe it or not, I have. Naturally, Pendergrast wasn't talking. So I called Gardner. He wasn't thrilled to talk to me. As you know, he holds a grudge against anyone who quits his department. But he's a political animal and he was willing to take the call. He faxed over these as a courtesy." Jerry held up a folder containing the family interview transcripts and some preliminary notes. "I haven't read them yet, but Gardner gave me a summary. He confirmed that neither victim had any criminal record or any known enemies. At this point, the police have no reason to suspect the families and they have no idea if the victims knew their killer or killers."

"Let me guess," said Kevin. "Gardner told you that he and Pendergrast were focusing the investigation on the park employees."

"You got it. That's the only reason he faxed me the family interviews. He was providing the background on why they need to investigate our people to encourage my cooperation. Not that they need it, legally, but it makes their lives easier if I do cooperate. I don't know if I should help them or not. I want the killer caught as soon as possible, but the minute they catch him, I'm history. Plus, Pendergrast will rub my face in it the whole time. They've already started interviewing cast members." Jerry ran a hand over his bald head, sweeping a few beads of sweat off. He tugged absently at his eyebrow. "Have you been able to find anything yet?"

"We're still reviewing the security tapes from the main gate. So far, we haven't been able to identify anyone who showed up on both days. I've got someone working on it and we'll keep looking. At this point, I agree with Gardner and Pendergrast. It's probably a cast member." Kevin told Jerry about the dry ice burns on both victims. This was a strong lead. It could narrow the field of suspects to just a few candidates. And they were getting the information at the same time as Pendergrast. If they played the lead right, the whole investigation could be over very quickly. Kevin leaned forward on the desk toward Jerry. "Can you get me a list of every cast member with access to dry ice?"

"That'll be a long List. We use dry ice for all kinds of things. It's used to keep retail food items cold. When you get it wet, it becomes a great theatrical fog, so we use it in our stage shows and we pump it into our rides for atmosphere. We probably go through a ton of it a year on just the Breakaway Toboggan ride alone."

Damn. That wasn't the answer Kevin was looking for. At best, the list would define the haystack they were searching through for the needle. However, at this point, he didn't have any alternative but to ask for the list, no matter how long it was. Jerry said it might take a day or two to get it, but he promised him he would.

"Do your cast members go through a background check before they get hired?" Kevin asked.

"Sort of. We do a felony check in the computer, but that's about it."

"So nobody working at Empire Realm has a felony record."

"That's right."

"So much for cross-referencing the dry ice list with a list of all the convicted murderers you've hired. I guess we'll have to work for this one."

Jerry offered a feeble smile and pulled on his eyebrow.

Kevin took the interview transcripts and found a seat in the cast cafeteria. He spent the remaining time before his shift reviewing them. The pages documented the face-to-face interviews with family members before they left Orlando and a series of subsequent phone interviews with various people. After the first few pages, Kevin hated to admit that Gardner's assessment seemed correct. Neither one of these guys seemed part of anything that would result in their murders. They appeared to be average Midwest Americans who happened to be in the wrong pace at the wrong time.

But that didn't make sense. The wrong place for what? They weren't robbed. They weren't raped. No money disappeared from their bank accounts. To anyone's knowledge, there was no reason for their murders other than to collect a single personal item from each: the sunglasses and the rental car key.

The common thread between the two widows was one of disbelief. How could someone have done this to her husband? He didn't have an enemy in the world. The second victim had a young son who was not interviewed except to confirm basic facts.

The first victim had an ex-wife who, although upset by the news of her ex's death, wasn't very charitable in her assessment of his character. She described him as selfish, slovenly, and egotistic. She claimed that he had a beard because he was too lazy to shave every morning. They ultimately split up because she wanted kids and he didn't. He had no desire to get up in the middle of the night and change a diaper. He was unwilling to sacrifice his lifestyle for a child.

None of this was particularly flattering but hardly a motive for murder. After the divorce, the ex-wife had re-married and had a child. She had moved on with her life. Just in case, Pendergrast had asked the local cops in Kansas City to check her out. She was clean. No record, a solid alibi, and no known unsavory associates.

The first victim worked as a sales manager at a Mitsubishi dealership in Kansas City. His co-workers had nothing bad to say. His finances were in good shape, although he was by no means wealthy.

The second victim was a marketing analyst for

DaimlerChrysler in Detroit. He had just been promoted and his colleagues were devastated by his death. He was on the corporate fast track, respected and popular. Parents and siblings were interviewed. Neighbors. Nothing connected these guys.

Wait—Kevin held his finger on his current page and flipped back to a pervious page. The first guy worked for a Mitsubishi dealership. The second guy worked for DaimlerChrysler. Both auto related. Did that mean anything? It seemed a stretch. They were completely different companies with home offices on different continents. One was a dealership and the other was a corporate headquarters several hundred miles away. It was something, but it was weak. As Kevin read on, he saw some of Pendergrast's notes. Pendergrast seemed to pick up on the auto connection too. He asked some pointed questions, about disgruntled customers, about if anyone had recently bought a Mitsubishi and traded in a Chrysler, about which Chrysler cars competed with which Mitsubishi models. He even spoke to the Chrysler dealers in Kansas City. None of them had ever heard of the victim from headquarters, although one manager knew the guy from the Mitsubishi dealer.

Kevin grimaced. Pendergrast was fishing. He might as well have based the victims' connection on the fact that they were both from the Midwest. Or white males. Pendergrast was just throwing out the widest possible net and hoping he caught something. It was desperate investigating, rather than focusing his efforts based on specific clues. But the clues were sparse. If a connection could be made between the victims, it could lead directly to the killer. Kevin shook his head as he read. Despite the inefficient tactics, Kevin didn't think he would have done anything differently.

Behind the interview transcripts was a packet of photocopied notes and documents. It appeared that Gardner had included several pages of Pendergrast's investigation notes. Kevin doubted that they were supposed to be sent with the interview transcripts and documents. Gardner probably handed Pendergrast's progress report to his secretary and told her to fax the transcripts. It looked like she just faxed the whole report over to Jerry without bothering to look at the actual pages. With these notes, Kevin was able to peek into Pendergrast's confidential investigation. Unfortunately, they seemed to offer nothing to help Kevin.

Nonetheless, Kevin skimmed through Pendergrast's notes, feeling a little like a voyeur. There just wasn't anything revelatory in there. Pendergrast was following a solid investigative path. So far, that path had led nowhere. Before he closed the file folder, Kevin glanced through the documents. There were photocopies of hotel bills, car rental receipts, airline receipts. Nothing out of the ordinary. Besides arriving three weeks apart, the victims had flown separate airlines, rented cars from different companies, and stayed in different hotels.

But then Kevin noticed something.

The first victim's documents contained a copy of a travel itinerary, printed on the letterhead of a company called Midwest Tours based in Indianapolis with offices throughout the American heartland. It outlined a fun-filled vacation at several Orlando attractions. If he hadn't been strangled and shoved into a topiary cow, he and his new wife were next going to Universal's Islands of Adventure.

There was no itinerary in the second victim's documents. But on the receipt for the airline tickets was printed *Issued by Midwest Tours*. It was small and printed in the corner of the. receipt, but it popped out at Kevin like a giant neon sign.

Was that the connection, the tour company? That seemed like a stretch, too. But Kevin felt it was stronger than the automotive angle. Pendergrast's notes made no reference to the tour company. Kevin didn't think he spotted it. Pendergrast probably would find it, eventually, but until he did Kevin had a slight edge.

Kevin planned to check out Midwest Tours as soon as possible. Find out how many Midwest Tours clients went away on vacation and never came back. Look into disgruntled employees. Complaint letters. Harassment claims. Anything, no matter how thin, that could be construed as a motive.

Kevin would make a few calls. Orange County had the dubious distinction of boasting more lawyers per capita than any other Florida county and Kevin had worked for most of the heavy firms. He had completed a job recently for a big firm downtown, tracking down witnesses in an expensive civil case. This particular law firm had offices throughout the U.S., including, if memory served, Indianapolis. Kevin would call and get a referral for a discrete independent private investigator in Indiana to start checking into Midwest Tours. A man on the ground would be able to get a lot deeper than Kevin could get on the phone. And there wasn't enough information to justify a break from the park investigation for Kevin to travel and start digging himself. He was sure that Jerry would cover the expense.

But the calls would have to wait a little while. At the moment, he was late for his shift.

CHAPTER 6

Part of the job description of being a loader was also being an unloader. Kevin spent the better part of an afternoon shift helping folks out of their mine cars and repeating the same warning about the moving floor over and over. And over. His voice got hoarse.

"The key is not to shout," said Sheila. "Keep it level. Keep it *cool*."

As monotonous and unfulfilling as this job was, Kevin actually found the work enjoyable. This was due entirely to the presence of Sheila.

She was attractive in a very natural way. She didn't wear much makeup (the Code of Conduct prohibited it), but she didn't need it. Her chestnut hair was not styled but cut simply, falling onto her shoulders. Her brown eyes were alert and just slightly mischievous. She had a smooth alabaster complexion. A small scar cut across an edge of her chin. She was slight of frame, not more than five foot three. But she could maneuver a crowd of fifty non-English speaking tourists on and off a ride like a seasoned cowboy would drive a herd of unruly cattle.

But it wasn't her appearance that made the work so enjoyable for Kevin. She had a way of not taking herself or her job too seriously. It wasn't that she didn't do her job well—she was clearly one of the most proficient loaders—it was just that she had a light, easy way of doing it. She was smart and funny and she went out of her way to make Kevin feel at ease in his new situation. It almost reminded Kevin of the casual camaraderie of two partners in a squad car.

Between chatting with Sheila and ruminating on his investigation, Kevin's shift seemed to fly by. The fact that the park was typically crowded kept him busy and also helped to pass the time.

The investigation. Kevin recounted to himself just where he was. He was tracking two parallel paths. The first path was that the murderer was a paying guest—an outsider. Pendergrast had the surveillance tapes from within the park, but, according to Jerry, they didn't show anything anyway. Kevin had Lucius poring over the security tapes from the main gate. If the killer were a paying guest, he would had to have come through that main gate. If he were on there, Lucius would find him. He hoped. Of course, just because someone came to the park on those two days certainly didn't mean he was homicidal. But it would be suspicious and somewhere to start. Then again, finding a match and then figuring out who the hell he was and where to locate him would be a whole different problem.

The second investigative path assumed that the killer was a park employee—an insider. This seemed to be the more plausible scenario. Why? Kevin mulled it over as he ushered a family of four off of a mine car. It's much more likely that an employee would be at the park on the two days in question. Even on his day off, an employee would have entry to anywhere he needed to go. An employee would know where the security cameras were and how to avoid them. An employee wouldn't arouse suspicion wandering the park grounds late at night after the park was closed.

And, perhaps most significantly, an employee would have access to dry ice.

Good old Violet. She was really sticking her neck out for Kevin and he knew it. She was a good friend, but that might not have been enough motivation for her to leak confidential autopsy results. Kevin was sure that it was not only her friendship but a passionate loathing for Pendergrast that had inspired her to be so helpful. However, when he really thought about it, Kevin also knew that a certain amount of guilt probably motivated Violet. She really *hadn't* been there for Kevin three years ago. Kevin certainly didn't blame her for that. He knew that he would have spurned any offers of sympathy or assistance. But Violet was a loyal friend and Kevin was sure she felt some internal obligation to make it up to him.

Kevin dismissed, at least for the time being, the theory that the killer was a friend of a park employee. Although a park employee would be able to sneak a friend in, that would mean that two people were involved. That would make it a conspiracy. And conspiracies were very hard to keep secret. If it were a conspiracy, what was it based on? The tour company? A disgruntled Midwest Tours employee coming to Florida, working with a cast member to kill customers while on vacation? It still didn't make any sense.

The truth was that, like Pendergrast, Kevin was struggling to choose the most likely investigative path. His resources were very limited. He had Jerry's support and Lucius' eyes watching tapes in a long shot gamble. That was about it. He couldn't assign junior detectives to track down multiple leads concurrently. He didn't have the depth of the Orange County Sheriffs Office or its sister agencies such as the Florida Department of Law Enforcement to speed the chase. No databases. No access to the families. He had to assess the available evidence, make a choice based on his experience and his gut, and hope he wasn't running down a blind alley.

At this point, Kevin's gut came up with a fairly vague suspect profile. Violet concluded that the killer was a large man, at least six-foot two or six-foot three, and strong, otherwise he wouldn't have been able to kill the victims as he had. Kevin assumed the killer was acting alone. Nothing in Pendergrast's reports or in Violet's autopsy supported more than one killer. Kevin knew he could be wrong, but he made the decision, for the time being, to assume there was only one murderer. The part he couldn't figure out was if the killer was an employee or a guest. Lucius was watching tapes, trying to cover the guest angle, while Kevin worked the park looking at employees. Finding the connection between the victims was the key.

Even seemingly random killings contain some sort of connection, perhaps only something as tenuous as the murder victims all being young women with their guards down. Kevin knew this from experience. He had investigated a serial killer case once while he was a detective. It had been a high-profile investigation for which the FBI had eventually been called in. It was while working with Special Agent Milt Benning that Kevin truly learned how to track a killer. Before working with Agent Benning, Kevin had been a good detective. He cleared murders. But those were mostly "regular" murders—drug deals gone bad, domestics, robberies. After working with Agent Benning, Kevin became the best detective in the department. He learned the process of profiling the killer, understanding the background, sensibilities, and physical attributes. He learned how to extract meaning from seemingly meaningless clues and to never under-estimate the value of forensic science. Most of all, he learned to look for the connections between the victims, or between the victims and the killer, because that would connect the investigative dots. In the case of the Mall Murderer, as Kevin's case came to be known, understanding the victims' connections provided the roadmap to the short-circuited killer's brain. Using the profile, Agent Benning was able to explain why the serial killer did what he did. Using forensics, Benning was able to figure out how he did it. It was Investigations 101—Motive and Method. Catching him was just a matter of time.

The case had Orlando gripped in fear for three months. Five women had been raped and sliced to ribbons in local shopping malls—one at the Orlando Fashion Square just a few miles east of Downtown, two at the Florida Mall on Sand Lake Road, and two at the West Oaks Mall on the border of Ocoee. Mall patronage dropped off a cliff and the local merchants opened every day to nearly empty corridors and atriums.

Agent Benning was part of the FBI's behavioral sciences section in Quantico. He was deliberate and patient and spent a great deal of time with Kevin, explaining their serial killer's profile and outlining the various motivations. In this case, the killer was a sexual predator, killing young, attractive women in an attempt to exert control in a world where he felt he had none. The killer endured a childhood of abuse at the hands of his mother and aunt and it was a recipe for carnage. Women were the controllers in his world, the dominators, and he was striking back. Even though what they were dealing with on a daily basis was nightmarish in its brutality, with Kevin, Agent Benning carried himself more as a college professor than as some hard-boiled federal agent.

The killer was apprehended when a single bloody fingerprint was lifted from a slashed and bloodied nineteen-year-old girl in the food court men's room of the West Oaks Mall. The fingerprint was smeared and of poor quality. But the match was eventually found. The killer had once been in the Navy and served for a time on a nuclear sub. He had been finger-printed years ago as part of his enlistment and security clearance. His name was John Tinker, an attendant at a downtown parking garage.

When Kevin arrested him, he offered no resistance. He was sitting alone in his apartment, watching Regis and Kathie Lee as if he had been expecting him. Waiting for him. He just looked at Kevin with tired, drooping eyes and held out his hands for the cuffs.

The public breathed a sigh of relief. The malls filled back up. The FBI got the credit. But the Sheriff knew who in his department had worked the case and made the collar. Kevin was personally thanked by Sheriff Gardner and given a special commendation in a public ceremony.

Kevin knew that he was just doing his job. Other than receiving invaluable mentoring from Agent Benning, Kevin had treated the investigation like any other, no different from his prior case of a dope dealer cut down by his crew for skimming cash. Kevin hated the idea of some overblown ceremony staged for the cameras. But Maria had been so proud and had even bought a new dress for the occasion.

So he went and he got on the local news at both six and eleven. His picture was in the *Sentinel* along with a long article detailing the investigation. A color graphic timeline illustrated the chronology of the crimes and investigation. He was a local celebrity for a few days.

But as Kevin returned to his duties everyone soon forgot about John Tinker, a.k.a. the Mall Murderer. Well, not everyone forgot. Pendergrast remembered.

Kevin and Pendergrast had never been pals, but they didn't have any real reason to dislike each other either. They each went about their business without getting in each other's way.

Kevin was the youngest detective in the homicide unit and Pendergrast had always harbored some level of resentment against Kevin for not having paid the same dues. Kevin made the mistake of once suggesting that Pendergrast had spent more time in uniform because he wasn't as good a cop and had more to learn. Pendergrast hadn't appreciated the observation to say the least.

When Kevin garnered all of the publicity and accolades surrounding the Mall Murderer case, whatever semblance of a relationship he had with Pendergrast dissolved. All that remained was a simmering mutual animosity that was felt much more strongly by Pendergrast. Kevin had no interest in being in an office jousting match with Pendergrast and just tried to avoid him. Pendergrast, on the other hand, went out of his way to undermine Kevin's ability to do his job. Pendergrast's actions ranged from the immature (replacing the break room sugar with salt so Kevin's coffee would be ruined) to downright sabotage (such as taking phone messages regarding Kevin's investigations and then deliberately refusing to relay them).

Kevin knew that Pendergrast was ambitious. He knew that Pendergrast wanted to be the primary on the Mall Murderer investigation. He also knew that Pendergrast felt Kevin was too young and green for such a high profile case. But Sheriff Gardner overruled him and assigned it to Kevin. Although Kevin knew that Gardner respected his abilities, he also knew that Gardner would prefer his younger, more attractive face on television than Pendergrast's older, puffier, balding visage. Gardner hadn't been reelected three times as Orange County Sheriff because he didn't understand the public image of the department.

So Pendergrast seethed as Kevin became the department's golden boy. Until Kevin started drinking. Kevin's colleagues had covered for him, tried to get him help. But Pendergrast, once he learned of Kevin's drinking problem, took it upon himself to inform Gardner, "in the interest of public safety." At the time Kevin was incensed and confronted Pendergrast in a Publix parking lot. He was drunk and grabbed Pendergrast's lapels. They got into a struggle and were pulled apart by a uniformed officer who happened to be buying bread and milk on his way home. Pendergrast wagged a finger in Kevin's face and declared that Kevin was finished as a cop—and the best part was that he had destroyed himself.

With the passage of time and the help of his twelve-step program, Kevin could no longer be angry with Pendergrast. Although Pendergrast's motivation for telling Gardner about Kevin's drinking was malicious, it was the right thing to do. And Kevin *had* destroyed his own police career.

No one had been happy about Kevin's resignation except Louis Pendergrast. With Kevin gone, he became the top homicide detective. He used different tactics than Kevin, such as bullying and coercion, but he closed most of his cases. And Gardner needed cases closed.

Pendergrast was a jerk, but he understood the mechanics of a homicide investigation. Kevin knew that Pendergrast was working the Empire Realm murders hard. He had the advantage of the department's resources, as well as the ability to interview cast members and the victims' families without blowing any kind of cover. It was merely a matter of time before he closed the case. Kevin's only chance of finding the killer first was to trust his instincts and commit to them.

Kevin had spent a few lunch breaks and after hours moments trying to casually interview some cast members in the Lonesome Gulch area. It was always under some pretext, usually wanting to learn more about the park (him "being new and all"). But so far, he hadn't learned anything that helped his investigation (although he did learn that, if interested, he could score some primo pot from a friendly rodeo clown named Zonko).

While Lucius watched security tapes until his eyes crossed, Kevin reviewed the list of cast members with access to dry ice. He first eliminated the women on the list. Then he concentrated on those members of the list who worked in the Lonesome Gulch area of the park (where both murders occurred) and were on duty on both nights in question. That was a pretty long list—almost seventy people. Kevin was in the process of trying to find out as much about each of the suspects as possible. He'd bump into them at the commissary and strike up idle conversation. He'd talk to co-workers. He'd soon get the combinations to their lockers from Jerry and do a little covert snooping. Who knows—maybe he'd find a length of rope and a receipt for the purchase of dry ice in someone's locker. Fat chance.

"Hey, Dreamy. You're up." It was Sheila, rousting him from his thoughts. A full mine car of guests was coming down the track.

"Right," said Kevin and he stepped over to assist their departure. A small boy was in the left front seat and he wasn't wearing the usual happy face that most folks, and especially kids, wore as they came to end of the ride. His expression was blank and he stared ahead at nothing in particular. "Howdy, folks," said Kevin. "Please step out of the car to your left. Watch your step, as the floor is moving at the same speed as the car. Be sure to gather all your personal belongings and take small children by the hand."

"Honey, are you all right?" the boy's mother asked him. The boy didn't respond. Kevin looked up and saw that he was quickly running out of room to get the folks out of their seats before the moving sidewalk ended and the car passed on to the loading area.

Kevin took the boy by the arm to help him out. "You okay, partner? Let me give you a hand there."

"Mom," said the boy, "I don't feel so good." The boy looked over at Kevin and opened his mouth. A fire hose of vomit gushed out and splashed all over Kevin's arms, shirt, and legs.

"Oh, sweetie!" the mother cried and put her arm around her son. The rest of family followed her off the car to comfort the boy. Sheila quickly directed them to a nearby bench and asked if they needed anything, such as a glass of water. The mother responded that they just needed a few minutes. He sometimes got sick on roller coasters.

Kevin just stood there slightly hunched, arms held frozen away from his body. He was in absolute shock and wasn't exactly sure what he should do next. He rode the moving sidewalk until he hit stationary ground. He managed to step off and find an empty spot near the ride control panel. A chunk of vomit dripped from the end of his fingertip and plopped to the ground.

Sheila strode over. "You okay?" she asked.

Kevin just looked at her wide-eyed, unable to produce a response.

"That, my dear, is a Code V." She pulled a walkie-talkie microphone from the control panel and pressed the button. "Hey, Chuckie, we got a Code V in unloading."

Chuckie's voice came back filtered through the speaker. "Acknowledged. I'll get custodial up here right away. Where exactly is the Code V?"

Sheila stuck out her bottom lip, considering her response. "Kevin's wearing it."

Chuckie's reply was brief but to the point. "Yucko."

There was something wrong with his ass. Mickelson may have been new to the job of detective, but he would have had to be a pretty sorry investigator to not know that Pendergrast had some type of ass problem.

His hamstring. Give me a break. Pick-up basketball. Right. If Pendergrast actually played pick-up basketball, Mickelson privately vowed to turn in his badge and devote his life to the ballet. Pendergrast bouncing the rock with the brothers in a game of pick-up basketball seemed about as plausible as Mickelson earning the lead in Swan Lake.

Could be some type of rectal fungus. Mickelson had seen a commercial on TV once that showed a montage of animals rubbing their butts to relieve "uncomfortable anal itching." A bear did the shimmy shake on an big old oak tree, a dog scooted along with its butt on the ground, pulling itself forward with its front paws, and an elephant leaned back into a thin tree and rubbed its gigantic ass with such force that the tree all but snapped in half. Mickelson remembered watching it and thinking to himself, "that poor tree."

Pendergrast could have "uncomfortable anal itching." Mickelson half wanted to buy him some over-the-counter cortisone cream and slip it in his coat. At first it was mildly amusing, but now watching Pendergrast pace around and squirm was getting mildly irritating.

Besides, rectal discomfort surely wasn't doing anything to improve Pendergrast's mood, which was foul to begin with. The guy was pretty hard to take under ideal circumstances. Add in the bonus ingredient of an ass problem and he was an unabashed dickhead.

Mickelson was intensely interested in solving these murders. He may be a green detective, but he was no fool. He knew what the implications were here. This potentially had national exposure written all over it and he couldn't believe he stepped into a case like this as his first assignment.

And Pendergrast may be an SOB, but he cleared cases. Mickelson vowed to learn as much as he could from the guy, not let his personality rub off on him, and ride this case as far as it would take him. At the moment, his assignment was to fetch Empire Realm employees for interviews.

"Everyone's a suspect, Mickelson," Pendergrast growled.

They had set up a makeshift office in a trailer "backstage," as the employees called it. They had a long list of people to talk to. They were beginning with everyone who worked in the Lonesome Gulch area of the park who was also on duty on the nights of both murders. They also had a list of people who worked with dry ice. The M.E. had dropped the interesting news on them yesterday that both victims had dry ice burns on their skin.

Detective Klymer was chasing down the dry ice leads while he and Pendergrast interviewed the employees who were working on both nights. Mickelson walked from the trailer to a large wooden gate and pushed it open. He couldn't help but smile. Immediately he was enveloped by music. It was the kind of music you might find in an old John Wayne movie, full of heroism and drama. The music was coming from the bushes.

As he walked down the old west street of Lonesome Gulch, he imagined that the music was the theme of the crime drama he was now starring in. He strode purposefully down the road, cutting his eyes at both the tourists and employees, wondering who the killer was. *Everyone's a suspect, Mickelson.*

He made his way up to Prospector Mountain and forced his way into the line.

"Hey, buddy," said a tall man in a WilberHat. The WilberHat was essentially a dressed up baseball cap, except there were two googly eyeballs on the front, long horse ears on top, and an extended bill, at the end of which were the trademark bucked teeth of Wilberforce the Wilberhorse. A pink felt tongue lolled off to one side of the bill. "The line starts back there."

How did this guy expect to be taken seriously admonishing him for cutting in the line? Staring at the hat and the anger in his eyes, Mickelson half expected him to whip out a cartoon gun, pull the trigger, and shoot out a flag that said, "Bang!"

"Relax," said Mickelson. "I'm here on official business. I'm not getting on the ride."

"You better not," said the horse man. His chubby kids looked up at him with a "you tell him, Daddy" expression. Mickelson rolled his eyes and continued pushing his way up through the line.

He received the same angry response from almost everyone he passed. He couldn't take it anymore. Why the hell should he keep explaining himself to these people? They were waiting to get on a roller coaster, for crissakes. He was investigating a *double murder*. He pulled out his badge and held it up like a beacon.

"Excuse me. Police coming through. Make a path. Police officer coming through. Watch your back. Excuse me. Police."

He quickly worked his way to the top of the hour and a half line, creating a buzzing wave of nervous chatter in his wake. He looked to the first employee he could find, some goofball dressed like a coal miner, and asked, "Hey, where's Chuckie?"

Chuckie was already on his way. He was a little guy and he appeared hopping mad. His face was red and he looked like he wanted to run but wasn't allowed. He walked stiff-legged toward Mickelson as quickly as his little legs would carry him. His arms were also stiff, elbows locked, swinging at his sides as he strode over.

"What the heck do you think you're doing?" Chuckie hissed.

"Hey, relax, *Chuckie*. I'm just doin' my job."

"Your job?" Chuckie was doing everything he could not to jump up and down. He jerked his head to one side and Mickelson followed him to an area out of the vision of the waiting guests.

"Your job is not to come up through this line waving your badge and scaring the heck out of all these guests. You were supposed to have an escort and come up through a cast member entrance in a discreet manner. You call *this*—" Chuckie waved his hand around imitating Mickelson's showing of his badge. "—discreet? For gosh sake, Officer!"

"It's *Detective*, Chuckie. And I don't know anything about an escort. Just point me towards Sheila Nelson and I'll be on my way."

Chuckle's lips tightened but he held himself back from another torrent of "hecks" and "goshes." "I'll get her," he seethed. "Stay right here. Don't move."

"I get the concept of 'stay right here.'"

Mickelson waited a moment while Chuckie fetched Ms. Nelson. He took a moment to scan the crowd of tourists waiting to get on the ride. They seemed so happy and eager for their fun. Mostly, they seemed innocent and vulnerable. Lurking somewhere in this park was a killer. If he and Pendergrast didn't find him in time, which one of them might be next?

Chuckie returned with Sheila Nelson. She was short, too. Are all the miners under five-five? Like some sort of requirement to go down into the tunnels? Ms. Nelson was a cutie, though, in a sexy soccer mom way. Mickelson had noted with pleasant surprise that there was a large population of hot women who worked at Empire Realm. He looked forward to interviewing all of them.

"Sheila will take you back the *proper* way, Detective," said Chuckie.

"I look forward to being taken the proper way," Mickelson said with a sly grin.

"Oh, brother," said Ms. Nelson. She rolled her eyes and headed for a door in the fiberglass mountain rocks. Mickelson hurried after her. He was sure she would be more interested once he explained the critical role he was playing in the murder investigation.

If not, there was a long list of dancehall girls from the Lone Star Cantina who still needed to be interviewed.

She didn't know anything. Pendergrast was wasting his time.

"So you didn't notice anything suspicious at all?" Pendergrast asked.

"You mean like a dead body lying in the middle of the park? Nope. Can't say I noticed that."

This Sheila Nelson was a bitchy one. She was cooperating but not pleasantly. Pendergrast might have suspected something was up with her, but if she were involved with the murders, she probably wouldn't be such a smart ass. Still, he'd run her name through the computer when he got back to his office.

He leaned against the wall and crossed his arms. The very thought of sitting caused his muscles to tense involuntarily. "Look, Ms. Nelson, I'm just asking questions here. Nobody's accusing you of anything."

"Can I ask you a question?"

"Of course," Pendergrast said, smiling. An interviewing technique he found particularly effective was the false sweetness and innocence bit. "Ask me anything you like."

"Why won't you sit down? I mean, I've been in here for almost half-an-hour and you haven't sat down once. Is this some sort of cop intimidation routine?"

Pendergrast's smile vanished. The sweetness and innocence bit was hard to maintain when the subject of his hemorrhoid came up, however indirectly.

"Why don't you just tell me who you saw wandering around inside the park when you came off duty?"

Ms. Nelson sighed. "I told you. I don't know who I saw. The usual crew of second-shifters coming off and third-shifters coming on. Landscapers working on the plants, street vendors putting away their carts, custodial guys emptying the garbage cans. I saw all kinds of people."

"Wait a minute," said Pendergrast. "Landscapers? Isn't the middle of the night a strange time to be working on the plants?"

"Actually, no. That's when we work on the plants. That's also when we mow the grass. We're open every day of the year and we can't have our guests see us doing all that maintenance. I would only be suspicious to see a landscaper working during the day."

"Oh," said Pendergrast. She was obviously one of those ladies that had a problem with men. She seemed to enjoy correcting him too much. Pendergrast decided to try a different tack. "Why don't you tell me a little about yourself, Ms. Nelson."

"Like what?"

"Oh, I don't know. Are you married? I don't see a wedding ring."

"They don't let us wear too much jewelry. It doesn't go with the costume."

"I see. But that doesn't answer my question."

"I don't understand how that information is relevant. I told you what I know about the nights those guests died."

"I'm just curious. You can tell me now or I can go back to my computer and look it up."

Ms. Nelson paused, thinking. Pendergrast had obviously touched a nerve. Good. She clearly didn't want to talk about her marital status. That put her off guard. That gave Pendergrast an advantage.

"Divorced," she said tersely, crossing her arms.

Pendergrast nodded. "Me too. Any kids?"

She looked at him with narrowed eyes. She was getting pissed. "Yes."

"How many?"

She waited a beat to respond. "Three."

"That's nice. Three kids. I don't have any kids myself. Boys? Girls?"

"Two boys and a girl."

Pendergrast nodded again. He wasn't sure where he was going with this. After her bitchiness, he just liked making her uncomfortable. If you fished long enough you could usually expose the seamy underbelly of almost anyone's life. "What are their names?"

At that she stood up angrily. "Look, you said that I would be in here for a half-an-hour. I've been here for a half-an-hour. I need to get back to my shift."

"Must be tough to raise three kids on the salary you probably get working here."

She glared at him. "I'm doing fine."

"I'm sure you are. But the mining industry is getting tougher. Mines closing. Miners getting laid off. Not to mention the cave-ins."

She put her hands on her hips and leaned toward him, her tiny body filling with anger. "This must be very amusing to you, Detective Pendergrast. Making sport of someone's life. I think it's reprehensible."

"So where's Mr. Nelson?"

"My time is up."

"No, lady, your time is up when I say your time is up. And I ain't done asking questions. This is a serious matter and your lack of cooperation is really starting to piss me off. Maybe the two of us take a ride to the station and we continue this conversation in a more formal manner."

She stared at him, thin-lipped. Pendergrast could tell she was about to respond. He could hardly wait to hear what she said. He'd love an excuse to haul her into the box and really ask some questions. This interview was nothing compared to how he could get when he smelled blood in the water.

Before she could respond there was a knock on the trailer door.

"Goddamn it, Mickelson!" Pendergrast barked. "I'm not done. What the hell kind of moron rookie detective are you?"

The door opened and Mickelson stepped in. "I brought the next interviewee."

"Goddamn it, Mickelson! Have him wait outside until I'm done."

"Uh, I think you're going to want to talk to him."

"I swear to God, Mickelson, I'm gonna—" Pendergrast swallowed the last half of his sentence.

Into the trailer walked Kevin Lonnegan.

And he was wearing one of those silly miner costumes.

Open mouthed and without realizing what he was doing, Pendergrast sat down in disbelief. Right on his ass.

CHAPTER 7

Kevin stepped into the trailer and saw a visibly upset Sheila standing across from Pendergrast. Pendergrast took one look at Kevin and plopped down in his chair. When he did, he winced and let out a stifled grunt.

"Are you okay?" Kevin asked Sheila.

"Yeah. I am now," she said, her eyes still boring into Pendergrast.

"Jesus, Lou," Kevin said to Pendergrast. "What's wrong with you?"

Sheila's brow furrowed to hear Kevin refer to Pendergrast by name. She shot Kevin a look that he didn't see. He was too busy staring down Pendergrast. In another moment, Mickelson had ushered her out the trailer door and shut it, leaving the three men alone.

"What the hell did you do to her?" Kevin demanded. Pendergrast stared at Kevin in disbelief. When he received no reply, Kevin continued, "What did you do to her, Lou?"

"Hello Lonnegan," Pendergrast said slowly, deliberately, regaining his composure. Pendergrast gestured at the chair opposite the small card table he was sitting at. "Have a seat."

Never taking his glowering eyes off him, Kevin eased into the chair.

"Don't worry about her," Pendergrast said, slowly pulling himself into a standing position. Kevin knew that seeing him was a shock. He also knew that as long as he didn't suspect the real reason for Kevin being at Empire Realm, Pendergrast would get an almost orgasmic pleasure out of Kevin's presence in that miner's costume. "Why's your hair wet?" Pendergrast said.

"I just took a shower. Long story." He really didn't relish the idea of recounting the story of the Code V to Lou Pendergrast.

"Hey, I got nothing but time."

What the hell, thought Kevin. He would pretend it was Pendergrast's birthday and give him a nice juicy present. It could only help his cover. After all, who, in his right mind, would endure that as part of any investigation, undercover or otherwise?

"Well, if you must know, a kid puked on me as he got off the ride."

To Pendergrast's credit he didn't actually wet his pants. But the expression on his face said it all. Eyebrows raised, a suppressed grin on his lips, like he was trying to be polite and stifle his smile, but this was just too good. He couldn't help himself. Pendergrast shook his head slowly.

"Goddamn, Kevin. Really. Goddamn."

"You know, Lou, it's tough enough being here without you enjoying it so fucking much."

"I can only imagine."

Mickelson hovered nearby. He cleared his throat awkwardly. "He wasn't on the list. But I saw him up there and thought he looked really familiar. Then it hit me. I mean, shit. Kevin Lonnegan." Mickelson smiled a mouthful of white, straight teeth. He was young, good looking, with light brown hair. Green eyes. A suit that fit his tall frame well. A crimson silk tie. He was the complete opposite in appearance of Lou Pendergrast. But

Kevin recognized a little of himself in Mickelson and thought it ironic that Gardner would have paired them together. Kevin immediately suspected that Mickelson was to be the media "face" for what would surely become a very high-profile case. Mickelson turned to Kevin. "I was still in uniform when you quit. But everybody knew about you. About why you left."

"Oh, it was quite the scandal at the time," said Pendergrast. "Wasn't it?"

Kevin ran a hand through his wet hair. Playing along to let Pendergrast believe he really worked here was one thing. That was to protect his cover. But Kevin was really not interested in dredging up his sordid past. He remained silent.

"I heard you were a P.I.," said Pendergrast.

"I was. I am." Kevin shifted uncomfortably in his seat. Might as well make this a good show. "You know how it is. Sometimes work is good and sometimes . . . well, when things get slow and I need the cash . . ." He gestured with both hands up and down his miner's costume. The truth was that Kevin usually turned down work. He had a couple of very steady clients—the insurance guys, the lawyers—and he was only interested in working enough to maintain his humble house on the lake and buy some food. But Pendergrast didn't need to know that. "When I need the cash, I sometimes call Jerry and he hooks me up with a job until something turns up."

"Jerry Engle."

"Yeah. He's been good to me. My P.I. work's been pretty scarce lately."

Pendergrast nodded solemnly. Like he really understood the hand-to-mouth existence of such a poor, lowly P.I. "I bet it's tough to find work at the bottom of a bottle."

"Fuck you, Pendergrast."

Pendergrast smirked, satisfied that he had pressed Kevin's button. "You know why we're here?"

"I assume it has something to do with the dead guy they found the other day."

"See? You're not such a bad investigator, after all," said Pendergrast with a Cheshire smile. "They oughta be lining up at your door." Pendergrast walked awkwardly to the edge of the table, almost like he had a limp. He was about to sit on the edge of the table but caught himself and decided against it. He put a hand in his pocket to lend a casual air. It just made him look uncomfortable. "So you weren't working on the night the guy died?"

"No, I wasn't."

"What about the night the other guy died?"

"What other guy?"

"Come on, Kevin, I'm not stupid. You know who I'm talking about."

Kevin nodded. "You mean the guy in the topiary. No, I wasn't working then either." Kevin paused for dramatic effect. Pretended to have a revelation. "You think they're related, don't you? Jesus, you're investigating a double murder."

"Now, Kevin, you know I can't discuss the details of an investigation with outsiders." He lingered on the word "outsiders," rubbing it in. He walked to the edge of the trailer and gazed out the window, lost momentarily in thought. "A kid puked on you. That's just . . ." He trailed off and shook his head. "I can't even begin to describe my reaction to that."

"So who are your suspects?" Kevin asked.

"Kevin. Kevin, please. You know I can't tell you anything." Pendergrast spoke to him like he was a child. "Those days are long over for you. Now, I just need to ask a few more questions and then we'll get you back to the mine. Okay?"

Kevin offered a resigned nod and settled in for the rest of the humiliation.

Sheila was waiting for him upon his return. "So?"

Kevin cocked his head at her. *What?*

She leaned toward him. "So what's going on? Who's your friend?"

"Pendergrast is not my friend. We just know each other."

"I don't like him," Sheila said, as if baiting Kevin for a reaction.

"Join the club. We're thinking of getting t-shirts made."

Chuckie glared at the two of them from his podium. They were standing around while guests were waiting to get on the ride. Sheila gestured a group into a car.

"So are you going to tell me what's going on?" she said.

Kevin locked the lap bar down in the last row of a mine car. "What makes you think I know anything?"

"You know something. I wasn't born yesterday. I want to know why he's asking me about my kids."

"Hey!" Chuckie hissed from nearby. "No chitchat. Stay in character."

Sheila whirled on him. "You know what, Chuckie? My character thinks that the foreman is in danger of falling down a mineshaft."

Kevin stifled a laugh.

Chuckie didn't find the comment amusing. "Watch it, Sheila. I don't want to write you up."

She rolled her eyes. "Like it would make any difference in my life."

Kevin leaned close to her. "After our shift. We'll go somewhere and talk." She gave him a "damn right" look. Chuckie remained, arms crossed, brow furrowed, until they got back to the business of loading cars.

Why had Kevin said that? Why had he volunteered to talk to her later that night? Chuckie had given him an easy out; he could have avoided the whole situation. But he got the feeling that Sheila wouldn't have given up that easily. He would have had to offer her some explanation eventually.

Plus, there was something else. Since he started working at Empire Realm, Kevin had grown quite fond of Sheila. He didn't know her very well. But he knew that he liked who she seemed to be. And he definitely found her attractive. He enjoyed joking with her during their shifts and surprised himself by doing some borderline flirting with her. It was an odd realization for Kevin. He couldn't remember the last time that he had flirted with anyone. And he certainly hadn't felt anything close to genuine attraction for anyone in more than three years.

So, if he was really going to be honest with himself, he didn't offer to talk with her tonight purely to answer her questions. He had a silly, boyish desire to get to know her better. This was just the most convenient excuse. He would have to be careful, though. He wasn't sure if he was really ready to dip his toes back into the dating pool.

He shook off these thoughts and was actually relieved for the distraction of his repetitive work. Loading guests and sending them down the track was definitely a better way to pass time than sitting in a trailer, eating crap dished out from Lou Pendergrast. Kevin chastised himself for not concentrating on his case. Running into Pendergrast was a potentially significant event. If Pendergrast even suspected Kevin's real reason for working at Empire Realm, he could be charged with interfering with a police investigation and have to contend with legal prosecution. Plus, Jerry Engle would probably be out on the street. Kevin knew that this wouldn't be the last time he ran into Pendergrast. He'd have to be careful.

Although he tried to think about his case, his mind kept wandering back to Sheila. His suggestion had been so spontaneous, he hadn't even thought about where they might talk this evening. Maybe over coffee. It would be a little late for dinner. Kevin felt a flutter in his stomach. He was starting to get nervous. Was this a date? What if she thought it was a date? What if she didn't? Did he even want it to be a date?

Jesus, Lonnegan. What a dope. He had served in the Navy, been a cop, dealt with the lowest of lowlifes, yet the prospect of a potential, maybe, what-if-it-really-is, date with a woman had him in knots.

When their shift finally ended, they drove separate cars and slid into a window booth in a nearby Perkins restaurant. Perkins had seemed an innocuous enough location and they were open late.

Sheila had a cell phone to her ear as she slid into the booth. "Not long. Make sure Billy does his homework. He'll say he did it, but check it. And don't let him fool you by showing you yesterday's homework. What did they have for dinner? Uh-huh. Yeah. Maggie should be in bed by now. Give them a kiss for me. Not long. Okay. Bye."

Kevin wanted to ask her who she was talking to. He didn't think she was married—no ring, a few clues dropped in their workplace conversations. But he didn't know what her status was. Involved? In love? As she spoke on the phone, he worked up enough courage to ask her. She finished her conversation and snapped the cell phone closed. Kevin's lips parted as he started to ask her who was on the other end of the phone, but she wasted no time and immediately launched into her line of questioning.

"So how do you know that jerk?" she said, leaning forward over her placemat.

The waitress appeared and Kevin quickly ordered two coffees. He asked Sheila if she wanted anything to eat. Maybe a piece of pie? She shook her head.

"We used to work together," Kevin said.

"Where? Charm school?"

Kevin smiled. "I used to be a cop."

This news seemed to catch her off guard. She opened her mouth to respond, but then decided against whatever she was going to say. She leaned back into the booth seat. "I wouldn't have guessed that."

"I'll take that as a compliment."

The waitress returned and poured them both some coffee.

"You know," Sheila said, "I think I *would* like some pie." Kevin got the distinct impression that she was settling in to hear more of Kevin's history. "You have key lime?"

"Yes ma'am," said the waitress, a polite, older woman with what appeared to be an entire can of hair spray applied to her graying locks.

"Is it real key lime or just lime?"

"Key lime, ma'am."

"They're not the same, you know."

"Oh, I know. I'll bring it out and if you don't like it, I'll switch it for the apple. That's good, too."

"You've got a deal," Sheila said, grinning. She turned immediately back to Kevin. "So why does Mr. Charm School want to know about my kids?"

"I sincerely doubt he does. He was probably just asking questions to get a rise out of you. It's how he gets his kicks."

Sheila poured some cream and what appeared to Kevin to be a half a pound of sugar into her coffee. "That's sick."

"That's Lou Pendergrast."

"I take it he's investigating the deaths of those two tourists."

"That's what he told me. Seems he thinks they might be more than accidents."

Sheila shook off a shiver. "He thinks somebody killed them. He thinks that one of us is the killer."

"Not you and me specifically, but I assume he's investigating a lot of cast members. Probably talking to the victims' families."

"There's a freaky thought. Somebody working right next to us could be a killer." It was the exact thought that Kevin had been contemplating since he started working at the park. "Maybe it's Chuckie," she said, raising her eyebrows conspiratorially.

Kevin took another sip of his coffee. "Chuckie? Why do you think it's Chuckie?"

Her expression changed, just slightly, but enough for Kevin to notice. She had clearly been joking. Kevin's question, although casual, had alerted her radar. "I don't really think it's Chuckie. I was just kidding." She paused a moment, considering. "What if it's you?"

Now Kevin's expression changed. He gave her a bemused look. But he didn't answer her question. She narrowed her eyes at him, taking him in. She stared at him intently, surveying him. He couldn't help noticing how the corners of her eyes crinkled as she squinted. Finally, she relaxed, sat back, and crossed her arms.

"It's not you," she declared.

"How can you be so sure?"

"I can tell."

"That's quite a gift. *You* should be a cop."

The waitress returned and placed the slice of key lime pie in front of Sheila. She surveyed it with almost the same intensity with which she had just scrutinized Kevin. The pie filling was pale yellow on a graham cracker crust. A dollop of whipped cream adorned the top. Sheila took her fork and sliced off the tip

of the piece. Upon tasting it she said, "That's not bad." The waitress smiled and, content in the knowledge that she had satisfied
a true pie connoisseur's palate, moved on to the next table.

Sheila took another bite and, chewing, said, "Used to be a
cop, huh? Surely there's a story in there."

Kevin sipped his coffee, put it down and stirred it absently
with his spoon. "There surely is."

CHAPTER 8

He was a good-looking guy. That, naturally, had caught her attention first. Tall—at least six feet, maybe a little more. He was in good shape, too. Thin, but certainly not scrawny. He carried himself confidently, like he knew he didn't have anything to prove. He had a shock of red hair, trimmed neatly, but a little longer than the Code of Conduct might dictate. Perhaps the feature that had most grabbed her attention was his eyes. A deep midnight blue. They were intelligent eyes. Kind eyes. Eyes like a starry night. But maybe a little too serious. Although, when he did laugh, his eyes lit up and changed his whole face. In those moments of laughter he wasn't such a sphinx. He was open and happy and Sheila allowed herself to think, *just maybe . . .*

Then she would catch herself. She wasn't interested in a relationship. For God's sake, that was the last thing she needed right now, what with the kids, her lame job, going to school, and her impending legal situation. But she couldn't help herself. Kevin seemed different. She found herself maneuvering to work with him. Chuckie was starting to get suspicious. So what, she told herself. Maybe Chuckie was interested in him.

The fact that Kevin was heterosexual (she assumed) was enough to make him different from a large percentage of the male cast members of Empire Realm. Sheila couldn't care less what someone's sexual orientation was. It was just that the large numbers of gay employees severely limited her ability to meet interesting, straight men. It wasn't like she had any other social life where she could meet them.

But who was she kidding? Like she was going to meet an interesting, straight man working the loading area of Prospector Mountain. It was a job for high school kids looking for date money or losers without any education or prospects. Plus, she *really* wasn't looking for a relationship. Just a little companionship. But then Kevin showed up. He was different in more ways than just the fact that he was interested in women. He was about her age. He seemed educated. Let's face it, he seemed like he could do a lot better than that crummy job. Of course, so could she. But there she was. There they both were.

So when he told her that he used to be a cop, it piqued her interest. Perhaps he had a story like hers. Both of them deserving better but finding themselves, for the moment, in a crappy job to get their lives back on track. Perhaps he was a kindred spirit.

Then again, maybe he was just a loser like the others.

"Do I get to hear the story?" she asked him, taking another bite of pie.

He shifted uncomfortably. Evidently, he was one of those guys who had trouble expressing his feelings. In other words, a straight guy. "Not much to tell, really."

"Uh huh. Why aren't you a cop anymore?"

"I resigned three years ago."

"Why?"

"I wanted to be a private investigator."

Hmmm. Sheila nodded. He was hiding something. She could tell. "So is that what you've been doing for the past three years? Until you started at Empire?"

"That's right. Work's been a little slow lately and I wanted to do something interesting until it picked up again. I have a friend in the Empire security department and he got me the job."

Sheila looked at him seriously. "So, let me get this straight. You define working as a loader at Prospector Mountain as 'interesting.' I must admit, that disturbs me."

Kevin smiled. His blue eyes sparkled and she saw that there was a real human being in there somewhere. "It's a pretty loose definition. You know, you're a tougher interviewer than Pendergrast."

Sheila poured herself some more coffee and added cream and sugar. She should be drinking decaf, but too late now. She knew she'd be up half the night. "So why'd you *really* leave the police?"

He choked slightly on his coffee. Putting down the cup, he looked at her. She could tell he was considering sticking to his story, but she stared right back at him. She would keep asking until he told her or got up and left. When she wanted to know something, not much would stand in her way.

"I had a drinking problem," he said. Uh-oh. Alarms went off inside Sheila's head. He continued. "I've been clean for three years." Sheila didn't say anything, being careful not to respond too dramatically.

"That's great," she said. "It must have been tough to do." She took the edge off her tone, softening it a little.

"Yes, it was." He poured himself another cup of coffee. She noticed that he drank it black. Clearly, he wasn't worried about the caffeine.

"Did you always have a . . . drinking problem?"

He waited a moment before responding. He didn't look up as he spoke, just stirred his black coffee with a spoon. She could tell he was uncomfortable discussing this, but she also got the impression that he wanted to talk about it. Like he was a little relieved and just needed some help opening up.

"No," he said. "I started drinking after my wife died."

Nice going, Sheila, she said to herself. She suddenly felt a horrible pang of guilt. In the course of a few minutes she had already dredged up the guy's two most painful things in his life. "I'm sorry," she said. She meant it. Although she knew what it was like to lose a marriage, she couldn't possibly know what that kind of loss felt like. "Do you have any kids?"

Kevin continued to look down, stirring his coffee. "No." He paused for what seemed like a very long time. Sheila was about to say something, anything, to fill the silence, when he suddenly continued. "My wife was pregnant when she died. It was a car accident. A drunk driver." He paused again, apparently aware of the cruel irony in that. "When my wife was pronounced dead, the doctors performed an emergency C-section and delivered the baby. He was about seven months along. Very premature, although he had a good chance of survival. But his injuries from the accident were just too severe. He died six days later."

Sheila's hand was on her mouth. She felt tears welling up involuntarily in her eyes. As a mother, she couldn't imagine what kind of horror that must have been. She immediately felt such sympathy for him, she wanted to slide into his side of the booth and put her arm around him.

He wasn't crying or showing any sign of emotion, but there was a change in his manner that told her that it was painful to recall these memories. But it also seemed like he wanted to tell her. Like it was somehow cathartic. Like he wanted her to know. He finally looked up at her.

"His name was Michael."

"Oh, Kevin . . ." She wiped away a tear. "I'm so sorry."

There was another awkward gap in the conversation where neither knew what to say next. What could she possibly say? Thankfully, the waitress appeared.

"How was the pie, honey? You didn't finish."

"It was fine. I'm just not as hungry as I thought."

"We'll take the check whenever you get a chance," Kevin said. Sheila cringed. She had pushed him too far too quickly. They barely knew each other and she had to grill him on all the tragic details of his life. She wanted to rap a fist against her forehead.

"It's getting late. I assume you have to get back to your kids," he said.

"I guess. My mom's watching them."

"Your mom." He repeated this as a statement, not a question. She almost imagined the flicker of a faint smile on his face.

"Look, Kevin, I'm sorry I brought up all that. I didn't mean to pry. I have a habit of sticking my nose where it doesn't belong and—"

"It's okay, Sheila. Really." The check came and Kevin laid down a ten-dollar bill. Sheila offered to pay but Kevin waved it off. He insisted on paying for the coffee and pie. "I'll see you tomorrow at work?"

"Yeah."

They got up and walked to the door, which Kevin held for her. As she got into her car, he turned back. "Maybe we can go get a real dinner together sometime. Maybe a movie."

She smiled. "I'd like that."

"I spent the whole time talking about myself. I want to hear your story."

She maintained her smile. But inside she was thinking, *no, you don't.*

It had been a long time since Kevin had talked about it. A long time. Maybe it had been too long. He had convinced himself that it was better to not bring it up, not discuss it. That way he wouldn't be reminded of it. It would be easier for him to move on.

But now, driving home on I-4, he wondered if he hadn't been wrong about all of that. Maybe it was harder *not* talking about it. Keeping it bottled up. Trying so damned hard to forget and not dwell on the past. Sometimes it seemed easier to let it come out, not force it back down.

The Reverend once said to him, "You can't deny what happened, Kevin. You can try, but it'll just stalk you. You'll spend your whole life looking over your shoulder for it, pretending it's not there, but always knowing that it is. Sooner or later, you're going to have to invite it into your living room, make it a sandwich, and get to know it. You don't have to like it, but you have to get comfortable with it."

The Reverend is a wise man.

Maybe tonight, for the first time in three years, Kevin had invited it in. And Sheila had opened the door for it.

Sheila. Despite the difficulty Kevin always had talking about the deaths of Maria and the baby, he wasn't upset with Sheila for prodding it out of him. She was tenacious. No, that was an understatement. She was *damn* tenacious. Tenacity, while being an infuriating character trait, was also one that Kevin respected.

He hoped that his sad story hadn't put her off too much. She seemed genuinely sympathetic, although that wasn't why he wanted her to know. The last thing he wanted was someone feeling sorry for him. He wanted her to know so that she would understand who he was, just like he wanted to understand who she was. He wasn't looking for sympathy. He'd had enough sympathy to last a lifetime. He just wanted her to know.

She hadn't run from the restaurant. Maybe she could accept him and his past. His alcoholism. Maybe—

Kevin shook his head. He knew he was getting way ahead of himself. *Slow down, Lonnegan.* Jesus, where was he, in high school? He put Sheila out of his mind for the time being.

But he couldn't shake his memories. Talking about what happened, inviting it in and making it a sandwich, it had brought up thoughts of Maria that weren't so easily brushed aside.

They met while he was still in the Navy. He had been stationed at Key West, not a bad posting for any serviceman. They had met in Sloppy Joe's, the bar made infamous by the patronage of Ernest Hemingway during his residence on the island. Actually, Kevin learned from Maria, the current Sloppy Joe's was not the one that Papa had frequented. That bar was around the corner, now called Captain Tony's. Maria had been a waitress at Sloppy Joe's when Kevin first saw her.

She wasn't dressed in anything particularly impressive: a black Sloppy Joe's tank top and a pair of long shorts. But she transcended her meager attire. She had long black hair that framed an attractive, oval face. Her large, brown eyes were striking, as were her full lips. Her Cuban heritage manifested itself in her olive skin, and the afternoons spent on the island's beaches did much to give her a tropical, bronzed complexion.

He was instantly smitten. It took a couple of weeks of regular visits to the bar before he worked up the courage to ask her out. They went to dinner and she introduced him to conch fritters. Their first date ended with a barefoot stroll on the beach and a goodnight kiss under a coconut palm. They were together from that moment on.

Kevin worked a fairly regular shift at the base and spent almost all of his free time with Maria, exploring the islands that make up the Florida Keys. He was a Lieutenant and owed the navy a few years of service for the ROTC scholarship that paid for his college education at the University of Virginia. But his hitch in the military was almost up.

As soon as he was a civilian, he bought the white Blazer and headed to Orlando. Maria's family lived there and the couple wanted to tell them in person about their engagement. Kevin had proposed on the beach, under the stars. She had said "yes" immediately.

Maria was the second youngest of a huge Cuban family, her father having immigrated with his own family when he was a boy, before Castro's rise to power. They were a loud, boisterous group and Kevin loved them instantly. And they felt the same for Kevin.

Kevin and Maria decided to settle in Orlando. Kevin had no desire to return to New Jersey where he had been raised. He was the youngest of four boys and his brothers had scattered to various parts of the country, starting their own lives. He loved his parents but his relationship with them seemed better when it was limited to the occasional holiday visits. Orlando was as good a place as any to get married, have kids, and enjoy life. The weather was great, the cost of living low, and he actually got a kick out of living so close to all the theme parks.

The wedding was a huge ceremony at St. James in downtown Orlando. It was a full Catholic Mass, both of them being of the faith, though his wedding was the first time Kevin had been to mass since college.

They honeymooned in the Bahamas, Kevin blowing what was left of his savings on the trip. Three days of lazing on the beach, sipping fruity cocktails, and making love. It was the best three days of Kevin's life.

When they returned, Kevin enrolled in the police academy, having always been interested in law enforcement. His college major was criminology and he took to the job naturally. Being the youngest of four rowdy Irish boys qualified him to endure almost any hardship and he excelled at police work. He quickly rose through the ranks, patrolling the streets, working robberies and sex crimes, until he made Detective in homicide.

Maria had been so proud. The day of his promotion she baked him a disaster of a cake. A delicious, lopsided brown mess with *Congratulations* scrawled illegibly across the top. Kevin's ambition was fueled more by his desire to make Maria proud than by any internal drive. Sure, he wanted to be good at his job. She made him want to be better.

When they found out that they were expecting a baby, Maria's family threw a huge party. They stayed up half the night singing and dancing and Kevin felt like this was exactly where he was supposed to be. This was the life he had always wanted.

Until a guy with too much vodka in his blood ran a red light and changed that life forever.

Kevin let the memories flood in. He couldn't push them away. He had invited them in and he was now suddenly afraid they would never leave. It was a Pandora's Box that he might never get closed.

He turned his truck off the road and into his driveway. Sitting in the truck, letting the engine run, he took a few deep breaths. No more memories. He had learned over the past three years to suppress those memories. If he had any hope of making it out of the car and into the house without breaking down into tears, he had to get some control of his thoughts.

God, he wanted a drink.

That's what he used to do when the memories poured in and he couldn't stop them. The alcohol would deaden his senses; keep his mind from going too far into areas he couldn't handle.

There was a bar less than five miles from his house.

It would be easy to drive down, find a stool. One drink. One drink would settle him down. One drink would give him the time he needed to get his memories under control. Just one drink. He needed it. He wouldn't have any more than that. He would make a deal with himself. One drink. That was all.

It was just before midnight. The bar would be open. He closed his eyes, making a decision. With his eyes closed he could see Maria smiling at him. She was in that blue bikini top as they headed North on US 1. The azure water of the Atlantic was behind her. The Blazer's window was down and her black hair fluttered in silky strands across her face. Her teeth gleamed white. She tilted her head back laughing, singing along to the Seger tune on the radio. She put her feet up on the dashboard and Kevin could see her long toes and blood red nails tapping to the music. The dashboard was the same charcoal gray it was now.

Smoky.

Kevin opened his eyes and turned to his right. The passenger seat was empty and dark. The only sounds were those of the truck engine running and the lake frogs croaking in the night air. The dashboard had since faded in color, but he could almost see the print of heat where Maria's foot had just been. Once been.

The bar was less than five miles away. Kevin lifted his hands from his lap and placed them on the wheel. *One drink. Just one drink.* He took his right hand and reached for the gearshift. He gritted his teeth and with all his might pushed his hand past the stick. His fingers rested on the ignition and he turned the key back.

The truck's engine went silent, leaving the air filled with the eerie croaking of the frogs. Turning that key had taken all of his strength. Kevin placed both hands on his face and couldn't hold back the sobs. Turning the key had used up all of his resolve. He couldn't fight off the grief. He stayed that way in the truck for ten minutes.

He opened the front door of the house and hesitated, startled. Lucius was laying asleep on the couch, his notes and videotapes laid out on the coffee table. Kevin smiled at him almost paternally. He pulled a knit blanket quietly from a linen closet and laid it over Lucius' sleeping form. When he did, Lucius stirred, turning over so that he was facing the back of the couch.

"Yo, Red . . ." Lucius said groggily, neither turning back over nor opening his eyes.

"Good night, Lucius."

Lucius mumbled something that Kevin couldn't understand.

"Whatever it is," Kevin said, "it'll wait until morning."

"I found him, Red . . ." Lucius was still facing the back of the couch, eyes closed.

Kevin leaned over to make sure he had heard him correctly. "Say again?"

"The dude on the tape . . ." Lucius said, still sounding asleep. "I found the motherfucker . . ."

CHAPTER 9

He had called her at four; late enough for it seem spontaneous, but early enough to allow her to make arrangements to be there. Pendergrast was always thinking like that. It was what made him such a good detective. You had to understand timing. You had to understand people's motivations.

Pendergrast was pretty sure he understood Carla Beck's motivations. She wanted a good story. All reporters want a good story. Well, he had a good story. He had a fucking bombshell.

But he wouldn't give her the whole story right now. He would draw her in, doling out a little here and a little there, like a trail of breadcrumbs that led right to his bedroom. He had been attracted to Carla Beck since the moment he met her. She had been a beat crime reporter for the Orlando *Sentinel*. He was investigating the heroin death of an affluent teen.

Of course, he was still married at the time, so she wasn't interested in his advances. But through Pendergrast's investigations and Carla's reporting, they had gotten to know each other over the years in a professional way. As a rule, Pendergrast ordinarily despised the media. Unless the media had blonde hair and long, tan legs.

Pendergrast felt that the time had come to finally make his move. The timing was critical. He couldn't give her the whole story now. He would give her just enough to get her interested, provide a reason to get back together to learn more. He would give her a reason to call *him*. To pursue *him*. That would give him the advantage.

She was a columnist now for the *Sentinel*, just recently promoted, and would be hungry for a killer story to establish herself. *Timing and motivation,* thought Pendergrast as he sipped a martini. He understood her motivation and he understood the timing.

He had suggested meeting at Gordo's, a trendy martini and cigar bar in downtown Orlando. Although they were to meet at seven, he arrived at six-thirty. Gordo's was off of Church Street, near Orlando's downtown entertainment center. Church Street featured various bars and restaurants, as well as Church Street Station, a complex of themed shopping, drinking, and eating establishments. You had to look for Gordo's to find it. A small sign pointed down a brick-lined alley. At the end of the alley was a set of masonry steps that led down to the subterranean martini bar. It was a small place, essentially a basement, but it was elegantly appointed in dark, polished wood and maroon carpet. Tuxedoed waiters and waitresses served a wide variety of specialty martinis, including such novelties as chocolate and mango. There was a separate menu for the cigar aficionado, and the discriminating smoker could choose from an impressive assortment of cigars from all over the world, including expensive selections from the Dominican Republic and Tampa's Ybor City. Gordo's' business was starting to drop as the martini and cigar fad of the late 1990's faded. But, as the last bastion of its kind in Orlando, its business was adequate and it could sometimes be hard to get a table on a weeknight as the lawyers and bank staffers mingled after work. Pendergrast didn't want to take any chances, so he had arrived early to secure a table.

At least, that's what he told himself. But the truth was that he was eager and a little nervous, like a kid on his first date, and he had arrived early to have a drink and settle down. He needed to appear calm and cool. Plus, his hemorrhoid was still throbbing and the alcohol would allow him to sit for a little while without squirming too much.

He checked his watch and determined that he had enough time to hit the men's room before Carla arrived. He relieved himself at the urinal and washed his hands thoroughly. Gordo's had scented soap and if Carla got a whiff of his hands, he wanted to make sure they smelled clean. Lavender.

Before he left, he took a moment to check himself out in the mirror. His scalp was clearly visible through the black hair on the top of his head and he winced at the shine as he moved his head back and forth, looking for the most flattering angle. He couldn't find one. He made a mental note not to look down if he dropped something or when he signed the check. He didn't want to let Carla see the top of his head.

He checked his waistline, which had expanded slightly since that first day he met Carla. Technically, he wasn't fat. Not technically. He was a little overweight, but if he carried himself right, dressed in the proper clothes, and made sure he stood at the appropriate angle, he looked like he still wore size 38 pants. He ran his hand through his thinning hair one last time in a futile attempt at more coverage and then checked his nose hairs, which had been trimmed less than an hour ago.

When he returned to his table, he saw Carla walk in. She literally took his breath away. He paused and exhaled, watching her for a moment before she spotted him. She was relatively tall for a woman, at least five-nine, looking taller in her high heel pumps. Her shoulder-length blonde hair was cut in a professional, sexy style, parted on the side, with the longer side hanging down, partially covering one cheek. Although he couldn't tell from this distance or in the darkness of the bar, Pendergrast knew she had striking brown eyes. She was wearing a bright pink silk camisole under a white business suit with a skirt that landed at about mid-thigh. Pendergrast's eyes wandered to the hemline. His mind wandered farther than that.

She caught sight of him and offered a friendly wave. He returned the greeting and gestured at his table. They both arrived at the same time and exchanged greetings. Being a gentleman, he waited for her to sit before he did. When he did, he landed squarely on his inflamed hemorrhoid, grimacing and trying to stifle an involuntary grunt.

"You okay?" Carla asked.

"Fine. No problem." He felt it best to distract her from his less-than-graceful start to the evening. "Would you like a drink?"

"I'd love one. A gimlet. Two olives."

Pendergrast waved down his waitress and placed the order. He ordered himself a second drink. The waitress turned to put the order in when Carla stopped her.

"Wait—" she said. "Can I get one of these, too?" She pointed at a selection from the cigar menu.

Pendergrast was stunned. "You want a cigar?"

"Sure. Why not? I'll take this one, the Managua."

The waitress nodded and noted the order. She looked at Pendergrast. "And you, sir?"

"Yeah. Bring two of those." Pendergrast hated cigars. He had tried a few in his life and thought they were more trouble than they were worth. They were hard to light, they got all wet and nasty, and if you actually finished one, you felt nauseous. He glanced at the menu. The cigars were nine bucks apiece.

"So, Detective," Carla said, smiling coyly, placing an elbow on the table and leaning on her hand, "I'm so glad you called. I thought that since I left the beat, our paths wouldn't cross like they used to."

"Well, I think it's important to keep in touch. Congratulations, by the way. I read the column you wrote on that school voucher thing."

"What'd you think?"

"Oh, it was great. Terrific."

She smiled again, alabaster white teeth set behind scarlet red lips. She pulled the long side of her hair behind her ear and sat back in her chair.

"So, Detective Pendergrast, I assume you called for a reason. What's on your mind?"

"I just thought it might be nice to have a couple of drinks. Talk about stuff."

She leaned towards him. She was definitely flirting, Pendergrast was sure of it. She smirked at him, processing what he just said. She was picking up the cues. This might just be easier than he thought.

"Working on any interesting cases?" she asked.

"Well, as a matter of fact, I am."

"Anything you can share with an old friend?" she said, lightly touching the back of his hand. Her touch was warm, gentle. He felt himself getting aroused.

"Off the record?" he confirmed.

She gave him a pouty smile that said she really wanted to talk on the record. *Not yet, Carla. Not yet, but soon.* "Okay. Off the record."

The waitress returned with their drinks and stogies. Carla clipped off the end of her cigar like a pro and quickly lit it up. Pendergrast watched her cheeks suck in as she puffed, getting the end to light. Seeing that cigar extending from her mouth, her cheeks concave, his mind wandered again.

"You going to smoke that or save it for later?" she asked him, eyeing his cigar and blowing a plume of blue smoke through her lips.

"Uh, I'll smoke it now." He fumbled with the clipper and the result was a ragged hole instead of a clean slice. He leaned forward trying to get the end lit. The damned thing wouldn't light. Carla watched him struggling and smiled.

"Here," she said, taking the cigar from his mouth. "Let me." She put his cigar in her mouth and leaned into the lighter, taking several long, sensual drags until the end caught and glowed orange. She handed it back to him, pursing her lips and exhaling the smoke.

Jesus.

Pendergrast just stared dumbly, finally taking the cigar. He couldn't think of a thing to say.

"You were saying about your case. . . ?" Carla said.

"Yeah," he blinked twice, getting his mind back on track. "You heard about the guy who died recently out at Empire Realm?"

"Of course. Tourist. Dropped dead in the middle of the park or something."

"Well, he might not have exactly dropped dead."

"You're kidding."

"Wish I was." He took a long, cool drag on the cigar and promptly erupted into a coughing fit worthy of a chronic emphysema patient. Carla snatched her drink from the table and quickly sat back in her chair, holding both her cigar and drink out of the line of fire.

"You okay?" she asked finally.

"Yeah," he said, clearing his throat. "I'm getting over a cold and just can't shake this cough."

She nodded her head, empathizing. "Vitamin C, Zinc, and Echinacea."

"Hunh?"

"That'll fix your cold. Stop at Wallgreens tonight and get some."

"Oh. Yeah. Thanks." He sipped his martini. *Goddamn agar. Nine goddamn dollars.*

"So who do you think did it?"

"Not sure."

"Any suspects?"

Now he smiled at her. She was following the breadcrumbs. "Not yet. But we've got some pretty strong leads."

"How'd he die?"

"Carla, Carla . . . You know I can't tell you that. The M.O. is a key piece of information. If we let that out it'll taint the case."

"You know I love this stuff, Lou. How 'bout a hint?" She lowered her head and looked up at him with those big, brown eyes.

"Well . . . Okay. I can tell you that he definitely wasn't shot." Carla smiled at him as if to say "come on, you can do better than that." He shook his head, also smiling. "That's all I can say right now. Remember, off the record."

She smiled and took a sip of her gimlet, followed by a long drag on her cigar. "I remember."

They eyed each other lustily, Carla chasing a story and Pendergrast chasing Carla. Pendergrast knew that he had planted the seed and given it the necessary water. Carla would call him next time and, if she wanted the rest of the details, she was going to have to do something for him. Tit for tat, so to speak.

Pendergrast chuckled to himself, amused at the double entendre. This was working out exactly as he planned.

* * *

Greg held up one shoe. He was wearing absolutely nothing from the waist down.

"Mommy. No shoe."

Sheila looked down at him. She was almost twenty minutes late getting out the door, she still hadn't packed lunches, and her hair was dripping wet. But she looked down at her three-year-old son and couldn't help but laugh.

"I think you need to make some underpants a priority over that shoe, Greg honey."

"No *shoe.*"

"Come on. Mommy will help you find your shoe. And some pants."

It was like this every morning. Barely contained chaos. Billy and Maggie needed to get to school, Greg to day care. Sheila had to get them dressed and ready, the two older kids to the bus stop and Greg into his car seat. She had to make lunches, sign homework, and clean up the disaster area she called her kitchen. She walked Greg through the kitchen to get back to his bedroom and noticed a half of a waffle adhered with syrup to the top of the dinette table. She pretended not to see it.

Plus, she had her own homework to do, usually crammed into the wee hours of the night after work, after dinner, after helping the kids with their schoolwork, after baths, after bedtime stories, after umpteen glasses of water . . . After, after, after.

So she would sit at the kitchen table, crack open her textbooks, and read bleary-eyed until she finally succumbed to exhaustion, placing her head into the book's crease. *Just resting my eyes,* she would tell herself, *just for a minute.* The minute would pass and she'd open her eyes to find that three hours had gone by. Then she'd shuffle down the hall to her bedroom and collapse into her bed. Right before lapsing back into unconsciousness, she'd have just enough time to notice that her sheets really needed to be changed.

Then she would get up and do it all over again.

She was studying elementary education at the University of Central Florida. She wanted to be a teacher. There was a genuine moment of magic that she had observed in all three of her kids when they learned something new. A widening of the eyes as a realization occurred, a connection made. Blue and yellow make green. Because of the Earth's axis, Australia celebrates Christmas in the middle of summer. When she could facilitate that magical moment, it gave her a charge of energy that would last all day. It was those moments that she lived for. She wanted to be able to provide those moments to other kids, too.

Teachers' salaries, especially in Central Florida, were depressingly low. Sheila was aware of that. Although the difference between $6.50 an hour and $12.00 an hour seemed dramatic, in its meager ability to truly improve her quality of life, it wasn't an equally dramatic step up. Occasionally, she thought she should have chosen a different major, something with more earning potential, like business or computer science. But she knew that she would love being a teacher, no matter what the salary. And she knew that once she got that Bachelor's degree and teaching certificate, she would be a professional, not a minimum-wage flunky at Empire Realm. At least she would have a career instead of a job. She would also be, for the first time in her life, self-sufficient.

Almost.

She still depended on every penny that Phil sent for child support and the mortgage. She would have no chance of making ends meet without it. Thankfully, so far, he had been diligent about his financial responsibilities. The divorce wasn't final yet, which meant he wasn't legally required to provide anything at the moment. Sheila supposed she should be grateful. But that was pretty hard to do.

Phil was an associate in the second-largest law firm in Orange County. He made excellent money and was well on his way towards eventually becoming partner. As a result, Sheila and the kids were able to stay in their nice, four-bedroom home in the affluent suburbs of southwest Orlando. She couldn't imagine moving. Taking the kids into a smaller rental apartment. Scraping by all alone on a freshman teacher's salary. The kids moving away from their friends, perhaps into a less desirable school district. The thought of it kept her awake at night, her stomach in knots.

And there was the sentimental attachment she had for the house. She and Phil had bought it before Billy was born, living out of boxes, slowly acquiring furniture, silverware, and all the other trappings of putting down roots. The night they moved in, they had made love in the cavernous, empty living room.

Even though those days were long gone—*long* gone—she still felt very sad about potentially leaving the house. It represented not just her home and the home of her children, but also what once had been a happy marriage. Or so she thought.

Like all ambitious lawyers on the partner track, Phil had worked almost inhuman hours. Out of the house before the sun came up, home after the kids had gone to bed. Every weekend. "Billable hours, Sheila," he used to tell her. Billable hours pay for this house. Billable hours allow you to stay home and not work. She hated the hours he spent working, even resented them. But she understood. She supported Phil's career unflinchingly. It wasn't his workaholism that had destroyed their marriage. There were other things that did that.

Sheila helped Greg put on his underwear and a pair of shorts. Then together they located the errant shoe under a wet towel in the bathroom. When she walked back into the kitchen, she was stunned to see Billy cleaning up the waffle that was stuck to the dinette table. Not only had he removed the waffle and put it in the garbage, but he was even wiping the table with a wet sponge. The sight of her ten-year-old son demonstrating such responsibility, performing a chore that his absent father should be doing instead, made her suddenly want to break down into tears.

She wiped her eyes and embraced him tightly. "I love you, Billy," she said.

"Thanks, Mom," Billy replied, giving her a look of amused affection. Mom was being weird again.

Of all three kids, Billy was the one she was most concerned about. He was the oldest and had the best understanding of the ramifications of a divorce. She was petrified that he would somehow blame himself and she went out of her way to reassure him that it had nothing to do with him. She'd never forget his response when she and Phil sat him down and explained that they were separating.

"If you can't be happy together, then I think you should still be happy," he said, essentially blessing the break-up. Billy understood, but he was clearly affected by it. He had become quieter and more withdrawn since the separation.

Sheila found Maggie brushing her teeth and hurried her to finish up. She then buckled Maggie's shoes, adjusted her tights, and ushered her and Billy to the curb just as their school bus was approaching. She kissed them both good-bye and handed each of them a paper sack filled with a turkey sandwich, an apple, and a snack-pak of potato chips. She reminded them that their Grandma was picking them up today because she had to work. Lingering just a little too long, Sheila watched the bus drive off until it finally disappeared around a corner.

She quickly loaded Greg, who was miraculously still wearing both his shoes *and* his pants, into the car seat and sped off to his day care. She dropped him off, chatted a moment with the day care manager to make sure he was getting healthy snacks instead of the cookies he got last week, and dashed off across town to catch what was left of her early morning class.

As she drove she told herself she was insane. She had enough going on in her life. Three kids, college, work, and an upcoming divorce proceeding with a soon-to-be ex-husband who refused to fade out of her life. The last thing she needed was to get involved in a new relationship. The last thing she needed was a boyfriend.

And she certainly didn't need to get involved with someone who had a lot of baggage. A drinking problem that had cost him his career. Not to mention the real problem. Let's face it, how could she possibly compete with a dead wife? It was a no-win situation. She knew that she would have to prevent this relationship from going any further. The time wasn't right for her. There was too much history for him. By the time she parked her car in the student lot and started walking towards the classroom building, she had made up her mind. She would focus on her priorities: family, school, the divorce—in that order. There was no room for more. She listened absently to the professor as he droned on about pedagogy and her mind kept wandering back to one thing.

Kevin's eyes. Smiling. Sparkling. She couldn't wait until she saw him later that day at work. *Sigh . . . Oh, well.*

CHAPTER 10

"See the blue shirt? There. Motherfucker's wearing a tie." Lucius pointed at the image on the television screen. "What kind of fool wears a tie to a theme park?" Lucius paused the tape and got up from the couch, crossing the room to the TV. He jabbed a finger again at the still image. "A tie, Red! Fucker put on his church clothes to go meet Wilber Horse." Lucius laughed at the absurdity of it.

Lucius had spent the better part of the last few days just watching tape. The same twelve hours from each day, spread across four tapes, over and over again. He thought that perhaps his eyes might literally fall out of his head. Kevin was giving him five bucks an hour to watch TV and it wasn't nearly enough. After watching twenty-four hours of the same security camera shit a couple of times, Lucius seriously considered giving up, telling Kevin he couldn't find the dude. He wasn't on there. He had had enough.

But there was another part of him that was stronger than the part that wanted to quit. That was the part that relished the challenge. The part that said, if you can beat crack, stare down the bitch, you can find some dude on a videotape. Lucius began with the premise that there was indeed a guy who went to

Empire Realm on both days. If he made that assumption, then it was just a matter of watching until he found him.

Kevin had told him to try to find a single man, going into the park alone, not part of a group. Kevin said he was tall and probably strong. Lucius didn't know what the dude did, but he figured it was no good, otherwise Kevin wouldn't be on his trail. But whatever he did, Lucius didn't want to know. He had seen enough shit on the streets to last the rest of his life. His youth on the pipe was spent teetering between trying to know everything he could about certain things and trying not to know anything about other things. It was a curious paradox and needed to be balanced carefully if you planned to survive on the streets. Those days were over for Lucius now. He preferred not to know about any more trouble.

He began his search by making copious notes. He tried to write down every solitary-looking dude who came through the turnstiles. But that was hard. Since everyone had to funnel down into a couple of single-file lines that fed through a row of turnstiles, it was difficult to tell who was alone and who wasn't. But the more he watched, the more he got a feel for who was by himself and who was probably part of a family or group of friends. The mornings on the tapes were the hardest to go through. There was almost a continuous stream of people coming through the gates until about noon. Then there would be scattered groups entering periodically as tour buses dumped out until, eventually, nobody was going into the park at all, just coming out.

After a while, he didn't bother writing everyone down. It just got too hard. Besides, if he wrote them down he'd fill a dozen pads with half-assed descriptions that he would never be able to find later. Lucius figured that the only way that would work was if he entered the descriptions into some type of computer database and searched based on certain characteristics. He read about databases in a book Kevin gave him when he said he wanted to go to college and learn about computers. Maybe he'd be a database administrator some day.

Pretty soon he got to know the people on the tape like they were home movies of his own family. As he watched, the people became so familiar that he began to anticipate their actions. He'd tense right before the little girl stumbled and hit her head on the side of the turnstile. He'd grin as he waited for the little boy to jam a finger up his nose. The fat guy who gets stuck in the turnstile. The lady who spills her purse. The newlyweds (he assumed) who kiss on each side of the turnstile. The guy who goes through backwards, pushing the bar with his butt. The redneck who spits tobacco juice. They became like old friends.

When he saw the guy in the tie, Lucius immediately noticed him. Light blue shirt, yellow tie, pressed pair of pants. That dude definitely stuck out from the rest of the folks in their T-shirts, shorts, and fanny packs. But Lucius didn't make the connection right away. The guy was wearing the tie only on the second day.

In addition, he assumed that anyone in a tie wasn't trying very hard to look like he was part of the crowd. If he were up to no good, he wasn't even being smart about hiding it. So Lucius had dismissed him as some Empire management employee or maybe a Mormon.

But as he watched the prior day's tapes again he stumbled across a discovery. It probably took him three or four viewings, but eventually he noticed a guy in a starched white shirt and suit pants. A cell phone was on his belt and a gold pen was in his breast pocket. At first Lucius thought he was the dad in a family of four that was coming through the gate. He was immediately followed by a pretty mom and two kids who looked a lot like him. But something was wrong with that picture. Lucius wasn't sure what was off about it, exactly, but he was drawn back to that time code on the tape to watch it again, some hunch gnawing at him. Lucius didn't see it at first, but when he did it was like discovering the nose on his face. It was there all along. The man was dressed very nicely, although his family was dressed like everyone else—in shorts, sneakers, and camera bags. Why was this guy dressed so differently from his family?

As Lucius rewound the tape and watched it again, he noticed another guy in the background with the family, before they approached the turnstile. As they got up to the gate, the other guy, who was dressed in shorts and sandals with white socks, stepped over to the next turnstile to get through more quickly. When he did, the dude in the nice white shirt stepped in front of the mom and kids and pushed through the turnstile at the same time as the dude in sandals. The well-dressed guy wasn't part of the family at all.

Then, seeing the nice shirt, the slacks, Lucius flashed back to the dude in the tie. They kind of looked the same. Dark hair, high forehead. Wirerimmed glasses that probably cost three hundred bucks. Clean-shaven. A long, sharp nose. Lucius popped each tape out and then back in, freezing the image and double-checking it. Triple checking it. The guy was only wearing a tie on the second day but it was definitely the same man. The dude in the white shirt and the dude in the tie were the same motherfucker.

He thought he could do it, get in twice without Lucius figuring it out. But Lucius did figure it out. If he could beat the pipe, then there was no way some fancy-dressed, rich white dude was going to beat him.

When he was sure he had found him, Lucius shouted at the TV, "I got you! I got you, motherfucker!"

Kevin's reaction had been complete surprise when Lucius

mumbled, half-asleep, that he had found him. Kevin shook Lucius awake on the couch. "You found him? Are you sure?"

"Hell yes, I found him. Who do you think you're dealing with? My name is Lucius Monroe," he said, tapping a finger proudly at his chest.

"Holy crap, Lucius. I can't believe it!" Kevin sat in a chair next to the couch Lucius was sleeping on. "You're something else."

Lucius held up his hands and cocked his head at Kevin, his expression saying, *Oh yes, I am definitely something else.* Rubbing the sleep from his eyes, Lucius got up from the couch and popped in the first tape. He wasn't upset that Kevin had woken him. In fact, he was glad. He knew how hard what he had been asked to do was and he was justifiably proud of his accomplishment. He wanted to strut a little.

He showed Kevin the images on the tapes. There was no denying it. They were the same guy. Kevin sat back in his chair and thought for a long moment, pursing his lips and drumming his fingers on the armrest. It was late and, in the stillness of the dark house, they could each hear the chorus of frogs croaking loudly from the lake. Finally, Kevin spoke again.

"You know, Lucius, I think you may have just saved someone's life."

"Damn, Red." Lucius smiled and shook his head. "Damn."

Kevin used some video capture software on his computer to obtain a fairly clear image of the man in the tie. Because the security camera was mounted above the entrance gate, the angle was looking down on the subject, offering a poor view. But Kevin was able to find a frame where the man glanced up, sort of, and most of his face was visible.

He e-mailed the image to the private investigator he had found in Indianapolis with instructions to see if anyone at

Midwest Tours recognized him. The investigator's name was Stan Tokarz, another ex-cop. Based on Kevin's phone interview Tokarz seemed like a pro and came highly recommended from Kevin's lawyer friends. The guy was already working the case and Kevin felt confident that if there was something to find at Midwest Tours, he'd find it. As expected, Jerry had no problem with the extra expense.

Kevin then printed off a dozen copies of the photo and went to visit an old friend.

He met Sarah Klymer at a downtown sandwich shop called Vinnie's. She had already ordered a turkey sub on whole wheat with lettuce and sprouts, no mayo. She smiled when she saw him.

"Hey, Sarah."

"Lonnegan," she said, grinning and wiping her mouth. "I already ordered you a Chicken Philly and a Dr. Pepper." She looked barely a day older than when he last saw her three years ago. Light brown hair with some streaks of gray, a tanned, weathered complexion. She was thin and healthy. Obviously, she was still running marathons. She wasn't wearing make up, but she didn't need it.

"Thanks," Kevin said, sitting down. He was holding a manila envelope in his hand. "How you been?"

"Great," she said, taking a big bite of sandwich. "The question should be how are *you?*"

He smiled at her. "Great." An aproned employee delivered his sandwich and drink. He took a bite of his dill pickle.

"Okay," Sarah said, chewing. "We've exchanged the obligatory pleasantries. What's up?"

Kevin slid the envelope across the table to her. With a questioning look, she opened it and pulled out the contents. It was the security camera image of the man in the tie, blown up into an 8 x 10 glamour shot.

"Who's he?" Sarah asked, sipping her bottled water.

"That's what I was hoping you would be able to tell me." Kevin paused, considering what he was going to say next and how he was going to say it. "I need your professional discretion here, Sarah. I could get into a lot of trouble."

Sarah continued looking at the image. Without moving her head, she tilted her eyes back up to Kevin. "That's the front gate at Empire Realm, isn't it?"

"You're still the best detective I've ever met."

"What are you up to, Kevin?" Sarah said, sharpening her gaze at him.

"I know you're helping Pendergrast investigate the murders out there. This guy—" he pointed at the image, "—probably paid cash and definitely went into the park on the same two days that the murders occurred. He doesn't look like he was dressed for standing in lines and riding rides."

"Where did you get this?"

"Let's just say I'm an interested party. I need you to do some checking. See if the guy matches anyone in the books or on the wires. I don't have access to that stuff anymore."

"I hope you're not playing cop, Kevin. As qualified as you are, you know the rules."

"I'm just a concerned citizen with a potential lead."

Sarah wasn't buying it. She was too smart. But Kevin had to risk talking to her. If this guy killed someone else while Kevin was holding his picture, trying to find him on his own, he wouldn't be able to live with himself.

Sarah considered. Slipped the picture back into the envelope. "I'll see what I can find." She shook her head. "Concerned citizen . . ."

"Thanks, Sarah." Kevin sipped his drink. "One more thing. I need you to keep this from Pendergrast. At least for the time being. If he knew about it, he'd have me in the cage so fast he'd have to write *himself* a ticket. I need you to work this one alone."

Sarah pushed her own sandwich away. She wanted to help him. But she was a good cop and she wouldn't do anything to jeopardize the case. She was clearly torn. "Okay," she said finally. "I'll keep it to myself. For now. I'll try to find this guy in the files or in the database. But if I turn anything up, I gotta tell Lou. He's the primary and I gotta respect that."

"Fair enough. I just hope you'll give me a warning before you do."

"Eat your sandwich before it gets cold."

"With a what?"

"A tie, Violet. A necktie." Kevin was in the employee parking lot of Empire Realm, talking to Violet on his cell phone.

"What did you find, Kevin?"

"Nothing definite yet. But maybe something. I just have a hunch. Is it possible that the two victims were strangled with a man's necktie?"

Violet paused. Kevin heard voices in the background. "Wait a sec. I can't really talk here. I'll call you back."

With that she hung up. Kevin checked his watch. He was running late anyway. He had to check in with Jerry before his shift and didn't have much time. He rode the cast member shuttle to the park and found Jerry in his office, looking at computer printouts and tugging his left eyebrow.

"Are those my locker combinations?" Kevin asked, sitting across the desk from Jerry.

"Yeah. Just keep these close. Please. I could get so fired for disclosing personal locker combinations."

"You could get so fired for letting people get murdered in your park, too."

"Good point," said Jerry as he handed the printed spreadsheet to Kevin. Kevin, in turn, handed Jerry an envelope containing the remaining pictures of the man in the tie. He explained that the man had gone into the park both days, probably paid cash (no matching receipts had turned up yet), and was clearly not dressed appropriately. Jerry's eyes went wide.

"Holy shit, Kevin. Is this the guy? The doer?"

"Slow down, Jerry. I don't know. Maybe. I've got Sarah Klymer running the picture through the system to see if he shows up anywhere."

"Klymer? Can you trust her? She's pretty by-the-book."

"I think so. I don't have much choice. If she finds anything, I think she'll give me a heads-up right before she tells Pendergrast. At least I hope so. Until then, she'll keep it to herself. In the meantime, the guy in Indy has the picture and will add it to the Midwest Tours angle. I'll keep investigating cast members. Maybe I'll get lucky with your locker combinations." Jerry had done exactly as Kevin had asked, prioritized the list according to the key criteria: (1) they were working on the same nights the murders occurred, (2) they had direct access to dry ice, and (3) they worked in the Lonesome Gulch area of the park. Kevin knew that there was a lot of room outside of those parameters for suspects, but it was a start. Then again, the killer could indeed be the man in the tie.

Jerry studied the picture. "Sick fucker. I assume you want me to post this."

"Yeah, but be discreet. If he comes back, we don't want him to see himself and get spooked. Plus, we want to keep this under Pendergrast's radar."

"No problem. Our cashiers are trained to keep an eye out for certain people—known scammers, mostly. Every once in a while we'll even post a photo inside each cashier's booth and tell them to call security if the person shows up and tries to buy a ticket."

"Good. That should work. Except have them call you. No one else. And then you call me. I'll keep my cell phone on twenty-four/seven from now on."

At that moment, Kevin's cell phone rang loudly. "Excuse me." He offered a smile to Jerry at the coincidental timing and answered.

"Maybe," said Violet's voice through the receiver.

"Maybe?"

"This isn't an exact science, you know. There's a lot of interpretive art. We know that they were both probably strangled with the same thing. It wasn't done manually, with just the hands. And, it definitely wasn't a wire or a coarse rope or anything like that. There wasn't any trauma to the derma that would indicate those. You know that our guess is a woven fabric of some sort, so, yeah, maybe. The murder weapon could be a tie. I definitely can't rule it out."

"Okay, Vi. I understand. Thanks. I really owe you"

"Hey, Kevin?"

"Yeah?"

"A necktie? Really? Who's the killer, Regis Philbin?"

With a click, Kevin snapped his phone off.

Kevin rushed from Jerry's office and bounded down the stairs. If he didn't hurry, he'd be late for his shift. He didn't feel like listening to Chuckie's scolds. He shouldn't care, this wasn't really his job, but it was annoying all the same.

He actually didn't want to be late to see Sheila.

With the news that Lucius had found the guy on the tape, Kevin had been too busy to think much more about Sheila. But with his shift starting in just a few minutes, he couldn't help but turn his mind toward thoughts of her. He tried thinking of a casual way to ask her out again, one that seemed spontaneous and unrehearsed. He couldn't think of anything.

He charged out the first floor door and turned to head toward the locker room. He ran right into Mavis DuBois—literally.

"My, oh my, you do know how to greet a woman," she said, adjusting the ample bustier of her costume dress and fixing her large, blonde hair.

"Excuse me, Mavis. I wasn't paying attention."

"Perhaps I should give you something to pay attention to, Handsome."

"Uh, perhaps. Right now, though, I'm late for my shift." He stepped past her and hurried off towards the locker room.

She called after him. "Come back when you have more time, Sugar!"

Kevin made his way to the locker room and quickly threw on his miner's costume. Because he was running a little late for his shift, he was in that quiet time after the current shift headed off for their jobs and before the ending shift drifted in to change back into their street clothes.

Kevin glanced around quickly and unfolded the printout of locker combinations. Might as well start at the top. He found the first name: Marcus Anderson. Locker 145. Kevin promptly found the locker and had it open within a few seconds. Inside were some clothes: jeans, T-shirt, sneakers. A wallet with forty-two dollars in it. A pair of sunglasses. And a gay pornographic magazine called *Stud*. But no murder weapon. Kevin didn't really expect to stumble across anything on his first attempt. He carefully replaced the locker's contents and moved onto the next name on the list.

He had just twisted the last number on the combination and slid the latch open when he heard the locker room door creak open. Not wanting to be caught snooping in someone else's locker, Kevin quickly sat on a bench and started tying his boot.

A tall man walked in, dressed like a cowboy. With the boots, he was probably six-foot three. He walked directly over to the locker Kevin had just opened. The cowboy took off his hat and untied the kerchief from his neck. Ran his fingers through dark, stringy hair. Started unbuttoning his western shirt. That's when he noticed that his locker door was ajar. He put a hand on it and swung it open curiously. He peered in silently, checking the contents. Then he looked down at Kevin, who was still tying his boot. Kevin didn't look up. The cowboy turned back to his locker, checked the contents once more and then shut it with a loud bang. Kevin finally looked up. The cowboy was staring at him with furious eyes.

"Hey," Kevin said casually. The cowboy continued to stare, not saying a word. Kevin gave him a friendly smile, stood, stamped his boot to adjust his coverall trousers, and headed out the locker room door.

CHAPTER 11

"Oh, honey, you're breakin' my heart."

Mavis stood over them, aghast.

Kevin smirked up at her from the table he shared with Sheila. "Mavis, I'll always have a special place for you."

Mavis shook her head. "Yes. A place on the outside lookin' in." She turned to Sheila. "What's *your* name, Sugar?"

Sheila put down a french fry and extended a hand. "Sheila Nelson. A pleasure to finally meet you, Ms. DuBois. I've heard so much about you."

"Flattery will get you everywhere, my dear. You take care of my Kevin. Because if you don't," Mavis ran a painted fingernail along Kevin's shoulder, "I most definitely will."

And with that Mavis moved off to mingle with the tourists. The park was within an hour of closing, so the crowd was starting to thin. Kevin and Sheila had come off a long shift and had just enough time to change into their civilian clothes and meet at the Lone Star before it closed.

It had been a strange afternoon. Strange but fun. All through their shift, Kevin and Sheila had been exchanging furtive glances and secret smiles, like two high school kids after a first date. Kevin had suggested a quick bite in the park before they each went home.

They talked for a few more minutes over fries and chicken fingers before leaving. Kevin learned all of her kids' names—Billy, Maggie, and Greg—their ages, their hobbies, what they liked, what they didn't like. Kevin had just asked about Sheila's hobbies when Mavis announced it was closing time and they were forced to leave. Mavis apologized profusely but she had an establishment to run, you understand of course, don'tcha, Sugar?

Kevin offered to walk Sheila to her car and they passed into the backstage area through a gate hidden by some shrubbery. As they closed the gate, Kevin noticed a set of concrete steps leading down below a nearby building.

"That's the tunnel," Sheila said, off his look.

"Tunnel?"

"Right. The tunnel is actually a series of tunnels that run underneath the entire park. You can get pretty much anywhere in the park you want without having to walk where tourists will see you. Ever wonder how Wilberforce can just seem to appear out of nowhere in the middle of the park? The tunnel."

Kevin nodded. He remembered now. Kippy had told him about the tunnel as part of his orientation class at Empire University.

"So you were going to tell me about *your* hobbies," Kevin said. He was dying to ask the big question, the type of question that she seemed to have no problem asking. But he didn't want to scare her off. He couldn't bring himself to ask about her husband. Ex-husband? Whatever. Where was he? What was his deal? Why was he not around now? Divorce? Death? Abandonment? He wanted to ask but couldn't find the right words. So he stuck to safer topics. Her kids. Her hobbies. It was lame, he knew, but she seemed genuinely pleased that he was asking.

"Hobbies?" She snorted. "Like I have time for a hobby. My life is my hobby." She went on to tell Kevin about the classes she's taking at UCF. About her dream of becoming an elementary school teacher. She said she wasn't sure if school counted as a hobby, but she'd list it as one anyway.

He was impressed. Three kids. No husband to help. Working at Empire Realm because she clearly needed the money. Going to school to realize an ambitious dream. She was juggling a lot of issues in her life and Kevin respected perseverance in the face of adversity. It took commitment and passion to stick with school despite all the other distractions in her life.

By the time they reached the parking lot, Sheila had a hand on Kevin's elbow, holding his arm casually. Meaningfully. Kevin had been out with a few women over the past two years, but it had been a very long time since any woman had touched Kevin in such a casually intimate manner. His first reaction was contained exhilaration. But he also had a healthy dose of guilt. Was he somehow betraying Maria with his interest in Sheila? He tried to put those thoughts out of his head. He knew he would have to deal with them eventually. But not now. Not tonight.

"Here we are," Sheila said, stopping in front of her green Honda. "Thank you, Kevin. I had a nice evening."

"Me too."

There was an awkward pause that lasted only a second or two but seemed like an hour and a half. Finally Sheila stood on her tiptoes and kissed him on the cheek. A little embarrassed, he looked away, into the parking lot. His eyes went wide.

"Oh shit . . ."

Sheila stepped back. "I'm sorry. I shouldn't have—"

"No—that was nice. Very nice. It's just, well, that's my car."

Sheila turned around and saw what Kevin saw. There, a few rows from Sheila's car, was Kevin's white Blazer. All the windows were smashed and "Fuck You!" was spray painted across the driver's door.

Kevin made his way to the kitchen, the morning sun peeking up over the edge of Lake Jessup. He poured himself a cup of coffee and grabbed his cordless phone. Out on the porch, he sat down, sipped from his mug, and went over the events of the previous evening.

Sheila had offered to wait with him after they discovered that his truck had been vandalized. But he declined, chalking it up—for her benefit—to delinquents or someone's bad idea of a joke. Kevin performed a quick survey of the situation. Windows smashed—probably with a baseball bat or other similar instrument. Nothing was stolen. His radio was still intact in the dash. He had some tools in the back that were untouched. Clearly, robbery wasn't the motive. And, in Kevin's police experience, impulse thieves rarely took the time to spray paint epithets on their victims' cars.

This was a message.

But from whom? Maybe the killer. Maybe Kevin's locker room searching and casual information-gathering conversations with park employees had made the killer nervous—assuming, of course, that the killer wasn't the man in the tie from the security tape. Maybe the man in the tie discovered that his picture was being posted in each ticket booth and somehow traced it back to Kevin. That was unlikely, but possible. Maybe it was Pendergrast. He certainly wasn't above it. If the rumors were true, he'd done a lot worse in his career. Kevin could just see him getting some twisted thrill by piling on to Kevin's perceived misfortunes, being forced to work at Empire Realm.

The more Kevin thought about it, the more pissed he got. That truck held a lot of sentimental value for him. Sure, the windows could be repaired and the side could be repainted, but it was still a desecration. It was like bending his wedding ring. It could be repaired but it was upsetting nonetheless.

Kevin didn't call the cops, of course. If Pendergrast were responsible, that would just add fuel to the fire. If it was the killer, then Kevin was at risk of blowing his cover and getting busted for interfering with a homicide investigation. He didn't call park security either, for the same basic reason. The wisest course of action was to just keep quiet—for now—and see if he could flush the vandal out again.

He took another sip of coffee. The surface of the glass-like water of the lake was aglow with the reflected morning sun. About thirty yards from shore, a big gator cruised by slowly, its rounded snout and wide ridged back cutting a wake of small ripples in the smooth surface. It was probably a twelve-footer, one of thousands of gators that called Lake Jessup home. A moment later the gator slipped below the water and was gone from sight.

Kevin checked his watch. 7:15. He lifted his cordless phone and pressed it on. If Kevin guessed right, he'd probably already be in the office. One last sip of coffee and he dialed the phone. He punched a series numbers to maneuver through the automated answering system and finally the extension rang.

"Special Agent Benning. May I help you?"

Kevin smiled. He knew he'd be there. "Hi, Milt. It's Kevin Lonnegan."

"Kevin! How are you?"

"I'm good. How are you?"

"The same." There was a slight pause on the other end of the line. "Someone told me you left the force."

"That's true. I took some time and got my life in order. But I'm doing great now."

"I'm glad to hear it."

They made small talk for a few minutes, taking a moment to reminisce about their work together to apprehend the Mall Murderer, aka John Tinker. Last month was the five-year anniversary of his arrest. Kevin had forgotten.

"So," said Agent Benning. "If that's not why you called, what's up?"

"I'm a private investigator now and I'm working on a case. A double murder."

"I'm all ears."

Kevin filled him in on the case so far, including the autopsy results and the concurrent investigative paths. Benning was quiet, listening.

"Has your guy in Indiana found anything yet?" Benning finally said.

"A little. He sent me an e-mail update last night. Seems that there have been very few Midwest Tours clients killed while on vacation. Besides the two here, there was a lady mugged and killed in Chicago last year and a husband and wife in a hotel in Kingston, Jamaica about two years ago. In both cases, the murder was the result of a bad robbery. The Chicago mugger was caught and is, at this moment, sitting in a cell in Joliet. The Jamaican cops never caught the Kingston killer. Over the past five years, three Midwest clients have died of natural causes while on a trip. The most recent was eighteen months ago when a seventy-nine year old woman had a stroke during a Mel Tillis concert in Branson, Missouri." Kevin paused, sipping his coffee. "That's all he's got so far. He's still looking into complaint letters, harassment claims, and recent employee terminations. And he's working the picture of the guy in the tie through their branch offices to see if anyone recognizes him."

Agent Benning was quiet again, probably tapping his pencil on his desk. "Curious . . ."

Kevin sat up a little straighter in his chair. Maybe Benning had a thought. "What's curious, Milt?"

Another pause. "I'm curious, Kevin. Look, you're a solid investigator. You've got good instincts and you know the mechanics. You're tracking two parallel paths and so far you seem to be making all the right moves. You don't need my advice. And you know it. So why don't you just tell me why you really called?"

Kevin suppressed a grin. That's what he got for being indirect with the FBI and, especially, Special Agent Milt Benning. "Okay, Milt. I've had a thought in the back of my head since I first started this case. I've tried to ignore it. I don't have any solid evidence to specifically support it. But it won't go away. And I want you to tell me whether or not I should drop it."

"This is more like it. What's your crazy idea?"

Kevin took a breath. "I think I may be dealing with another serial killer."

Benning didn't laugh. Didn't grunt. Didn't clear his throat. Didn't make a sound. Finally . . .

"Talk me through it."

Kevin nodded to himself. Milt Benning had taught him more about homicide investigation in the couple of weeks they worked together to apprehend the Mall Murderer than he could have learned in years under someone like Lou Pendergrast. Benning had a studious, professorial demeanor. As a result, Kevin had asked a lot of questions and Milt Benning had taught him well.

"Okay," Kevin said. "There are only two victims, so that's a problem right there. There are too many more probable explanations. Including that it's just a coincidence."

"Don't tell me why it's probably not a serial killer. Tell me why it could be."

Kevin closed his eyes, composing his thoughts. "There are only two victims, but, what if they're only the beginning?

Even Ted Bundy had to start somewhere. Or, what if there are others we don't know about? The victims were totally unrelated and I haven't been able to determine any pattern between the two, except that they were both on vacation. So far, there's no connection. No love triangle. No blackmail. No drugs. I think they might be randomly selected. The M.E. has concluded it's the same killer with the same M.O. with the same probable weapon. I think it could be a necktie—if the guy on the security tape is the perp. Both victims were found with differently sized and shaped dry ice burns on localized areas of their skin. The burns occurred at or just after the time of death. One of the victims had a long, brown synthetic fiber found on his clothes. Nylon. Nobody has any idea what it's from.

"Here's the big thing. No money was stolen from either victim. But a small personal item was taken. I think they're trophies. And both victims were hidden in spots where they would be easily found to create maximum effect on a large group of people. The killer didn't try to hide them to stay hidden."

"Have you worked out a profile?"

"Just the physical. The guy's size, the fact that it's a guy. I don't have the psych."

"The psych will be hard to get based on only two kills. Not enough to really map his world and explain the inexplicable need to murder middle-aged, white male tourists. If it is a serial killer, then there is a connection between the victims, even if you don't see it yet. It may not be direct. Maybe they remind him of his father. Or an uncle who sexually abused him. Whatever. It's something, even if it's only in the killer's head. That's part of the puzzle, too."

"So far," Kevin said, "I don't hear you telling me I'm crazy."

"Keep talking."

"Last night, while my car was parked in a lot, someone

spray painted it with an obscene phrase and smashed in all the windows. Although I doubt it, it's possible that the killer knows I'm snooping around and is sending me a message to back off. Would that fit the profile?"

Benning was silent a moment and Kevin could hear him tapping the pencil on his desk, lost in thought. "That's odd, Kevin. Is this a repeated pattern? Has he smashed up cars before?"

"Not that I'm aware of."

"Has he spray painted before?"

"Again, not that I'm aware of."

"What about calling cards?" Milt asked. "Messages left with the victims. Words written in blood or carved into the skin. Notes left behind. Tokens or symbols. Anything."

"Nothing that's apparent."

"Hmmm. No calling cards, no pattern of vandalism. It just doesn't seem to match, unless he's getting something out of the vandalism that we don't yet understand. Most serial killers are planners. Sure, they may choose their victims spontaneously— although not always. Sometimes they even stalk specific people for months. But, usually, even a random victim fits into a pattern and is subjected to a well-planned death ritual. Now, some serial killers like to leave calling cards because they subconsciously want to be caught. They're compelled to kill, but they crave some sort of recognition. The guy you're describing doesn't sound like he wants to be caught yet. He took things. He didn't leave anything. If he was going to send a message, he'd be a lot more likely to do it on or around the bodies than on your car. Why would he put himself at risk by smashing up your car?"

"But it's an angry, violent act. If I posed a threat to his ability to continue killing, he might want to stop me."

"Sure it's angry, but it seems personally motivated, not a manifestation of a psychotic impulse. Most serial killers would rather pull the wings off butterflies or douse a pet dog in gaso-line and light it on fire than to smash up a car. Look at the classic arrest scenario. When Berkowitz was arrested, he just went along peacefully. When we arrested Tinker five years ago, the same thing. Did he seem like the kind of guy who would smash up a car?"

"No, but he didn't seem like the kind of guy who would rape and butcher a bunch of young women either."

"I'm not saying that it's impossible a serial killer smashed your car. I'm just saying it's unlikely. If the killer smashed your car, he's probably not a serial killer." Another moment of silence where only the pencil tapping could be heard. "Dry ice, huh? That's an interesting one."

"This is a live one. The two victims were just three weeks apart. I'm afraid that, if it is a serial killer, my time is running out before he acts again."

"Just remember what we talked about during the Tinker case. Work the clues, Kevin. Dry ice. That seems huge to me. The murder weapon—a tie? That's huge, too, if you're right. And that synthetic fiber. It sounds like you have all the pieces of the puzzle. Find the connection between those three things and your killer will immediately become apparent."

"Gee, why didn't I think of that?"

Benning snorted a chuckle. "Like I said, you know what you're doing."

"Seriously, though, Milt. I do appreciate your insights."

"Any time. Let me know how it's going or if you think I should get involved. I could exert some pressure from this end to force my way in."

"I don't think that would go over too well," Kevin said, thinking about how Pendergrast might react to the FBI stealing his glory.

"Well, you've got me curious now. I'll start scribbling up a profile based on what you've told me. And keep me in the loop. You can call me day or night. You've got my number."

"Yes I do," said Kevin, glancing back at the lake surface. The gator was back, cutting a silent path from left to right.

Kevin went into work early and spent a couple of hours rifling lockers and chatting with employees. So far, he had turned up nothing. It was apparent, however, that Pendergrast's official interviews had alarmed most of the staff. They had quickly figured out that the deaths were not accidents and a general sense of concern was spreading through the ranks.

Just before his shift, Kevin called Sarah Klymer to check on the progress of her investigation. No luck there either. The guy in the tie didn't match anyone in the books or on the wires. Kevin didn't expect him to—he doubted the guy had a record of burglaries with mug shots to match the security tape image. Sarah would keep looking.

Stan Tokarz in Indianapolis hadn't come up with much more, either. No recent employee firings. No harassment claims. Tokarz commented sarcastically that it seemed like such a nice place to work, he was going to fill out an application. He'd start working through complaint letters, e-mails, and phone calls next.

Before his shift, Chuckie assembled the entire Prospector Mountain loading crew backstage and went over the plans for the upcoming Empire Realm 20th Anniversary Celebration. Extended hours. A new parade. A primetime special on CBS. A new Corral Pals live show at the Roundup Theater. Even Bruce Willis would be here. It was billed as "The biggest month-long hoedown in the whole wide world!" Kevin couldn't help but wonder how many other month-long hoedowns were going on.

Chuckie informed them that their schedules would be altered

and they could count on some required overtime to cover the extended hours. Sheila shifted uncomfortably.

"Chuckie, you know I have exams," she said. "Overtime is going to be hard to do."

"I'm sorry, Sheila," said Chuckie. "I've got to treat everyone the same or it wouldn't be fair."

"We'll talk about it later," Sheila said.

"There's nothing to talk about. I'll post the Celebration schedules next week." Chuckie turned to the rest of the group. "Okay, everyone. That's it. Have fun and be safe."

The crowd dispersed and headed for the ride loading area. Sheila lingered behind, lost in thought, chewing the inside of her cheek. Kevin approached her.

"I'll cover your overtime, if Chuckie lets me."

"Thanks, Kevin," she said. "How's your car?"

"Ventilated. I definitely miss my air conditioning. And I still haven't gotten all the broken glass out of the seat cushions."

"What did park security say?"

"Not much. They basically told me not to hold my breath."

She shook her head in disgust. She took a brief moment, something on her mind. "Look, Kevin, I think we should talk."

Uh-oh. It had been a while, but Kevin's experience with women told him that no good conversation began with "we should talk." He braced himself. "Okay."

She grimaced, not sure how to proceed. "My life is very . . . *complicated* at the moment. I just don't know if I have *room* . . . what I'm trying to say is, I don't have a lot of *time*—well, it's not that I'm not interested . . . it's just the timing and all—I *am.* Interested, I mean. It's not you. Really. It just isn't going to work out for us right now. Okay?"

"Sure. I understand. So would you like to go to a movie this weekend?"

"Yeah. I'd love to."

They smiled at each other and Sheila shoved his shoulder playfully. Kevin again felt like a high school kid flirting with a soon-to-be girlfriend. Their moment was interrupted by an angry hiss from behind them.

Chuckie glared at them and gestured forcefully for them to get to work. *Right this instant!* With a last furtive glance at each other, Kevin and Sheila made their way to their loading stations.

Kevin spent the next two hours working alongside a college junior named Seth. What had begun as a physical, monotonous job had turned into a fairly enjoyable routine. Kevin found himself in "the zone," efficiently loading car after car of tourists. It wasn't a very mentally challenging job and it offered him plenty of time to think about both the case and his budding relationship with Sheila. He felt a little off balance by both.

His "zone" was broken by the arrival of a man accompanied by a Seeing Eye dog.

"I'm sorry, sir," Kevin said, just as he'd been trained. "You're welcome on the ride, but we can't accommodate your dog."

"Like hell," said the man. "This dog is allowed anywhere I am. It's the law."

"I understand that, sir. But this is a roller coaster. Your dog won't fit under the lap belt. He'd fly out of the car on a sharp turn."

"I want to speak to your manager."

"No problem. But he won't let your dog on either. Hey, Chuckie."

Chuckie approached and surveyed the situation. "May I help you, sir?" he asked pleasantly. As the man began his argument to bring his dog on the ride, Kevin felt a vibrating sensation against his hip. His body twitched involuntarily to left, surprised.

His cell phone was ringing.

He had the ringer volume turned off and was wearing it on his hip under his costume coveralls. He let it vibrate for a few seconds, knowing that whoever it was would leave a message on his voice mail. It finally stopped.

And then promptly started vibrating again.

Something was up. Kevin stepped to the side, reached his right hand down into his coveralls, and brought the phone out.

Seth eyed him suspiciously. "Dude, you're not allowed to do that."

Kevin ignored him. But then Chuckie caught sight of him and went apoplectic. "*What are you doing?*" he barked in a barely contained whisper. "*Did the Old West miners have cell phones, Kevin? Did they? You are in serious trouble, buster!*"

Kevin flipped the phone open. "Hello?"

It was Jerry Engle on the other end. He was panting and it sounded like he was running.

"Kevin! Kevin—he's here. The man in the tie just walked in the gate!"

CHAPTER 12

Jerry had been in the restroom when the call came in. He kicked himself now for missing it. He had been whistling pleasantly, shaking the last drip from his johnson, while the killer was walking in the gate.

Jerry had made his way casually back to his desk, stopping long enough for a gulp from the water cooler. He was in the midst of checking his e-mail when he noticed the red voice-mail light on his phone. He punched a few buttons and began listening. His jaw literally dropped open.

"Yeah, hi. Mr. Engle?" came the recorded voice on the phone. The voice was female, young, cute. "It's Chrissy, from the front gate? Listen, I think I just sold a ticket to the guy in the picture. The guy in the tie? I didn't stop him, like you said. So I'm calling you, like you wanted. Anyway, he just went in. Okay, bye!"

The message was tagged from ten minutes ago. *Ten minutes ago!* Who the hell knew where he was by now? Oh Jesus—

Jerry sprinted from his office, tearing by his assistant, Louise, who looked up from her computer screen long enough to mutter, "Jerry?" But he was past her in an instant, charging down the office stairs two at a time. He pulled his cell phone from his belt, fumbling with it as he ran. He bobbled it right out of his fingers and the phone skipped along the hallway floor ahead of him. Cursing, he scooped it up and speed-dialed Kevin. Kevin hadn't answered at first, so Jerry kept calling while he ran, weaving his way through the Lone Star Cantina and out into the main park area. Finally, Kevin answered and Jerry relayed the news. He then promptly ran right into a husky female tourist from Wisconsin. She glared at him and his cell phone.

"It's bad enough people drive wit' 'em. Now they's runnin' wit' 'em. Causing accidents, don'tcha know," she said indignantly to her husband as Jerry picked himself up and continued his mad dash.

Jerry maneuvered through the crowd until he reached the main gate, all the while scanning the throng around him for the sharp-nosed man with the high forehead. Was he wearing a tie today? Jerry felt the anxiety surging through his body. Was the guy here to kill someone today? Jerry could *not* allow another murder to occur during his watch. He *had* to stop him. Today. Now.

Jerry found Chrissy's booth in the row of a dozen ticket booths and tried to open the back door, which was locked. He had rushed out of his office so quickly he hadn't grabbed his set of master keys. So he pounded on the door. "Open up! Hurry!"

A muffled voice from inside said, "I'm sorry. I'm not allowed to open that door. Have a nice day!"

"Damn it! This is Jerry Engle, Director of Park Security! Open the fucking door, Chrissy!"

There was the sound of a metal chair leg scraping the floor and the clicking of the door lock. The door swung open to reveal a seventeen-year-old blonde girl. Her face matched her voice—cute, with a couple of pubescent pimples on her cheek. She was horrified.

"You're not supposed to swear in front of the guests, Mr. Engle."

"Chrissy, please," Jerry said, panting from the sprint from his office. "The man you called me about . . . the one in the picture, where did he go?"

"Dunno. I sold him his ticket and just after he walked off, I noticed the picture inside the booth. Then I realized he was the same guy and called you. I guess he just went into the park. That's where he looked like he was going."

"What was he wearing?"

"Today or in the picture?"

"Today, Chrissy! Today!"

"He looked nice. You know, gray pants. Pleats. I like pleats. I want to be a fashion designer after college, so I pay attention to clothes. He has good taste. Pant legs even had cuffs—"

"Chrissy!"

Chrissy spoke quickly, Jerry's agitation making her nervous. "He had on a white shirt, no wrinkles. And a paisley tie. That's how I made the connection. He was wearing a tie again. He looked like a businessman or something."

There was a voice from behind Jerry. "Was he alone?" It was Kevin.

Chrissy eyed him suspiciously, taking in his Prospector Mountain costume. But upon seeing Jerry turn from Kevin back to her with widened eyes that demanded an answer, she said, "I think so. I didn't see anyone with him." She started to breathe heavily, looking as if she was going to cry. "Am I trouble? Did I do something wrong? If I get fired, my Mom will kill me, I swear—"

"No Chrissy," Jerry said. "You did fine. You're not in trouble. Go back to work."

She nodded, controlling her emotions, and closed the door. Jerry wiped the perspiration from his brow and turned to Kevin. "What do we do?"

Kevin's demeanor was direct and professional. "Get all of your folks out there in the park right now. Get some extra eyes on the surveillance cameras. Give your team his description and tell them to hold him until we get there—and to be careful. We don't know what he's capable of. As soon as you have him in custody, then we'll call Pendergrast. But it'll be *your* collar Jerry. You will have officially caught him."

"What do I do in the meantime?"

"Same as me. Start searching."

When Kevin heard Jerry's voice on the other end of that phone he knew he had to act quickly. Kevin immediately set a rendezvous point—the ticket booth—and took off for it.

Sheila looked up at him as he dashed off, surprise and concern on her face. Chuckie shouted after him to stop, told him that if he left not to bother coming back. Kevin ignored him and pushed his way through the waiting line of tourists. In an instant he had to decide whether to use the cast member door and circle around backstage to the front gate or take the more direct route, right down the winding queue of tourists in line for the ride. He went for the queue.

He charged into the crowd, weaving his way through the line like a salmon in spawning season. Fortunately, most folks saw him coming and tried to move to one side or the other. But he made contact with more strangers in those few minutes than he probably had in his entire life.

Soon he pushed his way out of the faux cave and into the bright summer sunshine. He paused to orient himself and determine where the main entrance was. In another moment he was in a full sprint down the main street of Lonesome Gulch, surveying the crowd for the man in the tie as he ran. He found Jerry and the ticket agent and arrived in time to catch that the man was again wearing a tie.

Jerry issued him a walkie-talkie and set it on the park security channel. Kevin and Jerry decided to limit their individual searches to the Lonesome Gulch area. Jerry would use his platoon of uniformed guards to canvas the rest of the park.

A minute later, Kevin was rushing through the Old West shops trying to locate the suspect. He had a folded print out of Lucius' security tape image that he shoved at everyone he could see—cast members and tourists alike. But no one seemed to recognize him.

Kevin was sweating profusely in the ridiculous costume, rushing around in the middle of an Orlando summer. Before long, he found himself standing in the center of the Corral Pals playground. Ironically, the same spot where the last body was found. Tourists milled around him bustling from shop to ride to restaurant to show. The recorded voice of Wilberforce the Wilberhorse intoned behind him: "Huh-howdy, Pardners! Are yuh itchin' fer some fun?" Kevin turned in a complete circle, looking all around for anyone wearing a tie. All he saw was a sea of T-shirts and shorts.

He approached an ice-cream vendor at the edge of the park. The vendor was tall and dressed like a cowboy—hat, kerchief, chaps, gloves, boots. Kevin recognized him from the locker room. Kevin placed the printed photo on top of the refrigerator-sized ice-cream cart.

"Have you seen this man?" Kevin asked.

The cowboy didn't immediately look down at the image. He just stared at Kevin.

"You're covering my cart," the cowboy said.

"What?"

"My cart. I'm trying to do my job here and I can't if you cover up my cart."

"Oh. Sorry." Kevin picked up the photo and held it for him. "I'm looking for this man. Have you seen him?"

"Why are you looking for him?"

"It's personal. Have you seen him?"

"No," the cowboy said, not really looking at the image.

Kevin shot him an angry, thanks-for-nothing look. Just as he turned away from the ice-cream cart, he heard a voice over his shoulder. Standing there was a middle-aged couple eating WilberBars. They could see the image on the page and were nodding at Kevin, saying something in German.

"Have you seen this man?" Kevin said, holding up the page for them to get a better look.

The German man nodded. "Yah."

"Where? Where did you see him?"

The German couple conferred a moment, presumably confirming their understanding of Kevin's question. "Yah. He vas valking . . ." The man turned and pointed a thick finger.

The man in the tie had headed toward Prospector Mountain.

Jerry was breathing heavily, his Empire Realm polo shirt drenched in sweat. Damn, it was hot. He chastised himself for being so out of shape. Next week he would start jogging again. Next week, he swore.

He paused to gulp a few mouthfuls from a water fountain near some park restrooms. Molten lava shot into his mouth. The initial blast of water from the fountain was scalding hot and Jerry jerked back with a yelp of pain. He let the water run for a few seconds until it was sufficiently cool to drink. He filled his mouth and swallowed three times, splashing a palm full of water on his face before moving on. His walkie-talkie crackled to life.

"Hey, Chief," came the filtered voice through the speaker. It was Jimmy, one of Jerry's security guards. Jimmy was nineteen and his enthusiasm for the authority of his position far exceeded his IQ. But that enthusiasm would be short-lived. After this summer, he was back to college and regular bouts of binge drinking. "I see a guy wearing a tie. You want me to grab him?" Jimmy didn't know who he was chasing, or why, but he knew the guy was up to no good.

Jerry squeezed the microphone button on his walkie-talkie. "Where are you, Jimmy?"

"On the north side of the Palace. Heading towards the Alpine Village."

"Do you see him now?"

"Yeah. He's like thirty yards in front of me."

Jerry started running. "Don't grab him yet. Stay with him. I'm on my way." Jerry turned up a small brick path lined with purple and green flowers. He was winding his way up the small incline towards the huge palace that stood at the center of the park. He raised the walkie-talkie back to his mouth. "Kevin— did you catch that?"

Kevin's voice came through the receiver. "I heard it. You go. I'm going to stay here and keep searching Lonesome Gulch. Let me know if it's him."

"Don't let him out of your sight, Jimmy!" Jerry shouted. He was just passing under the gated main arch of the Palace, its purple and green tiles sparkling in the afternoon sun.

"You got it, chief. His ass is grass."

Kevin bolted back up towards Prospector Mountain, his eyes darting from side to side, searching for any sign of his suspect. He shoved the photo back into his pocket. Now he just needed to find the son of a bitch. He probably also needed a little luck.

It seemed unlikely that the guy Jerry was tailing was their guy. He would have had to run—to sprint—to get to that section of the park so quickly. A man in a tie sprinting through the park would have attracted some attention. More people would have recognized him. And if Kevin's German friends were right, the suspect was heading in an entirely different direction.

Kevin cursed silently as he ran. Apparently, he and the man in the tie had passed each other as Kevin dashed towards the ticket booth at the front gate. If he had been more careful, if he had just worked the situation professionally, maybe Kevin would have spotted him. Instead, he ran off like some green rookie chasing his first collar. He was embarrassed.

Kevin assumed the guy wasn't armed. Both victims had been strangled. But how dangerous was he? This was a killer, after all. Even if he was a serial killer, they didn't all surrender peacefully like Berkowitz or Tinker. Sometimes they sat in a church tower and shot everyone they could see. At the prospect of being apprehended, no one knew how the guy would react. Maybe like a cornered tiger.

Kevin reached the base of the Mountain and paused. The afternoon sun was brutal and Kevin's hair was drenched with perspiration. The ridiculous coveralls didn't help. He had lost the miner's helmet somewhere between the ride and the front gate.

He took a long, deliberate look around. To one side of the ride was a path that led up to the Corral Pals live theater. Even from this distance, he could distinctly hear the folksy music and recorded singing of the Corral Pals characters. He pictured the big dopey costumes dancing across the stage, arm in arm, paw in paw. On the other side of Prospector Mountain was the Dixie Emporium restaurant.

The Dixie Emporium sat on the edge of a small, man-made lake. Actually, it sat *in* a small, man-made lake. It looked like a big paddlewheel boat but was really a concrete and steel building shaped to look like a paddlewheel steamer. Inside was a surprisingly good restaurant, a full bar and themed entertainment. If the man really did head in this direction . . . Kevin considered for a moment before deciding that the Dixie Emporium was a pretty likely place for a man in a tie—certainly more appropriate than the Corral Pals theater filled with exuberant six-year olds.

In another moment Kevin was walking through the front door of the Dixie Emporium waiting area bar. Albert Einstein walked up and smiled at him. The smile twitched as Einstein perused Kevin's miner costume.

"Well, you look a little lost, friend," Einstein said in a high-pitched, twangy voice. Then Kevin realized who he was, chastising himself silently for being so ignorant. Not Einstein, Mark Twain. The actor had the bushy white hair, the walrus mustache, and the trademark white suit and string tie. He even sounded like Mark Twain should sound.

"I'm looking for someone." Kevin produced the picture and showed it to him. "Is he here?"

Mr. Twain considered the image for a moment. "I don't recollect his personage on these premises. No, I surely don't."

"I'm going to take a quick look around."

The Twain actor glanced from side to side and then lowered his voice, speaking without the accent. "Who is he?"

"I'll let you know if I find him."

Kevin made his way through the bar, scanning faces. A Dixieland jazz banjo player sat on a stool in the corner, plinking out riverboat ditties. He was wearing a black vest, arm garters, and a straw hat, accompanying himself occasionally with a harmonica in a shoulder harness. Kevin circled back to the entrance. The man in the tie wasn't there.

The restaurant wasn't very crowded. It was too late for lunch and too early for dinner, but even so, there were more diners than Kevin would have predicted. Reservations were hard to get and if you really wanted to eat in the Dixie Emporium, sometimes your only choice was 3:30 in the afternoon.

A fast lap around the restaurant revealed nothing. Seeing Kevin's miner costume, an overweight male tourist with a plate of half-eaten pasta and scallops grabbed his arm.

"Excuse me," the tourist said. "We need some more bread, please. And refills on our drinks."

Kevin stared at the man. "Right," he muttered before moving out of the restaurant and upstairs to another, larger bar.

This lounge looked out over the lake and was appointed with stuffed leather chairs and red velvet wallpaper. Apparently, the theme was a riverboat "gentleman's lounge." Small gambling tables covered in green felt were scattered throughout the room. An attractive female dealer sat nearby doling out blackjack hands to a tourist family, explaining the rules of the game. They placed bets with what looked like Monopoly money.

Again, the place was mostly empty, it being a little early for the serious boozehounds. As Kevin searched the room, he paused when he spotted the assortment of alcohol bottles behind the long mahogany bar. They were stacked on shelves almost to the ceiling. Whiskey, vodka, gin, tequila, bourbon. Domestic, imports, premiums, well brands. The bottles stood in neat rows, all at attention, waiting to be called into service. Kevin was suddenly struck with a very odd sensation. Sadness.

But this wasn't his usual sadness, the one that had grown so familiar over the past three years. This was more of a vague, sad longing.

He realized that he missed drinking.

The bar downstairs hadn't triggered this reaction—it was basically a restaurant waiting room with cheery banjo music and kids with balloons. But this lounge looked like a real bar, like a classy hotel bar. Like the bar he and Maria used to go to sometimes in the Hotel Tropicale in Key West.

It wasn't even so much that Kevin had a burning desire to have a drink. That ache was always there, buzzing inside his head, at certain times much louder than at others. What Kevin now felt, suddenly and inexplicably, was a sad realization that he would never again be able to sit at a bar like this, order a drink, and pass some time. It wasn't the actual drinking that he suddenly missed but the sense of belonging, that he was a part of the scene. He knew that for the rest of his life he would be an outsider in places like this. The thought made him a little mournful.

He shook off the feeling, telling himself he had a lot of nerve to mourn the loss of his drinking past. Drinking had cost him his career and almost his life. Mourning it was selfish and not very smart. But, once Kevin was satisfied that the man in the tie wasn't there, he glanced once again at the long bar with the velvet stools and offered a silent farewell.

"Hey, Chief! He's talking to some other guy now!"

Jerry huffed his way out the other side of the Palace, turning towards the Alpine Village. He barked back into the walkie-talkie. "Who's he talking to?"

"Dunno," said Jimmy through the receiver. "But he looks pissed. I think he's yelling at the guy. He's pointing his finger at him now."

If Jerry could he would have started running faster. But he was moving as fast as his legs would carry him. Next week he'd start jogging. Ugh, it was *really* hot. Jerry recalled that the weatherman on the radio that morning had said it would be 96 degrees with a heat index of 104.

The sky above was just starting to darken with the daily summer thundershower. Angry, purple clouds were rolling in from the west. That would cool things off a little, but it would probably be too late to give Jerry any relief.

"Chief! Chief! They're going around the side of one of the shops! They're gonna be out of everyone's view!"

"Where? Where are they?"

"Around the side of the pastry shop. They'll be all alone, Chief! Should I grab him?"

"Can you keep them in sight?"

"Not anymore. Not without them seeing me. Either I grab him or I lose him."

"Is the other guy a tourist?"

"What? I dunno. There they go. They're moving around the building. Either I grab him now or never, Chief."

Jerry took a deep breath. "Grab him, Jimmy. Hold him 'til I get there. I'll be there in five minutes. And, Jesus, be careful. Protect yourself."

"His ass is grass, Chief." Jimmy's communications crackled to an end.

Jerry moved as quickly as he could through the Alpine Village, passing peaked white buildings with dark trim. This whole section of the park looked like something out of the *Sound of Music*, except without Julie Andrews and Christopher Plummer. Jerry reminded himself that the *Sound of Music* wasn't an Empire Studios film.

The pastry shop was just ahead, around the next corner. It was a favorite spot for Jerry. They sold rich, creamy eclairs and Napoleon slices. Jerry vowed to give up the pastries next week, too.

He heard the shouting before he turned the corner. Angry voices were raised and a serious argument was in full swing. Jerry raced around the corner to see a crowd of tourists huddled around Jimmy and his suspect.

Jerry knew immediately that something was very wrong.

Jimmy had a man face down on the cement, twisting his arm sharply behind his back. The man was struggling frantically, shouting at Jimmy.

"Get off me, you maniac!"

"Shut your pie hole, scumbag!" Jimmy shouted back.

Jerry pushed his way through the crowd and Jimmy spotted him.

"I got him, Chief! I got him just like you said," Jimmy shouted proudly, his face positively glowing.

"Oh shit . . ." was all Jerry could muster.

"Is that you, Engle?" the man on the ground said, unable to twist his head around.

Jimmy jerked his arm again, eliciting a high shriek of pain. "I told you to zip it, dirtbag! I swear I'll twist your arm right off. Chief, you know this guy?"

"Yeah, Jimmy. Let him go."

"Hunh? Say again?"

"Let him go. That's not the guy."

It took a good ten seconds for that information to sink into the creases of Jimmy's brain. "But he's wearing a tie."

Jerry's shoulders slumped. He exhaled a long sigh. "That's because he's Bill Oglethorpe. The President of Empire Realm."

Above them, thunder cracked from the approaching storm clouds.

Kevin came out of the Dixie Emporium, relieved to be out of the bar and back in the bright glare of the afternoon sun. Some dark clouds were rolling in and a loud boom of thunder punctuated the nearby screams of the Prospector Mountain riders as their cart swerved around a bend and back down into the tunnels.

Kevin looked back up at Prospector Mountain and suddenly had a thought. It would be pretty damned ironic if the man in the tie was in line to ride the Mountain. Kevin would have had a better shot at nabbing him by staying put rather than running all over the park like an idiot. It was then that he knew the man *had* to be in line. It would be the Universe's ultimate joke.

He strode purposefully towards the line, past the sign that declared "You must be *this* tall to go on this ride," past the posted warning for pregnant women and people with heart conditions, past the sign informing everyone that they had a 90-minute wait to look forward to before they even saw the loading area. He worked his way up through the waiting tourists, studying faces.

There was a fairly good chance that the man was no longer wearing a tie. It was possible that he wasn't even wearing any of the same clothes. He could have stashed some appropriate clothes somewhere in the park. Or, he could have easily purchased whatever he wanted inside the park. The only video they had seen him on was the entrance camera. Kevin wondered if he should have told Pendergrast, let him have someone watch all the tapes from the entire park from those days and see if they could track the guy's movements. Maybe he had a specific pattern or ritual he followed. Maybe he always rode the Mountain three times, bought an ice cream, and then killed someone. Kevin had wanted to protect his cover, to give Jerry the opportunity to nab him. But in doing so, had he possibly endangered someone else? If Kevin didn't find him, if the guy got away, there could be another murder today. If someone else died because Kevin didn't bring in Pendergrast, he would never forgive himself.

He had to find him *now*. In this line.

Kevin picked up his pace, moving faster up the line. Most people stepped aside, recognizing his miner's costume as authority to bypass the queue. He continued to scan faces, looking for the dark, receding hair, the sharp nose, the thin mouth. He spotted a couple of men who, from the back, were dead ringers. But as he came around he saw that none of them were him.

Kevin wound his way through the twisting caves, around the faux wooden beams that looked like they supported the rock walls. The folksy, Appalachian string music filled the tunnels, coming magically from speakers hidden in the ceiling. Muffled thunder could be heard over the music as the storm rolled in.

It was just as a loud crack of thunder struck that Kevin spotted him. He was standing a few yards up the line, wearing his white shirt and paisley tie. The man shifted his gaze and his eyes locked with Kevin's. There was a look in his eyes, a look that surprised Kevin.

It was recognition.

CHAPTER 13

"I don't even know where to start, Engle." Oglethorpe was rotating his right arm in a circle, making sure nothing was permanently broken. His eyes were wide, furious.

"Hey, I'm sorry, Dude," said Jimmy. "Really. I thought you were the guy."

"That's enough, Jimmy," Jerry said. "You're not helping."

Oglethorpe cocked his head at Jerry. "For God's sake, Engle, is this your idea of security? Assaulting people in the middle of the Alpine Village? This is how you're making our guests feel safer?"

"Perhaps we should talk about this in private, Bill."

"Sure. Why not? You can have your goon attack me in front of the whole fucking world, but let's go discuss it in private." Oglethorpe took a breath and realized that it probably would be best not to continue this discussion onstage in the park. He nodded at Jerry and gestured at a backstage door behind a privacy wall covered in painted ivy. Oglethorpe excused himself from the man he had been talking to before Jimmy pounced on him. It turned out that the other man was the manager of the pastry shop—whom Jerry knew well—and Oglethorpe had been lecturing him on the display of his eclairs. The pastry shop manager was trying unsuccessfully to hide his glee at having his lecture interrupted by the significantly greater ass chewing Jerry was about to receive. He raised his eyebrows at Jerry in a "thanks buddy" salute.

As Oglethorpe and Jerry made their way through the backstage door, Jimmy and the pastry manager handed out some merchandise coupons to the assembled gawkers, apologizing for the scene.

"This better be good, Engle," said Oglethorpe as they came through the door. "I swear to God, this better be good."

Jerry took a breath and prepared himself for the explanation. Should've taken a Xanax this morning. Should've taken two. He relayed to Oglethorpe how he suspected that the killer could be in the park right now. They had a description that he was wearing a tie. Jimmy had mistaken him for the man in the tie.

"Oh, great," said Oglethorpe. "Now my staff thinks I'm a fucking murderer."

"That's not true, sir. They just think you look like one." Jerry winced, regretting the words as soon as they left his lips.

Oglethorpe glared at him. "Can I assume that since you grabbed me, he got away?"

"Not necessarily. I have my best man still searching."

"Forgive my lack of confidence. Where are the cops?"

"I can't call them until I'm sure. I'm working on a hunch. If I called them now, I'd be exposing the park to potential litigation." Jerry knew Oglethorpe's buttons. Any threat of a lawsuit scared the crap out of him.

"Okay. Okay. But, Christ, Engle. If there's a killer in the park right now, you better find him. We can't afford another incident. The Anniversary is coming up."

"I understand." Cold bastard, thought Jerry. If someone's life really were at stake, the first consideration really shouldn't be its impact on the projected revenue. "If the guy's in the park, my team will find him."

"I hope so. For your sake, Engle."

Jerry took another calming breath. Please, Kevin. If ever there was a time to come through, it was now. It was definitely now.

As soon as he saw Kevin, he bolted. Kevin immediately charged after him. The guy was heading up the line, towards the loading area. The waiting guests screamed as he barged through, knocking them out of his way as he ran. Kevin followed in his wake, jostling more than a few tourists himself. Kevin considered shouting for someone to stop him, but instinct prevented him from doing so. If the guy really was the killer, the last thing Kevin wanted was to jeopardize some innocent bystanders' lives by having them grab him.

How did he know me? thought Kevin. There was no doubt that the man knew Kevin was after him. His eyes had clearly registered recognition. Then, when the man started running, Kevin knew for certain that his cover was blown. But how? How did he find out?

They raced through the winding tunnels of the ride queue, pushing off fiberglass walls and careening around startled tourists. The ambient music transitioned to an up-tempo bluegrass tune and the fast-paced song spurred Kevin more quickly up the tunnel. He was catching up to the man, whose progress was slower than Kevin's because he was crashing into waiting guests as he ran.

They came around a corner to a section of the tunnel that was open on one side to the loading area below. Rain was pouring down in sheets. There was a flash of lightning accompanied by a deafening burst of thunder. The waiting guests flinched at the sound. A toddler cried, frightened by the noise. Kevin saw the man in the tie vault over the railing and down onto the pebbled surface of the loading platform annex, a six-foot drop into the storm. Kevin was right behind him, leaping out into the rain, which pelted him with a million fat drops.

The man quickly oriented himself. He was on the annex side of the loading platform, a useless strip of dock to be used only in an emergency evacuation. Guests boarded the ride from the other side of the mine tracks. This side only offered a small platform with an access doorway behind Kevin. On the edge of the annex was the slate gray sky of the storm. A fatal fall over the Mountain's restraining wall was all that awaited the man should he try to escape that way. He made a feint in that direction but then thought better of it. Behind the man were the wide, electrified tracks of the ride. There was nowhere for him to go. Kevin had him.

"That's far enough!" Kevin shouted over the rain. The drops practically exploded at his feet as they hit the platform.

The man looked around wildly, like a trapped animal. His white dress shirt was plastered to his body, his tie swinging as he twisted, looking for somewhere to run.

"It's over!" Kevin said. "It's over."

Kevin's co-workers had gathered on the other side of the mine tracks. He could barely see them through the rain. A diminutive figure approached the edge of the loading area.

"Kevin!" It was Chuckie. A crack of thunder obliterated whatever else he said. Kevin thought it was something along the lines of "What do you think you're doing?"

"Chuckie!" Kevin shouted across the tracks. "Call park security! Now!"

The man in the tie leaned towards Kevin, his expression fierce. "Why couldn't you just stay away? This is *my* life!"

"It's over now. Just take it easy."

"No! I will not take it easy. This is not your life!"

Another short figure was moving on the loading platform. It was Sheila. She came to the edge of the electrified tracks. "What the hell do you think you're doing?" she shouted.

At the sound of her voice, both Kevin and the man in the tie turned towards her. The man hesitated a moment. Kevin couldn't see his face. Then the man suddenly started running. Directly towards the restraining wall at the edge of the platform.

Kevin took off after him. He had no intention of letting this guy fling himself out into the air and come crashing down on the asphalt in front of a horde of vacationing children. But he was too far away. Kevin wouldn't be able to catch him.

Just as the man neared the precipice he turned sharply and jumped—not over the wall, but directly into an approaching mine cart. It was empty, Kevin's scene with the man having distracted the loaders from filling it. Kevin chased after it desperately. If the man got on the ride alone, there were probably a half dozen places where the cart slowed enough to allow him to jump off. Once off the ride, there were myriad maintenance access doors that he could disappear through. Then the chase would be on again, except this time the man knew they were chasing him. He had to be stopped now.

Kevin was still several yards away. He squinted to keep the rain from his eyes. It didn't even seem to fall in drops—more like a giant bucket being tipped over and dumped on Orlando. Three more strides, two, one . . .

Kevin leapt for the receding mine cart and landed against its side, his hands finding a hold on the restraining bar inside the cart. The bar was wet and the thick foam pad was slick. He felt his grip slipping. His arms trembled as he tried to pull himself up into the moving vehicle. He knew he only had a few seconds before the car plunged down that first stomach-churning drop.

If he was still hanging onto the side when they dropped, he would easily be tossed down the track and very likely decapitated by the cart's wheels. Behind him he heard Sheila scream.

The cart hooked the conveyor and clacked up towards the top of the hill. Kevin's right hand slipped off the bar, with just his left hand clinging desperately to the foam. The cart was cresting over the top of the hill.

Kevin looked down at his feet and saw the fiberglass railroad ties passing beneath him as the cart reached the top of the hill. He would have to time it right. One, two, three, four—He stomped his left leg as hard as he could onto one of the fiberglass railroad ties, catching it between the gaps. With that leverage he was able to swing his right leg up over the side of the mine cart and drop into the back row. Just as he fell backwards onto the lap bar, which had already lowered into position, the cart careened almost vertically down the mine tunnel with an audible whoosh.

Knowing that a sharp turn was at the bottom of the drop, Kevin hooked an arm around the lap bar and held on. They hit the turn and the momentum pulled Kevin along the slick safety bar. He wedged his feet against the side of the vehicle and heard his suspect tumble across the front row of the cart, cursing loudly. Kevin pulled himself into a crouch, positioning his feet on the floor and his backside on the lap bar. The man was sprawled across the front seat, struggling to right himself.

"Hold on," Kevin said over the noise of the tracks, "or you'll get tossed from the cart."

The man looked back and Kevin couldn't quite read his expression. Fear. Anger. Confusion. Maybe all three. But he took Kevin's advice and grabbed the safety bar.

The cart swerved around another bend and into a series of sharp S-curves. The man struggled to hold on, losing his grip at one point and catching himself dangerously on the side of the cart.

The track leveled off and the folk music became audible again. On the ground beside the track a family of animatronic raccoons disturbed an abandoned miner's campsite. One baby raccoon with a silly grin repeatedly popped its head out of a coffee pot, the pot's lid resting on its ears like a hat. The man in the tie sat up and shifted his weight towards the edge of the cart. Kevin knew he was going to make a jump for it. This was a perfect spot to hop out. A red Exit sign glowed in a corner.

"Don't even think about it!" Kevin shouted and launched himself over the back of the cart's second row. He reached forward into the first row, grabbing for the man, trying to get a grip on his shirt or belt. But his shirt was drenched and clung tightly to his body. There was no loose fabric to grab. The man jerked his body aside to avoid Kevin's grasp and his paisley tie swung around. Kevin snatched it in mid-swing.

The man lunged for the side of the cart and Kevin yanked the tie. The man fell back into the row with a loud thud. Then the cart was moving more quickly again, falling down another curved section of track. Kevin rocked back into his own seat, releasing the tie to secure himself. The man in front of him grabbed onto his own bar. The two of them swerved and fell several more times before Kevin shouted, "Duck!"

They threw themselves down as the car passed under a low-hanging horizontal beam with a horseshoe tacked on it. The tracks exited the tunnel and swung out into open air. The rain pounded them for the few seconds they were exposed. As the cart turned back into the tunnel, a flash of lightning illuminated the dark passageway. A burst of thunder punctuated the lightning.

The car slowed again, climbing up another incline for what Kevin knew was the final twisting, vomit-inducing section of the ride. The man again moved to leap out of the cart but Kevin was ready. He reached over the back of the first row seats and caught the man around the neck with his right arm. He pulled the man back down into the seat roughly. The man struggled and clawed at Kevin's forearm, leaving three bloody gashes.

But Kevin held on, widening his stance for what he knew was a brutal portion of the ride. Holding onto the man in front of him, he wouldn't be able to secure himself.

"Hold on, pal," Kevin said into his ear. "This is gonna get interesting."

The cart toppled down the descending tracks, spinning grotesquely in a mad corkscrew. Kevin lost his balance but refused to relinquish his grip. The cart suddenly changed directions and tossed Kevin over the seat and into the front row. The cart continued its out of control spiral down. The man groaned as they tumbled down onto the floorboard together, Kevin below, his arm still clenched around the man's neck.

The cart finally leveled off, slowing to a crawl. They made their way towards the unloading area, passing some smiling animatronic prospectors who waved good-bye.

"So why did you do it?" Kevin said, still holding his arm around the man's neck.

The man struggled to respond, both from the pressure Kevin was placing on his trachea as well as the emotion that was now choking his voice. "Those are my kids, you son of a bitch . . ."

"Why did you kill them?"

But the man didn't even seem to hear him. He stopped struggling and shouted as loudly as he could, "Those are my kids!"

The cart entered the unloading area and stopped. An Empire Realm security detail of four guards was standing there with Chuckie, Sheila, and a few other employees. The officers pulled Kevin and the man from the cart and separated them.

"Is this him?" asked one of the guards, a big bear of a man with a southern accent.

"Yeah," said Kevin. "That's him. Have you called Jerry Engle?"

"He's on his way," said the guard.

"You're bleeding," said Chuckie, pointing at Kevin's arm.

The man turned in the guard's grip towards Sheila. "Those are my kids, Sheila. *My* kids!"

Kevin looked at Sheila. She was looking coldly at the man in the tie. But she said nothing.

"Sheila?" Kevin said. "Do you know this guy?"

Sheila turned to Kevin, slowly tearing her gaze from the man in the tie. Her expression changed to confusion. "Of course I know him," she said in a tone that suggested she assumed Kevin already knew this. "He's my husband."

CHAPTER 14

Almost the first words out of his mouth were, "I'll sue." "Oh God," had been Jerry's response.

They got him some dry clothes and he now sat in a small conference room down the hall from Jerry's office, dressed like a cowboy. Kevin and Jerry huddled in the hallway outside the room.

"Is he the guy, Kevin?" Jerry was at his eyebrow again. "Please tell me he's the killer."

"He's the guy from the tape. I'm sure of that. I just don't know if he's the killer."

"Oh Christ, Kevin. If he's not, I'm history. Should we call Pendergrast?"

"Not yet." Kevin knew that he probably should call Pendergrast immediately. But something held him back. A hunch. There was a lot more to this situation and he wanted to sort it all out before he let the sharks in.

The elevator doors opened and Sheila strode down the hallway, still dressed in her miner's costume. She was soaked from the rain.

"Mrs. Nelson," Jerry said. "Thanks for coming—"

"How did you know?" she barked at Kevin, who was taken aback by her tone. "Did he threaten you?"

"Not exactly," said Kevin.

"Wait until I tell my lawyer about this. You were both witnesses, right? Right? He was a lot closer to me than three hundred yards."

"Mrs. Nelson," said Jerry. "I'm not sure I understand—"

Kevin cut him off, quickly reading the situation. "Is the divorce final?"

"No. Almost," said Sheila.

"He said he'd sue," said Jerry. "Is he serious?"

"I'm sure," said Sheila. "He's a lawyer."

"Oh, God."

Sheila turned back to Kevin. Her tone softened. "How did you know about him?"

Kevin put a hand on her arm, gently. "I'll explain later. Can you wait in Jerry's office?"

"I guess."

Kevin turned to Jerry. "Come on."

"Wait," Jerry said. "I don't understand."

"Just follow my lead," Kevin said, pushing open the conference room door.

Sheila's husband, whose name they now knew was Phil Nelson, leapt to his feet, leaning forward on the conference table. "I hope you have some damned good lawyers on staff, Mr. Engle. Because I intend to sue you for assault. And I am a very good lawyer."

Kevin nodded and sat on the edge of the table. How many times had he done this when he was a detective? He felt the old juice coming back, the interview tactics being dusted off and brought back out of retirement. It felt good.

"Are you sure you want to sue, Phil?" Kevin asked.

Phil slowly turned his head and glared at Kevin. "Why the fuck should I answer anything from you?"

Kevin acted as though he didn't hear the question. "Sure, you could sue. Perhaps you'd even like me to call the cops. I could do that right now." He produced his cell phone and flipped it open.

"Yeah. Yeah, why don't you do that? I'd love to tell the cops about how you chased me and then assaulted me, putting my life in jeopardy on a dangerous roller coaster. You almost killed me."

"Okay. But, of course, I'll have to tell them everything. I'll have to tell them how you've been stalking your estranged wife. How you've been repeatedly violating your restraining order to stay the hell away from her. How I feared for her safety and intercepted you. I'm sure they'd be interested in the whole story. Shall I dial the number or would you like to?"

Phil narrowed his eyes and sat slowly back down in his chair. He said nothing, but the vitriol in his expression spoke volumes.

"No?" said Kevin. "Well, let me know if you change your mind." He made a show of flipping his phone closed and sliding it into his pocket.

"I want you to stay away from my kids. You hear me?"

"I suppose that's why you smashed up my car, right?" Phil didn't respond, but Kevin was sure he detected the faint whisper of a smirk on his face. "For the record, I haven't even met your kids. Yet."

Phil tensed and, for an instant, Kevin thought the guy might charge him. But Phil fought back the impulse and remained in his seat.

"Who the fuck are you, anyway?" Phil said.

"I'm just a guy who happens to be very fond of Sheila." Kevin stood up again and wandered absently to the window. He stared out into the wet streets of the park. The rain was finally stopping, leaving the whole area blanketed in a thick soup of humidity. Wispy steam rose from the asphalt in patches. "Besides, I wouldn't worry about me, if I were you," Kevin said, still staring out the window. "You have bigger problems."

"Yeah? Like what?"

Kevin made a point to exchange a meaningful look with Jerry. "Gate security cameras captured you coming into the park on May 29th. You were also seen entering the park on June 21st. You were pretty easy to spot, all dressed up for work. I assume that you came straight from work, right?" Phil said nothing. Kevin took his silence as concurrence. "Do those two days mean anything special to you?"

"If you think you can intimidate me by trotting out that ridiculous restraining order, you're wasting your time. You two work for the park. You have no authority to keep me here. I can leave whenever I want. I'm only here to make sure you understand to stay away from my kids."

Kevin pursed his lips. "Hmm. I think that you might be confused. You're the one a judge told to keep away. I'm allowed to go near anyone I want."

"I'm not kidding, asshole."

"Neither am I. What's so special about those two days, the two days that you decided to play hooky and stalk your wife, is that someone died inside the park on both of those days. They each died under very mysterious circumstances. It seems awfully coincidental that you just happened to be here on both of those days, don't you think? I mean, what are the odds?" Kevin smiled and sat back down on the edge of the table.

"You're kidding, right? You're not seriously suggesting that I had something to do with those deaths?"

"Seriously suggesting? I don't know. Jerry, would you consider this serious?"

Jerry remained standing in the corner, arms folded. "It's pretty damned serious to me."

Kevin turned back to Phil. "Well, there you go. I guess we are seriously suggesting it. Is there any other kind of murder except the serious kind?"

"Who the fuck *are* you?!"

"I don't suppose you can tell us exactly what you did while in the park on those two days and when you left?"

"What? I'm not telling you a goddamned thing. Not without a lawyer present. And I'm certainly not going to continue this slanderous line of questioning. I wouldn't have to take it from real cops and I certainly don't have to take it from you."

Kevin stood. "Sure, Phil. You're free to go. For the record, your picture will be posted at all of our ticket booths and gate entrances. You're no longer welcome as a guest of Empire Realm. Ever."

"The fuck I care." Phil stood and made his way towards the conference door. Just before he reached it, Kevin moved in front of him so that their chests were almost touching. Kevin leaned close into his face and spoke very quietly, but without any doubt about his sincerity.

"You owe me for the windows and paint job on my truck," Kevin said. "But I'll let it go. Just know that if you ever come near Sheila again, it won't be your *car* that gets smashed. That's a promise."

Phil opened his mouth to respond but then changed his mind and retreated out of the room. Kevin watched him intensely until the door shut.

"I'll call Pendergrast," said Jerry, pulling out his cell phone. "He needs to grab him and question him."

"Don't bother," said Kevin, slumping down into a conference chair. "He didn't do it."

Jerry's face was ashen. "What? How do you know?"

"Years of experience interviewing murderers. I just know. He doesn't fit the profile. Never did. I knew something was out of whack. Shit." As soon as they got off that ride, Kevin had known that Phil was innocent of the murders. Kevin would check him out, of course, investigate any alibis, but he was sure they would be dead ends.

"What about the video?" said Jerry. "He was here both days. That's grounds enough for Pendergrast to haul him in."

"Probably, but it would be a waste of time. It was just a coincidence. Sort of. I'd bet that if we watched more tape we'd find that our friend Phil comes to the park all the time."

"So he just comes here to spy on his wife?"

"Apparently. I assume the divorce wasn't his idea. He's obviously been following me and Sheila. He's the one who smashed up my truck. He's probably an asshole and a bully, but he's not our killer." Kevin planned to talk to Sheila next. He indeed had a lot to learn about her. This little episode certainly explained her reluctance to talk about her marriage.

Now Jerry slumped down into a chair. "Oh, God. I'm ruined. We're completely back to square one. We have no leads." The fingers were flying at the eyebrows again.

"We don't have any suspects, but we do have leads. Midwest Tours is still being checked out. Don't forget the dry ice. I think we have to go back to the theory that the doer is an employee. Sorry, cast member."

"Whatever," said Jerry, his head resting in his hands. "You think he'll sue?"

"Not unless he wants to be found guilty of violating whatever restraining order he's under." Kevin rubbed his arm where a large bandage covered his scratches. "I'll keep looking, Jer. I'll find the guy. I will. I just need a little more time."

Jerry groaned. "I'm afraid we may be out of time, Kevin." He closed his eyes. "At least, I am."

* * *

Sheila rubbed her face. She looked tired. "He used to beat me," she said, looking directly at Kevin, waiting for a reaction. Kevin offered no visible response. He had been a cop too long and had seen too much domestic abuse to be particularly shocked. "The list goes on," she continued. "Adultery. Long hours at work. Too much drinking. He was almost never around and then, when he was, I was terrified. At first for myself, but then, later, for the kids. He never hit them, but he came close a couple of times and I knew I had to get them away."

They sat on a bench not far from the Palace. The park had been closed for some time and the third-shift workers were scurrying about, trimming hedges, restocking shelves, and emptying garbage cans. Even at this late hour, Empire Palace was illuminated spectacularly, its purple and green exterior sparkling. Kevin saw workers high on the turrets polishing the wrought iron rails on the balconies. An eerie silence enveloped the park at night, one that was only noticeable once the ambient music was switched off and the crowds were gone. Sitting there, at the base of the Palace, the nighttime silence blanketing them, Kevin felt like he was in the presence of some ancient, gaudy cathedral.

"So why did you stay so long?" he asked her. "It just doesn't seem like you."

She sighed. "He didn't always hit me. That started later. He didn't deal well with the stress of his job. Ninety-hour weeks. His managing partner is a tyrant. Phil reached a breaking point and started taking it out on me. At first I tried to help him, to understand what he was going through. But I eventually came to realize that there was no excuse for that behavior. The affairs were the same thing. I always forgave him. Again, I rationalized that he was just coping with his stress, that since we were high school sweethearts and had never dated anyone else, the infidelity was understandable. I didn't like it, but I tolerated it. I was wrong." She paused, rubbing her finger where her wedding ring had once been. "I left him. Took the kids to my mother's. Through the lawyers, we negotiated for him to move out and the kids and I went back to the house. His lawyer felt it would be better for his case to make that good faith effort. But he didn't stay away. He started following me. I'd find him watching me while I was at the grocery store. See him sitting in his car, staring as I picked up the kids from school. He began threatening me, saying that I better stop the divorce or else. I was afraid he would do something. Given his violent history, I was able to get a restraining order. I thought that was the end of it."

"Apparently not. I have a feeling that he's been coming to the park and watching you for a while."

"God. That really gives me the creeps." She glanced away, absently watching a cast member push an ice-cream vending cart from the street to behind a building. "How did you know? I think you owe me an explanation."

Indeed he did. Kevin knew that. But how could he explain it to Sheila without compromising his cover? He didn't think he could. He could lie and try to convince her that he knew her husband had smashed his car and somehow figured out who he was. She was smart and convincing her would be hard to do. Plus, Kevin didn't relish the idea of lying to her. He genuinely liked her, liked her in a way that he hadn't liked anyone in a very long time. Even as he wrestled with the guilt of his attraction to her, he knew that he wanted to know her better, maybe even venture a relationship with her. That would be impossible if he began that relationship by lying to her. He didn't want to jeopardize his investigation. But he also didn't want to jeopardize what could be the first real relationship he'd had since Maria's death.

"Kevin?" Sheila said, leaning around to see his face. He realized that he had been staring straight ahead, lost in thought. He turned to face her.

"Sheila," Kevin said, taking her hand in his. "I really like you. And I think I'm starting to care about you in a way that is both scary and exhilarating. The last thing I want to do is lie to you." He paused, now gauging her face for a reaction. There was none. He continued. "So I won't."

"What's going on, Kevin?" Sheila's voice was cautious.

"Remember when I told you that I work as a private investigator? That when work gets slow I sometimes take a job here at the park to make ends meet? That's not entirely true. I am a private investigator, but I've never worked here before. I'm working on a case right now, undercover."

"Undercover?" She paused, processing that. "Like some spy? Is this a joke?"

"I'm afraid not."

"What does this have to do with my husband?"

"Actually, nothing, as it turns out. You were right about the two tourists who died here a few weeks ago. They *were* murdered. And it seems likely that they were both killed by the same person. That's why the cops have been all over the place, why Lou Pendergrast has been interviewing everyone."

"What are you saying? That you're still a cop?"

"No. Like I said, I used to be a cop. Jerry Engle and I were both on the force together. His job is on the line because of these murders and he asked me to go undercover and investigate."

Sheila said nothing for a moment, her mind sorting through this information, trying to make some sense out of it. She started to say something, turned away, then turned back with a mischievous glint in her eye. "I think I would have preferred it if you lied to me." Kevin smiled. She never ceased to surprise him. "Why doesn't Mr. Engle just leave it up to the cops? That's their job, after all."

"It's . . . complicated. You would have to know Lou Pendergrast."

"I know him as well as I ever hope to."

"If Jerry can find the killer before Pendergrast does, he'll be a hero and save his job, not to mention lives. But he can't investigate himself. He's too high profile. So he hired me."

"But what about Phil? How does he fit in this?"

"One of my associates . . ." Kevin smiled to himself, knowing that Lucius would appreciate being described as his *associate*, ". . . reviewed the security camera tapes from the front gate on the days when the murders occurred. Your husband was identified coming into the park on both of those days."

"Oh my God . . ."

"So when he came back, I was alerted and we grabbed him. The fact that he came into the park, alone, on both days, made him a suspect. I honestly had no idea he was your husband."

"You think he . . . he *killed* those people? I don't believe it. Phil is an awful human being but I just don't believe he could kill someone."

"I don't think he did it, either. I think it was probably a cast member. We're still looking."

The two of them sat there for a few more minutes, not saying anything, just watching the night workers go about their tasks. Finally, Sheila broke the silence.

"You must really trust me to tell me this," she said, still looking out over the park streets.

"I guess I must."

"I assume I'm supposed to keep this a secret."

"I'd appreciate it."

She patted his knee, her tone becoming more upbeat. "Well,

Kevin Lonnegan. Now you know the truth about me. I know the truth about you. There's only one thing left to do."

"Oh? What's that?"

"You need to meet my kids."

CHAPTER 15

He was odious. Truly. Physically unattractive, an abrasive personality. Just gross. But she agreed to meet him again for drinks.

Carla Beck sometimes wondered if she occasionally crossed the line of her journalistic ethics. Pressuring an anonymous source to go public was one thing. Or even using selected portions of a quote. But, really, pretending to be attracted to Lou Pendergrast was just plain wrong. It certainly felt wrong.

Even if Carla were interested in men at all, which she most definitely was not, Lou Pendergrast would not be the type of man she would pursue. Or allow herself to be pursued by.

Margo wasn't exactly thrilled with the idea of her meeting Pendergrast for drinks. Again. It's not that she was jealous—she and Carla were committed to each other and Margo trusted her. It was just that the idea of Carla sitting in a trendy bar while some Neanderthal ogled her wasn't exactly comforting. Plus, Margo had a real issue with Carla's discretion about her lifestyle. Just because she was in the public eye didn't mean she had to hide who she was. Perpetuating a veil of secrecy only made societal acceptance more difficult. Ellen DeGeneres could talk to Barbara Walters all she wanted, but it was the people in the communities who would really make the difference. Local celebrities like Carla needed to be on the front lines of acceptance.

Intellectually, Carla understood Margo's opinion. And in her heart she agreed with it. But change was slow in coming. Even with the sizable homosexual population in Orlando, there was still an established base of conservatives. Rednecks, religious zealots, bigots. And she had to recognize that they all read the Orlando *Sentinel*. The last thing she needed, especially in her new role as a features columnist, was to alienate any portion of her audience. She needed an attention grabber, a hot issue to write about. But she had no interest in making that hot issue her personal lifestyle.

So now she sat at Gordo's, again, nursing a gimlet. This time she was waiting for him. She was wearing a particularly suggestive outfit. Low-cut blouse showing some cleavage, just a peek at the lace trim of her bra. A black skirt with a small slit up the left side. She winced as she recalled selecting that ensemble. Her clothes were deliberately chosen to entice Pendergrast. It was manipulative and dishonest. But she did it anyway.

Pendergrast came through the door, immediately craning his thick neck to search for her. Carla was suddenly overcome with an urge to dive under her table and hide there until he went away. She might have even done that except Pendergrast spotted her and gave her a quick wave and sly smile.

He walked over to her and she noticed that he moved with an odd gait. It wasn't a limp, exactly, but a slight hesitation of sorts as he stepped. She decided not to ask him about it.

"Hi Carla," he said as he sat, somewhat cautiously, on the stool opposite her.

"Evening, Lou," she said, pulling her hair flirtatiously behind her ear. She had read in a magazine somewhere that you could tell a woman was flirting with you if she pulled her hair behind her ear. Carla thought it was stupid, but, hey, in for a penny, in for a pound.

He eyed her hair move like a predator. Maybe the magazine article wasn't so stupid, after all.

They made excruciating small talk for a few minutes, Pendergrast ordering a chocolate martini. *Uck*—whoever heard of a chocolate martini? Carla wasn't surprised when he declined a cigar, after he almost choked on the last one. She, too, declined. Finally, when Carla fell she had put in enough time making small talk, she got down to business.

"So, Lou," she said coyly, tilting her head down and looking up at him. "What's up?"

"Well, Carla, we've known each other a long time. Cops and reporters don't always get along the greatest, but I think that we each have a lot of professional respect for each other."

Carla shivered. "I couldn't agree more, Lou."

That response seemed to fortify his resolve. He clasped his hands and leaned across the table. "I've always felt a, *a . . . connection* with you. I think we really *get* each other, you know what I mean?"

"Sure." *Ugh. Oh God.*

"In the past it really wasn't appropriate for us to have this kind of conversation. I was married and it just wouldn't have been right."

"Of course." Carla distinctly remembered at least three occasions where Pendergrast had overtly hit on her while he was married. She had politely declined, claiming other commitments.

"So, now that we're both available . . . I mean, given the connection and all, I thought that we should pursue a relation-ship that's more than professional." He paused, waiting for her to react. He probably expected a big sexy smile and a response like, *what took you so long to make your move, big boy?* But she just couldn't bring herself to do it. She had crossed enough lines this evening and that was just too much for her.

"Well, Lou," she said, formulating a response. "I-I don't know what to say . . ."

He sensed her hesitation. "I understand this is a transition. To become more than just friends." She screamed silently inside her own head. Since when were they ever friends? Pendergrast went on. "I know you need to trust me. And I have to earn that trust."

Carla's head was spinning. This was going too far. Flirting was one thing but there was no way she could maintain this charade if he actually wanted to have a romantic relationship with her. The thought of it made her shudder. If Margo had overhead this, she probably would have punched him in the jaw. Carla realized that Pendergrast was still talking.

". . . the kind of thing that's very sensitive, of course. So I have to remain anonymous. At least for the time being."

"Right, Lou. Of course."

"But I would expect to be featured prominently once the whole thing comes out. Naturally, you would have an automatic interview with me."

"What exactly are we talking about here?"

"My case. The one I mentioned to you the other day."

"Right. Empire Realm. You think a tourist's death might have been a murder. Refresh my memory," she said, lightly touching the back of his hand.

"There were actually two deaths recently at Empire Realm. Both tourists." She knew what he was talking about. The other one was a little while ago—also a tourist. Found dead in a topiary bush. The *Sentinel* had mentioned it but not made a big deal. "What you don't know is that we believe that *both* were murders."

Carla's journalistic instincts kicked in. Two murders. Empire Realm. This sounded like a story.

Pendergrast glanced at his hand where she had touched him. He really was predictable. "Furthermore," he continued, "the evidence suggests that both were victims of the *same* killer."

Carla just stared at him. She couldn't quite believe what she was hearing. "You're saying that there is a murderer stalking tourists at Empire Realm?"

"That's exactly what I'm saying."

"Wait a minute . . . just so I understand . . . are we talking about some kind of *serial killer* here?"

"That is one of the working theories. In fact, that has become the primary theory."

Jackpot. The sexy outfit, the false flirting, the compromising of her ethics—this is what they had been for. "Jesus, Lou, who else knows about this?"

"Obviously, the cops on my team. Nobody else officially, but there are probably suspicions by the security guy at the park. Although he would never admit it." Pendergrast found that amusing and chuckled to himself.

"What about the media? Does anyone else know you're tracking a possible serial killer?"

Pendergrast paused meaningfully. He put his clammy palm on her hand. "Just you." He looked deeply into her eyes. "I'm sharing this with you to demonstrate my sincerity. My hope is that you will. . . . *share* things with me, too."

Carla almost toppled off her stool. Pendergrast was suggesting some sort of hideous *quid pro quo* for his information. Clearly that was never going to happen. *Nev-er.* But for a story like this—a serial killer stalking guests at Orlando's theme parks— she was certainly willing to continue the charade.

"Oh, Lou," she cooed, "I think we have a *lot* we can share with each *other.*"

Kevin had trouble with the clown's mouth. The windmill wasn't too bad and he had even two-putted the enchanted bridge. But that damn clown's mouth seemed to shrink every time his golf-ball got near it.

Sheila's kids thought that it was hilarious.

Kevin took twelve putts before he finally picked up the ball and dropped it into the hole by hand. That sent the youngest kid, Greg, into a fit of laughter.

Kevin knew that he was walking into an awkward situation when he agreed to meet them for miniature golf. He had never been there before. It was a fairy tale-themed course on International Drive. I-Drive was a spectacularly gaudy section of town that housed a series of hotels, shops, restaurants, themed attractions, and the gargantuan Orange County Convention Center.

The kids were quiet and shy, as he expected, but little Greg seemed to warm up to him pretty quickly. Although he was only three, Greg had an open, fun-loving personality. The girl, Maggie, was a little reticent but seemed to accept Kevin as, at least, her Mommy's friend. The oldest boy, Billy, was definitely a hard case. He was sullen and quiet the whole time. Kevin knew he couldn't push himself on him. He just gave Billy some space and tried to be respectful of him.

It was a tough situation for the kid. Kevin couldn't even imagine what it must be like for him. His own parents had been married for forty-nine years and were still going strong. He and his three brothers had grown up in a loud, Irish-Catholic house filled with arguments and laughter and a permanent, indelible sense of reliability. It was a house filled with love and stability and the concept of a divorce shattering that was incomprehensible. He tried to imagine how Billy must feel about the dissolution of everything he had ever relied upon in his ten years on Earth. It must be an awful, unsettling feeling that had left him trusting no one. Least of all Kevin.

Despite Billy's reluctance to accept him, Kevin fell that the outing had gone well. They were nice kids and Sheila had obviously done a good job raising them. Her prick husband clearly had nothing to do with their upbringing. After Kevin deposited the golfball in the clown's mouth, they took a short walk to a nearby ice-cream stand and everyone had a cone. Before he got into Sheila's car, Billy had even thanked Kevin for the golf and ice cream. Sheila whispered her own "thank you" into his ear and gave him a quick peck on the cheek before she and the kids left.

Kevin didn't go home right away. He took a walk through Pointe Orlando, a trendy, outdoor shopping mall, eventually finding himself in FAO Schwartz, the once-giant toy retailer now clearing its shelves due to bankruptcy. He wandered through the displays and shelves, listening to the happy music that filled the air. *Welcome to our world . . . welcome to our world . . . welcome to our world of toys . . .* He watched the smiling young families. He picked up plush, stuffed animals—a cross-eyed koala bear grinned at him. He held a Barbie doll and moved its arm up and down. He shot a Nerf basketball through an indoor hoop. He spent a long time there.

And all the while he wondered, *What if?*

That had been last night and it was all he could think about now at work as he loaded guests onto the moving mine cars. He tried to think about his investigation, but his mind kept drifting back to paths his life could have taken. Sheila was working alongside him. During their shift Kevin caught her stealing smirking glances at him, like a couple of kids in algebra class.

What if that drunken driver hadn't turned at that exact moment? What if Maria and the baby had survived? What if the just the baby had survived? Kevin thought about that indoor basketball hoop. He would have bought that for his son. During the pregnancy, Kevin had fantasized about all the things he wanted to do with his boy. Take him fishing. Go to basketball games. Teach him to catch pop flies.

He had eventually resigned himself to a life without a wife and children. That resignation was part of dealing with what had happened, of working through the pain, of moving on. Or so he told himself. He remembered what the Reverend had said one time when Kevin expressed his acceptance of his fate.

"That's not moving on, Kevin," he said. "That's holding on." The Reverend believed that he had resigned himself to a life alone because he was afraid of letting go of what he once had. If he let someone new into his life, Kevin would feel like he was pushing Maria out.

He caught Sheila winking at him as she assisted an elderly couple onto the ride. He gave her a quick smile. Now that he had met her, he realized that perhaps he could make room for someone new in his life. Even if Sheila wasn't the one he was meant to be with, his feelings for her made him realize that perhaps there was someone new out there with whom he *was* meant to be. And the time spent with her kids last night showed him that maybe he *could be* a father. Maybe you get more than one shot at the life you always imagined. Maybe.

Maybe . . .

"Kevin?"

It was a man's voice, a familiar voice. Kevin turned. Carlos was there, staring incredulously at him.

"Man, it *is* you," Carlos said, furrowing his brow. "What are you *doing* here?"

Kevin was so surprised to see him, so shocked at the timing of seeing him, that he was rendered unable to respond. Having Maria's brother appear just as Kevin was in the midst of contemplating a new relationship with Sheila filled Kevin with a sudden, overpowering feeling of shame. He felt like he'd been caught in the act of cheating on Maria and there was nothing he could say about it.

"Kevin, you okay?" Carlos asked. Carlos' wife and two kids were looking at Kevin as well, waiting for a response. An acknowledgement.

"Carlos. Lilly," Kevin finally said. "Yeah, I'm okay. You guys just caught me by surprise."

Carlos lowered his voice. "Man, why are you working *here*? Is everything okay?"

"Yeah. Everything's fine. It's a long story."

Chuckie was glaring at Kevin. A mine car had moved on empty while Kevin chatted with Carlos. Kevin guided them into the next car.

"When are you off?" Carlos asked as Kevin lowered the safety bar. "We're here all day. Meet us for dinner."

"Sure," Kevin said, not knowing what else to say.

"Seven o'clock at the Lone Star!" Carlos called back at him as the car disappeared down the track.

Kevin watched it clack off into the tunnel. He took a moment to try to calm down. He deliberately slowed his rapid breathing. But his heart was racing. And he realized his hands were trembling. Why? He hadn't done anything wrong. He had nothing to feel guilty about. But that was only part of it.

He hadn't seen Carlos since the baby's funeral. Carlos had tried to contact him, as had all of Maria's family. But Kevin shut them all out. It was too hard seeing them. He saw Maria's face in their faces. He heard Maria's voice in their voices. Even now, Carlos had Maria's eyes. Kevin shook off a shudder at the thought that, somehow, Maria had just been looking at him.

An image flashed before him—Maria's face looking up at him, her black hair cascaded like ink on a bare metal gurney, her full lips cold and pale, jagged cuts crisscrossing the smooth skin of her forehead and cheeks, her lifeless eyes staring up, past him. Through him. It was her death gaze. Those were the eyes that he just saw in Carlos.

Kevin felt his throat go dry and clenched his eyes shut to shake away the image. When he opened them he was startled to see Sheila looking up at him curiously.

"You okay?" she asked. "Who was that just now?"

Kevin tried to swallow. He couldn't. "Nobody . . ." he said.

"You don't look so good. Maybe you should take a break." She gave him a playful pinch on the arm. Although her pinch was soft and harmless, in Kevin's mind it felt like a searing hot stab. He jerked his arm back from her.

"I'm—sorry . . . I've gotta go . . ." he mumbled and left the loading area. He saw Chuckie and told him he didn't feel well. He was going home. He didn't turn back and look at Sheila. He couldn't.

Kevin pushed through the cast member exit and into a small hallway next to an employee break room. He was breathing more heavily now, bordering on hyperventilating. *Get a hold of yourself Lonnegan. Relax. . .* He lifted his hands and stared into his palms. They were both shaking. God, his throat was dry. He leaned over a nearby water fountain, gulping the cold, chlorinated water as fast as he could. He ran some water over his hand and splashed it in his face. He could feel his heart pounding in his chest.

He made his way to the locker room and quickly changed out of his costume. In a few more minutes he was in his truck, pulling away from the park property. Another image flashed in his mind. A car: Maria's Toyota. The driver's side was crumpled, the car's frame bent into a crooked heap. Maria's bloodied face leaning forward, her limp pregnant body held by the shoulder strap of the seat belt.

He had gotten the call while he was in an unmarked car on his way back from a witness interview. The first uniform on the scene had radioed in the license tag and someone in the office recognized the name that came up. Kevin was quickly notified that his wife had been in an accident and he sped off towards the accident scene.

He wasn't far away and arrived in time to see the fire department cutting away the driver's door. It had been smashed beyond any hope of opening it. He immediately knew it was bad. He had seen accidents Like these before, more than he wanted to remember, and this one had all the signs of a fatality.

He rushed towards the car and was intercepted by a uniformed officer. "That's my wife!" Kevin screamed. The cop held him back and told him to let the paramedics do their work. *But that's my wife . . .* The cop said nothing, but his eyes betrayed his sorrow. *No . . .*

What remained of the door was pulled away and Maria's motionless body slumped sideways, still strapped into the seat. Blood dripped from her sagging head. Shards of glass were littered all over her and the ground outside the car. Her legs were pulverized in the impact. Kevin could see the tattered crimson flesh and shattered bone below her skirt. Her maternity blouse was drenched in blood.

The next few hours were a nightmarish blur. Pacing the hospital corridors, sitting in a small, over-air-conditioned waiting area while a television blared Oprah at an unnaturally loud volume. Asking the nurses if there was any news. Other cops stopping by, asking how Maria was doing. Kevin had no idea. He had never felt so helpless in his entire life. He found the hospital chapel and prayed desperately.

Finally, after hours of anxious waiting, the doctor asked to speak with him privately. The doctor was young and looked tired. Bloodstains were dotted across the front of his surgical scrubs.

"I'm sorry, Mr. Lonnegan," he said. "Your wife's injuries were too great. We did everything that we could, but she died." Kevin felt the blood drain from his face and he put a hand against the cold cement wall to steady himself. The doc went on to tell him that they performed an emergency Cesarean section and delivered his son. The baby was just over four pounds, premature and weak, but alive. He, too, had been injured in the accident and suffered from massive internal bleeding. Early indications were that his spleen had ruptured. A neonatology surgical team was currently operating on him. His condition was critical and was complicated by the fact that his lungs had not finished developing.

Kevin's mind had completely shut down. His throat was dry and tunnel vision was setting in. He was about to lose consciousness when the doc put a hand on his arm. He had still been speaking, although Kevin hadn't heard him.

"Mr. Lonnegan? Did you hear me?"

Barely audible, Kevin replied, "What?"

"Do you have a name for your son?"

Kevin's eyes finally focused and he looked at the doc. The man who had just told him that his life was forever changed.

"Michael," Kevin said, not more than a whisper. "Michael William."

The doctor nodded and led Kevin down several hallways and through a door marked "Restricted Access." There, on a gurney, lay Maria, her body covered with a clean white sheet. Her face was badly lacerated, but someone had taken the time to clean the blood. And her hair had been brushed. Kevin ran a finger along her cheek, stroked a strand of black hair, and choked back his emotions. In the corner he saw a canvas laundry cart with bed linens crumpled inside. The corner of a sheet hung over the edge. It was stained bright red.

The doctor led him to a small room where a nurse guided him through two stacks of paperwork. It wasn't until weeks later that Kevin realized the irony of that paperwork. In one stack were all the forms pertaining to his wife's death. In another stack were the forms for his son's birth.

Baby Michael survived his surgery but was confined to the neonatal intensive care unit, or NICU. Kevin put on a surgical mask and was permitted to spend a few minutes with him. The baby was unconscious and his tiny body looked so frail and weak. He had Kevin's pale complexion but Maria's dark hair. He also had Maria's deep brown eyes. An IV line was strapped to his arm and a feeding tube led to his nostrils. His little chest heaved up and down to the rhythm of the mechanical ventilator. The ventilator tube ran into his tiny mouth. Kevin stayed as long as the nurses let him, which was a long time— hours. They knew what had happened to him today and were sympathetic. Kevin was allowed to touch his son gently and he ran what seemed like a huge finger along his short, thin arm. The baby's translucent skin was soft, delicate, and membrane-thin. Kevin was afraid it might tear as he brushed his fingertip along it.

He made the requisite phone calls. His parents. Two of his brothers. He couldn't reach the third. Maria's parents and two of her siblings. Her sister Francesca. And her brother, Carlos.

The next few days were spent in a numb no-man's-land

between the abject grief of his wife's death and the desperate hope for his son's life. He balanced funeral arrangements with visits to the NICU.

The day he buried Maria was the day his son finally died. The first and last time that Kevin was permitted to pick up and hold his son was only after the life had left his tiny body.

Kevin walked out of the hospital and gasped in the night air of the parking lot. His throat was dry. He was shaking. A short walk across the street was a restaurant with a large bar. Kevin found a barstool and didn't get up for three hours. But no matter how much he drank, he couldn't wash away the image of his six-day-old son lying lifeless in his arms.

Kevin's brother, Rob, who was in town for Maria's funeral, picked Kevin up from the bar and took him home. He stayed and helped Kevin through the next few days, making arrangements for another funeral.

Michael's funeral was the last time that Kevin had seen Carlos. Until today at the park.

Kevin looked up. He realized that he was no longer driving. His truck was in the parking lot of a shopping plaza. Directly in front of him was a sports bar called the End Zone. His mouth was parched.

In another minute Kevin was inside and on a barstool. He ordered a shot of whiskey and closed his eyes. The memories were flying at him now, flooding his mind. He hadn't faced a torrent like this since he went to that first AA meeting. He knew that he shouldn't be in this bar. He knew that he should call his sponsor. But the memories were too painful, and he also knew how to stop the pain.

The bartender placed the shot in front of him and Kevin stared at it for a full minute before reaching for it. SportsCenter was on a TV behind the bar, but Kevin didn't hear it. The sound of his own heartbeat thundered in his ears. He put his fingers on the glass and lifted it.

Trembling, he brought the whiskey to his chin and closed his eyes again. He hadn't smelled alcohol in a long time. The whiskey was woody and spicy, with a sharp, chemical aroma. He lifted the glass a little higher and pressed it against his lips. He took a breath and opened his mouth.

Just as he did, his cell phone rang.

Kevin froze. The shot glass was suspended. The phone rang again. Kevin shakily put the drink down. The phone continued to ring. Kevin's gaze broke from the drink. The sounds of the bar began to filter back in. The TV, some guys behind him shooting pool, someone a few stools down coughing.

He put a five-dollar bill on the bar and backed away. He pulled his phone from his pocket and answered it.

"Hello?" he said. His voice was hoarse, exhausted.

"Hey, Kevin." It was the Reverend. His deep, gentle voice also sounded tired. "How soon can you be here?"

Kevin clenched his eyes tightly, finally turning away from the drink. "Uh, not long. Maybe . . . twenty minutes. What's wrong?"

The Reverend sighed. "Lucius is back on the rock."

CHAPTER 16

"I got a call from a friend of mine in the neighborhood." The Reverend led Kevin from the front door of his modest residence to his living room. Lucius was passed out on the couch, the only indication that he was still alive being the slow rising and falling of his chest as he breathed. "I picked him up and brought him back here."

Kevin had no doubt that the Reverend meant that he had literally picked him up and brought him back. Like a great, towering savior he swooped into the crackhouse and delivered Lucius from its depths.

Kevin knelt next to Lucius and noticed the blistered and charred fingertips that gave away his evening's activities. Then Kevin looked into his unconscious face. He felt that, in a way, he was staring into a mirror. Less than thirty minutes ago Kevin had been on the precipice of falling back into his own addiction. It was only pure luck and the serendipitous intervention of the very same savior that prevented him from falling back into the abyss. So, as he looked into his friend's face, he didn't feel the disappointment he had felt whenever Lucius had stumbled in the past. Now he felt shame and fear and regret. Because he was no different from Lucius. He was only a little luckier tonight.

Kevin stood and walked with the Reverend to his small kitchen. They moved to a half-round dinette table pushed against one wall. The entire room was bathed in a soft yellow glow from the overhead lamp.

"You look tired," the Reverend said, placing a cup of black coffee in front of Kevin.

Kevin smiled wearily. "I am."

The Reverend nodded knowingly and joined him at the table. Neither one of them needed to say anything about Lucius. There was nothing to be said. Crack had its hooks back into him and they all needed to start over again. But he had made it more than four months this time. That was more than before. That was progress.

Kevin sipped the coffee and tried to swallow the guilt he was feeling. He was actually grateful that Lucius had succumbed to his addiction. Lucius' weakness had saved him from his own. What kind of friend was he, to be thankful that Lucius had gotten back on drugs? The Reverend seemed to read Kevin's troubled face.

"It's not your fault," he said. His baritone voice was soft and covered Kevin like a warm blanket.

"I know."

"He wouldn't have stayed clean as long as he did without your help."

Kevin nodded. "There's always more that can be done."

"True enough." The Reverend paused and peered at Kevin, perhaps sensing something. "But, ultimately, it's up to each of us to choose our own path."

Kevin had the distinct feeling that the Reverend was looking inside him, no longer talking about Lucius. He felt the Reverend somehow knew he had come from a bar; that he had given in to temptation. It was crazy, but such was the Reverend's effect.

He connected with people on a deeply personal level. Kevin had seen the Reverend work the streets, talking teenaged hookers into a shelter, facing down the toughest gang-bangers and reducing them to tears.

"True enough," said Kevin.

They sat up late into the evening, talking and catching up. They hadn't seen each other for a while, not since they last sat with Lucius to ride out his withdrawal. Kevin told him a little about Sheila, about the guilt he was feeling for pursuing a relationship. He felt like he was being unfaithful to Maria. The Reverend just nodded.

"Would Maria have liked Sheila?" he asked.

The question surprised Kevin and it took a moment for him to respond. "Why do you ask that?"

"I'm sure Maria would want you to be happy. I didn't know her well, but I knew her well enough to know that she wouldn't want you moping around, running from every chance to be happy. If Maria would have liked Sheila, if they could have been friends, then I think she would be okay with it. She would want you to get to know her."

Kevin considered it. "Yeah, I think that if they had known each other, they might have been friends. They're very different, but I think they would have definitely been friends."

The Reverend nodded with a satisfied smile. Kevin felt the weight of his guilt lighten just a bit. The thought of Maria and Sheila shopping together, eating lunch, and going to the movies, while absurd, was strangely comforting.

Lucius groaned from the living room. "I'll make him some toast," said the Reverend. "That should be mild enough."

"Remember," said Kevin. "No jelly. Marmalade."

"I remember," the Reverend said with a smirk, pulling himself up from the table. He seemed to fill the entire room.

Just then, Kevin's cell phone rang in his pocket. He looked at his watch. It was 4:35 in the morning. He and the Reverend exchanged a foreboding look. No good call ever came at 4:35 in the morning. Kevin flipped the phone open.

"This is Kevin."

"Kevin. It's Jerry." Jerry Engle sounded agitated. His words were spoken quickly in a clipped, nervous tone. "You gotta get out to the park. Right now. There's—Oh God—there's been another murder."

Pendergrast was snoring soundly when the ringing woke him. His mind was clouded with sleep and the first thing he noticed upon waking was that his ass was hurting. It was a painful throbbing in his rectum and his sleep-addled mind told him that the throbbing and the ringing were somehow connected. His ass was ringing and it hurt like hell.

Pendergrast shook the cobwebs from his brain and rolled over onto his stomach. That helped his hemorrhoid, a little, and allowed him to instinctively grab the phone receiver.

"Whu . . ." he mumbled, his eyes still closed. It was the kid, whatshisname. Mickelson.

"Hey, Boss. Wake up. It's showtime."

"This better be fucking good," Pendergrast grumbled, finally rousing to lucidity.

"Well, there's one person who it ain't so good for. There's been another murder at Empire Realm."

That did it. Pendergrast was now wide-awake. "On my way."

Pendergrast quickly threw on some clothes, shoved a handful of Tic Tacs into his mouth, and ran out the door. He tried in vain to squash down a cowlick jutting out from the side of his head.

He flew down the highway, his bubble light flashing. As he

drove, he began to wonder why Mickelson had called him. Why did Mickelson get the word before him? Pendergrast was the goddamned primary. He was home and accessible. He should've gotten the call. That bastard Gardner was up to something and Pendergrast would be goddamned before he got shoved out of the spotlight of this case. He had the experience. He had paid his dues. He was the most seasoned detective in the department. Besides, *he was the goddamned primary!*

If Gardner had assigned Mickelson because his pretty face would look better on TV, then Pendergrast was going to deal with it directly. Not with Gardner. He was too political and could make Pendergrast's life very difficult if he wanted. No, Pendergrast would ride that Mickelson kid so hard, he'll be begging for a job writing parking tickets. Anything to get out. This was Pendergrast's case and nobody—*nobody*—was going to get in his way.

He pushed his foot on the accelerator and the car sped off down Interstate 4.

The first thing that Kevin noticed was the man's tongue. It was blue and protruding from the swollen lips of his open mouth. The body was lying in an alcove of the faux mineshaft that served as the queue tunnel for Prospector Mountain.

When Kevin arrived, he saw several security guards standing at the entrance to the tunnel. He also noticed a few more guards positioned at the top of the tunnel near the ride loading platform.

Kevin approached wearing his street clothes and found Jerry directing several more security guards to position barricades around the ride area. A sign was placed out front informing the guests who would arrive in four hours that Prospector Mountain was closed today for routine maintenance. *We apologize for the inconvenience.*

Jerry gripped Kevin's arm and led him to the tunnel entrance. He spoke quickly in a nervous whisper as they walked. "Like I said on the phone, one of my guards found him and called me first. I got the basics from him and then, first thing, I called you. I waited as long as I could before I called the cops. Had to. Although, I knew it would take a few conversations before the news made it to Pendergrast. I bought you as much time as I could. But Pendergrast or some uniforms could show up any minute, so let's be careful."

Jerry led Kevin up the tunnel, which was illuminated by overhead lights. About a third of the way up the corridor they stopped. A nervous-looking security guard spotted Jerry and straightened his posture. Behind the guard was the body.

It was a man. Maybe in his forties. The tongue was poking out. The eyes were open, bulging, vacant. The scene was virgin, untainted. No photographer yet. No Medical Examiner. And no Pendergrast. The evidence was fresh. But Kevin knew he had to work quickly.

He held out his hand to the security guard and asked for his flashlight. After an approving nod from Jerry, the kid handed it over and Kevin approached the body.

Kevin was careful not to get too close and risk tainting the evidence. He flipped on the flashlight. Squatted low to the ground and held up the light. He moved it deliberately over the corpse. There was clearly some trauma to the skin on the throat. It was red and irritated. This guy had been garroted, too. The hands looked normal. No broken nails or other defensive wounds. No visible blood under the fingernails. The guy was probably taken by surprise, overpowered, like the others. He moved the beam of light up and down the body's arms and legs. The guy was definitely a tourist, dressed in a pair of shorts and an un-tucked polo shirt. There—Kevin spotted it. On the outside of the left leg was a mark. It was a burn, like the other victims. Kevin didn't need to guess what caused it. Dry ice. He found another burn mark, smaller and tougher to spot, on the back of the left hand.

He scanned the ground around the body, looking for a footprint, something dropped, anything. There was nothing. This was such a high traffic area, with literally thousands of people passing through every day. A footprint would be a pretty dubious piece of evidence. But it would be something tangible.

There was a commotion at the entrance to the tunnel and Kevin recognized a distinctive voice. He tossed the flashlight back to the guard, offered a curt "thanks," and walked quickly up the corridor towards the ride loading area. He nodded at Jerry before he disappeared around the corner, confirming that it was indeed victim number three.

Jerry offered a resigned nod in return and turned back toward the tunnel entrance. As Kevin rounded a corner, out of sight, he heard Pendergrast's nasal voice booming.

"Jerry, Jerry. We really must stop meeting like this. People will talk."

"Hello, Lou."

"Can I make a suggestion? Why don't you guys set up a kiosk out there next to the hot dog guy where you can sell special Empire Realm Life Insurance policies. You could capitalize on a market opportunity."

"Look, Lou, the park opens at nine and I expect any police tape to be down by then. I'll keep the ride closed so you can do whatever you need, but no crime scene tape."

"Well, that's really my decision, isn't it? My case. My decisions. Now I've got some police work to do here and you're contaminating my crime scene. Take your flunky and get lost. Now."

"I mean it about the police tape, Lou."

"And I mean it about the life insurance. Good-bye, Jerry. I'll keep in touch. I promise."

Kevin didn't listen any longer. As much as he would have liked to eavesdrop on Pendergrast's investigation, he couldn't risk being discovered. Kevin continued up the corridor until he reached the loading area. He offered a friendly nod to the two curious security guards and slipped out the employee exit.

Later that morning Jerry met Kevin at a Waffle House near the park. Jerry was in full eyebrow-pulling mode.

"I can't stay long," Jerry said. "It's a total shitstorm. PR, media, Oglethorpe. This is a nightmare."

"Do the media know it's a murder?"

"I don't know. I don't think so. But three deaths within a few weeks, even if they're only thought to be a freakish coincidence of accidents, that's still really bad. The only way it could get worse is if it comes out publicly that they were murders. We've got the whole Anniversary Celebration coming up, tour packages booked, tickets pre-sold. If people get spooked and start canceling, I don't even want to think about it."

They sipped coffee and Kevin salted a plate of scrambled eggs. "What can you tell me about this victim?"

"Nothing. Pendergrast has clamped down. I called Gardner and demanded that he take down the police tape before the park opened. He was a jerk about it, but he did it. You know Gardner. He understands that tourism drives this town. But Pendergrast was furious. He's not telling me anything."

Kevin nodded. He took a bite. "Here's what I can tell you," he said, chewing. "It's the same killer. He was strangled. There were also dry ice burns on his leg and hand."

More eyebrow tugging. "Shit . . ."

"Exactly when and where did the family report him missing?"

"That's the worst part. Since the last victim, I've had my security staff on alert for any missing persons reports. If any came in, especially at night, they were to immediately notify me and authorize a systematic, park-wide search. It's what we call a level one priority, like when a parent reports a lost kid. But the family didn't report him missing until hours later, after they were back in their hotel room. Evidently, they had split up and weren't expecting him back for a while. By the time they suspected something was wrong, the guy was already cold."

Kevin nodded. That was a bad break. "Since we eliminated Sheila's husband, I've been refining my opinion of the killer. I believe this is even worse than we thought."

The blood drained from Jerry's face. "Explain to me how this could possibly be worse."

"I think these killings were random, making them very difficult to solve. We have no idea what the motive is. All we have is limited physical evidence."

"Random?"

"Jerry, I believe that we're dealing with a serial killer."

"Oh God . . ." Jerry tugged hard at his left eyebrow. "Why do you think *that*?"

Kevin took a big sip of coffee and explained to Jerry what he had explained to Special Agent Milt Benning the other day. Kevin continued eating his breakfast.

"Okay," said Kevin, swallowing a bite of sausage. "That's the bad news. But here's what we do have: the beginnings of a profile. I spoke to Milt Benning at the FBI just before you came in. He's worked up a preliminary profile and we compared notes. Let's start with the psych. That's kinda tough, with only a couple of kills to use to map the landscape of the guy's demented mind. But Milt's come up with a little . . . some based on the FBI's behavioral science database and some just his best conjecture. The killer is unassuming. Quiet. Doesn't stand out in a crowd. Maybe even shy. He's just started killing like this, although he may have hurt other people in the past—just not in this way. He likes it. He likes it so much that he's done it three times in two months. He gets off on it, maybe literally. As a child, his parents were emotionally disconnected from him, maybe even physically disconnected. Milt even suggested that he might have been a foster kid or raised by another relative. He probably began by abusing animals. Hurting animals provided him with something, fulfilled some need. But as time went on, that wasn't enough. He fought his impulses, probably for years. But has finally given in to his needs. He's accepted who he is and maybe even feels justified in his actions. In fact, he's proud of what he's doing, so much so that he lifts a small, personal trophy from each victim. To remember his accomplishment. I spoke to one of your guards who told me that the guy found this morning was missing a baseball cap." Kevin stopped talking, scooping some egg onto a piece of buttered toast. Jerry looked like he was going to be sick. "You okay?" Kevin asked him.

"Yeah . . ." Jerry muttered unconvincingly, staring at Kevin's plate.

"All right," Kevin continued. "Let's talk about the physical profile and M.O. Our perp is a man, in his twenties or thirties. Caucasian. Looks like the guy next door. He's a big boy, or at least strong. He overpowers his victims, probably helped by the element of surprise. He comes up behind them and before they know what's happened, he's got something around their neck, a woven fabric of some sort. He's strong enough to make the kill quickly without being discovered. You're not going to like this, but he's definitely a cast member. He knows the park too well.

He knows where the cameras are and he knows where he can quietly ambush someone without being spotted. And then leave the body somewhere without being seen. His job or location in the park gives him access to dry ice. I don't think dry ice has anything to do with the actual murder—I think he hides the bodies somewhere near dry ice until he can drag them out and display them. Violet suspected that the dry ice burns were at the time of death or immediately post-mortem."

"Wait a minute—display them? These bodies were all hidden. Shit, one of them was even *buried,* for God's sake."

"Ask yourself: displayed for whom? I believe those bodies were hidden so they *would* be discovered. By tourists. He wants tourists to find them. Each of the victims was positioned and hidden just well enough to keep them secret from the casual employees working third shift but not so well that the crowds of tourists would miss them."

Jerry rubbed his face. This was definitely not what he wanted to hear. "But the body this morning wasn't discovered by a tourist. One of my guards found him."

"That's right," Kevin said, holding up his mug for a coffee refill. He hadn't slept all night and was postponing the inevitable crash. "Thanks." The waiter moved away. "But that was an accident. You told me earlier that your guard lost a key and was retracing his steps trying to find it. He had already done a security walk-through of the Prospector Mountain line tunnel and it was clear. When he went back in later, which was unscheduled, to look for his key he found the body. He wasn't supposed to go back in. The killer knew the routine. I talked to some of the third-shifters from last night and nobody saw anything. That body was put there to cause the maximum effect on the first tourists who got in line to ride the Mountain."

"But why? I don't understand."

"It's a message of some sort. I'm not sure what. Yet. It could be some sort of issue with Empire Realm. He could have a problem with tourists. But make no mistake, our boy is a compulsive killer and his jones is up. This is a lot of activity and he's enjoying it too much. I'll bet that buried in his past are other victims, undiscovered. But he seems to have found some special trigger here, maybe lying dormant until a few weeks ago. He'll kill again soon, I promise, unless he's stopped." Kevin shoved a half a piece of toast into his mouth, chewing vigorously. Perhaps it was the caffeine or the rush of his old skills being dusted off, but he felt suddenly reenergized. And famished.

Jerry, on the other hand, looked positively green. "This is awful, Kevin. How can you eat like that?"

"I've jerked around too long on this case. My judgment errors may have cost this latest victim his life. I wasted so much time focusing on the security tapes and the mysterious man in the tie that I lost focus. All this information has been right in front of me the whole time. But it took this morning for it to really crystallize."

"So what do you want to do?"

"I'm done screwing around in a pointless haystack search through people's lockers. It's risky because I've almost been caught a few times. And I haven't turned anything up there yet. Stan Tokarz in Indiana is still digging through Midwest Tours, but so far that's a dead end, further supporting the theory of a cast member killer. What do I want to do? Start with the facts. We know that dry ice was probably the cause of the skin burns. I want to know everything about how dry ice is used at Empire Realm. By the time I'm done, I want to be a freaking dry ice-ologist. Once I understand that, I can start working backwards and figure out who has access to the most likely areas. In the meantime, run another report on who worked all *three* nights that people were killed. That should narrow it down a little more. And let's keep targeted on cast members who work in the Lonesome Gulch area. That should also help focus the list."

"Okay. Anything else?"

"Yeah," Kevin said, craning his neck for the waiter. "I could really go for some pancakes."

CHAPTER 17

It didn't go as planned. It was wrong. All wrong.

There were some purple and green striped plastic park barricades out in front of the ride, and a few too many security guards, but the ride was closed. It had been since the park opened.

Someone had found him. Someone had found him before the park opened.

There would be no accidental stumbling over the body. No horrified realization. No fearful clutching. No screaming.

This wasn't the way it was supposed to be.

Some happy family from the frozen fucking North was supposed to waddle blissfully into the Prospector Mountain tunnel, wide-eyed and eager to sit in their safety harnesses and pretend to be frightened. They would be smiling in anticipation, fresh from their complimentary hotel continental breakfast. They would round the corner and see the feet protruding from the alcove. Mr. Happy Family would crinkle his brow. *Hmm. What's all this?* He would investigate. Lean into the alcove. The man's dried lifeless eyeballs would stare back at him. *Oh my God . . .* He would see the blue tongue jutting out of the mouth. Realization would sink in. *He's dead! Oh my God!* Mrs. Happy

Family would scream. The fat Happy Kids would clutch their mother's flabby legs and join the screaming.

That was what was supposed to happen. Now it never would.

Petey had been able to witness the discoveries of the previous two bodies. What an incredible rush. Both of them. He knew they would find the bodies before they even did. He stood and watched them, waiting for that moment of realization. His heart raced in anticipation. His breath came in short, shallow pants. Tunnel vision set in as he focused on the discovery. It was heady, sensual. There was an intense build-up of anxiety, to the point where Petey didn't think he would be able to contain himself. He felt like he would explode. And just at the point where it became the most intense, where his heart was thundering in his chest—that moment, that split second before the realization, where they've noticed something but haven't yet discovered what, when you know that in a few seconds they will, that it's past the point of no return—in that moment, where you can't swallow, where you can't breathe, where you alone in the world know what will happen next, at that moment, you can actually *see* the realization come over their faces, like the shadow of a passing cloud. They realize what it is that they've found. And as they stumble back in horror, or scream, or cry, like the little girl in the playground, you can start breathing again. Deep, gulping breaths, like recovering from a wind sprint. Then the intensity starts to subside and giddiness takes its place. Your heart continues to race, because you know that you are responsible for the screaming and the crying. You are the only person in the world who knew what was going to happen and witnessing it is the most gratifying thing you've ever felt. Ever.

Watching that little girl as she shuffled her sandaled feet into the playground, you couldn't have hoped for a better discovery. Somehow, somehow the body had lain there buried in the sand for half the day—*half the day!*—before she walked out there with her melting ice cream. You would never have predicted that it would go undiscovered as long as it did. Never. But it did. And then you knew deep inside that you must have put the body there just for her. It was hers to discover. *Her* body. And you knew that the time spent preparing, digging the hole, making sure no one was around, was time well spent. Because you were able to put the body there, hidden from everyone else, waiting for her to find it. Then you watched as her shuffling step stumbled and the ice cream slipped from her wet fingers. She bent down to pick it up, her little lip quivering in sadness because she dropped her WilberBar in the nasty sand. And when she picked it up, her hand ended up on the man's nose. *His nose!* That was too perfect. Then she realized. She was just a kid, but she knew death when she saw it. And the shadow moved over her face and she screamed. It was glorious. Petey's body actually trembled from the release. The anticipation was exquisite, a nervous intensity like he had never felt before, and the release was like Rapture. He trembled and felt transformed. Truly glorious.

But he wouldn't be able to feel anything like that today and it made him furious. All that effort. All that risk. For nothing. *Nothing.* He hadn't been able to sleep all night, imagining the fat Happy Family when they discovered the body in the tunnel. As he lay in bed, his heartbeat quickened at the thought of the discovery to come. When he came in this morning before the park opened, he positioned himself with a clear view of the ride entrance. He wouldn't be able to see the actual moment of discovery, but he would be able to watch the first guests go into the tunnel. He would feel the same anticipation, for he would know what awaited them. He would know their future. He would count off the seconds in his head and be able to see, in his mind's eye, their every step, their crinkled brows, their terrified realization. He would wait for the screams that he knew would come and he would bask, trembling, in the emotional release as people ran and police swarmed.

But none of that would happen now. The body had been discovered already. Sometime overnight. By a cast member. It was wrong. Petey hadn't even been there. He had missed it. And there probably wasn't even a scream. It was all wrong.

It was too much like his time in the restaurant. He, like so many in Orlando's service trade, had been a waiter at a national chain restaurant. He worked at Pepper's on Highway 436, just north of the airport. He had to wear a demeaning uniform consisting of a pullover shirt with thick blue and white stripes, complete with suspenders and an abundance of embarrassing buttons. And he had to deal with the rudeness of humanity. Every foul tourist on his way to a flight home seemed to stop at Pepper's to make his life hell. They complained. They were demanding. They didn't tip—why should they? They would never see him again. They were flying away in an hour and a half.

Most of all they were rude, like the guests at Empire Realm. They felt entitled. Entitled to unmitigated ass kissing. Petey did it, but it pained him. They demanded their steaks re-cooked. They complained to the manager about him. They called him names and laughed at him when he left their tables. He hated them.

Sometimes, when someone was being especially rude, he would pour powdered laxative into their iced tea. He would deliver it with a smile and wait until it was drained before refilling it. His heart would race and he would chuckle to himself at the thought of the powerful laxative kicking in at 30,000 feet over St. Louis or, even better, the middle of the Atlantic. The Europeans were the absolute worst.

But it was unsatisfying on a fundamental level. He was never able to witness the retribution he was doling out. He imagined seeing their ruddy faces as the intestinal cramps seized them. But it really wasn't the same as being there. He would look at his watch and wonder if they were in the plane's lavatory yet. He would smile at the thought of them standing in a long line down the airplane's aisle, waiting to use the bathroom, watching desperately for the *Ocupado* sign to go dim. He imagined the line moving slowly, as it tends to do, and them losing all control of their bowels right there in the aisle, their liquid filth running like a faucet from their shorts and down their pale, white legs.

But he never knew for sure. He always wondered.

As time went on, the laxative was sometimes replaced with other things. He would spend long hours at night crushing aspirin and Benadryl into fine powder. He even used some rat poison he bought at Home Depot a couple of times. The rat poison was saved for special patrons, truly deserving patrons. And Petey would close his eyes and imagine their last painful gasps of life. The ambulance whisking them away from the airport tarmac just after landing. But it would be too late. Too late . . .

He was never able to witness it, though. He just tasted what the anticipation must feel like, how intense it *could* be. How the inevitable release could consume him. He was just tasting it, like licking the peel of an apple. He wanted to take big, juicy bites, to swallow the fruit's flesh, to feel it inside of him.

He eventually quit Pepper's and bounced between a few other restaurant gigs before landing at Empire Realm. Every day at Empire Realm, thousands—*thousands*—of fat, entitled pigs streamed through the gates. Rude Northeasterners, stupid Midwesterners, angry Europeans. They demanded and expected and never, ever, showed a trace of gratitude.

Here. Here at Empire Realm, he would be able to bite the apple. Here he would taste the anticipation. Swallow the release. Here he would know the intensity he only imagined at Pepper's.

But he couldn't poison people at Empire Realm and still be a witness to their death and discovery. The timing would be too unpredictable. He wouldn't be able to feel the anticipation and eventual release of the body being discovered. Petey needed to control the circumstances of the death and placement of the body. He needed to have control of the body between the time of death and discovery.

The killing had to be done quickly and quietly. He hadn't thought before about how he might kill someone with his own hands. He had only used poison at Pepper's. It had been remote, antiseptic. Easy. A gun was out of the question. Too noisy. He also didn't like the idea of stabbing. It was closer and more intimate than a gun, which he liked, but it was too messy. He couldn't hide a body that was hemorrhaging all over the sidewalk. He needed a method that was quiet and clean.

As a teen, he had once strangled a neighbor's dog by tying a rope around its neck and swinging it in circles for twenty minutes. It had been a fascinating rush, an experiment in "what would happen if?" But Petey had felt strangely disappointed afterwards. The dog, a brown terrier, had just laid there, a hairy, limp mess. After the struggle of getting the rope secured and the physical rush of swinging it around, its body twitching and writhing at the end of the tether, the resulting limp, motionless dog seemed somehow anticlimactic. He placed the dog on the neighbor's front stoop and retreated to his bedroom, where he watched out the window for its discovery. More than two hours passed before Mrs. Hastings came home. She parked the car and Petey felt his heart race in anticipation. She walked up to the front door and there was the dog, Chipper, dead on the Welcome mat. Mrs. Hastings dropped her groceries and erupted into a fit of tears. Her children were grown and Chipper had been like a child to her. She cradled the dead animal in her arms and wept openly right there in the front yard.

Petey had watched the discovery unfold before his eyes with a breathless excitement that bordered on the sexual. He became aroused and found himself masturbating as he watched Mrs. Hasting weep next door. It was an amazing, transforming experience.

So, as he stood at his assigned position a few weeks after starting at Empire Realm, he decided that strangulation would be the best way. It was close and intimate. It was clean. And it was quiet. There would be no screaming to attract attention.

Petey was a big man. Six feet, four inches tall. And strong. He didn't work out; he just had a natural strength. He knew that he could choke almost anyone he chose and be able to control the entire course of events.

The first one had been in May. A customer had been particularly rude to him. She accused him of taking a twenty-dollar bill from her but only making change for a ten. She had definitely given him a ten. When Petey protested, she argued and said "if you think I gave you a ten, you're obviously a big, dumb moron!" They argued some more and eventually Petey gave her the change for the twenty. That night his till was ten bucks short and it came out of his paycheck. He was furious.

He became obsessed with strangling a tourist. He wanted to choke the woman, but she was long gone. But they were all the same. He would stand there in the park and watch them go by, imagining his hands around their necks, feeling their muscles tensing, seeing their eyes roll back in their heads, sensing the life draining from their bodies. In his mind, he killed them all.

He planned it carefully. There was a Men's room off a side

street in Lonesome Gulch. It was surprisingly secluded. No security cameras could reach it. In order to get to it, you actually had to walk around a corner and out of sight. A privacy wall separated it from the backstage area. Petey waited until shortly before the park closed and positioned himself nearby. He lingered and watched. As the evening wore on, the crowds grew thinner. Finally, he saw a couple approach heading to the exit. The woman went into the Ladies' room, which faced out onto the street and the man went around the corner to the Men's room. Petey knew the bathroom was empty because he had been watching it for some time. He blocked the path to the Men's room with a nearby "Out of Order" barricade (it was actually meant for a park ATM machine) and quickly followed the man into the restroom.

The man stood there at a urinal relieving himself. Petey didn't hesitate. Still wearing his costume's gloves, he removed his costume's kerchief and swiftly brought it down over the man's head.

"Hey!" the man yelled, startled and angry. It was the last word he ever said.

Petey pulled the blue scarf tightly around the man's neck. They stumbled backwards, away from the urinal. The man's hands reached up and clutched at his throat, clawing desperately for air. His stream of urine sprayed up onto the wall as he fought.

But Petey was strong, much stronger than the man. His gloved hands trembled under the strain, pulling the scarf as tightly as he could. The man's bearded face went pink. His legs kicked back wildly. But only for a few minutes. The man's complexion eventually turned bright crimson and all breath left his body. Petey felt the muscles relax and the joints go limp. But still Petey pulled the kerchief tighter. He had to make sure.

He couldn't have him waking up overnight in the box. After a few more minutes, he was sure the man was dead. Petey took a pair of sunglasses from the man's shirt pocket as a personal memento to remember him by.

Breathing heavily, he carried the man outside and hid him where he knew no one would find him. And then he waited some more. The man's wife hung around for a few minutes searching for him. She even went around the corner and opened the Men's room door a crack, calling his name. Finally, she gave up and assumed that she had missed him and headed for the exit. She never saw Petey and he, in turn, never saw her again.

It was odd. He didn't feel as energized by the killing as he thought he would. It was handled swiftly and efficiently. Almost businesslike. It was over so quickly and the adrenaline rush so strong, he didn't have time to experience any emotions at all. It was just something that had to be done.

Really, it was a means to an end. The real experience was in the discovery. The actual murder was a compulsion, but the placement of the body was a deliberate statement. Though Petey had expected to kill someone that evening, he didn't know for sure. It was an impulse of opportunity. The discovery, however, he could control. He knew it was coming and the exquisite anticipation of it was what drove him.

The next morning, the discovery had fulfilled his every expectation.

That's why today's disappointment was so troubling. Now there would be no exquisite anticipation, no intense excitement, no heart pounding, no afterglow trembling. It was like waking up Christmas morning and discovering that someone already opened up all your presents. Petey was livid.

He looked over at Prospector Mountain and saw several security guards lingering near the entrance to the tunnel. A chubby, balding guy in a wrinkled sport jacket walked past the barricade and into the tunnel. Petey recognized him as a cop—the homicide detective who had interviewed practically everyone in the park, Petey included. He wouldn't find anything to point him in Petey's direction. Petey was too careful.

Petey also saw a redheaded guy in a miner's costume walk up. He chatted briefly with one of the security guards and then turned around. The redheaded guy was familiar. Petey had seen him before—in the park, in the locker room—and he didn't like him. He asked too many questions. He wandered around too much. Petey didn't like him at all.

Petey didn't have any friends at the park, but he kept a pretty close watch on the happenings around him. He had never seen the redheaded guy before a few weeks ago. Not, in fact, until *after* the man in the sand was found by the little girl. And now, this body discovery had been ruined. Petey began to wonder if the arrival of the curious redheaded guy and today's debacle weren't somehow related. But how? He wasn't sure.

But one thing Petey was sure about: he needed to feed his cravings. The thrill of the discovery was too great a rush and the park was the perfect a location to facilitate his hobby. In his heart he knew that it was only a matter of time before the heat would become too great and he would have to move on. Nothing would put a crimp in his hobby more than getting caught. But he didn't want to leave before he absolutely had to. If the redheaded guy was somehow a threat to Petey's hobby or even Petey himself, that would not be tolerated.

Petey decided that he would keep an eye on the miner. If anything seemed suspicious, Petey would act swiftly. And decisively.

Petey continued to watch the ride entrance until a guest approached him and he had to get back to his job. That entire day, he performed his job satisfactorily, although distractedly. He was consumed in thought.

For the first time since he came to Empire Realm, Petey fantasized about killing someone other than a tourist.

CHAPTER 18

Kevin stood over his kitchen sink and ate a ham sandwich. Every time he stood at the sink and ate, he couldn't help but think about that old cliche of the bachelor who didn't have any clean dishes. But that wasn't why Kevin ate over the sink. Through the small window over the basin he had an unobstructed view of Lake Jessup.

He could look at the lake for hours. After he had purchased the house nearly three years ago, he would gaze out at the water for entire afternoons, sometimes on his back porch, sometimes here in the kitchen. The water, the reflecting sun, the passing egrets, the gators—they gave him peace at a time in his life when he needed it most.

He stood there, chewing, thinking about his morning. He was exhausted but too wired to sleep. After the Waffle House with Jerry, Kevin had reported for work, as scheduled. Chuckie sent him home, telling him that the ride was closed for unscheduled repairs. Before Kevin left, Chuckie threw in the comment "I don't know who you're sleeping with, but they must be pretty important." On Kevin's surprised but amused look, Chuckie explained that he had twice wanted to fire him and had twice been prevented. The first time was when Kevin had abandoned his post in the search for the man in the tie. The second time was the previous day when Kevin suddenly went home with the excuse of "being sick." Chuckie pressed him about who his angel was but Kevin just smiled and shook his head. *Thanks, Jerry.*

Kevin spent the balance of the morning learning everything he could about dry ice. Jerry arranged for one of his security guards, a young brunette woman named Gwen, to be his guide. Gwen was a recent graduate of an OSHA-certified dry ice safety seminar. She took Kevin to "The Freezer," a garage-sized cold storage room where the park's primary dry ice supplies were kept. It was here that the individuals responsible for handling dry ice came to restock.

The room was aptly named. When he stepped inside from the warm, humid outside air, the sharp cold caught his breath. Carbon Dioxide only stays frozen when it is -109.3 degrees Fahrenheit or colder. The Freezer wasn't that cold, of course (or people's skin could freeze upon entering), but the ambient temperature fell somewhere around zero. The room was ringed with deep freezer cabinets where the actual blocks of dry ice were stored. Each cabinet had grated screens set at two-foot intervals. White, smoke-like vapor wafted gently through the grates. Kevin could hear the loud whir of fans throughout the room. The fan noise seemed to be coming from behind a three-foot screen covering the lower portion of three walls.

Gwen explained: "Normal air is 78% Nitrogen, 21% Oxygen, and only about one-third of one percent Carbon Dioxide. If the concentration of CO_2 rises over about 5%, the air becomes toxic. Since CO_2 is heavier than air, it sinks to the floor. The screens have fans behind them to draw it out and vent it. Nitrogen and oxygen are pumped in from the ceiling. Rule number one is that nobody is allowed in here for more than three minutes. And if you start panting or breathing heavily, get your butt back outside pronto. The cold storage lockers there have screens because the sublimation of the CO_2 from solid to gas will cause an airtight container to expand and eventually explode. Not a good thing. The idea is that you come in, use those gloves and tongs to load up your blocks, and then get out. That's the Freezer in a nutshell."

While there, Kevin observed several cast members come and go, replenishing their dry ice stores. One young man came and packed a small trailer full of the blocks, handling the cargo with thick gloves. The trailer was pulled behind a golf cart and would carry the dry ice blocks to the Lonesome Gulch rides that used it for effects. When water is dripped or misted on a block of dry ice, it accelerates the sublimation process and creates a thick fog-like vapor. Dry ice was even used for a portion of the Prospector Mountain ride.

Another cast member placed several blocks of dry ice into a pushcart that served as a sidewalk ice-cream vending station. And another employee placed several blocks into a cold beverage-vending cart.

There was no Freezer guard or steward. Cast members accessed The Freezer individually via a cipher lock on the door. If the small, numbered buttons were pressed in a particular sequence, the door unlocked. There was only one combination and no record was kept of when it was opened. Pendergrast had the security tapes from the Freezer camera, but they were basically useless. There were just too many people coming and going at all hours to zero-in on any viable suspects.

After leaving The Freezer, Gwen took Kevin to several places in the park where dry ice was used. He was most impressed by the vast plumes of mist that rose up in the Ice Haus, simulating the cloud-shrouded peaks of the Alps. Kevin recognized a few faces as he traveled the park—faces from Jerry's list—but at the end of the morning he didn't feel any closer to identifying a suspect than he did at the beginning.

Kevin stopped by the Reverend's on his way home to check on Lucius. He was doing better. Not very talkative. He was ashamed of falling back into his habit and couldn't look Kevin in the eyes. Kevin tried to reassure him that it was just a temporary setback. Four months was a long time. That was definitely progress. He and the Reverend were there for him and would help him get through it. Kevin didn't stay long. He left as the Reverend placed a bowl of soup on the table for Lucius.

Kevin got a brief update on his cell phone from Stan Tokarz in Indianapolis. As instructed, Tokarz had abandoned the inquiries into the identity of the man in the tie. But he had continued digging for other leads, including any disgruntled former employees. Although a few folks had resigned from various Midwest Tours offices over the past two months, none of those resignations was particularly rancorous and none raised a red flag for Tokarz. Corporate HR had told him that no one had been fired in that same period from any office. Tokarz found that hard to believe, so he did some further checking—called a few branch offices himself, checked with several states' unemployment compensation offices—and, hell's bells, they weren't kidding. No one had been fired in two months. He even learned that there is an Internet community for former employees so they can keep in touch with each other and with their friends still at the company. Tokarz again said he was thinking about filling out an application. That was all he had so far and would next move on to hate correspondence: complaint letters, e-mails, and phone messages. Kevin thanked him and hung up just as he pulled into his driveway.

Kevin finished his ham sandwich and rinsed his fingers in

the sink. He was convinced that the key to finding the killer was figuring out where the bodies had been hidden before they were placed for discovery. At first Kevin had thought that they had been stored in the Freezer. But he had learned that there was activity there all night during third shift. A body couldn't stay undiscovered very long in there. He started to run through some of the other possibilities in his mind when there was a loud knock on the front door. He wasn't expecting anyone.

He opened the door to reveal Sheila standing on his front stoop.

"Well, at least you're alive," she said.

"Sheila . . ." Kevin was surprised to see her. He had never brought her to his house. She must have looked him up and found it on her own. His surprise at seeing her caused him to hesitate for a beat, still holding the doorknob.

"So, are you going to invite me in?" she said.

"Yeah—sorry. Please."

He led her into the small living room. She looked around, surveying the place, picking up all the tiny details—the humble furnishings, the lack of photographs, an empty pizza box in the trashcan. After quickly taking it all in, she wheeled on him.

"How do you feel?"

"I'm okay now."

"I left three messages on your answering machine. I was worried."

Kevin cringed. Between the bar and Lucius and the new body, he hadn't been home until just a few minutes ago. He just hadn't gotten to the answering machine yet. There was probably at least one message from Carlos on there, as well. "Sorry." He took her hand and led her to the living room. They sat on the couch.

He told her everything that had happened since yesterday afternoon, starting with the shock of running into Carlos and his family. He told her about the memories flooding back, about visions of the accident. About going to the bar and almost losing his sobriety. About the Reverend and Lucius. About the latest victim at Empire Realm. About the dry ice research this morning. He even told her about his ham sandwich.

Sheila listened quietly, nodding occasionally, stating concern about the killer still at large in the park. When Kevin finished, her face softened and she shook her head. "I'm sorry. You probably think I'm some kind of Fatal Attraction stalker or something. I just really was worried. That's all."

"Thanks. It's been a while since anyone was worried about me." He offered her a soft drink. As he poured her drink over some ice, he asked, "How did you know where I live?"

"Yellow Pages under Private Investigators. When I showed up this morning for work, Chuckie sent me home because the ride was down. Now I know why. So I ended up with the day off. The kids were already taken care of. I called you and when you still didn't answer, I got worried. I pictured you lying in the middle of your floor, all alone, stricken with dengue fever. I decided to drive up and make sure you were okay."

Kevin nodded, genuinely touched. He didn't know what to say. All he could manage as he handed her the drink was, "Would you like a ham sandwich?"

Sheila declined with a smile. Sipped her drink. They were quiet for a moment. Kevin sat next to her on the couch, watching her. Sheila gazed around the room again, lost in thought. She turned and looked at him earnestly.

"Can I ask a favor?" she said.

"Sure."

"Don't say 'sure' yet. This would mean a lot to me, but if you're not comfortable, it's okay."

Kevin cocked his head. What kind of favor was this?

"I'd like to see a picture of Maria," Sheila said.

Kevin didn't see that coming. He paused a moment to process her request. He thought suddenly about what the Reverend had asked him: *Would Sheila and Maria have been friends?* He remembered his response.

Sheila mistook his thoughtful silence for discomfort. "I'm sorry—I shouldn't have asked you. It's—"

"It's okay. Really. Wait here."

He disappeared into the bedroom. Sheila took another look around the living room. This was clearly a "man's" house. No candles or potpourri. No flowers. One neglected plant on the floor by the patio door. Dust on the shelves—not too thick, meaning that he *had* dusted, just not in a while. The end table could use a lamp or something. The dish soap on the kitchen counter was in the manufacturer's bottle. But despite all that, the place was neat and well maintained. Kevin Lonnegan was by no means a pig. On the contrary, he actually appeared quite neat. It was just clear that no woman had influenced the home's decor.

Kevin returned with a small box. He set it on the coffee table and lifted the lid. Inside was a stack of photographs.

"This is from our wedding," Kevin said, handing Sheila a photo.

"She was gorgeous," Sheila said. She meant it.

The picture captured a happy, smiling couple. Kevin looked slightly younger, but was almost unchanged. His hair was a little longer, perhaps. But Sheila was drawn immediately to the image of Maria. She was stunning in her white dress. Smooth, olive skin. Long black hair adorned with baby's breath. Full lips a ruby red in her wedding-day make-up. Her eyes were striking—a deep, vibrant brown, tinged with flecks of what looked like gold. This was a couple at their most joyous, filled with the expectant promise of the rest of their shared lives.

It was a beautiful and, knowing what eventually occurred, heartbreaking image. Sheila understood why Kevin kept it in a box.

He showed her several more photos, some of Maria alone—laughing on the beach, posing in front of Cinderella's castle at Disney World, standing pregnant in front of a Christmas tree—and some of the two of them together. There were also a few pictures of Kevin's family—his parents, his brothers, their families—and Maria's family, a large smiling clan of second-generation Cuban-Americans.

At the bottom of the box were two pictures turned face down. Kevin just stared at them. He made no move to pick them up.

"May I?" Sheila asked, searching his eyes. Kevin nodded. She reached in.

The first picture was from a prenatal sonogram—a blurry gray image on a black background of a baby in profile. Along the side of the picture were the words: "Lonnegan. Boy. 20 weeks." Sheila ran a finger over the profile, recalling the ultrasound images from her own pregnancies. The baby's nose and chin were clearly visible. A tiny hand was held up in what appeared to be a friendly wave. She reached into the box and lifted the last photo.

It was a picture of a tiny baby, obviously premature. He was lying in a warmer bassinet in a hospital, a blue and white-striped receiving blanket behind him. He had surprisingly thick black hair. His skin was a dark pink and his tiny eyes were clenched shut. Both an oxygen tube and a feeding tube ran to his nose.

An IV line led from his forearm. What was presumably Kevin's palm held the baby's entire tiny hand. Sheila swallowed.

"Is this your only picture of Michael?" she said. Kevin nodded. "He had your nose."

"And Maria's hair."

Sheila carefully placed all the photos back into box. "Thank you," she said. Kevin smiled a sad *you're welcome*. "Look, Kevin, if you're not ready for a relationship, I understand. I do. I'm not sure if I am either. I mean, my divorce isn't even final yet. Plus I've been with Phil since I was in high school. A relationship would be a big deal for both of us. I think you're a nice guy and I wouldn't mind being your friend. I just don't want to—"

Kevin took her hand in his. Looked directly into her eyes. "I'm not very good at expressing myself. But I really care about you. I haven't felt this way about anyone in a long time."

"But . . ." Sheila's eyes drifted over to the box of photos on the coffee table. A beautiful dead wife was hard to compete with. Kevin placed the cardboard top on the box.

"Maria's gone." He said it definitively, like he had made a decision. "She's gone." He held Sheila's hand in both of his. "You're right here."

He leaned slowly towards her and kissed her. Softly. Gently. Sheila's eyes closed and her lips relaxed to return the kiss. Kevin leaned back and fixed his eyes on her. She had no doubt that he was completely there with her. Intent on her. She felt her heartbeat quicken.

He leaned towards her again and this time she met him halfway. Again the kiss was delicate. Kevin lifted his hand and brushed her cheek, placing his palm on the side of her neck. The kiss grew more passionate. Hungry. Without even being conscious of it, Sheila's hands reached for Kevin's back and pulled him close. She heard herself utter a little moan as their lips parted and their tongues found each other.

In another moment, Kevin was leading Sheila into his bedroom.

Sheila lay in bed watching Kevin sleep. He was peaceful. Strong. Beautiful. He was a good lover, a little awkward from being out of practice, but gentle, and not at all selfish. She wasn't used to having a man care about her needs first. Phil was neither a gentle nor generous lover.

It felt good to have Kevin's lips on her lips. To feel his unshaven, sandpaper chin against her neck. To feel his hands on her body. Caress her. Touch her in a loving way. No man had touched her like that since the early days of her marriage, before the kids, when Phil still cared about her. And she cared about him.

She didn't even feel self-conscious about her body. She knew that she was in decent shape, especially after three kids, but she had issues with her breasts. Let's face it, girl, they're small. It didn't help her body image that every few months of their marriage Phil offered to buy her breast enlargement surgery. But now, lying here with Kevin, she actually felt good about herself. Kevin didn't seem to care. In fact, he had clearly enjoyed her body just the way it was. He had even told her she was beautiful.

Afterwards, they talked. Not about anything in particular. Her kids. A case he worked on last year. Her schoolwork. It was nice. Comfortable. She knew he hadn't slept in almost two days and she stroked his hair until he nodded off.

Now she lay in bed, thoroughly relaxed. Her mom had the kids. Her homework was actually done. She had just made love in the afternoon—on a weekday—with a wonderful man. All she was missing to make this a perfect day was a pint of Cherry Garcia.

She closed her eyes. She refused to go through her usual routine of *what if*? What if she fell in love? What if her kids didn't like him? What if he turned out to be a creep? What if he was the one that she could truly share her life with? What if he started drinking again? What if? What if? What if?

She took a deep breath and slowly exhaled, clearing her mind, just concentrating on her breathing. She committed to just enjoying the moment, not thinking about the future. Not worrying about anything. She rolled onto her back, pulled the sheet up, and closed her eyes. She was aware of her chest rising and falling. She smelled the floral fabric softener in the sheet. She heard the soft rhythm of Kevin's breathing beside her. The distant sound of birds out on the lake. A breeze rustling the live oak branches outside the window.

In a few minutes she was sound asleep, dreaming about Cherry Garcia.

CHAPTER 19

Murderland.

Christ. It actually said *Murder land.*

Jerry pulled his desk drawer open and rummaged frantically. There. He grabbed the bottle of Xanax and shook a pill into his mouth. He washed it down with the last swallow of yesterday's can of Diet Pepsi. A grimace. Flat, brown, room temperature sugar water.

The Orlando *Sentinel* was splayed out in front of him, open to the Editorial page. There, across the top, was the headline: *Murderland.* He had read the entire column three times and selected paragraphs several more than that. A few key quotes jumped out at him.

"Empire Realm seems more concerned about the marketing campaign for their Anniversary Celebration than they do about the safety of their guests . . . three murders in less than three months . . . apparently the work of a serial killer intent upon targeting tourists . . . if Empire management doesn't do something to ensure the safety of their paying guests, they might as well open a new pavilion and call it 'Murderland' . . . this needs to be stopped now, not only because people's lives are in danger, but because this lack of security will decimate Central Florida's lifeblood: tourism . . . not just an Empire Realm problem, but a Disney problem and a Sea World problem and a Universal problem . . . as a community, we cannot tolerate a whitewashing or a cover-up . . . we will see through the distraction of a multi-million dollar marketing campaign, and so will the rest of the world . . ."

The phone on Jerry's desk rang to life. Again. It had been ringing all morning. He placed it on "Do Not Disturb." He was in no mood to talk to the media. He was in no mood to talk to the tour group organizers. He was in no mood to talk to anyone.

He felt sick.

He had hoped that Kevin would have found the guy by now, but, in hindsight, that just wasn't realistic. Kevin didn't have the resources of the Sheriffs department and, as good a detective as he once was, he definitely had his problems. It was more than he could handle.

Jerry tugged at his left eyebrow and looked out the office window. From his second-floor view, he could see the main street of Lonesome Gulch and Prospector Mountain in the distance. Somewhere out there a killer was walking free, planning his next assault. And Jerry was helpless to do anything about it.

Who had leaked the story? Probably Pendergrast. The columnist, Carla Beck, was suspiciously easy on the cops in their inability to catch the murderer. She seemed to be laying all the blame at the feet of Empire Realm management. But it didn't matter who leaked it, it was bound to get out eventually.

Three deaths in less than three months? Of course that was going to attract attention. Pendergrast had interviewed half the park's cast members. Several of Jerry's own security staff knew as much as he did. There was no way the murders were going to remain quiet for very long. Hell, it was a miracle they stayed secret as long as they did.

Jerry rubbed his forehead. He had a headache that felt like flathead screwdrivers jammed into each of his temples. He would have to sell the house. He wouldn't be able to afford it once he lost this job. What would he do next? He had no idea. Forget about another Director of Security position. He was, after all, the chump who allowed three tourists to be garroted under his incompetent nose. He had a vision of himself sitting slack-jawed on a stool in a shopping mall food court, wearing an ill-fitting brown security guard uniform.

He put his head down on his desk.

"For God's sake, Engle. This is what you're doing? Perfect."

Jerry looked up. Standing in his doorway was Bill Oglethorpe. Great.

Oglethorpe probably thought he was napping. *Perfect* was right.

Oglethorpe sat down. "I see you're reading the paper," he said.

"Yeah. Love that new columnist."

"Do you have any idea what my morning has been like so far? And it's only nine-thirty? No, of course you don't, because you won't answer your goddamned phone. I tried calling you four times. Paged you. Tried your cell phone. I figured you were up to your eyeballs trying to handle our current situation. So I get my ass up from my desk on the other side of the park and haul it *all* the way over here, and this is what I find you busy doing? Jesus Christ, Jerry."

"I've been here since five A.M. I got a tip from a friend at the *Sentinel* and I came in. I've already worked with PR and Guest Relations to prepare statements for the press and our guests. I've briefed all of our security supervisors and I've drafted protocols for every scenario I can think of. You caught me at a bad moment."

"When are you going to have a good moment? I'm not filled with confidence, Engle. You don't know the avalanche of pressure I'm under. First, there's the press. CNN has called twice. All the networks. Both Katie Couric and Charlie Gibson have personally called and left messages. The fucking Travel Channel wants to put out a safety advisory. Then there's Marketing. McDonald's is threatening to cancel the Anniversary promotional tie-in. Pepsi is also thinking about backing out. Bruce Willis is demanding a whole battalion of bodyguards just to walk in the gate, let alone be our Grand Marshal. A whole tour package from Germany canceled this morning. More cancellations are expected. Have you looked at the stock market today? The exchange has only been open for a half hour, but Empire has fallen almost six percent already. Millions and millions of dollars, Engle. Hundreds of millions at stake. You think that you and I won't be sacrificed in the face of that? Huh? If I go down, I'm falling right on top of you, buddy."

Jerry just nodded. Millions of dollars. Not to mention three people's lives.

Oglethorpe continued. "Goldman Sachs, Merrill Lynch, Fidelity—shit, half of Wall Street is calling Jantsen right now. It's barely six-thirty in LA. They're calling him at home in Malibu. Jantsen doesn't like to be called at home, especially at five in the morning. Warren goddamned Buffet called him just a few minutes ago. Guess who Jantsen called right after that?"

Oglethorpe paused. He actually wanted Jerry to answer the question. "I don't know, Bill. Did he call you?"

"Don't be cute, Engle. You're in no position to be cute. You're goddamned right he called me. My ear is still ringing. So not only do I have the Empire brass in Hollywood screaming at me, but I've got every other attraction in Orlando screaming at me, too. It seems that tour groups are canceling all over town. Both

August Busch and Michael Eisner personally called to threaten lawsuits if this doesn't get fixed now. *Now,* Engle. And I don't think you're the guy to fix it anymore."

"I understand."

"No you don't. Although every fiber in my being wants to fire your ass right now, I can't. It would be a public relations nightmare. Although you'll eventually make an acceptable fall guy—and that *will* happen, believe me—it would reflect badly on the entire organization if we terminated you now. Even if you're incompetent, *we* hired you. Executive management would look incompetent by association. So, you stay. For now. And I expect your complete cooperation."

So Jerry would keep his job. For a while. Until the time came for him to become the "acceptable fall guy." It was just prolonging the inevitable. "What do you mean by 'cooperation'?"

Oglethorpe looked at Jerry for several seconds, not saying a word. Then: "A few days ago, Jantsen retained the services of an executive security consultancy. They arrived yesterday and have been getting up to speed on the park and the current situation. This damned newspaper column was an unfortunate development, but they're handling it. It's their show now. They report directly to Jantsen. And you now work for them."

Jerry closed his eyes. Waited a beat. Then opened them again. "Who did he hire?"

Oglethorpe pursed his lips. Then, without a word, he stood and left the room. He returned a moment later accompanied by a tall man in a pressed, black suit. The man was in his mid-forties, square-jawed and broadshouldered. His neatly trimmed brown hair was dusted with gray at the temples. His eyes were the color of steel.

"This is Vincent Coluccio from PRN Security Consultants," said Oglethorpe. PRN. Jerry had heard of them, of course.

Peirce, Robertson, & Neuberg. They were the premier corporate security firm in the world. Based in New York, they had offices in Chicago, L.A., Atlanta, London, Rome, Bogota, Rio de Janeiro, Tokyo, Berlin, Johannesburg, and Paris. They recruited from the FBI, Secret Service, Scotland Yard, Interpol, Mossad. A former KGB agent headed the Berlin office. They were large, serious, and exorbitantly expensive. "Vince, meet Jerry Engle."

Jerry stood and extended his hand cautiously. Jerry was no weakling—he used to be a cop, after all—but he felt his fingers crush under the iron grip of Vincent Coluccio. As Coluccio leaned across the desk, shaking his hand, Jerry caught a glimpse of a shoulder holster peeking out from beneath his suit jacket. Coluccio just nodded, his eyes locked onto Jerry's, and said nothing. But Jerry knew what he was thinking. He could read it in his expression. He even heard it inside his head. *So this is Engle? This is the guy who gave up three victims? Pathetic.*

Oglethorpe didn't take his eyes off Jerry, either. "Engle is going to provide you with whatever assistance you need, Vince. Whatever you need—employee records, timecards, security logs, even a fresh cup of decaf—you ask Jerry and he'll get it for you right away. He's at your disposal twenty-four/seven. Right, Jerry?"

Jerry had to concentrate to keep his shoulders from sagging. "Whatever you say, Bill."

Coluccio finally spoke. "Good. Thanks, Jerry." His voice was deep, confident. He handed over a business card. "Here are the numbers where you can reach me." Coluccio sat, followed by Jerry and Oglethorpe. "First order of business is to respond to this column in the paper. Corporate Public Relations in New York will issue a release announcing that Empire Realm has retained the services of PRN Security. It will highlight our qualifications and credentials and will be step one in reassuring the public that Empire Studios puts their guests' safety above all else. Step two will be to go on the offensive. Empire may be responsible for ensuring guest safety, but the police are responsible for catching criminals. So far, they haven't caught anyone. We enlist the corporate PR machine to point the finger of culpability at the local law enforcement authorities. Why have there been three killings with no suspects? Why haven't they called in the FBI behavioral science experts for help? They're clearly not getting the job done on their own. Why did that columnist neglect to lay any blame on the police? Because the police are probably the source of the leak. Let's have the public start asking *them* questions instead of us. Step three involves placing an undisclosed number of PRN field agents undercover inside the park, twenty-four hours a day. They will know the routines and habits of every cast member, especially those in the Lonesome Gulch area. If there is the slightest deviation from the normal routine, my agents will move in. They will be armed and prepared to act immediately to protect the lives of Empire Realm's guests and staff. Any questions so far?"

Jerry only had one question, but he decided not ask it. Do those mall security guys have to buy their brown uniforms or are they provided?

Bruce Willis rode Prospector Mountain three times.

Chuckie had his picture taken with him. Kevin didn't get the opportunity to meet him, not that he particularly cared. Kevin's exalted role thus far in the big Anniversary Celebration was loading nine of Mr. Willis' personal bodyguards into a mine cart. Chuckie let Mr. Willis and his entourage remain in their carts without being unloaded and repeat the ride twice more. The guests who had been waiting in line for over an hour weren't thrilled, considering that Mr. Willis had bypassed the line, but Chuckie didn't care. Bruce Willis was so enamored with *his* ride that he wanted to go on it three times. Chuckie offered a fourth opportunity but Mr. Willis passed, stating that "the ride is pretty cool, but I don't need to see myself barfing all over Entertainment Tonight." With that he left, surrounded by nearly a dozen huge bodyguards, several park security guards, a couple of special events escorts, a talent coordinator, a park media rep, and a video camera crew.

There was an unusual energy in the park. An anticipation of . . . what? It seemed to Kevin to be more than just the Anniversary Celebration preparations. It felt almost sinister, foreboding, like an approaching storm. New faces in the cast locker room. Nervous guests spooked by the column in the *Sentinel*. The whole park vibe was charged.

Sheila passed him as she helped an elderly couple onto the ride. They exchanged a secret smile as she went by. Kevin thought about the previous afternoon. It had been eight months since he had been with a woman and not since Maria's death that he had been with a woman that he truly cared about. Maybe even loved. He felt that he had finally come through a dark tunnel and was now facing a future full of unknown promise, rather than a past of unrealized potential. He missed Maria, and always would, but he had moved on. It was time to start living in the present. For the future. He and Sheila had eaten lunch together today like a couple of kids in a school cafeteria.

Kevin had tried calling Jerry this morning but couldn't reach him. He read the paper and saw Pendergrast's fingerprints all over the *Murderland* column. The sleazy bastard. With this publicity and the kind of heat that was probably already on both Jerry from the Empire executives and Pendergrast from Gardner, Kevin knew that his time was short. If he had any hope of finding the killer, it would need to be very soon.

Kevin had risen early and reviewed his notes prior to arriving at the park. According to Violet, the victims were all killed at night. But the bodies weren't discovered until much later the next day. That meant they had to be hidden until they were placed for discovery. That hiding place was also associated with dry ice. Violet had said that the burns on the skin were post-mortem. The killer's job probably involved dry ice somehow. After yesterday's education on the use of dry ice within Empire Realm, Kevin had a pretty good idea of where the bodies were hidden immediately after being killed. He cross-referenced the names from Jerry's list of the cast members on duty on the three nights of the slayings with the most-likely jobs involving dry ice, and got a roster of seven potential suspects, two of whom were women. He eliminated the women based upon Violet's assessment of the physical evidence. That left five legitimate suspects. A manageable number.

Kevin had already left two messages for Jerry. He needed to pass along those names and have all the suspects put under surveillance. Unfortunately, Kevin couldn't just grab them all and question them. He had no hard evidence, just an educated theory and some very circumstantial clues. Their case would never hold up in court. The only thing that grabbing them would do would be to alarm the killer and send him into hiding, maybe forever.

And God knew that he couldn't give the suspects' names to Pendergrast. The first thing he'd do is haul each of them into the box and interrogate them to the point of tears. That would accomplish nothing. Kevin felt like he was starting to know the killer now. He remembered the profiling exercises that he and Agent Benning had gone through in their hunt for the Mall Murderer. The Empire Killer was not going to be intimidated by Lou Pendergrast. He was unreachable, disconnected from the kind of emotional response Pendergrast would try to elicit. The only thing the doer cared about with any kind of passion was killing—or rather, having people discover his deadly handiwork. With no real evidence, all Pendergrast would do is scare him off.

Besides, if possible, Kevin still wanted to give Jerry the opportunity to save face and be the one to officially capture the killer. But Jerry would have to answer his phone first.

Chuckie approached Kevin and handed him a slip of green paper. "You're either the luckiest son of a gun I've ever met or you really are sleeping with somebody pretty important."

"What's this?" Kevin asked, scanning the paper.

"Your number's up. Tomorrow is your C-Day."

"C-Day? What are you talking about?"

"You don't even know what it is. C-Day. Your Character Assignment. Once a year everyone gets assigned to be a costumed character." Chuckie shook his head. "You've only been here a few weeks and your number comes up right on the same day as the start of the Anniversary Celebration. Unbelievable."

"I don't want to. I'll pass."

"Pass? *Pass?* Did you even see which character you've been assigned?" Chuckie thrust a finger at the paper. Kevin read a section of the form that said *Character Assignment: Wilberforce the Wilberhorse.*

"I don't care. I don't want to do it."

Chuckie just stared at him, open-mouthed, aghast. "You can't turn it down. I mean, it's *Wilberforce!* You've been assigned *Wilberforce?*"

"That's really not changing my mind, Chuckie."

"I'm sorry. There's no argument. When your number's up, you go. It says on the form where to report tomorrow morning. It's in the tunnel, Section G. This is an honor, Kevin, truly. Somebody must really be fond of you."

Kevin read over the form. At the bottom was a name he recognized from his orientation class at Empire University. *Recommending Cast Member: Kippy Whittaker.*

Thanks, Kippy. Thanks a lot.

CHAPTER 20

Gardner was screaming at him. But Pendergrast hardly heard him. He barely noticed the usual things he normally observed during a visit to the Sheriffs private office. Gardner's stale, rank coffee breath. The speck of powdered sugar from a jelly donut lodged in the corner of his mouth. The one long nose hair protruding from his left nostril. Pendergrast was a detective, after all. It was his job to notice things. But not this time. While Gardner lectured him, Lou Pendergrast could only think of one thing.

Goddamn. My ass is on fire.

Seriously. It felt like someone shoved a lit match in his anus and was twirling it.

Gardner was still going off. He was pissed because they hadn't found the Empire Realm killer yet. He was pissed because the list of potential suspects was still in the double digits. He was pissed because he was elected Orange County Sheriff on the promise that he would keep his corner of Central Florida safe for visitors and maintain that steady stream of tourist dollars (and pounds and yen and marks). He was pissed because next year was an election year and he needed this case solved. What he most definitely did not need was an editorial in the *Sentinel* titled *Murderland.*

Gardner gave Pendergrast three days to arrest someone before he pulled the investigation away and called in the Feds. Three days. Despite his burning backside, Pendergrast heard that.

"Do I make myself clear?" Gardner barked.

"Yeah. But arrest or not, you can't pull my case. I'm the primary."

"Primary? I can do whatever the hell I want. I can put you in a uniform and have you write jaywalking tickets for the rest of your career. If I don't see this case close quickly, I'll pull it so fast you'll get whiplash. Now get to work."

Pendergrast eased himself up from the poorly upholstered seat and waddled out the door. He would be goddamned before he let Gardner pull his case. Pendergrast had waited his entire career for a case like this. He'd been working it by the book, making sure he was thorough, making sure that nothing slipped, making sure he compiled the right evidence in the right way so that once they got into court the trial would just be a formality. There would be no O. J. here in Orlando. There would be no sloppy police work to allow reasonable doubt. But Gardner didn't want to hear that. All Gardner wanted to hear was that the case was closed. Gardner had never worked Homicide. He didn't understand the rhythms of a murder investigation, especially one involving a serial killer. He was a politician, which was only one rung up the evolutionary ladder from lawyers.

And, at the moment, reporters were only one rung above politicians. Carla's surprise column in the morning paper had infuriated Pendergrast. She hadn't told him she was going to write that. He certainly hadn't told her it was okay yet. It wasn't going to be okay until he whispered it into her ear as they groped under his bed sheets. That scenario now seemed pretty unlikely.

She had taken the few breadcrumbs of information he had offered and filled in the rest by herself—maybe taking an educated guess, maybe talking to some folks at Empire Realm. Whatever she had done, the result was a sharp stick jabbed into a hornet's nest. The press was buzzing. The mayor and county commissioner were buzzing. Gardner was buzzing. And they all had their stingers aimed at Lou Pendergrast.

He had called Carla at her office first thing this morning and left her what he later admitted was an "unpleasant" voicemail message. Thus far, unsurprisingly, she hadn't returned his call. Bitch.

Pendergrast made his way to the Men's room and found an empty stall. He pulled a tube of prescription cream from his pocket and squeezed a liberal amount onto his fingertip. Dropping his pants, he gently—*gently*—applied the cream to the source of his rectal pain. Goddamn, that hemorrhoid felt huge. He swore it was the size of an eyeball.

As he hoisted his drawers back up, the tube of cream slipped from his fingers and bounced under the stall door into the main bathroom beyond. Holding his unbuckled pants up with one hand, Pendergrast stretched his other arm out under the door, but the tube was just a half-inch too far. He stretched again, extending his arm and fingers as far as they would reach. His trembling index finger just barely brushed the end of the tube, spinning it slightly, but there was no way for him to get a grip on it.

He quickly stood and buttoned his trousers. He slid the door latch open and rushed out into the main bathroom. He reached for the floor but stopped himself. The tube was gone.

"Looking for this?"

Leaning on the row of sinks was Smitty, one of the narco detectives. Pendergrast hated the nares. In his experience, the only difference between the narcotics cops and the drug dealers they busted was that the former carried badges.

Smitty was a big white guy, looked like a biker. Shaved head. Fu Manchu mustache. On his shoulder was a tattoo of a dagger dripping blood. In his hand was Pendergrast's ass cream.

"Just give it to me," said Pendergrast evenly, holding out his hand.

"So what's the problem, Lou? Fungus?"

"Come on, Smitty. Hand it over."

"You know, I didn't hear the toilet flushing." Smitty inhaled deeply. "And I don't smell your signature aroma. What were you doing in there, Lou? Where *exactly* were you applying this?"

Pendergrast said nothing more. It was no use. He put his hand down and waited for Smitty to finish with his fun.

"Seriously, Lou," Smitty said, reading the tube. "What have you got? Herpes? Crabs? Yeast infection?" He paused a moment, to finish reading the writing on the tube. "'For temporary relief of hemorrhoid pain and itching, apply to affected area every three hours. Do not ingest.'" He looked up at Pendergrast and smiled, his crooked yellow teeth poking through the bushy mustache. "I always knew you were a giant pain in the ass. Now I know why."

Pendergrast snatched the tube from his hand and Smitty burst into a fit of laughter. As he exited the men's room, Pendergrast heard Smitty's loud guffaws echo off the tile walls. Before the door closed, Smitty shouted through his laughter, "For God's sake, Lou, *wash your hands*?"

Pendergrast grabbed his briefcase and headed for the front door. As soon as he stepped out into the bright glare of the morning sun, he noticed a crowd at the edge of the parking lot. It was the media, huddled with their video cameras and microphones around something. Curiosity drew Pendergrast over toward the crowd.

As he approached and saw who the crowd was huddled around, he grew furious. He actually felt his ears get hot. The hemorrhoid started throbbing painfully. Standing in the center of the crowd, answering questions, was Mickelson. The rookie.

"We're just not prepared to provide any additional information on the investigation at this time," Mickelson was saying. "We must maintain the integrity of the case. I'm sure you understand."

The reporters shouted a hundred questions in unison. One emerged a little more loudly than the rest: "Do you have any suspects?"

"Yes, we do have suspects, but I can't comment on the specifics."

More questions shouted. People called his name. "Detective Mickelson! Detective Mickelson! Is it true that the killer is now targeting Disney guests?"

"I haven't heard that one yet," Mickelson said. "Thus far, all activity seems to be localized within the Empire Realm park."

More questions. This went on for several more minutes, until Pendergrast felt like he was going to explode. That should've been *him* in there answering those questions. That should have been *his* face on those cameras. Finally Mickelson excused himself and headed over toward the Sheriffs office. He spotted Pendergrast seething nearby.

"Hey, Boss," Mickelson said. "You ready to roll?"

Pendergrast was furious. He was long past counting to ten to try to calm down. He was in the fifties by now and still livid. "Why were you answering questions from the media?" he asked slowly and deliberately through clenched teeth.

"Sheriff Gardner ordered me out here to do it. I didn't want to. I said, 'Detective Pendergrast is the primary. He should answer the questions.' Gardner told me you were busy and that he wanted me to get my butt out here and face those cameras. How'd I do?"

So Pendergrast's suspicion was right. Mickelson was assigned to this case because he was young and handsome. Gardner wanted his face on camera, not Lou's hard, aging, slightly bald countenance. No matter that Mickelson had never worked a homicide case before. No matter that he was green and stupid. All that mattered was that his teeth were white and straight. The whole thing made Pendergrast want to throw up.

His hemorrhoid, Carla, Gardner, Smitty, and now Mickelson. It was barely ten o'clock and already his day was deep in the crapper.

The partners climbed into their unmarked cruiser with Mickelson behind the wheel. "Where to, Boss? Back to the park?"

"Yeah," said Pendergrast shifting his weight to avoid direct pressure on his hemorrhoid. "I have a killer to catch."

"Don't you mean 'we'?"

"You just drive the goddamned car and keep your mouth shut. And watch the potholes or, I swear to God, I might just put a bullet in your empty, pretty head." Pendergrast closed his eyes and waited for the hemorrhoid cream to start working.

Kevin was five minutes late. A tall woman with unnaturally black hair scowled at him. She was the Wardrobe Mistress. In her early fifties, she was gaunt and wore too much makeup. The thick makeup and the dye job, clearly attempts to appear younger, just made her look even older.

"Sorry," Kevin offered. "I've never been down in the tunnel before. I got lost." This was true. He did get confused in the vast network of catacombs that crisscrossed the subterranean layer of Empire Realm. But another reason he was late was because he had tried again to contact Jerry. Kevin had reached a point in the investigation where he needed Jerry in order to move forward. Only Jerry could question the five suspects Kevin had on his list. He had to get Jerry that list. Since Jerry wasn't answering his phone (Kevin left messages at his office, at home, and on his cell), Kevin had shown up in person. But Jerry was out of the office and unavailable. Something was up. Jerry had always been accessible until now. Kevin had a bad feeling about this. He would keep trying.

The Wardrobe Mistress fitted Kevin for his Wilberforce the Wilberhorse costume. Wearing it, Kevin felt even more ridiculous than he did in the miner's costume, if that were possible. At least his face wasn't visible inside the character. The Wardrobe Mistress removed the horse head and replaced it into a row of Wilber heads arranged along the wall of the corridor. It was a fairly disturbing sight—to see a half-dozen decapitated heads from one of America's most beloved cartoon icons lying in a neat line on the ground. Kevin forced himself to look away.

The woman handed Kevin a different head that was a better fit and pointed him down the hall to the Character Services Department. There Kevin was greeted by a Character Escort. His escort was an energetic, elfin girl of eighteen named Carrie. She was dressed in the required escort wardrobe: dark blue slacks, white shirt, plaid vest. She had a walkie-talkie on her hip and a small speaker in her ear. She had strawberry blond hair, cut short like a boy's, but styled femininely. A couple of cute freckles dotted her nose.

Kevin was still in the air-conditioned climate of the tunnel and had been wearing the Wilber costume for only about ten minutes, but he could already feel a bead of sweat running down his back. And he wasn't even wearing the costume's head at the moment. How would he survive out in the hot sun where it was predicted to reach 96 degrees? This was nuts.

Carrie saw him wipe his forehead with the back of his brown, furry hoof. "Don't worry," she said. "You're only allowed to be onstage for twenty minutes at a time. And you only work once every hour. When you're not onstage, I'll take you back to the Character Lounge. It's an airconditioned trailer backstage where you can relax between performances. We'll have some drinks and snacks there for you and the other performers."

Carrie then gave him a crash course in character acting. Rule number one: no speaking. All of the Empire Studio cartoon characters have distinctive voices, especially Wilberforce. There was no way Kevin or anyone would be able to do an adequate imitation. Besides, silence added to the characters' mystique. Somehow, silence made them seem more alive and not just a big heavy costume on the back of a reluctant minimum wage cast member.

To communicate with the guests, Kevin would need to convey Wilber's emotions. To Kevin that seemed all but impossible without the use of speech and from within a static rubber head plastered with a frozen goofy expression. But Carrie walked him through a few of the basic pantomime movements.

Happy: place the thumb tips on each side of the face, palms facing outwards, and tilt the head to the left. Conveniently, Wilber's hooves also sported thumbs.

Surprise: place both hands on the side of the face, palms against the cheeks, and lean forward with interest.

Oh No!: same as surprise, but instead of leaning forward, look up into the sky.

Don't Cry!: twist a fist in the corner of one eye. Carrie made him practice that one. Evidently, when very small children first glimpse the seven-foot tall Wilberforce lumbering toward them, many of them will scream like Satan himself is bearing down on them.

Smile!: point both index fingers at the dimples in the cheeks and rotate the hands.

Nice to Meet Ya!: grasp the new friend's hand and give one exaggerated shake up and down.

Hello!: wave the palm of the hand from side to side with the elbow as the axis.

Bye-Bye!: wave with the fingers only, like trying to clap with only one hand.

And so on.

Carrie led Kevin down the corridor, past a huge room packed with Hispanic women sewing costumes, past the master audio room that controlled all of the park's ambient music, past large animal character costumes hanging on racks like sides of beef, and past a long steam-filled room stacked with churning washing machines. She led him on a fairly straight path but they went past at least a half dozen perpendicular corridors. Kevin was amazed at the beehive of activity that filled these underground halls. It was a whole subterranean community of support services that kept the public face of the park running smoothly.

The ground now slanted upwards and they worked their way up the grade. At the top of the incline was a garage door-sized opening leading to the park's backstage area. A wall of air rushed down from a vent in the top of the opening, allowing people and golf carts to pass through unobstructed, but keeping the cool air inside the tunnel. As they reached the opening, Carrie turned to Kevin and smiled. She lifted the goofy Wilber head and held it up for him.

"Now don't lose your head out there," she said, placing the costume head over Kevin's head.

"Cute," said Kevin, his voice muffled inside the rubber head. "Is that your standard joke?"

"Yeah. You like it?"

"I'm laughing on the inside."

"Don't worry about anything. I'll be right there with you. Can you see?" Kevin nodded. "Excellent. Okay, Wilber, let's go meet your adoring public."

She took his plush-covered elbow and led him out of the tunnel.

CHAPTER 21

Wilberforce the Wilberhorse was an institution. More than just a cartoon character, he was now an American icon, a corporate logo, and a marketing juggernaut. His grinning image was plastered on T-shirts, mugs, and hats. There were stuffed, plush Wilbers sold in shops around the world. He starred in major motion pictures that had multimillion dollar promotional campaigns with McDonald's and Pepsi. He had sing-along videos for the toddler set. He had interactive video games for the pre-teens. He was ubiquitous and omnipresent.

He first appeared in 1951 in an animated short called *Horsin' Around*. His original name was Wilberforce the Walking Horse, which had seemed clever in 1951. After a few years "the Walking Horse" faded away and audiences began referring to him as simply Wilber Horse. Then, in the early '70s, Empire made a concerted effort to reestablish their brand, promoting the character's true name: Wilberforce. Unfortunately, "Wilber Horse" was, by then, already a part of the cultural vernacular and he became known colloquially as Wilberforce the Wilberhorse, which made absolutely no sense. But it was a unique (albeit ridiculous) name and it scored well with the focus groups of kids set up by the Empire Marketing Department. So, rather than fight it anymore, Empire Studios grudgingly adopted the name Wilberforce the Wilberhorse, much as Federal Express finally officially changed its name to FedEx. It was exhausting and expensive fighting the image battle and, in the end, people were going use whatever name they wanted anyway, no matter how nonsensical.

Wilberforce was born when Empire Studios decided to develop a signature character in response to the phenomenal success of Disney's Mickey Mouse and Warner Brothers' Bugs Bunny. Their answer was a tall, somewhat dim-witted horse. It was an unusual character choice. Where Mickey Mouse and Bugs Bunny were always the smartest character on screen, the appeal of Wilberforce was that the audience always knew more than he did about his situation. If there was a banana peel lying directly in his path, or a bomb with a burning fuse in his picnic basket, or a rattlesnake hanging down instead of the pull cord for his office window shade, he was always the last one to discover it, and he usually discovered it the hard way.

However, Wilber's mental challenges were offset by his heart of gold. He may have been slow-witted, but he was always toiling for the greater good of society. In one film he helped raise money for the Lonesome Gulch Orphanage. In another, he had to build a bridge for the Union Pacific train carrying a car full of toys.

Wilber's primary occupation was Sheriff of Lonesome Gulch, although, as the years went by, he showed up in all sorts of situations, such as: being stranded on a desert island, climbing the Alps, starring in an Italian Opera, working as a lighthouse keeper, and piloting a rocket ship into outer space. He was tall, at least in relation to the other characters on screen, and walked around on two hooves. He had big, googly eyes that would literally pop out of his head when he was surprised. Two prominent buckteeth protruded from his mouth. And he always greeted his friends with the same catchphrase: "Huh-Howdy, Pardners!" It was the Wilberforce equivalent to "What's up, Doc?"

Wilber's efforts were assisted by his trusty corps of sidekicks, the Corral Pals. The Corral Pals always came through for Wilber and were continually looking out for his best interests, even if he was oblivious. The Corral Pals included Spunky the Chipmunk, Arnold the Burro (the real intellect of the group), Jasper the Skunk, and Sam the Tortoise. Their perennial nemesis was a fox named Abner Abernathy. Abner was forever scheming for his own profit. Sometimes it was stealing the gold from Prospector Mountain. Sometimes it was diverting the orphans' money. Sometimes it was breaking the dam so that he could sell lake-front property where the town once was. Later, he was responsible for stranding Wilber on a desert island or chasing him in a sleek and menacing-looking rocket ship. Abner always plotted for success and was always foiled by the Corral Pals. Always.

Wilber's innocent ignorance was sometimes his salvation when dealing with Abner, like when Wilber stopped suddenly to lean over and sniff a desert flower, just as his nemesis fired a cannonball at him. The cannonball, of course, flew right over the top of Wilber's bent body, smacked into a rubber tree (conveniently labeled for our information) and was slingshot right back into Abner's mouth and out his fluffy tail.

Wilber was by far the biggest star in the Empire Studios constellation. He was much more popular even than Bruce Willis. His appearances in the Empire Realm park were highly anticipated by the guests. Where and when he would appear was never announced, thus adding to the awe and mystique of his presence when he did materialize.

Kevin had some pretty big horseshoes to fill during the course of his C-Day.

* * *

Carrie led Kevin through a hidden door into the park. They stepped out directly in front of the one-third size Aztec Pyramids of the South American section.

By chance, a small boy stood immediately in front of him, holding his father's hand. The expression on the father's face was the same as if a thousand dollars just fell out of the sky in front of him.

"Look, Dave," said the father, pointing. "It's Wilber! It's Wilber! Go on!" The father released the boy's hand and gave him a nudge towards Kevin. He fumbled for his camera as the boy stood paralyzed. Kevin offered the boy a small wave. The boy responded with a loud, sustained wail of terror.

"But, Davey," the father pleaded, "it's Wilber!"

The boy screamed even louder, as if he were being impaled.

The father scooped him up and hauled him away.

Kevin stood there for a moment, not sure what to do. He had been Wilberforce for exactly ten seconds and so far all he had done was terrify a small child. Kevin turned to Carrie for guidance. She was looking away, down the sidewalk, with a distant smile on her face.

"Wait for it . . ." she said.

An instant later they swarmed in. Kevin was suddenly surrounded by a teeming throng of children and adults, all calling his name and pawing at him. He felt like the Beatles.

One by one he worked his way through the crowd, posing for pictures, patting heads, shaking hands, and doing little dances. Kevin recalled something a co-worker had said. When he had heard it was Kevin's C-Day, one of his fellow Prospector Mountain loaders had mentioned that the animal character costumes were the world's biggest asshole magnets. According to him, the characters attracted every jerk in the park like flies to manure. It was, admittedly, a pretty cynical assessment.

The Wilber costume had a long brown tail that was held upright by a thick, hard plastic rig, braced by a belt that clasped around Kevin's midsection. If anyone happened to pull on the tail, the belt was driven into his gut like a sucker punch. One obnoxious kid took it upon himself to continuously pull Wilber's tail until Kevin felt sure he would puke inside his costume. He finally grabbed the top of the kid's head with his left front hoof and held it tightly. The kid screeched in fright. Then the kid's mother started screaming: "Wilber's attacking my kid! Wilber's attacking my kid!"

At that point Carrie judiciously whisked Kevin away backstage.

The tail-pulling kid notwithstanding, his first tour of duty actually wasn't so bad. Almost everyone that approached him was truly happy to see him. Kevin realized that he had spent almost every minute of his time at Empire Realm looking suspiciously at everyone he met, wondering if they were a mad killer. He hadn't taken a moment in all that time to think about what the park meant to the average visitor. Despite the high admission prices and the exorbitant food costs and the long lines, Empire Realm was still a magical, fabulous place filled with small moments of wonder; moments captured in the eager faces of little children as they reached up to hug their favorite cartoon character come to life before their eyes. Kevin had never experienced anything like it before.

The rest of his shift went very much the same, with the same reactions, the same tail pulling, the same tears and laughter. The heat didn't even get to him as badly as he thought it would. Carrie was quite punctual about his breaks and would announce to the crowd that Wilber had to get back to the Corral for some oats. The crowd would make a collective groan and follow him longingly as he made his way backstage. The Character Lounge was actually quite pleasant. Lots of fresh fruit. Plenty to drink. Soft bagels. All in all, C-Day wasn't half bad and Kevin was glad he had had the experience.

But he would have enjoyed it more if he hadn't been so distracted thinking about his investigation. He tried calling Jerry again a couple of times throughout the day with no success. Kevin's list of five suspects needed to be checked out. He needed Jerry to research where they were today and where they would be the rest of the week. If they couldn't find a tangible link between one of those five suspects and the murders, Kevin would talk to Jerry about handing the list and Kevin's notes over to Pendergrast. At this point, it was more important to catch the killer than to save Jerry's job.

Although, nothing could be done unless Kevin could connect with Jerry. The esteemed Director of Security had apparently gone AWOL.

Back in the tunnel after his shift, Kevin thanked Carrie and ducked aside for a few minutes to try to call Jerry again. When he didn't reach him, Kevin called Stan Tokarz in Indianapolis. Tokarz told him that Midwest Tours was still clean. There were a couple of complainers, but Tokarz had tracked most of them down and all had alibis. None seemed like a murderer to him. And there was no good explanation why any of them would have targeted those two particular clients on vacation in Orlando. Tokarz's professional opinion was that he was driving down a dead-end road. He'd keep digging if Kevin wanted, but he recommended that they pull the plug on the Midwest Tours inquiry. Kevin agreed. The tour company connection was purely coincidental. Kevin thanked Tokarz for the work and told him he was done. All he needed to do was send his bill.

Kevin tried Jerry again, calling all of the numbers he had.

After that proved fruitless, Kevin made his way back to the severe-looking Wardrobe Mistress. He removed the big Wilber costume and watched as it was hung up on a rack next to several identical Wilber costumes, which were next to a row of Spunky costumes, and Arnold costumes, and Abner costumes.

Kevin found a low bench along one wall in the costume room and sat to tie his sneakers. As he laced up the second shoe, he froze. Moving his fingers to the front of his pants leg, he picked up a long, brown hair.

Only, it wasn't a hair. It was a familiar looking long, brown, nylon fiber.

It was from the Wilber costume.

He stared at it for a moment, watching it hang from between his pinched fingers. Like looking at a winning lottery ticket, joyously shocked. Kevin had the killer. He had the son of a bitch now. He found the connection. His cell phone was in his pocket. But before he could reach for it—

"Kevin Lonnegan?"

Kevin looked up. Standing over him was a large, tanned man in a dark business suit. The man had sandy blonde hair just turning gray and was clearly in good condition under that suit. He looked like a cop, except the suit was too nice. Maybe a Fed. Kevin put the fiber in his pocket.

"Yeah. I'm Kevin Lonnegan. Who's asking?"

"Would you come with me, please?"

Kevin paused. The guy deliberately avoided answering his question. Hmmm. This would be interesting. "No, I don't think so," Kevin said.

"You're saying that you won't come with me."

"That's right."

"I'm afraid that I must insist."

"And I must insist that you tell me who the hell you are."

The man sighed and looked to his side. From the hallway two more men appeared, one African-American, both dressed similarly. "If you don't come with me voluntarily, sir, I'm authorized to bring you involuntarily."

Kevin quickly sized up the three guys standing in front of him. They were all big and seemed to know what they were doing. They had immediately positioned themselves around him so he couldn't make a run for it. Their hands were at their sides, not threatening, but ready to be used. Their feet were shoulder-width apart, knees bent just slightly. Who the hell were these guys? Kevin knew that he could never take all three of them. No doubt they'd kick his ass.

Kevin stood and held up his palms. "Okay, guys. No need to make a big scene here. I guess I'm coming along. But, give me a break, okay? Who are you?"

The first guy relaxed his posture slightly. "We are field agents from the private security firm Pierce, Robertson, and Neuberg."

"And what do you want me for?"

"I'm not at liberty to discuss that."

"Okay. Who is?"

"The AIC. The Agent in Charge."

"I'd like to talk to the AIC then."

The agent smiled. "That's exactly who we're taking you to see."

He shook Mickelson's hand first in the mistaken assumption that he was in charge. Pendergrast quickly interjected himself and thrust out his own sweaty palm.

"Detective Pendergrast. I'm the primary."

The guy, Coluccio, shook Pendergrast's hand. Greeted him with respect but with no deference. Mickelson was impressed. He had only just met Coluccio, but he was already intimidated. This guy was all business. Until a few minutes ago, Pendergrast, jerk though he was, had been Mickelson's role model. The guy was a machine who had cleared more homicides than anyone else in the history of the Orange County Sheriffs office. But, having just met Coluccio, Mickelson might have a new role model. Coluccio had an air of confidence and quiet strength that was a stark contrast to Pendergrast's foul blustering. His physical appearance was imposing, as well, like a quarterback for a pro football team. Pendergrast looked distinctly troll-like standing there shaking hands with him.

Pendergrast was in a seriously pissy mood—and that was saying something. The guy was hard enough to be around on a good day. When he was on a tear, he was unbearable. Mickelson couldn't even imagine Coluccio behaving like that. He wouldn't yell and berate you. He would just drop you before you even knew what hit you.

Someone said he was ex-Secret Service. Maybe. Maybe former FBI. Mickelson had also heard that Coluccio was a Navy Seal Lieutenant. Had been part of the team that nabbed Manuel Noriega in Panama.

When the time was right, Mickelson would try to talk to him, find out how he could join PRN. Rumor was that those guys made six figures a year. That sure beat his cop salary.

Pendergrast finished shaking hands and sucked his upper teeth. He looked at Coluccio, waiting for him to make a move. Coluccio gestured and invited them both to sit. Mickelson did. The seats were uncomfortable, metal folding chairs arranged in a sparse trailer in the backstage area of the park. It wasn't so different from the trailer that Empire had set up for their own investigation.

"Uh, thanks, but I think I'll stand," Pendergrast said.

For God's sake. Not his ass problem, again. Mickelson was embarrassed in front of Coluccio. When Mickelson talked with

Coluccio later, he would make sure that he knew that he was not responsible for Pendergrast's behavior.

"Suit yourself," said Coluccio, sitting behind his desk.

Pendergrast sneered at Mickelson in betrayal. What, like he was supposed to stand, too, just because his partner had uncomfortable anal itching? Or whatever? What a dick.

Since Pendergrast had seen Mickelson talking to the press earlier that day, he had been a complete jerk. The newspaper column didn't help either. Mickelson tried to explain that Gardner had ordered him to talk to the press, but it didn't do any good. Pendergrast was pissed and that was that. Mickelson knew that if he had any hope of a successful career as a detective in the department, he needed to do whatever Gardner wanted. So, screw you, Pendergrast. Mickelson returned Pendergrast's sneer with a smug smile and defiantly crossed his legs, settling in.

Coluccio observed this silent exchange but made no comment. "Well, Detectives," he said. "First, let me thank you for taking the time from your busy investigation to meet with me. I truly appreciate it."

Pendergrast said nothing, unless you count the gross slurping sound of teeth sucking. Finally, Mickelson said: "No problem, Mr. Coluccio."

"Please, call me Vince. I'm not sure how familiar you are with PRN, but we pride ourselves on being the elite private security firm in the world. Given the nature of many of our assignments, we must work hand in hand with the local law enforcement authorities. We have an excellent relationship with many local, federal, and international law enforcement entities, and we are proud of our ability to assist and complement their investigations. In fact, many of our personnel came from the ranks of these very agencies. The bottom line, gentlemen, is that we will do nothing to hamper your investigation. If our agents, in any capacity, get in the way of your own activities, I want to know about it immediately so I can address it."

More teeth sucking. "Yeah. Okay," said Pendergrast. "Just stay out of our way. We're conducting a criminal investigation here."

"As are we, Detective Pendergrast. As we uncover pertinent information and evidence surrounding these homicides, we will, of course, share that with you."

Pendergrast put his hands on the back of his empty folding chair. "Look, *Vince*. That's great, but, really, don't waste your time. We're professional police officers. I've been a homicide detective for a long time. A long time. I know what I'm doing. If I can be frank, I think Empire is wasting a lot of good money on an unnecessary luxury. You know as well as I do that PRN isn't going to find and arrest the killer. I am."

Coluccio was silent for a moment, a faint smile on his lips that betrayed nothing about what he was thinking. "You will arrest him—or her—that's true. However, if *I* may be frank now, it's the finding part that you seem to be struggling with. You've been investigating these murders for two and a half months now and you're no closer to finding the killer than you were when you started. Your suspect list is still in the double digits. Mr. Jantsen of Empire Studios doesn't have the confidence in your abilities that you apparently do. He feels that retaining PRN was a prudent investment. And I agree with him. Let's face it, Detective. Despite your experience and abilities, all you've really done so far is allow two more innocent people to be murdered in cold blood."

"Go fuck yourself, Coluccio," said Pendergrast, practically spitting. "What do you know about homicide investigations? A fancy suit and hundred dollar haircut doesn't qualify you to do shit when it comes to real police work. Where do you get off lecturing me?"

"I would wager that I know at least as much about homicide investigations as you do, Detective. Furthermore, I feel confident that I have more experience in the pursuit and apprehension of serial killers than you will ever have. I, and the members of my team, *will* find this killer. I assure you. We're being paid to do just that. When we do, you can arrest him."

"You arrogant son of a bitch. We're through here. Come on, Mickelson."

Mickelson rolled his eyes silently at Coluccio with the same expression a kid might make to his buddies when his Mom calls him in for supper. He stood and followed Pendergrast to the door.

"If I may offer some unsolicited advice," Coluccio said. "Don't talk to the press anymore. Judgment errors like the one that appeared in this morning's paper will only help the killer. You could compromise both of our investigations."

Pendergrast's only response was to storm out of the trailer with Mickelson close on his heels. Man, thought Mickelson, Coluccio was the only person he had ever met who could shut up Lou Pendergrast.

He definitely had a new role model.

CHAPTER 22

Sheila was tired. She had been up until the wee hours the night before finishing a school paper on collaborative learning strategies in elementary education. She yawned her way through her shift and counted the minutes until she could go home.

Billy had an art project to finish, Maggie needed a dance leotard mended, and who knew what mess Greg had created. Her mom was watching the kids, as usual (God love her), but she wasn't able to do what Sheila would do. She was Grandma and that's all she was supposed to be.

Not that Sheila expected anything else. She was grateful to her mom for being there for her. With Phil out of the picture, almost, Sheila didn't know what she would do if she didn't have the support her mom offered. Life would be hard enough, but college and the hopeful teaching career would be impossible.

With her schedule so packed, she rarely had a moment for any kind of self-reflection. But every so often, in a spare minute or two—walking to her car, sitting at a stoplight, waiting for class to start—she'd find herself examining her life in small yet meaningful ways. That's what she was doing now as she left the employee area backstage at Prospector Mountain and made her way down the nondescript concrete steps that led to the ground level.

Most of all she felt sad that she was not providing her children with the family life she always dreamed for them. Discovering that Phil had been stalking her at work for God knows how long wasn't exactly Ozzie and Harriet. Her kids deserved a better sense of family with a loving, nonabusive father and a mother who was around once in a while.

Intellectually, Sheila knew that what they did have was far better now that Phil was out of the house. And she felt empowered by the fact that she was doing something about her life and prospects by getting an education. But, still, she grieved for what could have been.

However, now Kevin was suddenly in the picture. So maybe there was hope still for a decent family life. Maybe she could have with Kevin what she always wanted with . . .

Stop it.

Stop it right now. You're getting way ahead of yourself again, girl. Kevin was handsome and tragic and kind but who said anything about marriage? *Come on, now.* She wasn't even interested in that type of relationship. She wasn't even divorced yet, for God's sake.

But she couldn't help herself. The stupid schoolgirl fantasies just popped into her head unsolicited. Images of Kevin playing ball with Billy. Reading Maggie a bedtime story. Holding Sheila's hand during a sunset stroll on the beach. Sheila shook the images away, chastising herself.

Sunset stroll on the beach? That wasn't even original. Not only was she having unwanted romantic fantasies, but they were coming at her in cliches.

She reached the bottom of the steps and headed down a narrow path lined with tall hedges that led to a backstage sidewalk. She couldn't wait to get out of this sweltering miner's costume and back into her regular clothes. If Greg hadn't caused too great a disaster, maybe she'd try to take a bath. When was the last time she took a bath? Probably not since the early Clinton administration.

She vowed not to think of Kevin any more tonight. It was a vow that she almost immediately broke.

As she stepped out of the narrow path and past the tall hedges, she heard a shuffling sound from behind her and suddenly felt a large, strong hand over her mouth. Another hand went to her throat and squeezed tightly. She was unable to breathe, to scream, if any sound could have even been heard through the gloved hand over her mouth.

She felt herself being pulled backwards, towards the hedge. A thought of her kids flashed by, but was quickly replaced by a survival instinct. What would Kevin do? He would fight. She struggled to get free, clawing at the hands, kicking backwards. But she was too small and the man behind her was clearly large and very strong.

And the fingers on her throat were choking . . . she couldn't breathe. She felt the blood pressure building in her face as her attacker's hand squeezed her jugular vein. The edges of her vision were turning purple. She was on the verge of blacking out.

A moment later she was pulled behind the hedge and completely out of view.

"I don't think that's any of your business." Kevin was in the PRN trailer backstage. He sat in a folding metal chair across from Coluccio, who was leaning against the front of his desk.

Coluccio smiled coldly, his gray eyes disclosing nothing. "I'm afraid it is my business, Mr. Lonnegan. By virtue of the contract PRN has signed with Empire Realm, everything associated with the safety of the park's guests is my business." He held up a printout of a spreadsheet. "So I ask you again, why is it that in addition to your regular salary of six-fifty an hour as a ride loader, the Empire Realm Security Department has been paying Kevin Lonnegan Associates a stipend of one thousand dollars a week?"

This guy was obviously a pro. Kevin knew who PRN was and what the firm's capabilities were. He also knew the caliber of talent they had on staff and it had to be respected. He may not be able to bullshit the guy, but Kevin wasn't going to be intimidated either. "All right, Mr. Coluccio. Let's not play games. I'll guess that you already know why."

Coluccio paused, considering. He put the printout on top of the desk and then sat behind it. "Okay. Yes. I know why, although I don't know the details. That's what I would like you to provide."

"Sorry. I can't do that. I'm sure you understand."

"I'm afraid I understand a lot more than you do. According to my information, you have been working for the Empire Realm Security Department. Until further notice, the Empire Realm Security Department now works for me."

"I work for Jerry Engle."

"Who now works for me. So, if you follow my logic here, you now work for me."

"I'd like to hear that from Jerry."

Coluccio nodded. "You will. But Jerry is currently occupied and I'm not a man who likes to waste time. If you have information that is pertinent to the investigation of the three recent deaths in the park, you need to tell me everything. Now."

Kevin returned the cold smile. "Just the same, I'd like to hear it from Jerry personally before I say anything. What's he occupied doing?"

"I'm not at liberty to say."

"Then, I guess, neither am I."

Coluccio said nothing for what seemed like a long time. He just stared at Kevin, his expression unreadable. Kevin knew what Coluccio was doing. Silence is the best ally of an interrogator. People instinctively want to fill silence and will start saying things that they probably shouldn't. It was a basic maneuver and Kevin wasn't going to fall for it. He waited another few minutes. Finally, Kevin broke the silence.

"Look, Coluccio, we can sit here all night making love-eyes at each other. That's fine with me. But I'm not telling you anything until I talk to Jerry."

Coluccio sat back in his chair. He smiled again, this time a little warmer. "Y'know, Kevin, Jerry actually had surprisingly good instincts to set up an undercover operative. It was the smart move. But this is a big case and you're just one guy with limited resources and a closet full of skeletons."

So PRN had already checked him out. Damn, these guys were fast. Well, Kevin didn't care. His drinking was no secret. He had nothing to hide.

Coluccio continued. "Now, I don't know. Maybe you know what you're doing. You have to be better than the dynamic duo detectives. I remember the Mall Murderer case from a few years ago. That was good work. And my friend Milt Benning at the FBI tells me you're a solid investigator. I haven't seen enough yet personally to form an opinion. But I'll give you the benefit of the doubt. Let's say you are as good as Milt says. I'll bet that you've dug up information that's relevant to our investigation. Look, we have the same goal. We're on the same team here. If you just tell me what you know, we'll go catch the bad guy. Everybody wins."

Yeah, thought Kevin, *everybody wins except Jerry.* These PRN suits sweep in, piggyback on Kevin's work, and hog all the credit. Jerry's still screwed and collecting unemployment.

"As soon as I get the word from Jerry," Kevin said. "You and me can be pals."

Coluccio sighed. "All right. I'll try to get him on his cell." Coluccio picked up his desk phone and dialed a number. He waited as Jerry's cell phone rang.

Jerry never had a chance to answer.

The door to the trailer flew open and Lou Pendergrast charged in, followed by Detective Mickelson.

"Get up, Kevin!" Pendergrast barked.

"Go to hell, Lou," said Kevin.

Coluccio hung up the phone and stood. "Excuse me, Detective Pendergrast, but I'm in the middle of a meeting here."

Pendergrast ignored him and turned to Mickelson. "Cuff the fucker."

Mickelson produced a pair of metal handcuffs and moved quickly toward Kevin. Pendergrast made a point to unsnap the holster of the gun on his hip.

"What the hell—" Kevin said. Mickelson grabbed Kevin by the arm and jerked him to his feet. Kevin knew better than to resist. He had roughed over more than a few resisters in his days on the job.

Mickelson shoved him towards the wall. "You know the routine, Lonnegan. Spread 'em."

Kevin put his hands on the wall and widened his stance. "This is a joke, right?"

Mickelson ran his hands up and down Kevin's torso and legs. "He's clean." He then grabbed Kevin's left arm and twisted it sharply behind his back. Next, he pulled Kevin's right arm down and handcuffed his wrists together.

Coluccio was on his feet and coming around the desk. "Just what do you think you're doing?"

Pendergrast finally acknowledged Coluccio's presence. He shot Coluccio a smug grin. "What am I doing? My job, asshole." Pendergrast walked up to Kevin and grabbed the chain between the cuffs. He jerked up sharply and stabs of pain shoot through Kevin's shoulders as his arms yanked up behind his back. "Kevin Lonnegan, you're under arrest for three counts of first degree murder."

This can't be happening, thought Kevin.

But, as Mickelson read him his Miranda rights, Kevin knew that it was.

CHAPTER 23

Pull my case? No goddamned way. Pendergrast's thoughts were churning as he and Mickelson had driven out to the park from the Sheriffs office. There was no way that fat politician Gardner was going to pull the biggest case of Lou Pendergrast's career. Three days to close the case?

Fine.

He had a list of suspects. Yeah, it was a little too long, but he would just work it like any other case. Lou Pendergrast knew how to conduct homicide investigations. No one in the department could touch him. All he had to do was tie the physical evidence to one of those suspects. It was there, just waiting for him. Plus, he was due for a break.

Pendergrast considered himself a pretty straightforward guy in most aspects of his life. He took nothing for granted and based his decisions on available facts. That's part of why he was such a good detective. But he also believed that every case he investigated had its own unique rhythm. It was nothing he would ever admit to out loud, but he firmly held that no case could be solved before it was supposed to be solved. A good detective can speed an investigation along, but it still has to run its course. Every so often you come across a case where no matter how hard you work it, it's like pissing into the wind. There's nothing you can do. Then, one day, the answer just drops in your lap like a goddamn bird from the sky. An anonymous tip on the Crime Line gives up the shooter. An unrelated burglary suspect is found with the murder weapon. Some prisoner shoots off his mouth to a cellmate. Whatever. On cases like that, you would have been just as productive to sit watching ESPN and wait for it to fall into your lap than be out there pounding the pavement.

Pendergrast felt that the Empire Realm case was a lot like that. He had worked all the angles. He knew the evidence. But the killer was careful enough to have eluded him so far. But his time would come. The bird would fall out of the sky—it always did—and then Pendergrast would have him by the balls.

As he walked through the gate to the backstage area of Empire Realm, Pendergrast squinted up at the cobalt blue sky. Circling far overhead were a half dozen turkey buzzards. They were ubiquitous in Central Florida, living off the carrion of dead armadillos and other highway road kill. Pendergrast smirked. He took the presence of vultures as a good omen. He was closing in on the killer. He'd find him in the three days.

It was fitting that the bird that would fall out of the sky was a vulture.

Mickelson was beside him. They had just arrived at the park after Pendergrast's shitty morning with Gardner, Smitty, and Mickelson's press conference. It was a long, potholed ride to Empire Realm in Southwest Orlando, and Pendergrast's ass was throbbing. The hot summer sun seemed to make it worse.

"What are you looking at?" Mickelson asked, shading his eyes as he followed Pendergrast's gaze skyward.

Pendergrast ignored him. The less he told Mickelson, the less Mickelson could tell the press. From now on, Pendergrast was controlling the flow of information.

They passed through a crowd of tall stilt-walkers, who were followed by a group dancing elves. Pendergrast curled his lip. "What the fuck is this?"

"It's the staging area for the parade," Mickelson said. "Today is the start of Empire's Anniversary Celebration. Bruce Willis is here."

The moron was actually excited about Empire's Anniversary Celebration. They were working a multiple murder case and he was talking about Bruce Willis. Pendergrast might as well have been working alone.

They reached the wooden steps to the Sheriffs Office trailer and Pendergrast's cell phone rang. He looked at the Caller ID display: *Sheila Nelson.* Sheila Nelson? Where did he know that name? Then he remembered. The woman from the mine ride. Lonnegan's friend. The bitchy one. He flipped the phone open.

"Yeah. Pendergrast."

The voice on the other end was faint and hard to hear. It was a woman and her voice trembled like she was crying or frightened. She spoke haltingly but deliberately. Her breathing was labored. "This is Sheila Nelson . . . I'm afraid . . . It's Kevin . . . He did it . . . He's the one . . . Look in the cubbies . . . at Prospector Mountain . . . Oh God . . . He's here . . ."

And then she hung up. Not a hello. Not a good-bye. Pendergrast dialed back the number but no one answered. All he got was a perky message saying that he had reached Sheila's cell phone, so please leave a message. He did, telling her to call him back immediately and this better not be some joke.

"Come on," Pendergrast said to Mickelson. "We're gonna head for the mountains."

"Huh?"

"Just shut up and follow me."

They arrived at Prospector Mountain and emerged through the employee entrance to the ride loading area. The line was actually moving along well, a combination of the extra cast members assigned to handle the Anniversary crowds and the less-than-expected numbers of guests as a result of the negative publicity surrounding the murders.

Pendergrast turned to Mickelson. "Go find the little queer guy in charge."

Mickelson scurried off and returned a few moments later with Chuckie.

"Look officers—" said Chuckie.

"Detectives," interrupted Mickelson. "How many times I gotta tell you? Detectives."

"Sorry. Look, we're very busy. Whatever it is, can't it wait?"

"No," said Pendergrast. *Can't it wait?* With the clock ticking on his case nothing could wait. "Cubbies."

"Cubbies?" said Chuckie.

"Yeah. What are they, where are they?"

"You mean the cast member cubbies backstage?"

"I guess. Whatever. You got any other cubbies?"

"No. I don't think so. Follow me."

Chuckie led them through the cast member exit and into a stark break room where a couple of vending machines sat against a bare wall. Opposite the vending machines were a lonely card table and a few molded plastic chairs. The Sports section of yesterday's *Sentinel* was folded in the center of the table. At the far end of the room was a grid of boxes built into the wall. Each box had a printed name label below it.

"These are the cubbies," said Chuckie. "Each cast member has one to put stuff in during their shift. You know, car keys, lunch, anything they don't want to keep in their locker at Costuming."

Pendergrast walked up and looked in the cubbies. Most of them were empty. A couple of lunches. A woman's purse. A guitar magazine. This was bullshit. When he got hold of that bitch Sheila Nelson, he would make her pay for wasting his time. He ran a finger along the second row and found her name under a cubby. He peered in. It was empty.

"Is Sheila Nelson working today?" Pendergrast said to Chuckie.

"She was. Her shift ended a little while ago."

"Uh huh."

"Isn't this an invasion of privacy or something?"

Pendergrast ignored him. He scanned the names on the rest of the cubbies. All people he had already interviewed. He didn't recognize any from his list of probable suspects. He was about to leave when his eye caught a familiar name: *Kevin Lonnegan.* Pendergrast smirked and leaned over to see what Kevin had in his cubby.

At first he didn't see it. It was lodged back in the dark corner. Pendergrast put in a hand and pulled it out.

It was a crumpled plastic grocery bag. Pendergrast opened it and looked in. It took a few beats for him to make the connection. When he peered in, he thought he was just looking at some of Kevin's personal items. A baseball hat, some car keys, a pair of sunglasses, and a kerchief scarf. But then he noticed that the car keys were on a rental company key chain. And then it clicked.

These were the items taken from the murder victims. And the scarf was consistent with the M.E.'s murder weapon theory. Sheila's voice jabbed his memory like a poker.

It's Kevin . . . He did it . . . He's the one . . .

An accusation. Accompanied by evidence. Was it possible?

Still staring into the bag, not believing what he was seeing, Pendergrast asked Chuckie, "Is Kevin working today?"

"Yes. But not here. Today was C-Day for him. He got to be Wilberforce. Can you believe it?"

"C-Day?"

"Sorry. You see, every cast member gets to play a costumed character once a year. Kevin's day was today. So, he was working, but not here. He was out in the park."

"Is he still here?"

"I don't know."

"You find out for me, Chuckie. Right now."

"Okay . . ."

Chuckie walked over to a phone on the wall beside the soda machine and dialed a number. As he did, Mickelson leaned over.

"What's up, Boss? What's in the bag?"

Pendergrast didn't respond. His mind was going a hundred miles an hour. Could Lonnegan be the killer? Was that possible? Or was someone setting him up? Lonnegan was certainly physically strong enough and knew how to fight. He could have easily overpowered the three victims. His background as a cop would have allowed him to cover his trail. It would also explain why Pendergrast was having such a tough time finding the killer.

Lonnegan wasn't even an employee when the first two bodies turned up. But that didn't matter. He could have come in as a guest, cased the place, learned where the cameras were, and offed the tourists. Then he got a job here to be closer to his prey.

But why? What possible motive could he have? Pendergrast knew he was violent—he saw that firsthand when they were on the force together. Maybe he was drinking again and out of his mind. Maybe he resented having to work a shitty job like this and was taking it out on the tourists.

Could someone be setting him up? Who? Sheila Nelson had called in the tip. They seemed to know each other and when Pendergrast questioned her, Lonnegan was obviously protective. Maybe they were dating and it went sour. She wanted him to take the fall. But the woman wasn't the killer. Couldn't be. According to the M.E., she was too small and weak to have killed those men. Was she setting up Kevin to cover for somebody else? Her ex-husband? That didn't seem to fit. More likely she looked in Kevin's cubby and accidentally found the missing items. Although the fact that the killer had taken personal items from the victims had not been publicly disclosed, Pendergrast had no illusions that it was secret. Upon seeing them in the bag, Sheila was scared and devastated that this man she was dating—maybe even sleeping with—was the killer. That would explain her tone of voice and why she didn't want to stay on the line.

Or maybe Lonnegan confessed to her in some impulse of warped pride. Showed her his bag of trophies to impress her. Only it backfired and she was horrified. And when she called Pendergrast, Lonnegan caught her, cutting her off. Pendergrast knew he would need to find the girlfriend right away. If it wasn't too late already.

Pendergrast's considerable experience as a homicide detective had taught him that nine times out of ten things were pretty much how they looked. This looked an awful lot like Kevin Lonnegan had killed those tourists.

Fuck it. Gardner wanted the case closed. The DA would whine, but it was more than enough for an arrest. The possession of the stolen articles was enough to implicate him as a material witness—justifying taking him into custody. The accusation by Sheila Nelson directly pointed the finger of blame. It was the connection between the victims and a suspect that Pendergrast had been looking for. It was the goddamned bird falling out of the sky and into his lap. The fact that it was Pendergrast's old rival only made the collar that much juicier. Pendergrast would enjoy this more than usual. Not only would he close the biggest case of his career, but he would bring down Kevin Lonnegan in the process. It was a two-fer.

The only problem was the dry ice. How did that figure in? What did Kevin have to do with dry ice? Didn't matter— Pendergrast would sweat that out of him when he got him in the box for questioning.

"Boss?" Mickelson was still staring at him. "What's going on?"

Chuckie hung up the phone. "His shift just ended. But the Character Escort told me that three big guys in suits just walked him out of the tunnel."

Coluccio's agents. No fucking way Coluccio and PRN were going to get credit for nabbing Lonnegan. How did they find out already? There was no time to waste. Pendergrast grabbed Mickelson and dragged him out of the break room. They ran down the backstage stairs and commandeered a golf cart from a security guard. They raced through the gathered parade performers to the PRN trailer. Mickelson called for back up as they drove. In another moment the two of them were busting through the door and cuffing Lonnegan.

Coluccio stood nearby with his arms crossed. "You sure about this, Detective?"

"Go home, Coluccio," Pendergrast said. "You guys were just a big waste of money."

"We'll see."

Lonnegan looked at Coluccio. "Get Jerry on the phone," he said. "I need to talk to him as soon as possible."

"Maybe you should tell me what you need to tell Jerry," said Coluccio.

Lonnegan cut his eyes at Pendergrast. "Not here."

Coluccio nodded. "I'll do what I can."

By this time, Mickelson had pushed Lonnegan to the door. As they pulled him out of the trailer and onto the short, wooden staircase that led to the ground, Pendergrast said, "I always knew you were messed up, Kevin. I didn't realize that you're a total psycho. You know you're headed for Old Sparky, right?" Old Sparky was the affectionate nickname of Florida's electric chair in Starke.

Lonnegan just shook his head. "I don't know what you're basing this on, but you're making a big mistake, Lou. You'll regret it."

"Will I? Tell that to your girlfriend. She's the one who gave you up and told us about your little collection. Or should I assume you already know that? She didn't sound so good on the phone. Is she now your ex-girlfriend? I don't suppose you want to tell me where she is, do you? Was she breathing when you left her?"

The stunned look on Lonnegan's face was priceless.

"No?" said Pendergrast. "Suit yourself."

Mickelson held Lonnegan's arms, which were cuffed behind his back, and directed him down the stairs. Kevin put his foot on the first step leading down to the pavement, and suddenly, unexpectedly, he fell.

Kevin knew he was going to get only one chance. As he took that first step down, he twisted out of Mickelson's grip and threw himself on top of Pendergrast. Pendergrast was caught completely by surprise and barely had time to get his arms up to try to break his fall.

The two of them toppled down the four steps to the asphalt. The fall wouldn't win any style points, but it served its purpose. Pendergrast bore the brunt of the impact, which was made worse by Kevin's body weight on top of him. Kevin heard him curse loudly as he hit the stairs.

They smacked onto the ground and Pendergrast made a low groaning noise when Kevin crushed him against the concrete. What happened next occurred in an instant. Beneath him, Kevin felt Pendergrast's arm moving, reaching for his gun. Kevin had no doubts Pendergrast would use it. Shifting his weight slightly, Kevin was able to position his hand next to the holster. As the gun slid out, Kevin grabbed it.

Kevin never stopped moving. He rolled over Pendergrast's girth and got his feet underneath him. Then, with his wrists still cuffed behind his back, one hand gripping the gun, Kevin pushed himself up to a standing position, bracing his free hand on Pendergrast's face. In a matter of seconds he was upright and running.

Kevin ventured a glance back and saw Mickelson trip over Pendergrast as he reached the bottom of the stairs, fumbling for his weapon. Coluccio stood at the trailer door, incredulous.

Kevin knew he only had a few seconds lead before they would be on him. They would move faster because their hands weren't cuffed behind their backs. Kevin needed to get lost in a hurry.

He shoved Pendergrast's pistol under his T-shirt, into the waistband of his jeans, and weaved his way through a crowd of colorful Russian Cossacks—performers in the parade staging area—who were squatting and kicking. Quickly getting his bearings, Kevin recognized the parking garage directly in front of him. It was the same parking garage he was directed to use when he first came to meet Jerry. Turning left he saw the back of Jerry's office building. He dashed off towards it.

From the corner of his eye he saw Mickelson pursuing him, followed by two suited PRN agents and one guy dressed like a tourist. Probably an undercover PRN agent. This was going to be tough. Who knew how many more agents were out there? And Kevin knew Pendergrast would have called for back-up so it was only a matter of time before this place was crawling with uniforms, SWAT, you name it.

Twisting his body, Kevin was able to swing the door open. He charged in and hit the elevator button. Anything to throw them off. Maybe they'll think he went upstairs to Jerry's office. But Kevin knew that would be a bad move. All he would do is trap himself up there. He turned right and pushed his way through the cast member entrance into the Lone Star Cantina.

The place was bustling, as usual. A few feet away Kevin saw Mavis working the room, chatting with the tourists. He caught her eye and she approached. She tilted her head and spotted the handcuffs behind Kevin's back. She smiled lustily.

"My, oh my, Kevin, Sugar. This is more like it. I had no idea you were so . . . uninhibited. I have a break coming up in a few minutes, or did you already know that?"

"Mavis, I'm in a jam here. I don't have time to explain, but you have to trust me. I didn't do what some people think I did. In a few seconds, some very serious men are going to come through that door looking for me. They cannot find me. Do you understand?"

Mavis' eyes drifted behind Kevin to the door. There was a scuffling noise on the other side. She looked Kevin in the eye for a beat and then put her hand on top of his head. In one quick motion, she pushed him down to his knees and lifted up her wide blue skirt. She stepped forward, put one leg over his left shoulder, and dropped the skirt over him, covering him completely.

Kevin heard the door open and the sound of footsteps rush into the restaurant. Mavis adjusted her stance and squeezed Kevin's face between her petticoat-clad thighs.

"Hello, gentlemen," he heard Mavis say. "Can I help you with anything at all?"

The next voice was Mickelson's. "Police. We're looking for a redheaded guy. He's wearing handcuffs. We think he ran through here."

"Well, indeed he did. Not the kind of thing one sees every day, so it's bound to make an impression. He came through that door there, ran through these tables here, and out the front door into the street." Mavis turned her body to gesture at the front door, squeezing Kevin's face even tighter between her thighs. "Not even so much as a 'howdy do' or a 'pardon me.' Where are people's manners these days, I ask you?"

Kevin heard the group charge off through the restaurant and out the front door. He waited a moment, not daring to move.

"My, oh my . . ." he heard Mavis say. "Is it warm in here or is it just me?"

She released her grip on Kevin's face and started to lift her skirt back up. But she immediately stopped, dropping it again. She leaned forward, almost losing her balance, using the top of Kevin's head to steady herself.

Kevin noticed that his left foot was sticking out of the hem of the dress. He was about to pull it back when he heard Mavis clear her throat loudly.

"If you're with the rest of those gentlemen," she said. "They went through the front door."

"Which way?" It was Pendergrast.

"I believe they went both ways." Beneath her dress, Kevin saw that Mavis' foot was starting to tremble as she fought to maintain her balance. "How did you get that nasty scrape, Sugar?"

"I tripped." Kevin heard the distinct sound of limping footsteps. The footsteps reached the center of the restaurant and stopped. "I have an idea, why don't you come here and show me which way they went."

Now her foot was visibly quivering. She wasn't going to be able to hold her balance much longer. Kevin pressed the side of his head against her leg to provide her some support. But it wasn't much.

"I'd love to, Sugar, but I have a Cantina to run. Besides, I really don't know which way they went."

There was a pause. No footsteps. "Even so, I'd like you to come here and show me."

Mavis paused, struggling to stay upright and trying to think of a response. "Tell you what, Sugar, you come back later when my shift is over and I'll show you anything you like."

Again there was a pause, followed by the limping footsteps. But the footsteps were getting louder, not quieter. Pendergrast was coming back. He limped up right next to Mavis. Her leg was trembling uncontrollably. Kevin wanted to reach out and steady it with his hand but couldn't without losing his own balance. She was going to fall.

"Hey, Boss!" Mickelson's voice. "Come on! Out here!"

There was another long moment where Kevin knew Pendergrast was staring at Mavis. Then Kevin heard the limping footsteps again, this time receding.

Mavis called after him. "Do watch your step from now on!"

The footsteps disappeared out the front door.

Mavis toppled over, collapsing into a nearby chair. She let herself gasp for the breath she held while struggling to maintain her balance.

"Oh, Kevin, I so wanted to enjoy that. A pity."

"Thanks, Mavis. I owe you."

"Indeed you do. And I shall collect."

Kevin rolled onto his back and brought his knees to his chest. He pulled his cuffed hands over his backside so they were now in front of him.

"One more favor, Mavis. I need to get into the tunnel."

A wicked smirk appeared on her face. "I'll let that one go." She stood and smoothed her dress. "Follow me."

CHAPTER 24

She was a fighter. That would make things more difficult. Not impossible. Just more difficult.

Petey had waited for her behind the hedge in back of Prospector Mountain. It was a small, secluded spot and he knew he would have a few minutes of privacy. He grabbed her and dragged her behind the hedge.

For someone so small she had a lot of fight in her. She struggled even more than the three men did. Although Petey respected the attempt, she was no match for him. He was far too strong. The more she kicked, the tighter he squeezed her throat. After a minute, maybe two, she stopped kicking. She was gasping, trying to gasp, making that gurgling, choking sound. Her face was turning bright red and Petey's hands trembled as his grip tightened.

Just as she was about to pass out, as her eyes were rolling back, he let go.

She collapsed onto the ground, coughing and heaving, trying to get air back into her burning lungs. He was immediately on her chest, straddling her, pinning her arms at her sides. From his shirt pocket he produced a pocketknife and opened it. The setting sun caught the metal blade and it flashed. He stuck the blade under her chin so she could feel its point pricking her skin.

"If you struggle, I'll cut your throat," he hissed. He spoke quickly, his words charged with the adrenaline rush he felt right before he killed. He leaned in close so that his hot breath covered her face. "If you scream, I'll cut your throat. If you do anything at all, except exactly what I tell you, I'll cut your throat. You'll never see those kids of yours again. Do you understand?"

Her eyes were wide, her neck muscles tensed, as if they could somehow stop the knife from slicing into her skin. Her head gave the slightest twitch, indicating that she understood. He didn't want to stab her. That wasn't the plan. Too messy. But he would do it if he had to. It would just complicate things.

While Petey had been watching and following the redheaded guy, whose name he learned was Kevin Lonnegan, he observed how much time he spent with her. Her name was Sheila Nelson. They ate lunch together; they seemed to hang out together. They were clearly more than just friends.

And that's when he got the idea.

Petey didn't need to *kill* Kevin Lonnegan. That's what he thought he would have to do. But the more he thought about it, the more he realized that the murders were attracting an awful lot of attention. Especially after that column in the *Sentinel* came out. He was thrilled, of course, but it was one of those "be careful what you wish for" things. His very success at being able to pull it off was creating an environment where it was becoming more and more difficult to be successful.

So he changed his mind. Sure, he loved working at Empire Realm. He loved the access it gave him to deserving victims. He loved how he could be invisible in plain sight and watch the glorious discoveries unfold before his eyes. But there were other places where he could do that. There was too much attention now at Empire Realm. It was time to move on.

However, Petey was smart enough to realize that if the killings suddenly stopped after he quit, someone would notice it as a pretty big coincidence and start asking questions. It would only be a matter of time before it would all be over. And that was unacceptable.

But what if someone else were arrested at the same time Petey quit? Then it would look proper that the killings stopped. Then there would be no coincidence. No suspicions.

Based on the fact that the arrival of Kevin Lonnegan was the beginning of the end of Petey's run at Empire Realm, and the fact that Petey just didn't like him, he would be a good candidate. Petey had all but caught him snooping through his locker. Petey honestly wasn't sure what, if anything, Kevin Lonnegan had to do with ruining his hobby at Empire Realm, but, right or wrong, Petey had pegged him as the catalyst, and that alone made him a deserving scapegoat.

So Petey started following him. He eavesdropped on conversations at lunch in the commissary. Learned about Sheila Nelson's kids. Learned that they were sleeping together. Learned personal, intimate things.

So today he took a plastic Publix bag and placed into it the items he took from the three victims. The sunglasses, the car keys, and the baseball cap. It was hard to part with them. They were private trophies. Petey had placed the bodies for public discovery, had shared them with the world, but the items he took were meant just for him. So he could look at them later and know what he did. Hold them in his hands. Remember. They were personal validations of his success. But, as difficult as it was to give them up, they had to be sacrificed. It was the only way. He even threw in a storebought kerchief for good measure. Kevin's murder weapon.

Petey shoved the grocery bag into Kevin Lonnegan's cubby at Prospector Mountain, making sure that no one saw him, watching the backstage video surveillance cameras and only crossing their view with a group of people. He also kept his costume cowboy hat on to shield his face.

Then he hid behind the hedge and waited for Sheila Nelson's shift to end.

Now he was sitting on her chest, jabbing a knife at her throat. He reached down her leg and fumbled at her belt. *She probably thinks I'm going to rape her,* he thought. *She'll wish I did that instead.* He reached around her hip and found it. Her cell phone. He had seen her use it in the commissary and heard her talk to her kids. He watched where she clipped it when she was done. She must keep her purse in her locker.

Still wearing his costume gloves, he turned on the phone. The battery was almost dead. But he wouldn't need much time. He rested the phone on her chest and produced a small piece of paper from his back pocket with his free hand. He made sure to keep the knife poised under her chin. He held up the piece of paper for her.

"Read this." He saw her eyes moving over the paper. That's not what he meant. "Out loud!" he hissed. "Read it out loud. But not too loud."

She opened her mouth. "I can . . . hardly breathe . . . crushing me . . ."

Petey leaned in close again. He pressed the blade harder against the pale skin under her chin. "I'm not moving. I don't trust you. You read this fucking paper or I'll cut your throat from ear to ear, I swear to God."

"Okay . . ." With strained breathing she read what was written on the slip of paper. "This is Sheila Nelson . . . I'm afraid . . . It's Kevin . . . He did it . . . He's the one . . . Look in the cubbies . . . at Prospector Mountain . . . Oh God . . . He's here."

"Good," Petey said. "Again."

"No . . . Not Kevin—"

"Do it!" Petey hissed, dragging the blade an inch along her jaw, slicing the skin and drawing a line of crimson blood. Sheila winced in pain and read it again.

"Okay," Petey said. "Now you do it just like that. If you don't do it just like that, I'm going to kill you. Then I'm going to get in my car, drive to your house, and kill your kids, your cat, and your dog. Do you understand?"

". . . Yes."

Petey dialed Detective Pendergrast's phone number. He had memorized it after Detective Pendergrast gave Petey a business card during his interview. The detective had interviewed half the cast members in the park and had given almost all of them business cards, asking them to call him if they thought of anything or noticed anything strange. Petey saved his card. He thought it was funny.

Petey listened to the phone ring and heard Detective Pendergrast answer. He pushed the phone at Sheila Nelson's mouth and held up the slip of paper with his knife hand. The knife rested on her chin as he held the paper.

She swallowed and read the words again, struggling to get air into her lungs. "This is Sheila Nelson . . . I'm afraid . . . It's Kevin . . . He did it . . . He's the one . . . Look in the cubbies . . . at Prospector Mountain . . . Oh God . . . He's here—"

Petey hung up the phone. Switched it off. "Good," he said. "Good." He again reached into his back pocket, this time pulling out a plastic grocery bag. He wadded it up and shoved it into Sheila Nelson's mouth. Then he took his costume scarf and tied it as a gag tightly around her head, making sure it passed through her teeth, forcing the plastic bag back towards her throat. There was no way she could make a sound.

Then, without another word, Petey placed both hands on her throat and started squeezing. The realization that he was going to kill her set in and her eyes went wide. Her feet kicked wildly, but they couldn't move Petey's heavy body. Her fingers scratched desperately at the sides of his legs but her arms were pinned and her short fingernails did no damage against his blue jeans. He heard the muffled, barely audible grunts that were supposed to be screams. After two or three minutes of this, her feet fell still.

Just then there was laughter on the other side of the hedge. Shift change. A group of Prospector Mountain cast members were heading up the stairs for their shifts. This had taken longer than Petey wanted. His window was closing. He looked up to see if anyone had spotted him. He didn't think so.

He looked down and realized that Sheila Nelson had stopped moving. Her eyes were closed. Was she dead yet? Maybe. He didn't have time to check. He quickly untied the gag and shoved it into his pocket. That couldn't be found with her. It belonged to him. With the plastic bag still in her mouth he lifted her up—she was extremely light—and carried her to the border of the hedge. Glancing out, he saw that there was now no one in sight. The group must have turned the corner for the stairs. He covered the two strides to the cart, opened the lid, and dropped her in. Unfortunately, the cart was empty and clean, but he didn't need to preserve this body. He wouldn't be around for the discovery anyway. He tossed in Pendergrast's business card and the cell phone.

The cops would piece it together like this: Sheila had figured out that Kevin was the killer because she found the grocery bag in his cubby. Concerned, she called Pendergrast. But Kevin attacked her while she was still on the phone.

Petey knew it was a flawed plan. It was only meant to buy him time—maybe a few weeks, a few months—to disappear and be completely forgotten. Too many witnesses probably saw Kevin and Sheila at the right times in different places. But Petey had set it up well enough that there would definitely be questions and an investigation. Kevin would go to trial. Maybe even get convicted. Meanwhile, Petey would slip quietly away, get in his car, and head for I-10. He'd take a nice, leisurely drive across the lower half of the country, eventually ending up in California. Maybe at Knott's Berry Farm. Or Universal Studios Hollywood. Or maybe even Disneyland, the granddaddy of all theme parks. And if he felt the itch along the way to resume his hobby, he was sure he could find a nice, crowded shopping mall somewhere in Texas where he could place a body in a trash can and sit in the food court to watch the discovery while eating a Chick-fil-A sandwich and some waffle fries.

Petey closed the lid and flipped down the latch to hold it in place. He was breathing heavily, just starting to come down from the adrenaline rush of the kill. He looked at his gloves and saw that there was a bloodstain on his left thumb from cutting Sheila Nelson. He would have to destroy them. He'd fill them with rocks and throw them in a roadside retention pond on the way home.

Normally he liked to hold the victims' throats longer, make sure they've truly asphyxiated. But he didn't have time to do that here. He couldn't control the environment like he could when the victim was random. No matter. Inside the airtight box with only a limited supply of oxygen, even if she wasn't dead yet she would be shortly.

Pendergrast had a large bloody scratch on his left cheek. His right arm twisted under his body when he fell, and it felt like he had pulled a muscle in his shoulder. The aforementioned shoulder was in process of developing a world-class bruise where it impacted the first step. But that wasn't the worst. The worst was that the fall somehow inflamed his hemorrhoid to the point where he wished he could drink an entire bottle of bourbon and lie on his stomach for a week.

Rubber band ligation. Ass surgery. Whatever the doc wanted. As soon as he had Lonnegan booked, he was going to see his doc and ask him—beg him—to fix his ass. He didn't care any more what the guys in the department would say. He was sure that Smitty already had the word out anyway. He just had to end this horrible pain.

"Hey, Boss!" It was Mickelson. Goddamn rookie. If Mickelson had a proper hold on Lonnegan, like any normal prisoner, he wouldn't have escaped—and caused Pendergrast such intense physical pain and embarrassment. Lonnegan even took his weapon, goddammit. There was no telling what he might do now. Scared. Running. Armed. Pendergrast, eyes narrowed, turned towards Mickelson. "Boss! The PRN guys say that the shops on both sides of the street here are clear. He must have headed deeper into the park."

Idiot. "Or, he doubled back and is backstage right now, heading for his car."

Mickelson's brow furrowed. He hadn't thought of that. "So what do you want to do?"

At that moment, there were a lot of things Pendergrast wanted to do, but couldn't. *Punch you in your perfect goddamned face. Spit on that bitch Carla Beck. Sit my bare ass in a sitz bath. Tell Gardner to go fuck himself. Beat the living shit out of Kevin Lonnegan.* Pendergrast turned to the senior PRN agent standing nearby. "Call Coluccio." He turned back to Mickelson. "When you took off after Lonnegan, I called for additional back-up. We have a Crisis Response Team en route, along with a half dozen sharpshooters. There are only two ways Kevin Lonnegan is leaving Empire Realm. In custody or in a body bag."

The PRN agent handed Pendergrast his cell phone. Coluccio was on the other end. As he talked, Pendergrast looked around at the tourists. The last thing he would permit was Kevin Lonnegan taking another victim. Or escaping. "Listen, Coluccio, you really want to help? I'm sealing the park. No one leaves without going through a checkpoint. Pull however many agents you need and put them on the backstage exits. I'll get some uniform deputies on the main exit gate."

"That's a tall order, Detective," said Coluccio. "There are a lot of ways out of here backstage. Kevin probably knows most of them."

"It's time for you to earn your goddamned money."

"We'll cover as many of the backstage exits as we can. But we want to be on the main gate exit. That's how tourists leave the park. Keep in mind that Empire is in the middle of a highly promoted Anniversary Celebration. PRN agents checking exiting guests will be a lot less conspicuous than uniformed deputies."

"Conspicuous? I don't give one shit about conspicuous! I'm trying to catch a serial killer here! Apparently, I'm the only one. You do as I tell you. In a few minutes, I'll have enough real cops here to cover all the exits and you guys can go back to drinking lattes and talking into your wrists." Unbelievable. Pendergrast wanted to throw the phone in a nearby horse water trough. Didn't anyone understand what was at stake here?

"And don't take Lonnegan lightly," said Pendergrast. "He's dangerous, armed, and obviously not afraid to use violence to escape."

"Listen, Detective, are you *sure* it's Lonnegan? He really doesn't fit the profile."

"Someday I'll give you a lesson in something that we in law enforcement like to call *evidence*. Plus, he ran, Coluccio.

Not something innocent people usually do. And he took my weapon. And his *girlfriend pinned it on him!* We've checked and there was plenty of time after he was done with his shift and before he got picked up by your goons to have gotten to her. Furthermore, I know Lonnegan. I've personally seen what he's capable of. Since his wife died, he's always been just one branch away from snapping. He's the doer."

"We'll find him," said Coluccio.

"And you'll hold him for me. Don't underestimate him."

"I understand."

Pendergrast exhaled. "And send that old gas bag Jerry Engle to see me."

"Okay. Why?"

"Because Kevin Lonnegan is his friend and he's going to help me catch him."

CHAPTER 25

Mavis led Kevin through the kitchen, past a row of deep fat fryers that sizzled and radiated an intense heat. The Spanish-speaking hourly kitchen workers didn't even look up at the handcuffed man rushing by. Mavis pushed the back door open, glanced around quickly, and gestured for Kevin to follow.

They moved behind a large, aromatic dumpster filled with half-eaten hamburgers and discarded onion rings. Behind the dumpster, along a cinderblock wall, was a narrow set of concrete steps leading down into the tunnel.

"This'll put you in the Red area of the tunnel," Mavis said. "Section B. You know how to get where you need to go?"

"I think so," said Kevin. "I'll find it."

"What do they think you did?"

"Killed some tourists."

"That's a crime?"

Kevin smiled. "Thanks, Mavis. You're the best."

"Be careful, Sugar." Mavis grabbed Kevin's face with both hands and pulled him towards her. Then she kissed him hard and deep. It was an aggressive, hungry kiss and Kevin was so surprised that he froze. After a few seconds, Mavis pulled her face back. "For luck," she whispered, her voice husky and throaty. She whirled around and disappeared back into the kitchen.

Kevin nearly fell down the stairs. But he quickly composed himself and bounded down to the tunnel, taking the steps two at a time. He emerged into the underground corridor and oriented himself.

The tunnel was actually a series of tunnels set up as a subterranean web. Three concentric tunnels ran in rough circles under the park like a bulls-eye. These were the Blue, Red, and Yellow tunnels. The bulls-eye pattern was sliced into uneven wedges by crisscrossing tunnels that connected the concentric circles. These were the alphabet tunnels. Kevin found himself in Red B. He needed to get to Yellow G.

He turned right and started running. He tried to keep his handcuffed wrists low and concealed. But he didn't want to sacrifice speed for style. It was only a matter of time before the tunnel was crawling with cops or PRN agents, if they weren't down here already.

He pulled out his cell phone and called Sheila. He got her voicemail and left a message to call him immediately. He had a very bad feeling about this.

Next he tried Jerry's cell phone. He listened to the garbled ringing as he ran. No answer. He got Jerry's voicemail. Again.

"Jerry—" Kevin said into the phone while continuing to run. "It's Kevin. I know who the killer is—or I will in a few minutes. And it's not me. Call me as soon as you get this."

Kevin knew running was a dangerous move, as was grabbing Pendergrast's weapon. He would pay for those actions later. He hadn't thought—didn't have time to think. Instinct took over and he just acted. Pendergrast's description of Sheila and her message was all wrong. *Was she breathing when you left her?*

Something had obviously happened to her—maybe even something he couldn't bear to consider.

There was no way Kevin was going to trust Pendergrast to find her and help her. Pendergrast thought *he* was the killer, after all. Nothing Kevin said would be given any credibility. If anyone was going to find her, it had to be Kevin. He had a very small window of opportunity coming out of the trailer and he took it, not thinking it through, still reeling from being arrested.

With the discovery of the nylon fiber on his pants leg, Kevin now knew how to get the killer's name. Once he had that, it would lead him to Sheila. He said a silent, desperate prayer.

Kevin turned right sharply into the F tunnel. He weaved through some cast members heading home after their shift, turned left into the Yellow tunnel, and found what he was looking for.

Character Escorts. It seemed like a week ago he was here, but it was just barely two hours. He opened the door into the character escort area. Six small cubicles filled the windowless room. Fortunately, no one was here. The night shift escorts were out with their charges. With the Anniversary in full swing, there was an extra character presence in the park.

Kevin walked through the cubes and found Carrie's desk. There, hanging from a peg on the cube wall was a clipboard. Kevin had seen it earlier, had noticed that Carrie filled in his name, character, and shift. He also noticed that Carrie was responsible for all Wilber assignments.

Kevin grabbed the clipboard and flipped pages back. It was the first murder, the one in May he needed to find. He got to the last page. The pages on the clipboard only recorded Wilber assignments for this month. He needed May.

He looked around her desk. If the assignment log was kept on her computer he was screwed. He wouldn't be able to log in and access her files. Just then there was a noise in the hallway outside the escort office.

Kevin crouched down below Carrie's desk. One of the escorts came into the room and settled into a cubicle on the other side of the thin, fabric wall. Kevin heard the sound of a drawer opening and junk being rummaged. He heard a male voice mumble something about *damn keys.*

While crouched, Kevin saw, stowed under Carrie's desk, a row of binders stacked along the floor. Each was neatly labeled on the spine by the month and year. He saw the binder for May.

In another moment, the guy in the other cube found his keys and rushed out of the office. Kevin grabbed the May binder and opened it on the floor. With his cuffed hands, he flipped pages as quickly as he could until he found the date of the first murder. He ran a finger down the page. There was only one Wilber assignment that day. And it was a name he recognized from his suspect list.

Peter Andrews. Petey.

The synthetic brown fiber that was found on the first murder victim looked just like the fiber Kevin found on himself after his shift. His instincts told him they were identical. He didn't need to call Violet. He didn't need to compare them. He knew.

The fiber got on the victim because the fiber was on the killer. The killer had been Wilberforce the Wilberhorse that day.

Petey Andrews was the murderer.

Kevin knew who he was. A big, tall guy. Quiet. Stuck mostly to himself. One of the cowboy ice-cream vendors. Dark hair. Small eyes set deep under a heavy brow. Wore gloves as part of his costume. Was definitely strong enough to choke the victims—

Wait a minute—ice-cream vendor. Ice-cream vendor . . .

The ice-cream vendors sold their wares from behind large, refrigerator-sized carts with wheels. The carts were stocked with

WilberBars, Chipwiches, juice pops, and ice cream sandwiches. When someone wanted to buy a WilberBar, the vendors just lifted the rubber-sealed lid, grabbed the snack, and handed it over. They made change with a belt moneychanger.

Kevin's mind raced back to the day he spent learning about the park's use of dry ice. The ice-cream snacks were kept frozen with blocks of dry ice, which were slid into slots positioned around the inside of the cart.

Jesus. That's it. Petey killed the tourists and then stored the bodies inside an ice-cream cart until he could place them. That's where the dry ice burns came from. That's why they were post-mortem.

Kevin had to find Petey. Now. That would lead him to Sheila. And he *really* needed to talk to Jerry. Just as Kevin thought that, his cell phone rang on his hip. Kevin flipped the phone open.

"Jerry—" he said.

But it wasn't Jerry.

"Kevin . . ." It was Sheila. She sounded hoarse and in pain. "Please, Kevin . . . help me . . ."

When Sheila woke she was groggy and disoriented. She felt like she had a bad hangover. And she wasn't sure if her eyes were actually open. It was just as dark with them open as closed. The only way she could tell that her eyes were open was by squinting them shut and then forcing them open as wide as she could. The world was completely black.

And silent. She could hear absolutely nothing. No voices. No insects. No ambient air conditioning hum. Nothing. It was also hot. *Very hot.* Well over a hundred degrees.

For a moment, Sheila panicked and thought she was inside an oven. It was that hot. And she was cramped into a small space. In the dark it felt like a box. She couldn't straighten her legs or even sit up. It was maybe four and half or five feet long, maybe two and a half feet wide and about the same height. She felt the walls around her. The ceiling and floor were smooth, maybe metal. The walls also felt like metal, but had large square holes cut every inch or so almost like a fat mesh. With her fingers she could feel another smooth wall about an inch or two through the mesh. The walls were hot but not burning. She wasn't in an oven. She was in a box somewhere, probably sitting directly in the sun. She pushed against every wall but couldn't get any to budge.

Was it even still light out? How long had she been in here? She had no idea, but given the temperature and the stale air, she guessed not long. If she had been in here for any length of time, she would already be dead. And if she stayed in here much longer she knew she was going to die. If not from the heat then from the carbon dioxide she was exhaling into the confined space.

Her first instinct was to yell. But her mouth was filled with a crumpled plastic bag. She immediately removed it, coughing as she tossed it aside. She was about to scream, but then wondered if her attacker was still nearby. Maybe he was standing right outside and when he heard her muffled cries, he would finish what he started. Sheila hesitated a moment, considering whether or not she should scream.

It was *really* hot in there. Her body was drenched in sweat. She was going to die if someone didn't get her out.

She yelled a terrified cry for help. But her voice was extremely hoarse and her throat ached where she had been choked. The gash on her jaw stung as sweat dripped into the wound. She continued screaming for help, even though she knew she probably couldn't be heard outside. If she couldn't hear noises from outside, then anyone outside probably couldn't hear her.

Oh God, what if she was in some sort of coffin . . . buried alive? Oh God . . . Sheila's breath started coming in short, panicked gasps. The thought of dying buried somewhere was just too awful to bear. She screamed until her voice was raw and capable of nothing more than a ragged whisper.

Tears welled in her eyes as she tried to cry out, eventually breaking down into a frightened sob. She told herself to stay calm. That becoming hysterical wouldn't help her get out of this. But the fear and panic were hard to control. Sobbing, she kicked and pounded on the walls.

And she thought she felt the box move. Just barely.

Did she imagine that? She kicked and pounded again and there was no mistaking it. She had caused whatever box she was in to rock just slightly, almost imperceptibly.

What did that mean? Probably that she *wasn't* buried alive somewhere. Maybe she was somewhere where someone could see the box moving. She couldn't scream anymore. She could barely speak. Kicking out her legs and thrusting her body forward and back, she was able to make the box rock again. She repeated this over and over for what seemed like a very long time, but was probably no more than a few minutes.

She had to stop. She was panting, exhausted from the physical exertion in the roasting temperature. Sheila knew that with the heat and the perspiration literally pouring off her in sheets, dehydration was quickly setting in. And she was rapidly filling the tiny space with carbon dioxide. She couldn't keep this up much longer.

But she had to try. Again she kicked and rocked her body, grunting with the effort. It worked, but barely. Someone would have to be pretty observant to see the slight tilting of whatever she was in. She continued for another minute or two. She had no concept of how quickly or slowly time was passing.

Finally collapsing, exhausted, Sheila realized that she couldn't continue. Gasping for breath, sweat stinging her eyes and her open cut, she laid her head back on the floor, her knees bent uncomfortably. Her arms fell limp at her sides.

Her left hand rested on something lying lodged in the corner where the floor met the mesh wall. She picked it up. In the darkness, she couldn't see it, but it was very familiar. It was her cell phone, laying face down. The antenna had been caught in the mesh.

Immediately, she pressed it on. The green display seemed to glow brighter than she had ever noticed before. She tried to use the display light to survey her surroundings, but it was too weak to illuminate anything. From what she could tell, she was indeed trapped inside a cramped, airless box. She saw no signs of a door or a latch. No visible means of escape.

Looking back at the display, Sheila saw that she was barely getting any signal in here. And her battery was dangerously low. Why hadn't she charged it last night like she wanted to? Because Greg wasn't feeling well and wanted her to read him the same story three times. Then she had homework and forgot to plug in the charger.

Oh Greg . . . Sheila's mind suddenly flashed to her kids and the very real possibility that she would never see them again. Phil would get custody of them. Maggie . . . Billy . . .

Fighting back tears, Sheila tightened her grip on the phone. With so little charge left, she would probably only get one call. She didn't hesitate.

In another moment, the phone was ringing and she heard Kevin's voice answer.

"Jerry—" he said.

"Kevin . . . please, Kevin . . . help me . . ." she said, her voice scratchy and barely audible. Thick static crackled on the line.

"Sheila? Are you okay?" His tone was alarmed.

"I'm trapped . . ."

"Sheila—I can hardly hear you. Where are you?"

"In a box . . . I think. I was attacked . . ."

"Do you know where you are?"

"No . . ." The emotions were boiling to the surface. She had to keep from crying. She couldn't. "It's so hot Kevin . . ." She was sobbing now.

"Tell me . . ." She couldn't hear the rest of what Kevin said. There was too much static and the signal got garbled.

"Kevin? Kevin! Are you there?"

There was more garbled noise. She had no idea what he was saying. Finally his voice became clear enough to understand. "—when you were attacked. Can you hear me? Sheila? Where were you exactly when you were attacked?"

"I was . . . behind Prospector Mountain. At the bottom of the stairs. He made me use your name—" She heard a distinct beep in her ear. Her battery was about to die.

"Do you know when you were attacked? How long ago?"

"No . . . right after my shift . . ." She was still crying, but she fought to compose herself. "Kevin, it's so hot . . . and I can't breathe. I don't think I can stay conscious. Please . . . tell my kids how much I love them. I want them to stay with my Mom, not Phil. Please . . . promise me . . ." The rest of her sentence was swallowed in sobs.

"Sheila! Sheila, listen to me." Kevin sounded like he was moving. Running or walking quickly. "I'm going to get you out of there. Do you hear me? I'm going to get you out. I think you're inside an empty ice-cream cart somewhere backstage. Keep your breathing slow and shallow. Don't panic. I'm on my way."

"I can't breathe . . . Kevin. It's so hot . . ."

"Sheila. Stay awake . . . don't close your eyes. Sheila—" Kevin's voice cut out with another loud beep. The battery was dead. Sheila tried pressing the power button a few more times, but it was no use.

She was so tired. Lying back, she felt her eyes involuntarily close.

So tired . . .

The last thing she thought of before slipping into unconsciousness was the cruel realization that she was going to die by melting inside an ice-cream cart.

CHAPTER 26

Pendergrast stood in the center of the ivy-covered gazebo just inside the park's front gate and watched the Crisis Response Team guys swarm in like commandos. About goddamned time.

There were at least a dozen of them, all clad in black, wearing helmets and body armor. Along with their .45 side arms, they each carried a high-powered Remington 700 rifle. Pendergrast knew that they were all deadly sharpshooters and at least four were Class A certified snipers. The crowd of tourists looked on curiously, not sure if they were real or part of some attraction.

Lieutenant Dan Howard approached. Howard was a 12-year CRT veteran, built like a linebacker. Weathered face. Crew cut. Chewing gum. His creased eyes were cold slits. "Okay, Lou," he said. "Where's the runner?"

"That's the problem. We don't know."

"That's beautiful, Lou."

"Save it, Howie. Let's just do our jobs here. We arrested him for killing three tourists. As we were transporting him, he escaped. We were backstage, over there." Pendergrast pointed at a nearby door leading behind Lonesome Gulch.

"Backstage?"

"Behind the scenes. Not out here in the park." Pendergrast

winced as his hemorrhoid throbbed. "Listen, Howie. He's dangerous, he's armed, and he's scared."

"Armed?" Howard said. "Didn't you say he was in custody? Armed with what?"

Pendergrast was silent for a moment, his lips pursed. Finally, "He took my gun."

Howard stared for a second. Then shook his head in disgust.

Pendergrast continued. "This place is crawling with innocent bystanders. I don't know what he'll do. If he's holding that gun and you get a clean shot, take him down. Do you hear me?"

"Loud and clear. Is Gardner on board?"

"This is my case. Let me handle Gardner."

"Okay. We won't risk hitting a bystander, but if we perceive an imminent threat and get a clean shot, we'll take him out. On your orders."

"On my orders."

"So do we get a physical description or do I have to guess?"

"Six-one. One-eighty, one-ninety, maybe. Was handcuffed when he took off. Don't know if he still is. Wearing blue jeans and a gray T-shirt. Red hair. Some of you guys may know him."

"Yeah? Who?" Howard glanced around at his men. How could they possibly know a serial killer?

"It's Kevin Lonnegan."

Howard knew him. The blood drained from his face. He leaned in towards Pendergrast, his voice low and serious. "Christ, Lou. Kevin Lonnegan?"

"He's the doer."

"Christ. You're kidding."

"Wish I was."

"Christ . . ."

Pendergrast sensed Howard's hesitation. "Do your job, Howie. You're a professional. If you get a clean shot, you take him down."

"You better be fuckin' right, Lou."

"I know my job."

"You better be fuckin' right."

Kevin was still in the tunnel, just inside the door of Character Costuming.

"Sheila—Sheila? Sheila!"

It was no use. The connection was gone. He called her back and got her voice mail. He tried again. Still no answer. Again.

Kevin tried to piece together what must have happened. That would help him find her. She had been attacked right after her shift, coming down the stairs behind Prospector Mountain. She had been forced to call Pendergrast and implicate Kevin. Something had been planted somewhere to incriminate him, obviously by the killer. Sheila's attacker had put her into an ice-cream cart—probably. That would be consistent with the killer's MO. But she didn't know where she was or how she got in there. Perhaps she had been blindfolded. Or the attacker choked Sheila, which would also be consistent, until she passed out and he thought she was dead. Maybe he was interrupted. Maybe he was in a hurry. Then he threw her in the cart and left her to be found later. But she wasn't dead. She woke up and called Kevin.

She didn't have much time. If Kevin didn't find *her—fast—* she would probably be dead within fifteen minutes. She was the only woman he thought he could love since Maria. He couldn't face losing her, too. Not after they had become so close. Not like this. He thought of her kids.

Kevin slipped back into the darkened Costuming room, sliding between the long metal garment racks hanging with huge, deflated Chipmunks and Skunks and Turtles. Finally he reached the rack of empty Wilber carcasses. He was alone.

The Wardrobe Mistress must have slipped out for a cigarette or maybe to stir her cauldron.

Kevin found the costume he was looking for and slid his legs into it. It was difficult wearing handcuffs, but he managed to get the tail belt fastened and the suspenders mostly over his shoulders. He zipped up the torso (it zipped from the inside) and, reaching out through the neck, grabbed a rubber Wilber head.

With his hands cuffed, Kevin couldn't put his arms into the costume's arms, so Wilber's brown horse arms just hung limply at his sides, like some kind of cartoon equine stroke victim.

Before Kevin could slip the mask over his head, his cell phone rang again.

He immediately dropped the costume's head and grabbed the phone from his belt. It had to be Sheila. Please let it be Sheila.

It wasn't Sheila.

"Kevin. Where are you?" It was Jerry Engle.

"Jerry—Listen. I need your help. I know who the killer is and he's got Sheila. She's gonna die within a few minutes if we don't find her."

"Okay, Kevin. Calm down. Just tell me where you are and I'll come get you."

"Nevermind where I am. You need to find Sheila. She's trapped inside an ice-cream cart somewhere, probably backstage of Lonesome Gulch. I need you to send out everyone you can to look for her."

"All right. We'll take care of it. What about you? Are you okay?"

"What? Yeah. I guess. Jesus, Jerry, she's only got a few minutes. Please."

"You're in some pretty hot water, you know, Kevin."

"It's bullshit, Jerry, and you know it. I know who the killer is now. I have his name. We need to find Sheila first and then you can go after him."

"Okay. Just tell me where you are and we'll take care of it."

Kevin paused, just for a beat. Something was wrong. "Why do you keep asking where I am?"

"I'm concerned, Kevin. I want to help."

"Yeah . . ." Kevin paused. "Pendergrast is standing right next to you, isn't he?"

"Look, Kevin, I know it's bullshit, but running is only making it worse. You stole a police officer's gun. Let me help you. Please."

"You disappoint me, Jerry. I forgive you, because I'm sure you weren't given any choice, but I'm still disappointed. Please, just promise me you'll look for Sheila. She's trapped in an ice-cream cart and she's almost out of time. Please, Jerry, I can't let her die."

"Kevin—"

Kevin hung up the phone.

He put the Wilber head on, secured it, and charged back into the tunnel, the costume's empty arms swinging limply at its side. He moved quickly toward a nearby park entrance.

"Kevin, look—" the line was dead. "Kevin? Kevin?" Jerry was nauseous. He pulled at an eyebrow.

"Where is he?" Pendergrast demanded.

"I don't know. He wouldn't say." Jerry hung up his cell phone.

"Goddamn it, Engle. *Goddamn* it! Can't you do anything?"

They were standing near a topiary chipmunk just inside the park entrance. Dan Howard was nearby, as was Vincent Coluccio.

"Jerry," said Howard. "Did you hear anything in the background that would give you a clue?"

"No. It was quiet. He got suspicious and hung up."

Pendergrast's face was getting red. "Did he say *anything*?"

"He said he knew who the real killer was. He said that the

killer had trapped his girlfriend in an ice-cream cart and, if we didn't find her within the next few minutes, she was going to die."

Pendergrast rolled his eyes. "Oh, that's rich. Of course he knows who the killer is! He's the goddamn killer!"

"You're wrong, Lou," Jerry said.

"I swear to God, Jerry, if you give me any trouble, I'll arrest you, too. For aiding and abetting."

"You know what, Lou? I don't care anymore. Arrest me. Do whatever you want. But Kevin Lonnegan isn't the guy. You're wrong."

Pendergrast leaned into Jerry's face and shouted, "How do you know? You were a shitty cop on the job and you're a shitty cop now. What the fuck makes *you* so smart?"

"Because I hired Kevin to go undercover and help me find the killer."

Pendergrast was about to scream at Jerry again, but caught himself as Jerry's words registered. Eyes narrowed, mouth open, all he could manage was, "What?"

"You heard me."

Dan Howard cut his eyes at Pendergrast. "You didn't know that, Lou?"

Pendergrast wheeled on Howard, pointing a finger. "My orders still stand, Howie. This doesn't change anything."

"I'm calling Gardner," Howard said.

"Like hell." Pendergrast was furious. "You carry out your orders on my authority. Kevin Lonnegan is the doer. I've got physical evidence. I've got his girlfriend turning him in. He ran, for crissakes! *He stole my fucking gun!*" Pendergrast turned to face Jerry. "Mickelson's picking up the girlfriend now. If she's really locked up somewhere, then Kevin's the one who put her there. She turned him in, so he had to eliminate her. Telling you about it, Jerry, is just covering his ass. If he told you, she's probably already dead. Kevin Lonnegan is the doer. She told me herself. He's the doer."

The other three men were silent for a moment. Pendergrast had a pained expression on his face. Finally, Dan Howard gripped Pendergrast's arm and pulled him aside, saying, "Lou, can I speak to you for a second?"

Coluccio turned to Jerry. "What do you think, Jerry? Do you believe him?"

"Who? Pendergrast?"

"No, Kevin. Do you believe he's innocent?"

"Hell yes."

"What about the gun?" Coluccio said, his voice just slightly lower.

"Pendergrast was probably going to shoot him."

"And the ice-cream cart? Is that connected?"

"I don't know. Probably."

"What about the girlfriend?"

"I think she's in trouble."

Coluccio took a deep breath. Glanced over at Pendergrast and Howard, who were gesturing and pointing at each other. "Okay. Pendergrast has all of my agents and your security officers tied up with a park lockdown. We've got people on every exit. I can't spare anyone for a search. Pendergrast wouldn't allow it and we have to follow his orders. But, I want you to go, grab one of your officers, and look in every ice-cream cart you can find. Now."

"Thanks."

"Good luck."

Jerry turned and ran off towards the nearest backstage exit. Adrenaline pumping, his heart was pounding his ribcage.

He prayed he wasn't too late.

* * *

Wilber emerged from behind a privacy wall near the entrance to the Anaconda Roller Coaster. He popped out unexpectedly, and without the customary Character Escort.

A seven-year-old girl nearby spotted him and squealed in surprise. She flung her half-eaten cotton candy to the ground and ran toward Wilber, arms outstretched. Wilber looked at her for half a second and then turned and ran. She called his name. *Wilber! Come back!* But he kept running.

Her mother spotted her and caught up, grabbing her hand. The girl started to cry. *Come back, Wilber!* But he didn't come back. He didn't even turn around. They watched him run off down the sidewalk, dodging around a group of surprised guests who were walking along looking at their park map.

As she watched him run, the mother thought to herself, *what's wrong with his arms?*

CHAPTER 27

Kevin knew he had no time to waste. And he couldn't rely on Jerry to help him. He was Sheila's only hope for survival. He popped up out of the tunnel in the South American section of the park, between the Anaconda roller coaster and the Amazon River Expedition.

He was going on a hunch. He had no idea where Sheila was, but he was working the clues. She was probably locked in an ice-cream cart. But where was the cart? He figured it was back-stage. An abandoned ice-cream cart would be suspicious within the always-perfect onstage park grounds. But where could it be backstage? Based on Sheila's description of how hot it was, Kevin suspected that the cart was somewhere in the open sun, which was just starting to sink in the west. Where could an abandoned ice-cream cart sit backstage where it wouldn't attract attention? Kevin could think of only one place.

The Freezer.

Situated around the Freezer was a parking lot of inactive vending carts. Ice-cream carts, beverage carts, lemon ice carts, snow-cone carts. Each waiting its turn to be loaded with dry ice and stocked with refreshments for the paying public. A cart could sit there for a long time before anyone noticed that something was wrong. It could be days before the suspect cart was put back into active rotation.

The Freezer was backstage on the border between Lonesome Gulch and the Asian Experience. He thought about just dashing through the tunnel to the exit closest to the Freezer. But the tunnel was probably going to be crawling with cops and PRN agents. They were probably already down there. And the tunnel wasn't even the most direct route to the Freezer. Because of its web-like design, Kevin would have had to make several turns and run an arced corridor to his destination. The fastest way across the park was a straight line, which could only be run from within the park.

So Kevin emerged just Northeast of Empire Palace, quickly got his bearings and started running. He knew the Wilber costume would attract attention, but if he kept moving, he could keep a good pace. He would also be hidden from immediate view of Pendergrast and Coluccio. He prayed no one would notice Wilber's empty, limp arms dangling at his sides as he jogged through the park.

Kevin passed through the Palace breezeway and turned down the main Old West street of Lonesome Gulch. Tourists pointed and some approached, hoping for a quick photo with Wilber. Kevin kept moving.

Then he stopped suddenly.

Out from one of the shops along the road ran a black-clad member of Orange County's Crisis Response Team. The man carried a sniper's rifle, charging across the road right in front of Kevin and into a shop on the other side. Looking up, Kevin saw another CRT member positioning himself with a rifle on a shop rooftop. Jesus. They were going to shoot him.

Kevin took a deep breath and continued moving.

* * *

"Hey, Boss." It was the kid, Mickelson, on Pendergrast's cell phone.

"You better have good news, Mickelson."

"Good news, bad news, Boss. I can't find the girlfriend anywhere. She clocked out on time, but never made it to the employee locker room. It looks like she's still here. Her car's still in the parking lot."

"If that's the good news, I'm going to personally break your thumbs."

"The good news is I think I have a bead on Lonnegan. The Costuming lady down in the tunnel told a PRN guy that one of her Wilber costumes is suddenly missing. If you recall, Lonnegan spent all day today dressed up in a Wilber costume."

A mirthless grin grew on Pendergrast's face. The thought of Lonnegan lumbering along, trying to escape in a horse costume was too perfect. It was actually smart enough to work. But they had him now, the son of a bitch. He couldn't hide in a giant horse costume.

A twinge of doubt flashed through Pendergrast's mind. Engle had hired Lonnegan to go undercover to find the killer? Could that explain the items in the cubby? Or was it possible that something so ironic as Engle hiring the killer to find himself had actually happened? Pendergrast had seen plenty of weird coincidences in his career. It could happen. But could Lonnegan be innocent?

Sure. Of course he could be innocent. But the evidence in hand said that he probably wasn't. The evidence said that he was guilty. Probably. Lonnegan had a violent, alcohol-fueled history. The girlfriend *said* he was the one. The victims' stuff *was* in his cubby. And when he was arrested, Lonnegan stole Pendergrast's weapon and ran, not exactly an innocent man's behavior. Gardner wanted the case closed. Pendergrast had seen stranger circumstances than this in other cases.

Lonnegan was the killer and he was going down. Howard's shoot orders still stood.

Lonnegan was the killer. Pendergrast repeated it to himself, a mantra, reinforcing it in his own mind, trying to push out any seed of doubt. *Lonnegan was the killer.* The more he repeated it, the more he assured himself of its truth. *Lonnegan was the killer.*

"You find him, Mickelson," Pendergrast said. "You find that horse costume and you put him down. He killed three people. He made you look bad. More importantly, he made *me* look bad. And he has to pay. Understand?"

"I understand," said Mickelson and he hung up the phone.

Lonnegan was the killer . . . Lonnegan was the killer . . .

Mickelson had two deputies and a PRN agent with him when he turned the corner into Lonesome Gulch. He was coming from the main gate area and was running along an onstage perimeter road towards the Dixie Emporium and Prospector Mountain. Seeing the group of serious men, two in suits and two armed deputies, the crowd of tourists shrank back, clearing a path for them.

As he ran, Mickelson caught sight of a blonde hottie in white shorts. She was watching them rush by and he made eye contact. He set his expression with the appropriate mix of seriousness and mission. She was definitely watching him. Blonde ponytail. Maybe twenty-five years old. Bronze, sculpted legs. He wished he could take a moment, slip over, and get her number. Maybe if he were alone . . .

That's when he saw him. The horse. Wilber. Maneuvering through a crowd in front of the Dixie Emporium. His back was to them. He was moving away and had no idea they were coming up quickly behind him.

"There he is," hissed Mickelson. He pushed himself out into the lead. He was the detective, after all. Plus, he wanted to impress the PRN guy. When word got back about how he tracked down the fugitive and apprehended him, perhaps he could write his own ticket with PRN. Six figure salary. Expense account. And if the cute blonde happened to be impressed with his actions, well, hey, that wouldn't be so bad, either.

"He's armed and dangerous, so don't take any chances," Mickelson said, just before breaking into a full-out sprint. "Draw your weapons. This scumbag is mine."

The four of them charged down the walkway, cutting a swath through the crowd. Mickelson hurdled a baby stroller at a full sprint. He felt it was a nice touch.

Lonnegan's back was still to them, moving away in that ridiculous costume. Mickelson was only a few feet away now. "Hey, Wilber!" he shouted. Wilber turned around just in time to see Mickelson leave his feet.

Mickelson hit the horse hard in the chest, just like he used to do as a second-string cornerback for the University of Central Florida. Lonnegan was so surprised he crumpled, toppling over backward, hitting the pavement hard. The hit was a thing of beauty. Both the PRN agent and the blonde had to be impressed.

In a second Mickelson was kneeling on the costume's neck, his 9mm Glock pointed directly at the head. The horse's goofy expression and floppy tongue stared back at him silently.

"Thought you could get away from me?" Mickelson shouted, the adrenaline coursing through his body. "Take off with my handcuffs? Push my partner down the stairs? Steal a cop's gun? You're gonna fucking pay, asshole. You hear me?!"

Mickelson jammed the gun between the horse's two big white eyes. The only response he got was the low gurgling sound of someone trying to speak while someone else has a knee shoved into his larynx.

Still aiming his weapon at the character's head, Mickelson addressed the deputy on his right. "Get him out of this stupid costume."

The deputy reached down and grabbed the head's ears. He gave them a tug. The costume head pulled off revealing Kevin Lonnegan's frightened face staring into the muzzle of Mickelson's gun.

Only it wasn't Kevin Lonnegan.

Mickelson was so surprised, he almost squeezed the trigger. He was looking into the terrified face of a seventeen-year-old girl. She was tall—had to be to wear the Wilber costume—with brown hair and a few too many adolescent pimples. Her green eyes were wide in abject fear. She continued to make the gurgling, choking sound.

Mickelson just froze there, stunned. He was sure it was Lonnegan in the costume. How could it not be Lonnegan? What the hell?

"For God's sake, Detective," the PRN agent said. "Get off her windpipe."

Mickelson immediately hopped off. He and his comrades stood there, staring down at the girl in confusion.

She burst into frightened tears. "What do you want?" she wailed. "Please don't hurt me . . . Oh my God . . ." The horrified Character Escort appeared through the crowd, mouth agape.

The PRN agent knelt down and helped the girl into a sitting position. "We're not going to hurt you. There's been," he shot a furious look at Mickelson, ". . . a terrible mistake. Are you all right?"

She was still crying uncontrollably. "I couldn't breathe . . . Ahggg . . ." *Sniffle.* "Oh my God, he was going to *shoot* me . . . Oh my God . . ."

"No, he wasn't," the PRN agent said softly. He turned to Mickelson. Less softly, he said, "Were you?"

"Hunh?" was Mickelson's response. He was still staring dumbly at the girl, unable to understand how she was in the costume and Lonnegan wasn't.

"Tell her you weren't going to shoot her," the PRN agent barked at Mickelson.

"I thought she was Lonnegan . . ."

"Oh my God! . . ." the girl wailed. Everyone standing around her noticed the darkening of the costume's crotch with urine.

"Very nice work, Detective." the PRN agent said. Then he turned back to comfort the girl.

Mickelson looked around. His two deputies glared at him like he had just beat up a girl. Which, of course, he had. Mickelson spotted the cute blonde standing nearby, staring aghast with her hand over her mouth. So much for getting her number.

He now had no idea where Lonnegan was. Or Sheila Nelson. And he probably just got the department sued. And forget the six-figure salary. The worst part was that he was going to have to eat even more shit from Louis Pendergrast. He *really* hated that guy.

Mickelson holstered his gun before he did something he would regret.

The Freezer was maybe thirty yards away now. Kevin ran—at least as well as he could in the bulky costume. There were six ice-cream carts parked in one row beside the Freezer. They looked like horizontal refrigerators with wheels and handles. Nearby were other inactive vending carts—beverages, snow cones, popcorn, cotton candy.

As Kevin approached the first ice-cream cart, he tripped over the costume's big feet. He pulled off the head and kicked off the rest of the costume. Still handcuffed, he sprinted up to the first cart.

"Sheila!" he shouted. "Sheila! Can you hear me?" No answer. He immediately flipped the lid open.

Empty.

He threw himself at the next cart and tore open the lid. "Sheila!" Also empty, except for a discarded ice-cream wrapper. His breath was coming rapidly as his panic set in. *No no no*—He reached the third cart. Grabbed the lid.

Empty. "Sheila! Can you hear me?!" His breath was coming more rapidly now. Moved to the fourth cart. Opened it.

Empty. *No . . . Please no . . .* The fifth cart—

Empty.

"Sheila!"

Please God . . .

He reached the last ice-cream cart, his heart pounding, afraid of what he would find inside, afraid of what he wouldn't find inside, afraid of—

Empty.

No . . .

He had guessed wrong. She wasn't here. The cart was hidden somewhere else. Unnoticed behind some dumpster or a van or a hedge. Or maybe it wasn't an ice-cream cart at all. Either way, he had guessed wrong and because of that, she would die. He put his face in his hands, fought to keep from breaking down into sobs.

"Kevin!" It was a voice behind him. Kevin didn't look up. It didn't matter now . . . "Kevin!" Then he felt a hand on his shoulder. Jerry Engle's hand. "Kevin, are you all right?"

"I don't know where she is, Jerry . . . It's too late . . ."

Jerry squeezed his shoulder. There was nothing to say. "We'll keep looking."

"Sir!" It was another voice. One of Jerry's security guards was a few yards away, standing next to several beverage carts. He was young with neatly trimmed black hair. "I think I found something!"

Jerry gave Kevin a nervous glance and then was up, moving, zigzagging through the carts. Kevin was right behind him.

"Sir," the guard said. "Look. There's another cart shoved in here." There, crammed between two beverage carts, was an ice-cream cart. "And look." The guard pointed at the lid latch. Unlike the other ice-cream carts Kevin had opened, this cart's latch had a small piece of wire wound through the eyelet. Kevin pushed himself in front of the guard.

"Hey," said the guard. "What's with the handcuffs?"

Hands trembling, Kevin unwound the wire and pulled it through the hole. He lifted the latch and swung the lid up.

Sheila was lying motionless in the bottom of the cart.

She was drenched in sweat, looking like someone had dunked her in a pool. Her perspiration covered the shiny metal floor of the cart in a glistening sheen. A crumpled plastic grocery bag lay next to her dead cell phone. Because she was taller than the space, her legs were bent awkwardly, as was her neck. Her head leaned unnaturally against a floor corner where she had passed out. Coagulated blood covered one side of her lower jaw.

"Dear God . . ." the guard said.

"Help me get her out!" Kevin ordered. Jerry and the guard helped Kevin lift her out of the box and lay her on the ground. "Call 911. Now!" Kevin said to the guard. Kevin leaned down and pressed his fingers on her neck. "Please . . . please . . ." He adjusted his fingers' position—"Come on, Sheila . . . Please . . . I can't find a pulse, Jerry. I can't find a pulse—"

Jerry placed his fingers on her neck. Adjusted them. Finally, he said, "There. It's faint. But she's alive."

"Jesus . . ."

"We'll get her straight to the hospital. She's extremely dehydrated."

Kevin was trembling. He moved a strand of Sheila's hair that was stuck to her forehead. "You're gonna be okay, Sheila. Just hang in there." He told Jerry Sheila's mothers name and asked him to find her number and call her. Jerry promised he would.

"Please, Jerry, make sure she gets to the hospital. Make sure she's okay."

"I will. I promise."

"I need your help for one more thing, Jerry."

"Kevin, you gotta wait for Pendergrast. He and Coluccio have sealed the park, both the main gate and all the backstage exits. You can't get out. Listen to me—Pendergrast has Howie and the CRT here. They've set snipers for you."

"I know. I need you to call HR and get me the home address of Peter Andrews. He's an ice-cream vendor here at the park."

"He's the killer?"

"Yes. Get me the address."

"Kevin, I can't. They're going to kill you. I can't do that."

Kevin exploded. "Just get me the fucking address, Jerry! Do it!"

Jerry considered for a moment. Then relented. "I'll get it, but we're giving it to Pendergrast," he said. He punched some keys on his cell phone and got an administrator in Human Resources. He identified himself and asked for Peter Andrews' home address. He waited a moment, nodding. Then his eyes went wide. "You're kidding," he said.

"What is it?" Kevin asked.

"I got his address, but . . ."

"What?"

"According to the HR electronic timecard system, he's here. He's in the park right now, working a scheduled shift."

Before Jerry could say another word, Kevin had vaulted a nearby beverage cart and was sprinting toward an onstage entrance.

CHAPTER 28

Pendergrast stood to the side of the park's main exit, shifting his weight from foot to foot. His hemorrhoid throbbed painfully. As he scanned the throngs of guests exiting through the turnstiles, he vowed again to call his doctor first thing in the morning.

So far he hadn't spotted Lonnegan or the girlfriend trying to slide out amongst the guests. He cut his eyes at the two uniformed deputies. They were watching the tourists closely, following his orders. Apparently, his threat of getting them reassigned to parking enforcement if Lonnegan slipped past them was an effective motivator.

"Detective Pendergrast?"

Pendergrast turned around. Standing behind him was Bill Oglethorpe, President of Empire Realm. Fortunately, Pendergrast hadn't had to deal with him too often since starting his investigation. He was kind of a weasely corporate suit who always wanted "the current status."

"Yeah?" Pendergrast said.

"Is it true that you've sealed my park?"

"Yeah."

"That's a fairly drastic measure, don't you think? Why did you do that without consulting me?"

Great. Like I have time for this. "I didn't realize I had to consult you on how to do my job. You don't consult me on how much to charge people for those Wilberhats. But, as long as we're talking, I think they cost too much. I mean, come on."

"Look, Detective. We're in the middle of the biggest event in the history of Empire Realm. This police presence is very unsettling for our guests."

"So is a homicidal fugitive running loose in the park."

"I'm sure that there are more discreet ways to handle this. Please don't make me call Sheriff Gardner."

Pendergrast felt his blood pressure rising. Who was this guy to criticize and threaten him? The same guy who would scream if the killer escaped. "You wanna call Gardner? Go ahead. The fuck I care. Now get outta my face so I can do my job. Or maybe you want I should go home and let our friend keep strangling your guests. Your choice, Oglethorpe."

"Keep your voice down—" Oglethorpe spit through clenched teeth, his eyes intent on the exiting guests.

Ignoring Oglethorpe, Pendergrast lifted his walkie-talkie to his mouth and pressed the talk button. "Mickelson. You hear me? Report. You find the horse yet?"

"The horse—?" Oglethorpe said.

There was no response from Mickelson. "Mickelson, you there? Report, Goddamn it." Another few seconds of silence. Then—

"Hey, Boss."

"Mickelson." Pendergrast said. "What's your progress? You find the horse?"

"Uh, not exactly." Mickelson said.

"What the hell does that mean, 'not exactly'?"

"We found a Wilber, but it wasn't Lonnegan. We're still looking."

Oglethorpe craned his neck towards Pendergrast. "What's this about a Wilber? What are you taking about?"

"You better find him, kid," Pendergrast said into the microphone. "For your sake."

There was suddenly a new voice on the frequency. "I found him."

"Who is this?" Pendergrast said.

"This is Turner." One of Howie's CRT boys. "I'm on a rooftop in the Old West section of the park. I've got the runner in my scope."

The next voice was Howie's. "Give me a confirmed ID, Turner."

"Red hair," Turner said. "Blue jeans. Gray T-shirt. Pair of police-issue bracelets. He's running down the middle of the street. Looks like he's in a pretty big hurry."

"What about the gun?" Pendergrast said.

"I can't tell from this angle. Too many people—wait—I see it. I see the gun. He's holding it up in front of himself. Shit, it looks like he's aiming it at a group of tourists in front of him."

"Do you have a clear shot?" Pendergrast asked.

"Negative. Not yet. But give me three seconds. He's approaching a gap in the crowd. Confirm shoot authorization."

"Confirmed," shouted Pendergrast. "When he's clear, drop him!"

"Holy shit," said Oglethorpe. "You're not—"

"You got that, Turner?" Pendergrast said.

"Got it. Confirmed shoot authorization. He's definitely raising the gun . . . almost in the clear. He won't make it out of the street."

Oglethorpe was literally jumping up and down. He grabbed Pendergrast's arm. "You're not going to shoot someone in the middle of my park, are you? You can't do that!"

Pendergrast turned and looked directly at Oglethorpe. "Watch me."

* * *

It didn't take Kevin long to move from the Freezer to the nearest onstage entrance. He covered the distance in a few sprinting strides. In another moment he was through the door and into the park, oblivious to Jerry Engle's calls behind him.

Sheila would be in good hands with Jerry. The best she could hope for, in her condition. She was still alive. Thank God. But who knew what kind of permanent damage had been done? She had been in that box for too long with too little air and too much mercury in the thermometer.

Kevin emerged into the park on the far side of Prospector Mountain, close to the Asian Experience. He was running as fast as he could, swinging his handcuffed arms back and forth in front of his body in a rapid, rhythmic motion. Now that he was out of that stupid costume, he felt like he was flying.

He rushed past the entrance to Prospector Mountain, turning left before he reached the Dixie Emporium. After rounding the next corner, he would be on Lonesome Gulch's main street. It seemed like a million years ago that Jerry had first walked him down that street and offered him the job.

Kevin chastised himself. Somewhere along the line he had screwed up and been made. Somehow, Petey Andrews knew what Kevin was really doing, or had guessed correctly. Kevin's mistake had gotten him arrested for triple homicide and almost cost Sheila her life. Kevin was ashamed. And he was pissed. No, he was way beyond pissed.

He was consumed by rage. A white-hot anger at what that bastard had done to Sheila burned behind his eyes. Kevin suddenly felt Pendergrast's gun pressing into his hip, like it was expanding, throbbing. Like some kind of living organism. Reaching around, Kevin removed the gun and held it out in front of himself. He wasn't thinking anymore. His pulse thundering in his ears, adrenaline coursing through his veins, Kevin felt like he had been pushed down a mountainous ski slope. Barely maintaining control, moving quickly, and no way to stop until reaching the bottom.

Kevin wasn't exactly sure what he was going to do when he reached Andrews, but he knew it wasn't going to be pleasant. He hoped he wouldn't gun him down in the middle of the park, but Kevin honestly didn't know if he could restrain himself. He just knew that he had to get there. He had to be the one to reach him first. This was no longer just a case. This had become personal.

Petey Andrews worked as an ice-cream vendor at the edge of Lonesome Gulch, in the shadow of Empire Palace. Kevin knew who he was. Tall guy, stringy black hair, dark eyes, with a small, roundish nose that seemed out of proportion to the rest of his wide face. Pale complexion despite working in the sun all day. He was on Kevin's short list of five suspects and fit the profile. Worked on the same days as the murders, male, big enough to commit the crimes and succeed, no known family, had access to dry ice so he could store the bodies after killing them and before displaying them. Kevin had crossed paths a few times with Petey—in the locker room, in the park, in the commissary. He was quiet, maybe a little creepy, liked to stare, never hung out with anyone. But being a creepy loner was far from being a serial killer. Otherwise, Kevin would have had to suspect every computer programmer he had ever met. Besides, how many times had some psycho gone on a killing rampage only to have his neighbor recall what a nice, friendly boy he had always been?

Kevin continued charging down the street, weaving his way through startled tourist families. Someone running through the park as hard as he was running was unusual. Someone running like that, wearing handcuffs and holding a pistol definitely raised a few eyebrows. Rounding a corner up ahead, Kevin saw the Anniversary Celebration Parade snaking its way down the street toward him. A half dozen giant, happy moths danced and flapped around a slow moving float that looked like a big, plastic garden. Insane calliope music blared from somewhere in the garden float. Maybe they were supposed to be butterflies.

Kevin reached a patch of street that was clear of tourists and used the space to lengthen his stride, his arms swinging. He tightened his grip on Pendergrast's gun, raising it up, preparing to see Petey Andrews at any point. He had to reach Andrews before Pendergrast. Or Coluccio. Or before Andrews got spooked and disappeared. The fact that the guy was brazenly working his regular shift after almost killing Sheila further enraged Kevin.

Kevin ran as fast as he could in the open gap between tourists. He got two or three steps into the clearing when he felt his left foot slide out from under him, sending him to the pavement. He had stepped on a stupid WilberBar melting on the ground. Like some dumb cartoon character, Kevin had put his foot down, in full stride, right on top of the slippery ice cream mess. He hit the pavement hard, catching his right elbow on the cement, a sharp stab of pain radiating through his arm. The gun slipped from his hand and clacked to the curb, out of immediate reach. The instant he went down, he saw, from the corner of his eye, a slat in a wooden park bench next to him splinter apart.

Kevin knew immediately what it was.

Jerking his head around, Kevin saw the CRT sniper on a rooftop across the street, the long black barrel of his Remington 700 peeking over the edge. The sniper adjusted his grip and reset his aim.

Shit!—Kevin rolled upright and lunged toward a nearby

cluster of South American tourists. He realized how he must have looked with that gun in his hand. Evidently, Howie's team had shoot authorization. *Thanks, Pendergrast.* Those guys were good. If Kevin hadn't been such a klutz, he'd be dead now. That damn WilberBar saved his life. If he had a clear shot, Kevin knew that the sniper wouldn't miss again. Did the sniper see him drop the weapon? He couldn't know for sure. Kevin couldn't assume that just because he lost the weapon they wouldn't take another shot at him. It depended on how big a threat Pendergrast convinced them Kevin was.

For half a second Kevin considered giving himself up, offering Petey's name. But it was too late now. They'd grab Kevin and while they listened skeptically to his story, Petey would slip quietly away. No, Kevin believed that he was the only option to reach the real killer.

They wouldn't risk a shot with civilians nearby. Kevin's only hope was to find protective cover behind people. Abandoning Pendergrast's gun, he charged into the middle of the South Americans, who stared at him in surprise, wondering what he wanted. An older guy said something in Spanish or Portuguese, but Kevin wasn't listening. From the middle of the group, peering over shoulders, Kevin quickly surveyed his situation, turning in a wide circle. In addition to the shooter on the roof, Kevin saw two more CRT positions. There had to be more he didn't see. It would only be a few minutes before the wrath of the Orange County Crisis Response Team was bearing down on him. They were probably already on the ground and on their way.

Kevin dove out of the South Americans and directly into the passing Anniversary Celebration Parade. He dodged around the dancing butterfly/moths and ran right up the middle of the parade. A uniformed security guard blew a whistle and motioned for him to get out of the street. *No crossing during the parade!*

Like some spawn-hungry salmon, Kevin pushed his way up through the oncoming parade, passing under stilt walkers' legs, between twirling plates, and over confused elves. He dashed between floats, grabbing a fairy princess by her shoulders and pulling her along with him across an open patch of street.

He continued charging through the parade until he reached the last float. This one was decorated like the surface of some distant moon. It was promoting Empire Studios' latest roll of the high-budget movie dice, a $170 million science fiction gamble called *Earthbound.* Standing in a crater, laser pistol holstered on his leg, military uniform crisply pressed, Bruce Willis was waving to the crowds on either side of the street. Mr. Willis looked down and spotted Kevin, their eyes locking for a beat. Confusion passed over Mr. Willis' face when he saw Kevin's handcuffs. He cocked his head curiously, not sure if Kevin was some incarceration-themed part of the parade. Kevin offered a perfunctory salute and kept running.

There was a clearing in the street in the moon float's wake, a small gap between the end of the parade and where tourists were filling back into the road. At the edge of the clearing, Kevin spotted him.

Peter Andrews stood innocently behind his ice-cream cart, handing some woman a frozen juice bar. Anger and adrenaline surging through his entire body, tunneling his vision, Kevin lunged for him.

CHAPTER 29

Petey had no intention of going home. After putting Sheila Nelson in the box, the least-suspicious thing he could do was remain in the park and work his shift. It was brilliant, really.

His plan was now in full motion. After tonight, he would resign his position, break his apartment lease, and start driving west. Although he wasn't pleased that he had to leave, he *was* looking forward to a new chapter in his life, filled with opportunity and surprises.

Unfortunately, the first surprise of this new chapter was a right hook to his jaw.

He was facing the other way, handing some fat New Yorker her fruit pop, when he felt the blow impact his chin. His teeth cracked together painfully and he went down, catching himself with his right hand on the corner of his vending cart. Twisting his head around, Petey saw the redheaded guy, Kevin Lonnegan, standing beside him, his eyes crazed. Lonnegan's arm was across his body from the punch and Petey saw that Lonnegan was wearing handcuffs.

In less than a second, Petey's mind put it together. Lonnegan had been arrested as planned, but somehow he got away. He fingered Petey as the real killer and came after him in some antiquated attempt at vigilante justice.

Lonnegan swung his arm around to backhand Petey. But Petey was expecting this blow and managed to deflect it. He grabbed the chain between Lonnegan's wrists and, using his body weight, pulled it around the cart, swinging Lonnegan into the bushes behind the sidewalk.

Petey debated for only a moment about what to do next. He could wait for the cops to show up. Obviously they had put the handcuffs on Lonnegan and suspected him as the killer. But if he waited, Lonnegan would point his finger and there would be questions that Petey couldn't answer. What he really wanted to do was to choke Lonnegan now. Stomp his booted foot down on Lonnegan's throat. Maybe he could claim self-defense. But he knew that would be impossible here in the middle of the park. No, he needed to disappear right now instead of at the end of his shift. His car was packed. Full of gas. He had a new driver's license and Social Security card for his new identity. He had bought a hair bleach kit from Walgreens this morning. He was prepared to be a whole new man. There was really only one thing Petey could do now.

He ran.

He headed deeper into the park. The crowds were thinner than along the parade route and there was an entrance to the tunnel at the base of Empire Palace. If he could make it into the tunnel, he had a good chance of slipping away. He knew every twist and turn of that subterranean maze and could just vanish.

But he had to get there first. Behind him, Lonnegan was pulling himself from the bushes. Lonnegan wasn't as tall as Petey but he was obviously strong. That punch to the jaw hurt and as he ran, Petey tasted the salty, metallic tang of blood in his mouth.

Petey crashed through a group of teens and cut across a patch of grass between sidewalks. He glanced back and saw Lonnegan charging after him. Lonnegan was running quickly, making up the distance between them. In another few strides Petey reached the massive arch of the Empire Palace breezeway. A twenty-foot tall passage cut right through the center of the Palace, serving as a central conduit to all four major sections of the park.

Petey ducked inside the arch and threw himself behind a wide column covered in a mosaic of small, glittering purple tiles. Lonnegan was approaching quickly and Petey realized that he was probably going to be overtaken. Petey couldn't afford Lonnegan chasing him through the tunnel. He had to stop him now. If Petey could get down into the tunnel without being followed, he knew he could escape.

Mounted on the column was a medieval battle axe with a long wooden handle and a cast-iron blade. The blade was permanently affixed to the pillar with a metal bolt and clamp, but Petey was able to get his fingers behind the wooden handle. He gave a mighty pull and the handle came free from the axe blade with a loud crack that echoed through the archway. Two passing newlyweds jumped at the sound.

On the other side of the column Petey heard Lonnegan's footsteps run into the passage and stop. He could hear Lonnegan's labored breathing as he walked, searching for Petey hiding within the neat row of tiled columns. The door to the tunnel was ten steps away, against the interior wall of the archway, leading down below the Palace.

Lonnegan was now only two columns away. He would come around this column in just a moment. Petey adjusted his grip and with both hands raised the wooden handle over his head like a club. As soon as he saw Lonnegan's red hair peek around the edge of the column, Petey brought the handle down with all his strength.

* * *

Kevin didn't see the club until it was almost too late. He got his hands up but not in time to cross them and block the stick with his forearms. The club came down between his hands, headed right for the top of his head.

Fortunately, the handcuff chain suspended between his wrists caught the brunt of the blow and kept the stick from splitting his skull completely open. The club connected with his forehead at the hairline and sent a screeching ring through his ears. The impact would leave an impressive welt and give him a nuclear headache but Kevin's brain remained safely inside his skull.

Kevin staggered backward and saw Petey Andrews raise the stick over his head again. *Jesus, he's a big son-of-a-bitch.* But this time Kevin saw it coming and managed to grab the club as it swung down, stinging his hands. This must have caught Andrews by surprise because Kevin was able to give the stick a sharp tug and yank it out of his grip.

Now it was Kevin's turn to start swinging. Kevin felt a rush of intense, primal rage unlike anything he had felt since the night he had assaulted Lucius. His emotions affected his reactions because he missed Andrews with his first swing. Andrews was a big target, but he was agile. He dove around the column and Kevin chased him.

On the third swing Kevin connected with the side of Andrews' head, sending the big man out from behind the column and into the center of the arched passage, knocking over a plastic trash receptacle. Andrews tried to move past Kevin, his eyes focusing on a wooden door in the wall marked "Cast Members Only." But Kevin was able to keep him at bay by wielding the stick.

"Give it up, Petey," Kevin said. "It's over." He concentrated to regain control of his anger. In his state of mind, with the right opportunity, Kevin could easily kill him.

Andrews' chest was heaving, maybe from the exertion,

maybe from the realization that he was caught. His eyes locked onto Kevin's. Cold, hollow eyes; dark and too small for his face.

"It's over," Kevin repeated. His professional instincts were taking over. *The suspect is cornered. Backup is presumably on its way. Just keep him here. Keep him focused on me to prevent him from hurting anyone else.* Kevin lowered the stick just slightly in an attempt to be reassuring.

Andrews turned and bolted. Kevin was right behind him. Andrews ran into an ornate alcove and disappeared into shadow. Kevin followed him in and saw that it was a secondary exit from the four-star restaurant at the top of the Palace. A spiraled staircase snaked up through the Palace turret as an alternative to those adventurous diners who didn't want to wait for the elevator. There was no sign of Andrews but the only way he could have gone was up.

Kevin threw aside the stick and charged up the stairs, taking the steps two at a time. The winding ascent through the window-less staircase induced dizziness and Kevin occasionally steadied himself against the fiberglass castle bricks as he ran. In the back of his mind he was vaguely aware of a harpsichord minuet piped in through invisible speakers.

Upward he ran. Kevin lost all sense of distance. Three floors? Ten floors? He had no idea. He could sometimes hear the pounding of feet running above him. Finally he reached a landing with a small porthole-sized window. Judging by the view, Kevin assumed that he had run nearly to the top of the Palace.

Next to the window was a door that led to the lobby of the Palace Restaurant. Kevin hurried into the restaurant and spotted Andrews pushing his way past a tuxedoed maitre d' and into the dining room. In another moment Kevin was crashing after him, careening around tables covered with white linen. The harpsi-chord music continued into the restaurant and gave the room a subdued, formal ambience that was completely shattered by the two strangers bounding through.

Based on his body language and facial expressions, Andrews was starting to panic. He reached the edge of the dining room, a wall of plate glass offering an eagle's view of Empire Realm and the surrounding Central Florida landscape. Kevin stood across an occupied table to confront him. He held his cuffed hands in front of his body, trying to keep Andrews calm.

"There's nowhere to go, Petey," he said.

With eyes like a caged animal's, Andrews worked his back along the glass until he reached a door marked "Authorized Personnel Only." Beyond the door was a small balcony that led along the outside of the glass, where costumed characters strolled for the amusement of the guests while they dined.

Andrews bolted through door and onto the balcony. Kevin was immediately after him. It was surprisingly cool outside. The sun was sinking in the west and the height of over one hundred feet provided a breeze that the ground didn't offer.

Andrews ran along the balcony, seemingly unfazed by the dizzying drop on the other side of a thin, waist-high wrought iron rail. He reached an exterior wall of the Palace that effectively ended the balcony. He had nowhere else to run. Andrews leaned out over the rail, looking for another perch, somewhere to escape to. There was nothing. Kevin feared he would jump.

"Just relax, Petey," Kevin said. "Relax."

Andrews' eyes were wide. "You ruined it! It was so perfect . . ."

"What was perfect, Petey?" *Keep him talking.*

"Everything! All of it . . . nobody else could do what I did. Nobody! And it was all perfect until you showed up!"

"How many more were there, Petey? How many before you came to Empire Realm?"

"You don't understand. It was different before. I couldn't be there when they were found. But here—here, I could watch the whole thing from the front row. I picked the star, I set the stage, and then I watched it unfold. It was perfect."

"It was murder."

Andrews rubbed his hands over his head in frustration. He was on the verge of crying. "It was so perfect . . . It's not fair." He beat his palms on his face, going from despondent to furious disturbingly quickly. "It's not fair! You ruined it! You! IT'S NOT FAIR!"

He launched himself at Kevin, his massive hands reaching for Kevin's throat. Kevin tried to maneuver out of the way, but there was precious little room on the narrow balcony. They slammed up against the restaurant window. The glass buckled with a reverberating boom but didn't break.

Kevin struggled to get his hands up between himself and Andrews, who was leaning all his weight against him. Andrews' fingers closed around Kevin's neck. Squeezing. Kevin knew that he had to do something quickly or he would soon be victim number four. The pressure on his airway was causing his vision to blur. Andrews leaned in pressing Kevin's back hard against the glass. Their upper bodies were too close for Kevin to get his hands up between them. Andrews' grip tightened. Kevin imagined the horrified reactions of the guests watching the struggle on the other side of the glass.

There was just enough room, however, for Kevin to jab a desperate knee into Andrews' side, breaking the big man's concentration momentarily. Kevin used the opportunity to thrust his palms up and into Andrews' chin. Andrews staggered backwards for a step. Kevin clasped his hands and delivered a hard, two-fisted blow to the midsection.

But Andrews recovered quickly and grabbed Kevin's arm. They grappled with each other in the confined space, Andrews using his superior size to turn Kevin around, now forcing Kevin's back against the wrought iron rail. With his hands cuffed, Kevin couldn't get any leverage to shift Andrews' weight. Kevin felt himself tipping backwards over the precipice.

There was no way to stop the momentum. Andrews leaned harder. Kevin resisted, using every muscle in his back and abdomen to keep upright, to keep from going over the side, but he was overmatched. Andrews knew it, too, and pressed all his bulk against Kevin. Another inch or two and gravity would carry Kevin over the rail. Kevin had one desperate chance. Stretching, he wrapped his left leg around a vertical bar in the railing, wedging his foot behind the rod.

Then he stopped fighting.

He let himself get pushed over the top of the barrier. The purple and green spire of the palace roof swished by and was gone, replaced by thin white clouds against an orange sky. Kevin's left leg held, swinging him over the side but not out into the air, his knee acting as a pivot point on the horizontal rail.

When Kevin suddenly stopped resisting, Andrews' momentum carried him over the side also. Except Andrews didn't have his leg secured in the rail. A look of terror washed across his face as he realized what was happening. Andrews twisted his body when he went over, clutching desperately at Kevin as he fell.

Kevin's back slammed against the railing—sending crimson splotches bursting into his vision—and his arms were nearly jerked from their sockets. Hanging upside down, arms stretched out below him, he saw that he had hooked Andrews around the neck with the handcuff chain. Kevin's right leg kicked wildly up into the air while his left knee burned under the bent strain of supporting the weight of two bodies.

Andrews twitched madly as the chain cut into his windpipe.

His hands clawed at Kevin's arms but in his panic he was unable
to get a grip. Kevin heard the rasping gags of Andrews choking
between his wrists. Kevin tried but didn't have the strength to
lift Andrews or even himself back up over the rail. The strain
was so great that Kevin was afraid his arms would literally be
pulled from their sockets or his knee would snap off if he didn't
get help soon. Kevin could actually feel the ligaments in his
knee stretching painfully, reaching their breaking point.

Andrews continued to writhe, bumping his body against the
shining purple wall of the Palace. He was thrashing so much
that Kevin feared the handcuff chain might slip from his throat
and send Andrews crashing to the pavement. Kevin gritted his
teeth and held on, a groan of intense pain involuntarily escaping
from his lips. He looked out over Empire Realm, upside down
from his current vantage. The sun was setting, casting the entire
park in a golden blanket, reflecting off the waters, drenching the
streets in amber. A distant crowd of onlookers pointed at them
from the ground.

After a moment, the gagging sounds ceased. Then Kevin's
arms stopped moving from Andrews' twitches. Now, the only
movement was the slight trembling of Kevin's muscles trying to
support Andrews' silent, dead weight. Again looking out over
the inverted park, Kevin saw a gathering crowd staring up at
him and the motionless man, pointing fingers, covering their
mouths. Kevin also saw a group of uniformed deputies running
through the crowd toward the Palace.

In another moment, Kevin felt hands grabbing, helping
him back over, and helping him haul up the lifeless body of
Peter Andrews. Two male dinner guests and a waiter pulled
them both back over the rail. As soon as he was safely on the
balcony, Kevin's knee buckled and he collapsed onto the floor,
breathing heavily, registering the pain in his wrists, shoulders,

and knee. His head pounded where Andrews connected with the stick.

Andrews' limp body flopped to the floor next to him. His empty eyes were wide open. Staring.

Still watching.

CHAPTER 30

With help from a dinner guest, Kevin pulled himself into the restaurant and fell into a chair. He rubbed his aching left knee, wondering if it was just sprained or if there was permanent ligament damage. His arms trembled like a detox patient's. The man who helped him inside handed him a glass of water.

"Thanks," Kevin managed and brought the trembling glass to his lips. Through the window he saw the other guest and the waiter kneeling over the motionless body of Peter Andrews, checking for a pulse. In another minute the restaurant erupted into a storm of activity as cops and security guards swarmed in.

A kid in a CRT uniform leveled the barrel of his rifle at Kevin's head. Kevin really couldn't care less. He continued to sip his water. Pendergrast walked up, followed by Dan Howard, Walter Mickelson, Vincent Coluccio, Bill Oglethorpe, and Jerry Engle.

Kevin turned to Jerry. "Sheila—"

Jerry gave him a thumbs-up. "Paramedics took her to Sand Lake Hospital. They said she had a close call but she'll be okay. I called her mother and she's on her way to meet her. She's going to be in the hospital for a while, but she'll be fine."

Kevin closed his eyes and let his shoulders relax. *Thank God* . . . "Thank you, Jerry."

Jerry gave him a nod. "EMTs are on their way to check you out, too."

Pendergrast took in the scene silently, deliberately: Kevin sitting at the white linen table; Andrews' body on the balcony beyond the glass. He wasn't sure what exactly to make of it or what exactly to do about it. He sucked his teeth as he considered.

Kevin made eye contact with Dan Howard. "Howie. How you been?"

Howard nodded. "Good, Kev. You okay?"

"Never better." He tilted his head at the rifle barrel pointing at him. "Is that really necessary? I'm not going anywhere."

Howard motioned for the CRT kid to lower his weapon.

Oglethorpe pushed his way between them and addressed the police. "Can someone please tell me what the hell's going on here?"

Pendergrast shot Oglethorpe an icy look. Then he turned and wandered over to the window. Looked at Andrews for a long moment. Turned back to Kevin. Pursed his lips.

"The murders are over, Mr. Oglethorpe." It was Coluccio.

"So is he the killer?" Oglethorpe said, pointing at Kevin, whose handcuffs jangled as he sipped his water.

Coluccio exchanged a look with Pendergrast. Pendergrast winced and looked at his feet.

"No," said Coluccio. He pointed out the window at Andrews lying on the floor of the balcony. "*That* man was the killer."

"Then who is this guy?" Oglethorpe said, again indicating Kevin.

"He is a private undercover security operative," Coluccio said. "He's the one who identified the killer and stopped him."

"Christ Almighty . . ." Oglethorpe said. He looked at Pendergrast in disgust. "Am I glad we finally hired PRN."

Coluccio looked at Kevin and offered him a tired smile. "Actually, sir, he doesn't work for PRN. He's independent."

"Independent? I don't understand."

"You see," Coluccio said, stepping aside to make room for Jerry. "Jerry hired him long before PRN ever became involved at Empire Realm. He's been working under Jerry's direction for several weeks now."

Oglethorpe leaned forward, as if he hadn't heard him clearly. "Jerry?"

"Yes, sir," Coluccio said. "If Jerry hadn't taken action when he did, the killer might still be at large."

Oglethorpe turned to Jerry. He opened his mouth but was unable to say anything. Jerry smiled sheepishly, obviously grateful for Coluccio's integrity. PRN could easily have grabbed the credit since they currently controlled Empire Realm security.

Oglethorpe turned and walked away, muttering to himself. He grabbed the restaurant manager and started issuing orders to get the guests out of the dining room.

Kevin offered Coluccio a salute with his water glass. Coluccio nodded and shook Jerry's hand.

Mickelson looked at Pendergrast. "Boss? What now?"

Pendergrast pinched the bridge of his nose. A migraine was apparently surging through his skull. He said nothing.

Howie stepped forward. "I suggest you take those damned handcuffs off him before he sues the department for wrongful arrest. As soon as his girlfriend regains consciousness, I'm sure she'll ID the stiff out the window as her attacker."

Mickelson looked to Pendergrast for guidance. After a few seconds, Pendergrast nodded.

"While you're at it," Howard said, "Why don't you apologize and thank him for doing your job."

Mickelson leaned over and unlocked the handcuffs. "Uh, no hard feelings, Lonnegan. If you forget about us cuffing you like that, we'll forget about the resisting arrest and assaulting an officer."

"Sure," Kevin said. "Whatever." He rubbed his wrists. They were bloody and deeply bruised where the cuffs had cut into them. They had supported the entire weight of Peter Andrews as he dangled over the rail.

Kevin stood and limped shakily to the window. Standing next to Pendergrast, he looked at the body of Peter Andrews on the balcony. Neither man said anything for a long moment. Kevin finally broke the silence.

"So, Lou, are we done here?"

"I'll need a statement," Pendergrast said.

"Sure. No problem."

They looked out the window for another few seconds.

"Find your gun?" Kevin asked.

Pendergrast nodded slowly. He blew a mouthful of air through his lips. An angry sigh.

"You've been out of the department for three years," Pendergrast said. "And you're still grabbing all the glory."

"Hey, I'm just a P.I. It's officially another case closed for Lou Pendergrast."

"Yeah . . ." Pendergrast rubbed his forehead.

"Y'know, Lou, when I told you that a kid puked on me . . . that was true."

Pendergrast nodded. "Thanks, Kevin. That helps."

"Sure."

A team of paramedics moved into the room and helped Kevin back to his seat. Kevin closed his eyes. He was looking forward to his next routine workers' comp case.

* * *

He saw him in the shed, adding oil to the engine.

"Lucius!" Kevin waved his hand to get his attention. Lucius looked up and grinned to see his friend. He wiped his hands on a rag and hurried around the big mower.

"Red! What are you doin' here?"

"I'm meeting Sheila. You've met Billy, right? Sheila's oldest boy." Kevin put a hand on Billy Nelson's shoulder.

"Yeah. Wassup, B?" Lucius tousled Billy's hair.

Billy smiled. "Not much. Kevin took me fishing."

Lucius rolled his eyes. "Oh no. I *been* fishing with the man. Did he push *you* outta the boat, too?"

Kevin shook his head. "For the last time, I didn't push you. I told you not to stand when we went through that other boat's wake."

Lucius held up his palms. "Tell it to the judge, Red. Tell it to the judge." He turned to Billy. "How'd you do?"

Billy's eyes lit up. "Good. I caught three bass."

Lucius nodded in approval.

"So," Kevin said. "How's the job, so far?"

Lucius tried to suppress a smile. "Good, Red. Good. You know I love mowing that grass. I look out and see that lawn looking trim and neat and I say, 'that's *my* grass, motherfucker—'"

"Hey," Kevin said, nodding at Billy. "The mouth."

"Sorry . . . It's all good, Red. Except, you know they mow the grass in the middle of the night? That's some crazy sh—stuff, man."

"They don't want the guests to see anyone mowing. They're supposed to just show up in the morning and find everything perfect. Like magic."

"Yeah," Lucius said, wiping his hands on his rag. "I'm gettin' used to it. Not as hot at night. And it keeps me outta the 'hood after sundown. I'm gonna stay clean this time, Red."

"I know you are, Lucius." Kevin had pulled some strings with Jerry and gotten Lucius a job in the landscaping department at

Empire Realm. Jerry was glad to do it. He was so grateful for Kevin's help with the investigation that he would grant almost any favor Kevin asked.

Jerry's stature had suddenly risen within the theme park community. Word spread about how he coordinated the killer's capture. Employment offers came in from across the country. Jerry had debated what to do and decided that the time was right to make a move. Opportunity might not knock again. He weighed his options and eventually accepted a V.P. of Security position at Dollywood in Tennessee. It was a smaller park with a lower profile, both of which appealed to him. A little more money. Plus, his wife's parents lived three hours away. But the real reason, he had confided to Kevin, was the fact that Jerry was a huge country music fan and would occasionally get to work directly with Dolly Parton herself.

Then Jerry sprung his last piece of news. He had recommended Kevin to replace him as Empire Realm's Director of Security. Oglethorpe didn't know who to hire and wanted to avoid an expensive recruiting effort. He was willing to accept Jerry's recommendation. In addition, Kevin's role in stopping Andrews had given him credibility and he was now already a known commodity to Oglethorpe.

Kevin was stunned. Jerry told him to think seriously about it. The job was more about prevention than investigation, but Jerry had never regretted working there. He had really loved it. Kevin was told that no matter what his decision was, he never had to pay park admission for the rest of his life.

Kevin promised Jerry he'd think about the offer. And he would. Just not today. Today he was content to keep his park involvement limited to meeting Sheila after her shift. He was delivering Billy to her after a day spent fishing on Lake Jessup.

Over the last couple weeks, since Sheila's recovery, Billy and

Kevin had spent more time together. And they were starting to really like each other. Billy especially liked hearing stories about Kevin's experiences in the Navy—places he visited, people he met. They shot hoops together. Went fishing. Just hung out.

Kevin said good-bye to Lucius and led Billy to the backstage entrance to Prospector Mountain. They turned a corner and came face-to-face with Sheila, who was coming down the cast member stairs. They laughed when they saw each other.

Sheila gave Kevin a peck on the cheek and walked with them to the locker room. She heard all about Billy's three bass. As they walked, Kevin thought that Sheila had never looked more beautiful, even with the new pink scar under her chin. She showed no signs of the trauma she'd suffered.

Of course Empire Realm had paid all her hospital bills and continued to pay for sessions with a stress counselor. Sheila didn't think the counselor was necessary but went because the company was paying for it. Because they were afraid of getting sued, the Empire Realm brass also decided to pay for Sheila's entire college education. Plus a generous lump sum if she waived rights to all future litigation.

They reached the door to the women's locker room.

"I'll just be a minute," Sheila said. She put her hand on Kevin's arm. "Mom's got Greg and Maggie and is meeting me and Billy at Bennigan's for dinner. You want to join us?"

"I'd like that," Kevin said.

Sheila smiled and went into the locker room. Kevin sat with Billy on a nearby bench. While they waited, they talked about their day of fishing, the Orlando Magic's next season, and Billy's baseball team.

Kevin promised to teach him how to catch pop flies.

ACKNOWLEDGMENTS

I'd like to offer my most humble thanks to all those who provided me with valuable assistance during the writing of *Murderland*. Whether you read drafts, provided structural advice, offered editorial support, or supplied research expertise, your input was vital and very much appreciated. I thank you all.

ABOUT THE AUTHOR

Thomas B. Cavanagh spent several years in film and television entertainment where he wrote award-winning children's television programs for producers such as Nickelodeon, the Disney Channel, and Anheuser Busch Entertainment. He has taught graduate level courses focused in e-learning and technical communication, and holds a PhD in Texts & Technology from UCF and a graduate degree in creative writing from the University of Miami. He is currently the Vice Provost for Digital Learning at the University of Central Florida. Cavanagh has written and managed numerous multimedia programs for Fortune 500 companies, the US government, and the military. Cavanagh lives in Florida with his family and two cats.

THOMAS B. CAVANAGH

FROM OPEN ROAD MEDIA

OPEN ROAD

INTEGRATED MEDIA

Find a full list of our authors and
titles at www.openroadmedia.com

FOLLOW US
@OpenRoadMedia